RICHARD STONE

I0686076

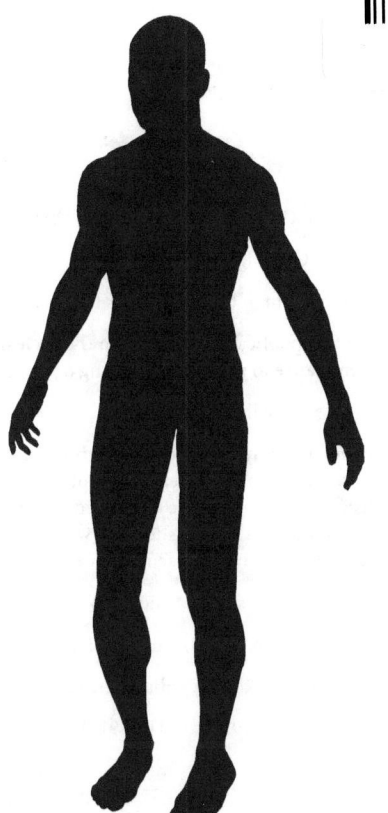

REJUVENANT

Typeset in Minion Pro

Design, typesetting and publishing by UK Book Publishing

www.ukbookpublishing.com

ISBN: 978-1-914195-91-4

REJUVENANT

Much has been written about the outbreak of youth violence at the latter end of the twenty-first century, particularly in the wealthiest economies of the west. Like many such dark explosions, the causes seem obvious only in retrospect. The global population had risen above nine billion some time before, but for several decades had been flat or falling; the use of radical life extension technologies was commonplace only in a few advanced economies; and the massive increases in global consumption by the expanding middle classes were masked by the economic problems of low-growth economies, and by ingenious efficiencies in resource usage.

A few voices were raised predicting planetary disaster, but the world had successfully come through energy crises and climate crises and was not inclined to listen. It was the Asian nations, now politically and militarily dominant, who began to understand that the populations of their old rivals in the west were growing again, because their citizens were failing to die, and that this process had profound implications. Suddenly over-population, resource depletion, a planet in danger, were back on the agenda, a popular concern, the crisis du jour. Demonstrations and protests became widespread, especially in the less-developed world. International bodies met, debated, made their rulings: population growth had to stop; reckless consumption of resources had to stop. Those countries whose citizens cheated death must limit births.

The United States had no choice. Guilty, with other rich countries, of previous despoliation of the planet, no longer militarily supreme, we were also by this time the biggest offender in terms of extending our citizens lives. We signed the treaties. Thus, in the United States, the Population Management Agency was founded, becoming by 2072 a major controlling force: terminating pregnancies and issuing reproductive rights by lottery.

This was one key element in the oppressive conditions leading ultimately to youth rebellion in the west. The other arose naturally from the demographics. As people lived longer and longer, and as fewer and fewer babies were born, the population aged. This was a process that had been apparent in the twentieth century as well; but it began to accelerate in the middle of the twenty-first century when the lifespan of most individuals was increasing rapidly. By 2085 the median age in the United States was 58, compared with 17 in 1820, and 35 in 2000. Elderly candidates won elections. The old retained power, wealth and jobs. The young were disenfranchised and largely unable to reproduce. The conditions for violent action had evolved out of slow processes of change, and were suddenly upon us.

Jeff Savage, *The Methuselah Paradox*
(Johns Hopkins University Press, 2086)

PROLOGUE: A DEATH IN SYRACUSE

Rose was spooked by the call, even though she'd been expecting it. She knew there was nobody at the other end: it was just a voice, telling her that her pregnancy check was due; but the artificial tones resonated in her head like a witch's curse.

She said she'd be there, and closed the call, and tried not to panic. Just a voice, she kept telling herself. But she knew the voice was connected to other things, systems, agents, police. People who didn't let things go.

She grabbed her cat, Flint, and huddled up on the couch. She wasn't going to go to the center tomorrow, of course. She'd go away, hide somewhere. She'd go all the way to Canada if she had to.

Melanie had laughed when she'd told her that she was pregnant. But Melanie wanted to think that if anyone was pregnant, it was her. Because how much did it cost to buy baby rights on the open market? Millions and millions of dollars! A waterfront home in Florida! A lifetime's savings! No wonder Melanie was jealous.

After a sleepless night, Rose felt her nerve giving way. Eyes widening in fear, she gazed at her balcony window, her hallway, the heating-cooling grid, expecting to see the silvery flash of bees.

She rushed around the apartment looking for Flint. She had to get out, go somewhere, but not without her cat. She found him in the kitchen, staring at his empty bowl. He looked at her with startled eyes, hunched down ready to spring, but she swooped him up and hugged him tightly to her chest.

She ran to her bedroom, trying to think what she would need: her purse; a coat in case it got cold later. She nearly lost Flint as she was

1

unlocking the door. She flung her coat and purse out into the hallway, and used her free hand to pull the door to and press the touchpad.

Her eyes dancing up and down the hallway looking for bees, she scooped up her purse and coat and ran awkwardly to the elevator.

◇◇◇

The Syracuse office of the Population Management Agency noted Rose Mickelburger as non-compliant with her voluntary attendance program and issued a mission directive to its team of MAIMs, Micro Airborne Intelligent Machines. Swarm 117 entered Rose's apartment through the ventilation ducts and spread out into the three small rooms, looking for cells and molecules. After two minutes they re-assembled and linked filaments, pooling data and analytical power.

The swarm concluded that Rose was probably not pregnant, but that confirmation was required. The swarm broke up into its constituent bees and rolled under the door of Rose's apartment like silvery smoke, picking up the scent of Rose and the cat in the hallway outside.

◇◇◇

Rose was distraught. She had lost Flint. The cat had grown increasingly disturbed as she ran through the streets towards the interstate, and had finally given a cry of fear and twisted out of her grasp.

Alone, she recoiled from her surroundings. The buildings were grimy and there were junked appliances scattered around. Few people lived here any more. The deep throbbing from the interstate was starting to get into her head. But there were some abandoned apartment blocks further on where she thought she might hide, maybe even lay up for a day or two. Until she had decided what she was going to do.

"Rose, what's going on? Where are you?"

Melanie's voice. Maybe she had tuned in to her breathing, her pumping heart. "I'm okay. I'm not waiting around for bees, that's all."

"Jesus, Rose, is this about the baby? Listen to me. *There isn't any baby.* You're imagining it. You do that, remember? You imagine things. Go back home."

Suzanne's voice cut in: "Tell me where you are. Or tell your genie to tell me where you are. I'll come and get you. I'm free right now. Rose?"

She felt a sob building up in her throat. She mustn't listen to her friends. They didn't understand. They didn't want to understand. She really was pregnant, and she had to defend her baby.

She reached up awkwardly as she ran and pressed a stud on one of her earrings, disconnecting the audio link. Now she was completely alone. The telcom floater, hovering somewhere up above her, would move away, keep tabs on its other clients.

She stumbled around the overgrown precincts, looking for a building she could get into. She saw only one other person and it gave her a shock. It was an old person, a woman probably, and she looked old in a way she'd hardly ever seen before: lined face, stooped body; as though she'd been shrunk, dehydrated, had the life sucked out of her.

Rose shuddered and turned away. Her baby. She had to think about her baby. But the old person, she realized suddenly, had come from somewhere. She forced herself to turn back and look more closely at the apartment block behind. She noticed at once that the roll-down door to the parking garage was half-raised. She looped around the old woman and ran down the ramp and eased her way under the door.

She maneuvered around the wreck of a car and pulled open the door to the stairs. It was pitch dark in the stairwell. She fought off panic and started up, slowly, then faster, desperately, tripping a few times, not stopping until she was pushing open a door to the roof.

The flat roof was covered in decaying leaves, greasy underfoot. Ventilator ducts reared up around her like solemn statues. The noise from the interstate hit her like a muffled scream. She could see the vehicles now, chasing each other in close-linked convoy at a hundred miles per hour.

She moved away from the noise, watching the stairwell housing and the ventilator ducts, every nerve tensed. Had she escaped? Could bees find her here? And then her gut gave a kick of pure fear as she saw that half-visible dust, that iridescent swirl, appearing from around the door of the stairwell.

She tried to run, her legs slow and wooden, but she slipped and fell on the greasy surface. She rolled over and looked back. The bees had formed themselves into black letters:

HI ROSE
PMA PREGNANCY TESTING SERVICE

They were going to swarm all over her, invade her, analyze her. She struggled to get up. They'd half disappeared again, but they were coming for her, she seemed to feel them on her body, in her nose, under her clothes.

She scrambled up and ran in terror and collided with the rusting barrier around the roof.

◇◇◇

Swarm 117 followed Rose twelve storeys to the ground. She landed on a playground wheel. The air was suddenly dense with cellular material and molecules. The swarm circled cautiously. It determined that the death of the target human had occurred, and that resuscitation was unlikely to be viable. The head of the human had struck the central axle of the playground wheel, and extensive physical brain damage was occurring.

The swarm rose up and formed into a dish and made a secure upload of data to the PMA satellite. It provided a visual record of the accident.

Its mission was successful, it concluded. In the final seconds of her life, the swarm had confirmed that Rose Mickelburger was not pregnant.

PART ONE: ONE–NINERS

CHAPTER 1

Alan Connacher reached out and put a hand on the shoulder of his dying friend. The deterioration in Phil's condition over the last few days shocked him deeply. Nobody expected this kind of health crisis any more: the world had moved on from all that: lost spouses, mourned colleagues, the drawn-out battles with disease. Young or old, people expected to live, not die.

Except that here he was, Phil Springer, one of his oldest and closest friends, someone he'd known for almost seventy years, lying in a Washington hospital bed, the novelties of sickness and suffering written on his face.

He gave his friend's shoulder a squeeze, and sank down on the bedside chair. "You're looking good," he lied.

The familiar high forehead, winged with spikes of white hair, was drawn tight and filmed with sweat, but the pale blue eyes were bright. "They say I'm not doing well. Which is kind of ironic, under the circumstances. I thought ninety was the new fifty."

"We'll find an answer, Phil," Alan said. "The medics will work it out."

"You'd better put me in one of your machines and rejuvenate me."

Alan looked closely at his friend, not sure whether he was serious. "You're going to have to hang on a while for that. But I'm finally authorized for trials, and it goes without saying that I'll get you in the program if you want me to."

Phil shook his head gently, as though the concept of a new start, a younger body, was beyond him. His mouth opened and he seemed to struggle with a wave of nausea. Then the breath went out of him and he sank back on the pillows. Alan looked beyond him to the robot on the other side of the bed, which was connected to Doug's body by a series of probes. His friend was suffering from a novel form of immune system breakdown, which left him prey to a deviant form of *e coli*. Machine antibodies and targeted antibiotics had twice cleared the rogue *e coli* out of his blood and tissues, only for it to return. It was as though his immune system had hidden it, or re-created it. Phil was unlucky enough to have discovered one of those increasingly rare conditions that proved resistant to medical technology.

"You always used to talk about rejuvenation," Phil said, reviving suddenly, a touch of color surfacing on his cheeks. "Even at Harvard. And here you are. You stayed with it all that time and got a result."

"Not yet, I didn't."

"But you contributed to all that's happened... delays in the onset of ageing... life extension procedures..."

"Others did more."

Phil took a deep breath, his expression wistful. "Who could have known, back then, when we were students, that we'd all be still around, pursuing our careers, in our nineties?"

"Nobody. And we're going to go on pursuing our careers in our hundreds. So don't even think about dying on us, Phil. We value you too much."

Phil looked away, his energy fading, pain in his eyes. "I'm not going to make it, Alan. I understand that. And you know what? I'm not sure I really care..."

Alan stared at his friend, affection for him bringing him close to tears. In a year or two, he thought, I could do something for you; my trials will surely get done, one way or another. I'll have a proven, viable procedure. You're dying on me too soon...

In his ear, his telcom genie said, "Joe Lempit wants to talk with you, Alan."

Alan sat up in his chair, controlled his emotion. "Okay" he said quietly. "Tell him I'm on my way."

He reached out again to his friend, took hold of his emaciated arm. "I've got to go, Phil. But hang in there, okay? Dave's going to come by later, and I'll see you again tomorrow."

He turned around at the door. Phil had leaned back and was staring at the ceiling. Alan watched him a moment and then left the room.

◇◇◇

As he approached the building housing his business, Life Extension Sciences, he saw that the eight above-ground stories were pulsating in waves of harsh colors, and that a thousand or so demonstrators were thronging outside in the twilight.

He told his vehicle to park underground. From there he went four floors down to his Security Office, where wall screens were monitoring the building and the demonstrators. He got a briefing from Joe Lempit, his Security Chief, and watched for a few moments as a dark silhouette advanced up the smooth, curving, face of the building. He said, "Do we know who he is?"

"No. He's wearing a suit. A recent model, probably. If we cut out the data input from the wall itself..." Joe pointed at one of the wall displays and moved his finger; the main display of the climber on the wall suddenly changed. "...and just look at him through an outside camera, he's more or less gone."

Where they knew the climber to be, harsh waves of color like those of the surrounding wall had appeared. Only a hazy silvery profile tracing the outline of his body, noticeable when he moved, gave him away.

"So he thinks he's invisible," Alan said.

"From out there he *is* invisible." Joe restored the missing data and the climber came back into view.

Alan pushed away from the door jamb and moved closer to the displays. The demonstrators, all young, had broken through the outer security gates and were milling around the walkways at the front and sides of the building. A pair of guards from the Science Park Administration were looking on, not attempting any action. The demonstration was peaceful so far, just signs and raucous singing. Labor Day a few days before had put them in a good mood. As he watched, a couple of illegal sign-writing petards were thrown in the air: these wrote a phrase in the air in black smoke, and then re-wrote it in fire, like a fuse, as the smoke ignited.

"NEW BIRTHS NOT REBIRTHS".

"NO REJUVENATION WITHOUT NEGOTIATION".

"ROSE MICKELBURGER LIVES".

Alan sighed and turned away. He liked to think he had some sympathy with the plight of the young. They were increasingly marginalized and outnumbered, and that sometimes meant they got a raw deal. The recent rise in activism wasn't entirely surprising, nor even, if it was peaceful, unjustified. But since the death of Rose Mickelburger, actions had become more extreme, including bombs at businesses not employing their quota of young people. There was even a group which had taken her name, the Rose Mickelburger Faction. He didn't think he was in line for bombs and violence just yet, but he got exasperated by protests against life extension technologies; youngsters seemed to forget that without a few pioneers like him, they would still be living in a world with death as its main determinant.

He raised his eyes to a monitor in the corner. "Ken? You up to speed with this?"

Ken Tidy, Alan's liaison at the Wheaton Police Department, had a direct pipe into the security system, and was watching events from police headquarters in Wheaton. His face on the monitor seemed to be smiling. "What do you want me to do?"

Joe Lempit, still watching the big displays, said, "He's on the roof."

Ken Tidy, on the monitor, said, "I could send an aircar."

"Let's wait a moment," Alan said. "He may just want to hang another sign from up there."

Joe said, "He's at the roof pod door." One of the big screens showed a glistening figure close-up, just visible against the pale remains of the daylight.

"What's he saying?" Alan said.

Joe made an adjustment.

A tinny, male voice said, "I want to talk to the director. This is a peaceful mission."

"You're talking to him," Alan said.

"I climbed your building. You could at least let me in."

"Nice try, buddy," Joe breathed.

"Frightened to climb back down?" Alan said.

"I had sponsors for this climb. Students. I have a petition. Three thousand, five hundred and twenty-eight digital signatures. I need to deliver it to the director in person."

"What does it say?"

"It says what you'd expect it to say. It says we need to talk and negotiate."

"Spare me," Alan muttered under his breath.

"The thing of it is," the tinny voice went on, "you wouldn't want the media running a story about how you refused a petition."

Alan thought about his grandson Zeb, who did his PR and lobbying. No, Zeb wouldn't want him to refuse a petition. And not because Zeb sided with the activists. There were a lot of older people who liked to see youth treated respectfully.

"Plus I'd rather not climb back down."

"Maybe you should have thought about that before you climbed up," Alan said. He thought for a moment. "Okay, but no discussion. Just give me the petition."

"I need some video of you receiving the petition."

"Wait a minute," Alan said. He waved at Joe to cut the audio link and glanced at the monitor showing Ken Tidy. "What do we think about this? I've probably got to receive this petition and the guy sounds harmless. Joe, I assume you can scan him for bombs and guns before you open the inner door up there?"

"Yeah, that's no problem. If you really want to do this."

"What choice have we got? Any misdemeanor and we'll detain him. Ken?"

"I can send bees. Just to be a hundred per cent safe. I've got a couple of swarms on standby."

"Can bees get inside that suit?"

"Probably not," Ken said. "But they can identify air intakes and discharge chemicals into them, which should be equally effective."

"Okay. Let's get this over with." He waved at Joe to restore the outside audio link. "Spiderman? The inner door will open when you've been scanned. Walk down one floor and wait in reception."

They watched as the wraithlike figure waited and then entered the roof pod hallway. Internal cameras picked up the surveillance. The intruder was still using the intelligent camouflage, but the cameras were deciphering the flaws: the body shape of an athletic male could be seen walking down the stairs.

Alan stood up straight. He wondered briefly about taking Joe up with him, but thought better of it: Joe wasn't exactly quick on his feet, and he might see threats that didn't exist. "Stay here and watch," he told him. "When you've done the final checks, put him in my office." He turned back at the last minute. "Maybe I'll take your stun gun. Just to wave at him if he gets carried away."

◇◇◇

The reception area was spacious, with Italian leather couches in pale blue, and machines for free drinks and snacks: it was empty at this time on a Saturday, but in any case Alan didn't pay for human receptionists; it was tough enough paying for the technical guys he really needed.

Alan paused when he got to reception and said, "Is he clean?"

Joe's voice said, "He's wearing a small backpack which contains the suckers he used for the climb… no safety tackle, by the way… a couple of those little sign-writing petards… No bombs. No guns. A couple of floaters. Could be for the video or for the petition itself. But he looks kind of jumpy. Spaced out. Take it easy in there. Or wait for the bees. Should be here in a couple of minutes."

"I'll be okay. Keep a watch on us."

Alan patted the gun in the pocket of his suit and steadied himself and approached the door of his office. It was closed. He nodded and it opened and he went in. The door slid to behind him.

The suited figure in the middle of the room jumped and tensed like a cat.

Alan stood still. Tall, sheathed in black, the figure looked like something out of a fantasy game studio. The eyes, camouflaged but visible, were dangerous, the pupils small, as though he was on some kind of drug; the drug he had used, perhaps, to give him strength and courage, drive him up the face of the building.

"You saw me?" the kid said, as though following his train of thought; "you saw me climbing the building? You thought I wouldn't make it?" The voice was hollow, artificially disguised, but there was a hint of pride in it.

Alan felt his irritation increasing. "Shall we get this over with? Where's the petition?"

"There isn't one."

"Excuse me?"

"I made it up. To get inside your building."

Alan took a deep breath. He felt the first stirrings of unease and also a flash of anger. Part of him wanted to leap on this impudent invader and march him straight back up to the roof. He turned away, biting his lip.

"So why are you here?" he said.

The kid's eyes roamed about the office for a moment and then came back to him. "'Cause of this place. 'Cause of what you stand for."

"And what's that?"

"Rejuvenation! You're going to do it, aren't you? You've got a trial planned."

Alan kept his gaze steadily on the young man. For the first time, it occurred to him that he might be more than just a daredevil kid representing an ordinary student body. He might instead be a member of one of the new activist groups, and therefore a good deal more dangerous.

"Yes," he said in neutral tones, "a human trial is planned."

"That's not going to happen, man! We'll stop it. Because you know what it means to us? Young people everywhere? It means we'll be sidelined, junked, ground down even more. That's what rejuvenation will do to us. You understand? Take me. I'm in sports, man. I have a shot at the big time. You know? I'm good. I'm very good. But you bring back the heroes of the past. Rejuvenate them. Where am I? You guys will be the big stories. You guys will be the glamour. You guys will get the training. You guys will win the matches, the medals. Because you'll have the youth *and* the experience. You'll cream us. You know what I'm saying? We'll be nothing more than the ritual sacrifice. The gladiators. You can't do this to us!"

The kid was shouting now, as though, behind the mask, he was losing control.

"That's pathetic." Alan suddenly felt his anger spilling out. "When you have the advantages of new brains and youth? Start your own leagues! Learn new techniques! Challenge the old guys!"

"When it's the old guys running the networks and the venues, and the old guys paying to watch matches? You think they want to see their heroes beaten by a young guy? Get real."

"I am real. And your premise is wrong. How many old-timer sports stars want to go back and re-start their careers when so much in sports has changed?"

"All of them! All of them! And it isn't just sports, either. My sister, man... My sister does a boring job, a normal job, okay, selling stuff, fashion items, mostly to old folks, and she does pretty good, but if you guys come flooding back, with your connections and your money, okay you don't buy a pretty dress from an old person, but if it's an old person who looks like a *young* person... You see what I'm saying? She's out of there! Finished! Just like me! You can't do this stuff!"

Alan waited a moment, hoping the kid would calm down. Then he said:

"Suppose I take you down to the ground floor and let you get back to the demo."

"Suppose I take you."

"Excuse me?"

"Suppose I take you."

"I don't think so," Alan said. "Bees are standing by."

"No... fucking... bees!" the kid screamed. He whirled suddenly and scrabbled something out of his bag, a small sphere, the size of a ping pong ball, which he tossed into the air with a jerk of his hand. The sphere took flight and moved straight for Alan's head, veering away and passing out of sight.

Alan blinked, moved his head slightly. Something touched the hair at the back of his head, retreated.

Alan turned his attention back to the kid. He was leaning forward, concentrated, something of the sportsman in him now, as though he'd thrown a brilliant line pass and was waiting for the catch.

Not a robotic floater, then: the sphere was clearly under the kid's control. Like most youngsters, he'd grown up making things work with brain waves: games, screen pointers, even telcom genies. There'd be permanent connections from his scalp to some kind of wireless device, concealed in his suit.

Alan felt no fear: just a time-stopping moment of tension, like a high-pitched sound. He almost laughed at the thought of the gun in his pocket. Talk about old technology...

"It's a bomb," the kid said. "I guess you understand that. It'll blow up if I let it. Very localized damage. But then again, if it's up against the back of your head? I think it will do the trick. Blow out a piece of your brain. And the thing of it is… I really have to concentrate. Even as I talk, I'm concentrating. To stop it blowing up. If I get distracted, it'll blow. Understood? And bees are very distracting. So no… fucking… bees! Okay?"

Alan watched him for a moment. "Keep concentrating, okay? I'm going to talk to the cops."

"I'm concentrating."

"Ken? You in the loop here?"

"I'm here."

"Where are the bees?"

"Right overhead."

"Better keep them there."

"I want to see them," the kid said. His eyes were still on Alan.

Alan could feel the sweat now, under his arms, on his back. This kid seemed to be making it up as he went along. And did he really have the control he thought he did? Could he manage these two lines of thought?

"Joe?" he said to his Security Chief. "Can you give me an overhead surveillance shot? On a screen behind me?"

Alan's office was twenty feet square, and the lighting was artificial: no light was getting in from the outside wall, the apertures blinded because of the material's defensive posture: but he could sense the light from the screen behind him, sending new colors across the rug.

"Wheaton PD," the kid said, his eyes flickering aside and back. "Okay. Just hold them there like that."

Alan glanced around quickly. The bees had formed themselves into the Wheaton PD logo and were hovering, visible in the light beamed up from the roof.

"You understand this, Wheaton PD?" the kid said, still looking at him. "You distract me with bees, or anything else, and you got a dead guy in here."

It seemed to Alan he had to wait a long time for the response. Then he heard, "Understood," from Ken.

"He says 'Understood'," he told the kid.

"Get the word out. If you want to live. Make sure the whole building knows."

"Joe?" Alan said.

Joe said, worry in his voice, "Sorry, Alan. I thought we had everything covered."

"You're saying this thing could be a bomb."

"Well… I don't think we want to risk it. The scan signature could be much the same as the sign-writing petard."

So much for sticking with Joe as security chief, Alan thought, instead of hiring a young guy; we old guys just don't keep up.

"Joe? This isn't your fault, okay? Put the building on defensive alert. Nobody goes in or out. Brief everybody, including the robots. No distractions. Nobody comes near us. Okay?"

"You got it."

Alan looked at the kid. "Looks like you're in charge. Maybe you'd like to move this thing back to a safe distance. I'm not going anywhere."

"Yes you are too. You're taking me down to your labs."

CHAPTER 2

As Alan led the way on to the elevator, down towards the lab security module, pictures from long ago came into his head. He saw his daughter Trudie, six years old, flirting and grandstanding and arguing for another ride on his shoulders, at the beach at Cape Cod. He saw his wife, skin young, hazel eyes shining, looking seductively at him over a glass of wine at the Mirabelle. Further back, still a boy, he was in the science museum in Boston with his father, an MIT academic, staring into a souvenir box of colored minerals.

These images vanished as they entered the security module controlling access to the labs. He was back in the present, back with his dilemma. Adrenaline flooded his system: there were some choices here, and somewhere at the back of his mind he had been preparing.

"Take us into the lab," the kid said.

They were in a platinum-alloy chamber, color-coded lights on the roof, a gentle movement of air.

"Impossible," Alan said. "In the first place, you need approved status, which requires guarantors and a couple of days to arrange, and then the usual DNA check to confirm identity. Then we would need to be scrubbed over, and a ping pong ball in my hair would cause some problems. Third, the spiderman outfit, the bag, would have to go."

"You can over-ride all that."

"No. The system works like an independent robot. It makes its own decisions. Is that right, lab security?"

"Yes, Dr. Connacher," a measured, artificial voice said.

Alan could feel his heart pumping, fear making his throat dry. He was pushing the kid, and he knew the dangers of that.

"And I'd like to suggest again," he added, "that you move this bomb away from my head. While you think about what I'm saying."

"I don't want to do that. Just in case it blows up. Your head will dampen the blast. Safer for me. Meanwhile, I'm waiting."

"Waiting for what?"

"For you to figure it out. Get us in there. Whatever it takes."

"Don't you understand what I'm saying? It's out of my control."

"Work it out, Mr. Director. I'm not waiting for ever."

Alan stared at the suited figure. He wasn't showing real signs of doubt or agitation. The eyes were intense, determined. Had the drugs left him with a false sense of power and confidence?

"If you kill me, your chances of getting out of this building are minimal."

The kid's eyes glittered. "Are you listening to this, Mr. Security Director?" he said, and waited a couple of seconds. "Answer me!"

"Don't get involved, Joe," Alan said.

"Answer me!" the kid shouted.

"Yes," Joe's voice said. "I hear you."

"Then open the fucking door! Because your boss here is trying to get himself fucking killed!"

"Sorry, Alan," Joe's voice said. "I think I have to do this."

A framed opening appeared in the wall. A roof light turned green.

Alan didn't waste time questioning Joe's decision; but he balked at leading a saboteur into the heart of his personal territory. He stood still, immobilized.

He felt a foot in his back, shoving him towards the doorway. He nearly swung round and attacked. He could taste the fury in his mouth. But his death would help no-one except the enemy. He allowed himself to be propelled through the doorway, and controlled himself by focusing on the familiar surroundings.

There was the wet shower, the dry shower, the lockers, the rack of billowing intelligent gowns, and now, as the doorway sealed behind them, the swarming attentions of SAIMs, Small Airborne Intelligent Machines, the smallest bees licensed for commercial civilian use.

Alan turned his head, curious how the kid was reacting to these: was he suspicious? No, he seemed unworried, prepared. So this is all planned, Alan thought; he knows exactly what he's doing. I let him in the building, and everything follows.

"Dr. Connacher, you're advised to have a dry shower. Your visitor is clean."

"I'll skip it," Alan said.

"Yes sir. The floaters in your personal space and in your visitor's equipment contain explosive material. They must be disposed of in type B containers."

"Security Director?" the kid said, his voice rising dangerously.

Joe's voice said, "Just ignore it."

"Yes sir," the artificial voice continued smoothly. "Please put on gowns."

Although lab security had made no specific reference to the gun in his pocket, Alan had by now decided that it was a liability: he didn't want anything distracting the kid's attention. He took off his suit coat, the gun weighing down the pocket, and dropped it in a bin. He picked a gown off the rack and put his arms through the sleeves: the gossamer weightless material settled around him without apparently touching him. Alan indicated to the kid that he should do the same. The kid shook his head.

Alan didn't argue. "My visitor is wearing a closed suit," he said.

"Yes sir."

No further objections: Joe was keeping the over-ride in place.

The lab doorway opened and they passed through.

◇◇◇

Alan wasn't used to the labs being so quiet and empty. Even on a Saturday evening, there were usually a couple of die-hards trying to crack a problem or earn some Brownie points. They had been rounded up and escorted out, probably, by Joe's deputy. And what could they do? Except fatally distract his captor?

Alan was wondering how likely it was that the kid's threats were real. Okay, the explosive was real; the lab's detectors had worked better than Joe's, and the contents of the ping pong ball had been confirmed; but would the bomblet explode if his concentration was disturbed? It made a good story, a good deterrent: but it was a tough mental balancing act that would limit the kid's ability to react to outside events. There was a good chance, surely, that it was a bluff. Or that triggering the bomblet would be delayed by several seconds, so that he could have momentary lapses of concentration without immediate consequences; killing Alan wasn't going to help his cause.

Or maybe it would. Maybe it was part of the plan. Maybe the kid was going to kill him and find another hostage to get himself out of the building.

Either way, it might be worth taking advantage of any suitable moment to grab the bomblet. If he could get his hand round it before it exploded he would probably avoid brain damage. He would lose a hand: but a hand could easily be replaced; a brain couldn't.

The kid stood poised at the railings, the lab, built as a succession of open-plan floors and access walkways, opening out below him. He looked as though he wanted to jump the barrier, swoop across the space like Tarzan, become again the daredevil climber who had penetrated the building.

"Give me the tour," he said, pointing downwards.

"Where are we going?" Alan said.

"I'll tell you when we get there."

Alan walked down the black-treaded stairway to the first working area, a place mostly of screens and workbenches, from which all manner of robotic micro-labs, housed a couple of floors below, could be activated and monitored: nano-assembly of molecules and machines; biotic simulations; through to experiments on live laboratory *arkanes,* the pseudo-species created for humane laboratory use. Normally home to 20 or more researchers, those who needed direct rather than remote oversight of experimental results, the space was as empty as everywhere else, apart from a couple of idle gofer robots.

Alan walked steadily between the benches, not looking back, and down the half-dozen stairs to the next work space, indicating it with a wave of the hand, then turned and kept going, down the open stairs to another level. Here there was just a corridor, lined with access ports to the sealed micro-labs. Alan kept walking. The tour, to which the kid had referred, was something he was used to providing, to all kinds of dignitaries and associate workers; but his usual pride was soured now into fury and disgust, and he offered no guide or explanation to the features they were passing.

The kid prowled effortlessly behind him and asked no questions. Alan tried to think where his interest might lie: presumably in the level to which they were now descending, the clinical level, where rejuvenation technologies were actually being tested and applied. This was the obvious place to attempt an act of sabotage.

This level had independent access for medical staff and regulators and, one day, volunteers. Alan had determined that the technology must be developed and tested in-house, despite the temptation of using the facilities and backup of an outside research institution. In fact he had struck a deal with the Johns Hopkins Department of Biomedical Engineering, to provide medical oversight and backup, and some research activity, and there was a frequent movement of personnel backwards and forwards between the two sites. But today it was quiet. In fact it had been quiet for months, but not this quiet.

They joined the incoming corridor and passed without checks into another holding area and then on into the clinical work area. It was a big room, occupying most of the building's footprint. There were tables and chairs and screens on the right, and on the opposite side two very large installations, ten feet high, like huge Egyptian catafalques, except that the body, when these installations contained one, was hidden deep within, embalmed in liquid, and fed from a myriad of surrounding processors and tubes; clutter extended, at the moment, by a variety of monitoring devices, clinging like minor acolytes to the central hulks.

Referred to humorously by researchers as the coffins, to Alan they were instead the product. In his dream, he saw thousands of these ultra-sophisticated pieces of equipment spread out in hospitals and clinics throughout the country, restoring life to millions, particularly those suffering from age-related conditions still untreatable over the very long term; and earning him a little money in the process. But so far he had received far fewer orders than he had hoped for, as healthcare agencies weighed up the cost, assessed the disincentive effects of youth protests, and waited for successful human trials: and Alan had begun to see these behemoths with a jaundiced eye.

He had grown up with the absolute conviction that only a much longer lifespan could redeem life, rescue it from the demeaning, trivializing effects of premature ageing and death. But the doomers, as these youngsters called themselves, ironically invoking the boomers of the last century, didn't seem to understand that even with the life extension technologies they were currently using, they would one day grow old. They saw only that they couldn't freely reproduce, and that their numbers were declining.

"Don't you understand about death?" Alan wanted to shout at them. "Don't you care that first your parents, then you and your friends, will one day cease to exist?"

And as he turned to face his captor, this bizarrely-suited exemplar of youthful selfishness, he felt not only fury at him for attacking, invading his business, but fury at him for not understanding his role in the wider human enterprise.

◇◇◇

"Keep going," the kid said.

Alan stared at him blankly.

The kid waved at him impatiently. "Let's go. The tour. Move it."

Then Alan understood what the kid was after, and the bile rose in his throat.

He began walking, past the glass portals of the immersion tanks, past the screens, the seminar room, the cafeteria at the end, and down the stairs to the lowest level.

This, the monkey habitat, was a different world. Pathways wound through landscaped savannah, with grass slopes, oak trees, banana trees, play areas, a large pond. The pathways were segregated from the habitat by wire-mesh fencing, but volunteer seniors were usually to be found within the habitat, interacting with the nine rhesus monkeys currently in occupation, checking their health and well-being. Robots provided basic maintenance and replenished food supplies.

The interaction between robots and monkeys was one of the entertainments for visitors: if a higher-ranked monkey, particularly a female, felt that a robot wasn't bringing the food quickly enough, she would chatter away at him, like an infant seeking the attention of its mother. The monkeys, in fact, had figured out that the robots were an inferior species, although of what precise characteristics they never seemed entirely sure, shying away in alarm if a robot came upon them unawares.

As he started down the pathway into the habitat, Alan gave a quick glance around to check on the locations of the monkeys. The volunteer workers knew the personalities of all nine, and kept detailed notes of their social organization. Alan didn't have time to follow this fully, but he usually recognized individuals and knew their status. Doris and Annie, for instance, hung out together and did a lot of mutual grooming, and one of the males, Boris, was a trouble-maker who was not above stealing a tempting-looking banana from the hands of a lower-ranked member of the troop.

Only one of the present troop had been rejuvenated. A total of eight individuals had been treated during the past two years, all of them 25 to 30 years old, noticeably weakened by ageing; seven of those had been relocated, secretly, to other research institutes, where their health and behavior had been monitored carefully. The information issued to the public described these animals, correctly, as entirely normal, with the added benefits of improved health, energy, strength, eyesight, hearing.

Of particular interest was the reaction of the other animals, most of them young, to their rejuvenated troop member: they clearly recognized the individual as a monkey they knew, but they also understood that changes had taken place; changes which required a good deal of inspecting, vocalizing, grooming, and sometimes hostility before the phenomenon of their reborn friend could be incorporated into their social and personal psyches.

One of the findings not released to the public was that rejuvenated individuals were likely to end up higher in the complex dominance hierarchies than they had typically been before rejuvenation.

"Okay, which one is it?" the kid said.

Alan had spotted Doris and Annie swimming in the pond, another female swinging on the branches of an oak, Boris screaming, just for fun, it seemed, at a robot. The monkeys, accustomed to interacting with humans, were aware of their presence and were showing off.

Alan took a deep breath and faced the kid. "Which one what?"

Alan felt the hairs at the base of his neck stirring and the small sphere appeared directly in front of him and took a run at his forehead, veering past his eyes and swinging out of sight again.

The kid seemed to enjoy that. "Which one of these fucking monkeys is rejuvenated? And don't get any clever ideas about hiding it, because

I'll kill them all, one by one, if you fuck me around."

The kid had turned on his camouflage kit again, and he was now a shimmering, barely visible presence: but the distorted harshness of his voice had generated interest, a hint of alarm, in the monkeys. There was an outbreak of screeching and squeaking. Doris and Annie stopped swimming and held on to each other. Boris ran over bravely and climbed up the wire fence a few feet from where they were standing, brown hair bristling, pink face accusing, and gave a short, high-pitched bark, which Alan recalled was a response to threat.

Alan was struck dumb. He could not face identifying a particular monkey for destruction. Neither did he imagine, watching the tense determined eyes of his captor, that he could get a hand on the little sphere behind him before the kid would move it or detonate it.

Suddenly the kid, losing patience, pulled another sphere from his bag, held it up for Alan to see, and at the same time gave flight to the one at the back of his neck, sending it darting along and through the fence, to where Boris was clinging. Boris froze, reached cautiously behind him, found nothing, and began angrily shaking the fence.

The kid released the second sphere, which flew to the familiar spot behind Alan's head.

Just as Alan was trying to make sense of that, returning his gaze to the kid, there was a loud pop back to his left. He swung round, fear wrenching at his gut.

Boris had no time even to scream: his small head half-obliterated by the blast, he fell to the ground on his back, and lay twitching.

Alan jumped towards him, stopped helplessly, leaned onto the fence holding the wire, thinking he was going to be sick.

Boris stopped moving.

There was screaming and chattering from the other monkeys, and then quiet, as though they had suddenly recognized the seriousness of the event. They approached skittishly, running towards Boris and then turning back.

"Gee," the kid said. "I must have lost concentration. That can happen when you've got two of these things in the air."

The dominant female, Sally, was leading the ragged approach to the body, screaming at the two humans, either to warn them off, or demanding their help. She ran forward the last couple of feet and

23

dipped a finger in the blood still flowing from Boris' carotid arteries, tasted it, and retreated again. Doris and Annie hung back behind her, Annie grasping the hair on her back.

"That's the one, then," the kid said.

Alan looked up, startled.

The kid nodded, a halo of movement, only the eyes clearly visible. "The dominant female."

Alan could no longer restrain himself. He leapt at the shimmering figure, trying to get some purchase on the suit. The kid went down, but wriggled free, whirling around and kicking Alan in the side of the head. Alan sprawled, head ringing, half-unconscious. Too late, he scrabbled for the sphere behind his head, but it was gone.

"Don't do this stuff!" the kid screamed. "You're not rejuvenated yet, you old fart. And never will be, if you're dead!"

Alan stayed down, putting up a hand to feel his head.

He heard another loud pop. He couldn't bring himself to look. How did he know? He wondered. How did he know that the dominant female was the rejuvenated one?

There was another outbreak of screaming from the monkeys.

He felt a kick in his side.

"Get up! Get up!" the kid shouted.

Alan pulled himself up to a sitting position. His vision was blurred, but he knew what he was seeing when he looked through the wire into the habitat: two bodies; two little bundles of sandy-brown hair.

The other monkeys had disappeared, retreated to safe havens in the trees.

Alan felt beaten: he had been useless at saving the monkeys, perhaps useless at saving himself. He struggled to his feet.

"Alan?" Joe's voice said. "You okay?"

"He's okay," the kid said. "And nothing has changed. You distract me, and your boss is dead. Just like the monkeys."

"Alan?" Joe said again.

"I'm okay. Just keep a lid on things a while longer."

"It's your *ideas* we're fighting," the kid said, out of the blue. "As for the monkeys: that's as much your fault as mine."

Alan said wearily. "Where to?"

"The main entrance."

Alan set off, his head still ringing, no coherent plans to fall back on. He went back up to the clinical level, took an elevator, led the way out through visitor security controls. They reached the main lobby. Like everywhere else they had passed through, it was empty of people. But outside, Alan could see the demonstration was still in progress, crowding the walkways around the entrance.

The camouflaged wraith beside him said, in a voice Alan thought now slightly subdued, "Remember, you're my ticket out of here. If I go down, you go down."

Alan nodded.

"Someone out there is going to take control of this floater." The bomblet buzzed around in front of his eyes and then returned to the back of his neck. "You won't know who it is. There's a hundred people out there. One of them. Okay? And then I'm going to disappear. Are you listening to this, Mr. Security Director?"

"Yes," Joe said.

"If anyone or anything comes after me, tries to stop me, if you bring down those bees or any other bees, or surveillance floaters, the one who's looking after this floater is going to get distracted. Understand? Very distracted. And you know what happens then. You got all that?"

"Yes."

"Let's go."

The wraith took the lead now, barely visible in the brightly-lit lobby, showing up in silhouette as he reached the final set of glass doors, then passing through into the crowd. Alan followed rapidly behind him, and was suddenly outside in the warm evening air, the kid already gone, the mass of young people ebbing and flowing and masking his passage.

Alan stopped, uncertain. He had caught the attention of a number of demonstrators: but there was no sign which one of these youngsters held his life in his hands, or rather in the electrodes taped to his scalp. He looked up. The bees, still in their 'Wheaton PD' formation, waited, high above the roof.

And then something stirred at the base of his neck and the bomblet floater spiraled past his eyes and up, disappearing into the night sky. There was a flash and a bang, and Alan sat down on the steps of his building and took deep breaths of fresh sweet air.

CHAPTER 3

T here was something *not right*, Jay Kirilenko thought, about being beaten at cubechess by a girl who looked about sixteen years old. It offended his sense of propriety; and it made him feel old and past it, which, at forty-five, was hardly the case. Not these days. But with eighty year olds going around looking much as he did, there were too many things which were *not right*; things which irritated him profoundly.

Monkeys getting killed. That was not only deeply unpleasant, but a sign of order and values collapsing all around him. Threatening him personally, as well as his organization. His life's work, in fact. That was definitely *not right*.

He tried to concentrate on the one-meter-sized virtual cube in front of him. He would certainly lose to this upstart if he didn't keep his mind on the game, which moved at a frighteningly fast pace. The cube already contained more of her red and yellow icons than his own blue and white ones. He raised his eyes, searching the girlish face, which the player notes said was twenty-three years old, for weakness; but all he could see was naïve excitement and enthusiasm.

Okay, he thought grudgingly, she's a phenomenon; and this is not my day. After a couple more defensive ploys went wrong, he gave in to her aggressive assault without much further resistance. He stood up and peeled off the glasses and the cap containing the sensors. He gave her hand a perfunctory shake. Time to face up to the ugly business of the evening.

The club had an extensive bar area, as well as two other cubechess installations. There were lots of people here, mainly players and hangers-on, almost all young. He had instructions and advice for several of his lieutenants, assembled from several locations around Philadelphia. The worst possible thing would be to allow a sense of being outdone, outshone, to percolate around his organization. His principles of non-violence, of slow and steady groundwork, of responsible protest, would win in the end, not the spectacular stuff, killing monkeys and planting bombs. Not this Rose Mickelburger Faction, as they were calling themselves: that was going to end badly; or so he hoped.

He got a beer and moved between several tables, chatting briefly about cubechess, then taking his chance of a few words with one or other of his local organizers. Yes, they didn't like what was happening either; although in one or two cases he sensed some ambiguity. Is this the way we have to go? Is this the only way to combat the overweening smugness of the one-niners? That was the underlying doubt. To which he wanted to bang his fist on the table and shout, No, if we give up the moral high ground we'll lose the argument, we'll be damned by the decent majority.

He played another cubechess match, against a seasoned veteran, a member of his own organization, in fact, one of those who had been on the original demo at the Mars Three Habitat; he lost again, which felt bad, because he was used to winning, but he'd caught sight of Kate, hovering at the edge of the group of spectators, that bright, challenging look on her face, and blind rage had swallowed him up for a couple of moves. When he could see again, it was too late.

He stalked her between matches, this time clutching a lemon soda, finally pinning her down with a couple of women whom he supposed were functioning as security.

"Kate, we need to talk."

He had never entirely pinned down the story of her Japanese American origins: but the look in her eye of permanent provocation, as though everyone should expect attack rather than defense, was as lively as ever. Jay had slept with her once, and didn't like to think about it. He didn't like to think about anything much in their relationship, but he knew that she had now become too powerful, and too ambiguous, to ignore.

"You want to figure out why you lost?" She said it with a tilt of the head that indicated she wasn't just thinking of the cubechess match.

"That's right. Also maybe what you're doing in Philly."

"I've got as much right to be in Philly as you have."

"Well, that's true. But can we have a talk about it?"

"Oh my, Jay. You're drinking lemonade. What's going on?"

"Kate…"

"Okay, okay." She stood up. "Let's find a corner of the bar." As she turned away, she said to her companions, "Stick around, okay?"

The surface of the bar showed baseball games which the customer could flick through. They went to the quieter end, a space not surrounded by people they knew.

"Mine's a bourbon," Kate said, idly changing the game taking place on the bar from the Phillies to the Red Sox.

"Kate, we're at cross purposes here."

"What, bourbon, lemonade?"

He took a steadying breath. "Operations. You can't expect to put on your kind of show, like this thing yesterday, and still swan around at my events, benefiting from my infrastructure. You just can't do that. You're bringing in a whole new level of risk."

"Ah, it's the risk, is it? I thought so. You were always were too cautious. Anyway, I don't know what you're talking about."

"Yes you do, Miss Rose Mickelburger. Don't fuck me around. Some of the earlier stuff might have been ambiguous, but this one is too close to home. You're personally involved at Connacher's place. You're going to get questioned. Let me be clear. You can't run these rogue operations off the back of M3R. I won't allow it."

"What are you going to do? Call the FBI?"

"Kate, you've got your own group, and your own name, so take the people you've recruited and go. It's a reasonable request."

He was trying to control his anger, but he felt it washing over him, seeping into his voice. He wasn't helped by the condescending look he was getting from Kate.

"You're such a fucking dinosaur, Jay, you know that? You're good at the small stuff, M3R is a pretty smooth machine, you're national, dozens of tight little cells, morale is good, I'll give you all that: But you're still doing these tiddlywink operations after what, ten years, when the situation among the hard core young like me has got a hell of a lot worse. I'm the way forward, when are you going to realize that?"

"Never. Never. It's a matter of principle. If you give up on non-violence, you'll lose the support of the vast majority of the decent citizens of this country."

"Baloney. The couple of things we've done here, on the East Coast, has got us more attention, more respect, across the whole country, than everything you've ever done put together. Right? Of course I'm right. So don't fucking diss me for moving on and showing you where you should be going."

"Kate, I'm just asking you to take your people and set up your own structure, your own meeting places." He made an effort to keep his voice down. "For God's sake, don't ruin my organization because of your recklessness and carelessness."

"Your organization is dying, and as for the structure... well, the structure is useful. I tell you what. I'll let you take your people and set up something new. That's my best offer."

Jay feared for a moment that he was going to strangle this contentious woman. He heard his voice tremble. "Okay." He stood up. "Okay. I'll cut you out of everything. And everybody I can associate with you. You'll find out who's got the power."

"Yes," Kate said. "Yes. I think we will."

CHAPTER 4

A lan could barely remember the last time he had gone to see his grandson Jason at home. Jason's apartment discouraged such visits: it was a small one-bed in an older building, in need of new carpets, fresh paint, and an energy makeover.

He rode up in the elevator and walked the corridor to Jason's door. He hadn't slept much in the last few days, and he felt mired in depression and inertia. As well as the invasion of his labs, his friend Phil Springer had died. He suspected he was in need of counseling: he had moments of sudden fury followed by a sense of helplessness. The picture of himself being herded around his building by a kid in a camouflage suit sat in his mind like some shameful image of debauchery, disturbing and persistent.

Jason opened the door and gave him a suspicious look and turned aside with a barely audible greeting. Alan had mumbled something on the telcom link about a catch-up meeting being overdue, but clearly Jason had picked up on his tone of voice and was expecting something less agreeable. Alan entered the apartment and stopped, wondering how to proceed. As usual, the contrast between Jason's living conditions and his own stirred a sense of guilt. It was Jason's choice, of course, but somehow, these surroundings said, his family had failed him.

Sam appeared at the door of the bedroom and looked at him solemnly. Again, Alan felt completely at a loss. It was nearly a year, he calculated, since he had seen the boy, and he hardly recognized him. And Sam, clearly, hardly recognized him either. Or didn't recognize him at all. How had he allowed that to happen? His only great-grandchild within range and he had consistently failed to make contact. Not that Jason was exactly encouraging the relationship, but of course that was his fault too: he, and even Trudie, Jason's mother, had made it clear what they thought of spending several million dollars on something, anything, you couldn't really afford.

Sam suddenly ran across the room in front of Alan and picked up a small robot car beside the couch and stood holding it, looking back at Alan.

Unlike his father, who was busying himself with something at the kitchen worktop, there was no suspicion in Sam's eyes, only a question.

Alan felt a surge of emotion that startled him. He was normally resistant to the charms of small children. They had become so rare, so valuable, that they were treated like little princes and princesses, their every word and gesture a miracle of nature. In the world in which Alan had grown up, this equated to being irredeemably spoiled. But Sam had a pleasing face, thick black hair falling over his eyes, and instead of that irritating assumption of royal privilege, there was a hint of diffidence in the way he looked up at his great-grandfather, mixed with a solemn intelligence. On impulse, he took a pace forward and squatted in front of the boy.

"Hey Sam. You remember me?"

"No," the boy said, shaking his head slowly and emphatically back and forth, but without retreating.

"Sure you do."

"No," shaking his head still, but now there was a hint of a smile, as though this denial of acquaintance might be a deliberate tease.

"Well, I'm your great-grandfather. We've met a few times."

"Okay."

"You know what a great-grandfather is?"

"It means you're a very old person."

"That's true."

"And I'm a very young person."

"That's true too."

"I was five three weeks ago. I really was."

"Good for you."

"I got this robot for my birthday. You can hold it if you like."

Sam handed his robot trustingly to Alan, who took it carefully.

"I'm the only one who can work it. I have to use my mind."

"Are you good at that?"

"I'm very good. I'm very very good." The boy nodded solemnly, as though merely stating a fact.

Jason called over: "Sam, your great-grandfather hasn't come to play robots. Leave him alone, please."

Sam looked at Alan as though debating the exact meaning of this.

Alan recognized the double meaning of Jason's words: he was being told not to interfere. *Don't pretend you care about my son.*

Alan returned the robot to Sam and stood up. "I'll see you later, Sam."

Sam ran around the couch, clutching the robot, and headed for his room. Alan watched him go.

Jason, in the kitchen area, suddenly put down the kettle he was holding and let forth an angry oath.

Alan saw that Jason's gaze had moved to a point behind him. He swung around. He saw nothing at first, but then picked up the familiar blurring of background objects. A swarm of bees had entered the room. The patch of haze swirled and looped, and then flowed to a blank stretch of wall, where the bees turned black and coalesced into letters:

PMA

CHILD ID AND HEALTH-CHECK SERVICE

Jason took a step towards them, his expression murderous. "These damn things, they don't have to come this often. Sam!"

The boy was already back in the room, watching.

"It's okay, Sam, just another check."

But the boy wasn't afraid: in fact, his face was full of awe and excitement. He ran towards the bees, waving his arms. They enveloped him decorously, moving as he moved, like a diaphanous silver cloak. Sam spun around, grabbing at them, clutching his fists, and they flowed away, vanished, as his fingers closed. He laughed and tried harder, but they eluded him without effort.

Then the game was over. The bees withdrew, turned black, wrote, "Thank you for cooperating," on the wall, and disappeared.

"God, that makes me mad," Jason muttered.

The boy danced around the room, trying to see where they had gone, inspected his hands in case he had caught one, got down on hands and knees to examine the carpet, and then ran over to Jason.

"Daddy."

"Yes Sam." Jason put his hand on his son's shoulder, his anger under control.

"Where do they go when they disappear like that?"

"They don't go anywhere. They change color to whatever is behind them and you can't see them. Then they leave through the ventilator."

The boy chattered on, eyes bright. Alan thought, Jason is not so bad with this kid. He treats him respectfully, but not like he's a king-in-waiting. And the kid is smart.

Watching the two of them, he could clearly see the genetic link. The 60% random dip into Jason's viable gene pool, rather than nature's 50%, gave that extra emphasis to Jason's paternity. The remaining 40% seemed to have hit the Pacific region: Sam's black hair, Alan thought, had come from East Asia, surely, and something in his face as well, although Jason's Caucasian features were dominant.

After Sam had fully rehearsed the reasons for the bees' visit with his father, he went back to his room and Jason went on with his kitchen preparations.

"I've made some peppermint tea," he said at last, crossing from the kitchen and handing Alan a mug.

Alan accepted it with a muttered word of thanks. Did Jason remember that he didn't drink peppermint tea, or any other kind of tea for that matter? Probably. Jason, his expression now closed up again, made a reluctant gesture in the direction of the couch, and Alan sat down and placed the mug on a side table.

"Jason, you know what happened at my offices last week?"

Jason was still standing. He nodded slowly, not meeting Alan's gaze. "Of course."

Alan waited to see if any expression of sympathy would follow.

At last Jason raised his eyes. "I'm sorry you got… you know… some lunatic… Those monkeys didn't deserve that." The eyes veered away.

"But I did?"

"I didn't say that."

"You seemed to imply it."

33

"No. It's just that… No."

"Were you at the demo at my offices last week?"

"No."

"Any ideas about the kid who climbed the building and used those floater bombs so effectively?"

"What do you mean?"

"I thought the style, the method, the skills might ring some bells."

Jason's eyes narrowed suspiciously. "Is this an interrogation?"

"I just thought you might be able to help."

"Look. I support organizations like Fair Deal for Youth. But this guy who killed the monkeys, that's different. I don't support that. And I've no idea who it could be, or what organization he's part of."

"You've spent some time at my offices recently, Jason."

"With good reason. As I've explained to you."

"A project. For this course you're doing."

"Yes."

"There is no such project. I've checked with the school."

Jason frowned into his mug. "It's unofficial."

"There is no such project, Jason!" Alan felt his anger breaking through, and he dampened it down by picking up his mug and tasting the unpleasant contents.

Jason shrugged and said nothing.

"Are you going to sit down?" Alan asked him.

"Listen, Granddad, if you've come here just to - "

"Sit down, for God's sake." Aware of the boy in the bedroom, Alan struggled to keep his voice level.

Jason moved his head around, staring at the ceiling, as though bored and frustrated by his impudent grandfather, but then he sat down.

Alan waited until he felt he had Jason's full attention, and then he went on: "The point about this kid, whoever he is, whatever organization he represents, is that he didn't jump into this operation unprepared. He knew what he was doing. He knew about my security systems, building layout, which monkey had been rejuvenated. In a word, he had inside help. Jason, I'm sorry to have to tell you that Cap Olsen, the National Security Director at the FBI, thinks that you provided that inside help."

Even much later he could remember the stages of Jason's response: shocked attention, a moment of absolute stillness as disbelief gathered, then a flush of anger spreading up his face.

Alan only half listened as Jason began a defensive tirade against this "bullshit accusation".

"Okay, okay," he said, holding up his hands, "I believe you. But why did you invent this project?"

Jason stared at him and relapsed into sullen silence.

"Jason, the FBI are going to be all over you because of that, so maybe you'd do better to tell me first."

Jason remained silent, his expression of defiance gradually winding down, until Alan saw the troubled youngster beneath: the graceless man who lacked his brother Zeb's charm, whom the family chose to ignore or treat as second-class; the man struggling to make his way in a difficult world; the man who had defied everybody to become a father.

"Jason," he said in a softer tone, "I know I probably wasn't a lot of use to you when you were growing up, or since for that matter, and I apologize for that, but I never had any problems with you visiting me at my offices. You knew that. Why did you make up this project?"

Jason stared at his tea, the mug clasped in both hands. "I thought it would be easier... to find out certain things."

"What things?"

"Financial data. Whether you were making money. Whether your business was worth something."

"The answer is probably no, because of debt levels. But why did you want to know all that?"

Jason seemed to shrink further into himself. "Granddad, you must know... In my world, people practically make a joke of it... You're a target, aren't you? Because you're sticking your neck out over rejuvenation... You're the sort of guy that youth extremists..."

"Want to kill?"

Jason gave a little shrug.

Alan had received too many shocks over the last few days for this one to cut deep. He was half-relieved that Jason had a motive unconnected with the plot against his monkeys.

"You want to know if there'll be anything to inherit?"

"But not for me." Jason glanced up quickly. "For Sam. Sam is..." Jason was too choked up to continue.

Alan sat still for a couple of minutes and then tried another sip of the peppermint tea. It tasted worse. He put the mug down. He studied Jason's expression for a while, thought through what he had said, and made a decision.

"Jason, as you probably found out, I'm not in good shape, financially. However, I will find some money for Sam. Okay? I'll get my accountant to speak with you." Alan paused. "In return, I want just one thing. If you have any idea who could have provided insider information about my security system, tell me. Or tell the FBI. Is it a deal?"

Jason stared at him for a moment. "Did you ever wonder about Yinghua?"

"Yinghua?"

"I think you know that I know about you and Yinghua. And that's okay. We'd already... broken up... so that's not the point. The point is what she is."

"And what is she?" Alan said the words with difficulty, his mouth suddenly dry.

"Don't get mad about this."

"Jason: say what you want to say."

"You know how seriously she takes things. Maybe you don't know how much she... gets involved in things."

"Youth things?"

"That would be my best guess."

"Are you saying she spied out my lab and passed stuff on to the Rose Mickelburger Faction?"

Even as he put the question, Alan was rejecting the possibility, putting it beyond consideration. This was just Jason working out his resentments. During the six months of his clandestine relationship with Yinghua, she'd never shown any sympathy for the youth activists. And he was sure they had communicated at the deepest level.

"You showed her around, didn't you?" Jason said. "Answered her questions? She had the opportunity."

"You need to give me more than opportunity."

Jason hesitated. "I just had the feeling... when we were together... that she had things going on... a hidden agenda, if you like..."

"You figured she was spying on you?"

"I don't know. I really don't know. I just didn't understand her. She'd disappear for a day or two at a time, no explanation. She had connections with people whose role and identity I didn't know, and which she didn't seem to want me to know."

You were mismatched, Alan thought. The truth is, she was out of your league.

He had recently developed a theory about Yinghua's relationship with his grandson: childless herself, she'd fallen for Sam; for his bright intelligent face and his black Asian hair. Jason had just been the intermediary.

"Okay," he said, "I appreciate the thought. I'll pass it on to Cap Olsen at the FBI. Anybody else you can think of?"

Jason shook his head. "Can I ask you something?"

"Go ahead."

"Why did you and Yinghua break up?"

He looked away, not wanting to get into this painful territory with his awkward grandson. He knew what he thought was the reason, but he occasionally wondered whether it was more to do with his ageing brain, his loss of emotional stamina.

"She's only forty, Jason," he said. "And however young I am in functional terms, I'm in fact 89, and the world sees us as very far apart. The young world, anyway. As you know, we had to keep our relationship secret. So for her sake, her career, I decided, in the end, that... it would be better if I let her go free."

"So it wasn't her idea."

"No. I don't think so."

"But you hurt her, and therefore it's possible..."

"That she betrayed me? I don't think so, but like I say, I'll mention it to Olsen."

In his heart, he knew he'd do no such thing. Yinghua revered her ancestors in the Chinese fashion. She talked about reconciliation between young and old, not about insurrection. Whatever it was she had chosen to hide, it wasn't a link with the Rose Mickelburger Faction.

On that issue, he was no further forward.

CHAPTER 5

O n the long drive north through Michigan, the man who called himself Kronos worried about his companion, Merko. Was he going to break down into a dysfunctional wreck? Become someone he might have to kill?

They were driving along an old logging road in the dark, washboard ribs of impacted dirt under the tires, walls of conifers on each side looking silver-grey in the beams of the truck's headlights, dust billowing up in the tail lights behind. Kronos was aware of Merko in the passenger seat, shifting nervously, piping some god-awful noises into his ears, and using brain-wave control to create a haze of color on his wrap-around shades. His chameleon jacket was doing its tricks, even here inside the cab, showing a skeleton, or writhing snakes, or slogans about the disenfranchisement of the young.

Kronos tried to control his irritation: the truth was, he couldn't manage without Merko. Merko was going to supply the technology behind the biggest assault on its self-satisfied elite that this country had ever seen. Merko, in fact, was the reason they were here in the first place. But did Merko know what it was like, when people started dying? Or was he still in a dream-world, expecting it all to be clean, anaesthetized, impersonal?

He had a dark and depressing vision: maybe everything Merko had ever told him would turn out to be a dream; he had no special powers, had made no remarkable discoveries during his time at NSA. He was a fantasist. A fantasist with brilliant intellectual capabilities, but a fantasist all the same. In which case he really would kill him. It would be a matter of simple justice.

Three miles later the logging road forked. His route-finder told him to bear right. An old sign on a pole said 'Long Lake'. After another mile he was told to slow down, and a moment later he was bumping down a narrow track, spruce needles brushing the side of the truck. He turned off the lights and put on glasses giving him an intelligent mix of light and infra-red. He took it slowly. It was ten minutes before the route-finder told him he had reached the designated location. He stopped the truck and killed the engine and jumped out.

He walked around to the right-hand side of the truck and opened the cab door. Merko was adjusting his glasses, probably thinking them into infra-red mode.

"Let's go," Kronos said roughly, and went to the rear of the truck and unlocked the tailgate and opened the back of the box. Heat from the engine, decoded by the glasses, showed the contents in sharp silhouette: at the back, taking most of the space, was a small robot excavator; at the front, some hand tools, a couple of old-fashioned rifles, and the backpack containing the beehive.

Kronos stood still and listened. He could hear the breeze stirring the tops of the trees, the faint creaking as trunks moved, the whine of cicadas, the shuffling of life amidst the brush and debris on the forest floor. Nothing else.

It was going to happen. Steady and professional. No other emotions. Just get it right.

He looked for Merko. His silhouetted figure, hands waving, appeared around the truck, like a ghost.

"Should've brought fly dope, man."

Kronos swung the back pack across his shoulders and picked up a rifle. "Come on. It's about a mile. Stay behind me."

Kronos walked carefully. It had been dry for days and the track was hard. The light amplifiers in his glasses, combined with infra-red, gave him a clear black-and-white picture of a tunnel through trees.

They heard the generator first, then saw light. Kronos left the track and circled through the trees, glad of the generator noise, covering any sounds they might make. When they were close enough, he hunkered down and waved for Merko to do the same.

They were looking at a small cabin of unpainted plywood sitting on concrete blocks. Leakage of light from a small window and infra-red from the stovepipe gave enough information for Kronos's glasses to construct a well-lit picture of the area in front of the cabin. It was rough ground, dotted with tree-stumps, littered with junk. There was an old boat engine, rusting oil-drums, wood stacked under the cabin and beside the cabin, as well as the two ancient trucks. Wooden stairs led up to a door at one end of the cabin.

Kronos nodded to himself, satisfied. This guy doesn't matter, he thought. He's marginal, not connected. Nobody's going to miss him when he's gone. And going by the wrecked truck, he's old. He's kind of the enemy anyway.

He didn't articulate these thoughts to Merko, recognizing that his ability to make ruthless calculations, like the excitement now alive in his gut, was something best concealed.

Kronos stood up and circled around through the trees until he was as close as possible to the cabin door without breaking cover. There was a line of light under the door; almost certainly, therefore, the point of access the bees would choose.

He looked around for Merko. At first he didn't see him: then he remembered the chameleon jacket, now in camouflage mode, and he focused in on the white globe of Merko's face, suspended in space like a Halloween floater. Merko's eyes, behind the glasses, looked jittery, but not yet panic-struck, which was about as good as he could expect.

Kronos eased the pack off his shoulders and opened it and took out the domed ceramic chamber and set it in front of Merko. The myriad channels engraved on the dome's surface, seen through the special glasses, seemed to glisten like a snake's back. Merko squatted and reached out and tapped a tiny device into a socket at the base of the chamber. His expression became concentrated, his glasses now data screens, and he began a muttered dialogue with the bee-control systems in the hive.

Kronos waited. "Happy?" he said at last, pointing at the sky. He was mainly concerned about the MAIMCOM surveillance system, ready to report on unlicensed bees, but they also needed to know if any of the scattered residents of the bush-country had personal floaters, telcom floaters, hovering within range.

Merko didn't seem to hear him; but a moment later he nodded.

"I will wait five seconds," Kronos said, "And then I'm going in. You wait here."

Merko nodded, his eyes still distracted, reading his glasses.

"Merko?"

Merko looked at him.

"Wait here."

Merko nodded.

"Let's go then."

Merko didn't say anything or do anything, but suddenly the dome of the chamber seemed cast in shadow and there was a faint hiss. Kronos froze in watchful anticipation. He could see nothing, but he knew that bees were flooding out of the canister, each one programmed with Merko's mission parameters, each one using wireless contact with its neighbors to optimize camouflage and efficiency. The whole swarm should execute its deadly assignment inside a couple of minutes; at least if Merko had got things right.

He saw the seconds counting in red at the edge of his visual field: 2, 3, 4… On three there was a darkening of the band of light along the bottom of the door of the cabin. The bees had found a gap there and chosen that as their point of ingress. So far so good.

On seven he stood up, still holding the rifle, and moved rapidly and carefully across the rough ground to the door of the cabin. The door had an old-fashioned handle and he turned it but the door held fast. He flicked an intelligent key from his lapel and inserted it in the keyhole under the handle. There was a click and the key turned. He turned the handle again and the door opened. The seconds count stood at 17.

Inside was blinding light. Then the glasses adapted and everything came to life in color. His eyes jumped around the room, noting but ignoring the old couch, the dirty strip of carpet, the wooden table, looking for the bees, finding them almost at once, near to the floor to his right, where a human form lay spread-eagled. 21 seconds gone.

It was a man and he was lying between the table and an old-fashioned kitchen range. Probably he had been standing when the bees entered. They would have released a chemical payload in his nose even before he knew they were there.

He had fallen on his back, arms spread wide. The bees, now bunched in a tight swarm over his head, fluoresced with black and red highlights, bloodied by their mission. Kronos took a step closer, cursing the fact that the lock had delayed him. He would get a detailed audit later, but he had wanted to watch the process live, learn whatever needed to be learned.

The bees had gone in through the eyes and the nose. Already, he could see through the screen of bees, the eyes had been completely destroyed. The brain was being excavated, tossed out of the eye cavities of the skull, by a thousand tiny egg-beaters, in a growing mist of blood and cellular debris that was settling over a range of several feet.

Kronos checked quickly back down the body: tartan work shirt, micro-fabric jeans, boots; more or less as expected; a loner; a guy who fished and hunted and liked to live in the bush.

He suddenly felt the floor boards move and heard a creak behind him. He whirled, bringing up the rifle. Merko was standing there.

"Oh God. Oh no." Merko was aghast.

"Get out of here!" Kronos shouted at him, furious at the intrusion, furious at the breach of instructions.

"Oh God. This is gross. This is…"

Merko was crumpling, gagging. Somehow his brain wave link with his jacket had set it flashing a bilious green.

"Merko, get out of here!" Kronos leapt at him: They had enough of a clean-up problem without Merko being sick in the cabin. Enraged, he nearly pushed Merko out through the door. But stopped himself. Merko injured would be the last straw. They had a body to move and bury. He grabbed Merko's jacket firmly by the collar and herded him through the door and down the steps. He gave him a restrained shove and left him gagging. He jumped back into the cabin and closed the door. The counter in his glasses said 58 seconds.

The bees had gone. He cursed Merko again, but at least the timing was within their estimates. Now the bees would be going through self-cleaning and inspection regimes, and they'd have an overall mission time when they returned to the hive. It looked okay. It looked like a success. Merko might be a pain in the ass, but he had delivered.

Kronos stared at the body for an exultant moment. It looked gruesome: with the eyes gone, the sheen of blood covering the face and spread over a two-foot circle of floor, it looked like something out of a horror movie. Imagine that in newscasts, in magazine downloads, across the country, across the world. Repeated twenty, thirty, forty times. Imagine, under the blood, the face of that bullshit senator in Falls Church, or his friend The Great Rejuvenator in Wheaton; any of those sanctimonious one-niner bastards.

It was dynamite. It was going to scare the shit out of the whole clan. And it was going to put all those other feeble activists, those crap bomb-makers, those Rose Mickelburger people, firmly in their place. He, Kronos, would be top of the heap.

This is it, he thought; *the revolution starts here.*

He strode forward and kicked the boot of the dead man. "Okay, so I killed you, you dumb fuck, but you're part of history. Does that make it better?"

CHAPTER 6

L ulled by the quick and clever sounds of his car's motor and control systems, as he flew in the dark up the lanes and underpasses of highway 29 towards Wheaton, FBI Director Cap Olsen quickly glanced through plastic download pages of the *Washington Post*, some articles changing even as he watched. Finding nothing of interest, he put them aside and tried to concentrate on what he was going to tell Alan Connacher.

Very little would be good. Nothing at all would be better. But given how sharp Alan was, he was probably going to have to acknowledge that his special team had made a breakthrough and identified the guy who had killed his monkeys. On the other hand, he didn't need to admit that Alan's hunch about cubechess had been correct: yes, the activist guy was a cubechess player, and cubechess was the way his cell recruited and communicated internally; but his own team of investigators would have seen the connection between cubechess and the brainwave control of bomblets, so there was no point feeding Alan's egotism.

He had to keep his own fingerprints on this one. There was only one grade higher he could go within the FBI; to the recently-created post of secretary. He didn't care whether he got to be Secretary or not, from a functional point of view, but he sure as hell didn't want to get shunted out of his directorship. Even at 87, he had a long working life ahead of him.

A good result here could give him a chance to prove his worth; even those committees over on the Hill, testifying before which was his least favorite activity, would be impressed. Maybe, ultimately, this operation could secure his job, keep himself out of the retirement hell his brother Charlie was going through.

Charlie, 92 years old, had been talked into an executive rotation scheme by his employer, and was facing five years, minimum, of so-called "alternative duties". He was doing voluntary work and traveling a lot and he said he liked it, but Cap saw the look on Charlie's face sometimes and he knew what he was thinking: are they really going to let me back in to proper work? And if not, what the hell am I going to do for the rest of my long life?

Cap knew that some seniors had gone back to waiting tables, like they were students again. Jesus Christ. No wonder everybody like him, in a job they loved, got nervous, over-cautious. No wonder they cheated a little, favored their own, gave the young what must have seemed like a raw deal.

He glanced at the clock on the dashboard. It was now even later than he had hoped and planned. Alan had been at one of his daughter's lavish parties, and his telcom genie had finally given him a meeting time close to midnight. That was irritating, but Cap was determined not to be put off. He was looking at a tight schedule tomorrow, and he wanted to pursue the basic concept tonight, while it was fresh in his mind.

His car paused at the barrier across Alan's driveway while probes checked underneath. He put his hand out the window and felt the light suction of the ID probes moving over his fingers. A few seconds later the barrier rose and his car took him on to a visitor parking slot in front of Alan's porch. Connacher himself let him in to the house and took him through some empty-looking spaces to a den at the back, with a desk and a couple of stuffed chairs and a food and drink facility.

Cap hadn't seen Alan since they'd met at his office at FBI Headquarters, over a week ago, and he was struck by how bad he looked. He'd lost weight, his tall frame seemed to slouch a little, and his strong features were etched harder on his face. On top of that he didn't seem very pleased about having a late night visitor.

Cap said, "Okay, it's a bad time, but there you go. Can I sit down?"

Alan waved at a chair.

"I'll have coffee, black," he said as he sat down. "Cap Olsen."

"Twice," Alan said.

"Yes, gentlemen," the drink facility said.

Alan collected the two mugs and gave one to Cap and sat down.

Cap took a sip. He raised his eyes for a moment and watched the floater he'd brought with him darting around the room checking for bugs. "Let me start with some obvious stuff. Please bear with me for a moment. You, your company, pretty much leads the field in terms of whole-body rejuvenation. You've rejuvenated monkeys. You have permission for human trials. As a matter of fact, if you had the right volunteers, you could start rejuvenating humans tomorrow. Isn't that correct?"

"Not exactly."

Cap made a face. "What's the problem?"

Alan leaned back in his chair and looked upwards, visibly making an effort to bring his mind to bear on the issue. "If we had to start from scratch with a new volunteer, it would take about three months, with the volunteer attending the lab three times a week, to prepare what we call The Procedure, that is, the cell-by-cell program that goes into effect when the volunteer goes into the coffin."

"The coffin?"

Alan shrugged. "That's what we call it. Actually it's more like a very large, above ground, burial chamber."

Cap digested that for a moment. "Three months? No way round that?"

"No. We have to know a great deal about the individual, the genotype and the extant phenotype, before we can start rejuvenation."

"Suppose you threw all your facilities at it and had the volunteer seven days a week, round the clock?"

"We might get it down to six weeks. No guarantees. In the end, we'll get it down to a week, but this is early days. We have to go carefully."

"Okay." Cap nodded slowly. This was a problem. "And these volunteers you had lined up... before Spiderman blew your program to pieces... you'd done this... Procedure for them?"

"Yes. Unfortunately yes. We put a big investment into that."

"And who else?"

"Myself, of course. I was the guinea pig."

"No-one else?"

"No."

"All your volunteers withdrew?"

Alan shrugged wearily. "Pending a re-evaluation of security. Which we need to do some time. Cap, where is this going? Why are we having this conversation at one o-clock in the morning?"

"Because I decided it was in the national interest to do so," Cap said gruffly.

"By national interest I presume you mean us, the ageing majority?"

"I mean the elected institutions of government."

Alan said nothing.

"You got a problem with that?"

"Not really. Especially not at one o'clock in the morning."

Cap was silent for a moment. He checked the floater again: it had finished its inspection and was glowing green.

"Alan, we're in a situation of mounting extremist activity. You of all people should be aware of that."

"I am aware of that."

"And I have a job to do in responding to that situation."

"Explain to me what particular job you are doing at this particular time of night, and how I am involved in that."

"What you can do for us is what I'm here to talk about."

"Then please explain yourself."

Cap Olsen felt a growing irritation, and a growing sense of defeat, but he wasn't ready to give up just yet. "I think I should tell you we've made some progress in the Spiderman investigation."

"I'm listening."

"I can't give you details."

Alan put down his mug. His face was suddenly animated. "But you're here in the middle of the night to ask me about rejuvenation. You must have something. You must have something big. Have you identified him?"

Cap hesitated. "I can't tell you that."

"Wait a minute. Wait a minute. I get it. Rejuvenation. Whether you've got Spiderman or not, you think you've identified a network. A Rose Mickelburger network, presumably. And you think you're going to use rejuvenation to set up one of your agents for the job of penetrating the network. Am I right?"

Cap bowed his head, wishing he was working with a scientist who was less of a smart-aleck. "You know as well as I do," he said slowly, "that it's useless trying to penetrate these youth groups with genuine young people, no matter where you get them or how you train them. Their cover is blown in about ten minutes. And they won't do it anyway. Age loyalty is that strong."

Alan now seemed fully awake and engaged. "All the same, I've got to tell you that rejuvenating an old guy is a pretty ridiculous idea. You'd have lots of problems. Not just the three month lead time. What about ID? You'd be identified by the DNA checks as someone who's supposed to be old. What about disguise? You may look young after rejuvenation, but you're still recognizable, especially to family. And how the hell do you think you -- me -- could rejuvenate someone without my entire staff knowing?"

Cap said nothing.

Alan said, a weary look returning, "Anyway, I wouldn't do it. What kind of a clinical trial would that be? No matter what risks your guys were willing to take. Medical status, post rejuvenation, has to be monitored day and night."

Cap said acidly, "Even if the President asked you? Nicely?"

"So I'm right," Alan said.

"I was getting around to telling you."

"It didn't sound like that."

"Any chance of some more coffee?"

"Two more coffee," Alan said.

"Yes, gentlemen," the machine said.

CHAPTER 7

Merko needed to find a washroom fast. These frigging drugs, that's what they did to you. Here he was, waiting for the bees to take the bait, respond to his call, and all he could think about was taking a piss.

Because he was alone! Alone in this frigging car park in Annandale somewhere, in the middle of the night! With this entire frigging operation depending on *his* control systems, *his* satellites, *his* frigging god-like knowledge, *his* mission statements… While that inflated prig of a man stayed up there in Bethesda issuing orders like he already ruled the world.

"Jesus!" he screamed and jumped out of his truck and took a couple of paces and urinated into the ornamental shrubs bordering the asphalt.

Frigging drugs.

Merko zipped up and returned in a rush to the truck. He could feel his whole body trembling.

Jen. He needed Jen beside him. But his Big Leader had told him he couldn't talk to Jen just now.

The same Big Leader who planned to kill him if he fouled up. Oh yeah, he could see that clear enough. Well, Big Leader better watch out. One final mission and he could take out Big Leader as easy as writing *you're dead* on his glasses. That would fix him for thinking he's god.

Merko put a hand on the door of his truck and tried to stop his body trembling. He forced himself to look around, all directions, make sure, one more time: nobody, nothing happening, just the school, dead, not even a light, their alarm and surveillance systems not bothered by a parked truck. Even the weather was playing along, cool and dry, stars in the sky, comms working fine.

Kronos's voice said, "Merko, you okay?"

Merko's heart jumped. "Yes!" he shouted. "Leave me to concentrate!"

"I don't see anything."

"We're fishing! It takes time!"

"Okay. Take it easy."

"Stay off this channel!"

Merko went around to the back of the truck and stared at the dish pointed at the sky, his link with his borrowed satellite network. Above him, his satellite was pointing a tight wireless beam at a sequence of sites around Washington, and reeling off a hundred swarm identities using the PMA protocol request for contact. He had read somewhere that the one-niners, long ago, had done this kind of thing when they were illegally searching for phones to clone; phishing, they called it. So maybe what he was doing was swishing: looking for swarms to acquire and bend to his service. If he could find any. If Big Leader left him alone. He stamped back to the cab and got in and slammed the door angrily.

Big Leader had no idea how complicated this was. Big Leader thought his servant Merko could do everything on his own, without help, without support. Jesus!

He clamped his hands on his knees to stop them shaking and thought his way back into the multiple screens projected in three dimensions by his glasses. He began mumbling to himself, adding sub-vocalizations to the brain wave data input to his glasses, steadily regaining his concentration. His glasses were linked by wireless channels to the dish in the back of the truck and showed him what was happening at the two dozen target sites. All the basic procedures were pre-programmed, but he had to move through every information source to follow results, see what worked, what swarms responded.

PMA swarms at this time of night were on routine missions: surveillance, exploration; no pregnancy tests, not much human contact; so he should be able to grab some for a few minutes. As long as he'd correctly calculated the odds, chosen the site areas, got the protocols right. As long as-- Yes! He'd got one! A bite!

He whirled around through the data, checked the upload. Another one! Jesus, they're coming too fast, he seemed to feel them, see them through his glasses, pressing on him, objecting, resisting... No, the first looked okay, right there near the targeted Georgetown site, taking the mission suspension, the reset, the special loop, the new mission, *done,* now the second, this one Bethesda... another new one... Jesus, this was moving, this was happening, *he had them,* he'd fished them out and they were his, for a moment, and then...

Then they were Kronos's children. Off on their missions. Making their own decisions. Nothing to do with him. Doing their thing and vanishing back into the night sky...

"Hey Merk! I think I picked up a trace! Way to go, old buddy."

"Shut up! Keep this channel closed."

"One giant leap for mankind..."

"Shut up!"

Big Leader thought he was making history. Big Leader could think what he frigging well liked. Merko clamped his hands tighter and tighter on his thighs, bruising the flesh beneath.

"They're your missions!" he shouted suddenly. "I'm just the idiot technician!"

"Merko..."

"And stay off this frigging channel!"

◇◇◇

The swarm of Micro Airborne Intelligent Machines, PMA MAIMSWARM 32C4, spread itself thin and flat as it approached the target home, avoiding security lighting and other radiation hot-spots, keeping low to the ground for maximum camouflage.

Working independently, the bees surrounded the house, testing for air movement and temperature, moving up the air-flows to check for filtration systems. They rendezvoused under the front porch and linked filaments and decided that the best way in was through a poorly-closed window on the second floor.

They went in like a tail of smoke sucked inwards, dropping to the floor and spreading in a wave from room to room, under doors, collecting human cells and biotic molecules, according to their special skills. Their movement generated only a faint background drone, too weak to rise above ambient noise levels.

They chose an unoccupied room for another rendezvous, staying beneath a large chest, and linking themselves in a tight structure, multiple filaments connected. Their data showed there were two humans present in the house: a male and a female. Both were lying on beds, in different rooms, vital signs indicating sleep. They pooled their analyses of cells collected and assembled DNA profiles of the two humans. Mutating briefly into a wireless radiator and collector, they used a telcom link with the national identity database to relay the DNA data and obtain the names of the humans. They confirmed that the male was their target, General Clem Anderson.

The attack profile agreed, the bees split up and flowed along the floor and into the room where the target was lying naked on a bed under a sheet. About 200 bees flew into the nasal passages and discharged their tiny payloads. The General seemed to catch his breath, made a nose like a snore, half-lifted his head, then fell back limp and unconscious, his head lolling to one side.

The bees whirled around him now like dervishes, forming a dense cloud over his face, combining in dagger-shaped strike teams to penetrate the surface of the eyeballs, then using spinning Catherine wheel formations to displace and eject material from the eyes, grinding deeper and deeper into the eye socket, and on into the brain.

The swarm's Temporary Mission Directive required them to destroy and displace the frontal cortex on the basis of size and depth approximations, leaving an un-patterned display of cellular debris and blood on the face and immediate surroundings of the target human. When wireless signals from specialist bees indicated full completion of the mission, the swarm withdrew from the partly-excavated skull and spread flat again, hugging the floor. They spewed out around the frame of the poorly-closed window, swooping down to a water butt at the back corner of the house and churning through the surface water in a first-stage cleaning process.

Time elapsed since the swarm's arrival at the General's home was 3 minutes and 32 seconds. Leaving the area, the swarm used low-lying cover for several blocks and then flew upwards. Finding themselves within the time parameters of their temporary mission, the swarm formed a dish and relayed video material from their mission via a specially-designated satellite channel. A few seconds later the swarm received an Identification Friend or Foe challenge from a MAIMCOM monitor, and paused to validate its existence by exchanging the daily MAIMKEY with the monitor. It then experienced a memory reset which removed the temporary mission from its databanks and filled the vacated timeslot with routine search maneuvers. Restored to its original mission, it flew on towards the banks of the Potomac.

CHAPTER 8

Cap Olsen began to feel his mental faculties slipping away from him, as fatigue and irritation and too much coffee began to blunt the edge of his concentration. Alan was keen to know who Spiderman was, and in particular who his connections had been inside his business, and Cap decided to tell him that their suspect had a link with Johns Hopkins University's Whitaker Institute. Alan employed a few research academics from that source. They discussed some of the implications. Alan agreed that a couple of the Johns Hopkins people might have been able to get into the security system and suggested a couple of names.

As Cap stood up to go, he was beginning to consider an extreme option: using Alan Connacher himself as the agent.

Connacher had let slip that he had done the preparatory work on himself. Therefore, he was ready. He was a candidate. Not the ideal candidate, but a candidate. At present, the only candidate.

There were a couple of things going for him, apart from the essential quality of being old, one of the tribe: he was motivated because of the attack on his labs, and he had various special capabilities, mainly his science background, that would help him blend in with a group of cubechess-playing smartasses.

Even better, it would shut him up, put his over-active intelligence to work, and bring him under the control of the FBI.

Cap realized he wasn't in a fit state to evaluate this idea, and he said nothing to Alan.

His attention suddenly focused on his telcom link: a short beep had signaled a high priority call, and without any preamble from his genie, he found himself listening to a voice he knew, the night duty agent at Headquarters.

"Director, since you're up, I think this one is for you. I've got Senator Winkowski's bodyguard on hold. He says the Senator is dead."

Cap thought he must have misheard. "Say again?"

"Senator Winkowski's bodyguard, sir. On the line. An emergency, apparently. The Senator has been attacked."

"You're sure? I mean, you've checked him out?"

"Yeah. This guy is for real."

"Shit. Okay, patch him through."

Cap sat down again and tried to get his brain to focus. He listened as the background ambience changed. He could hear someone breathing fast, a voice in the background. "Hello?" he said.

"Yes, hello. Sir… Who am I with?"

"I'm Cap Olsen, FBI."

"Okay, good. Sir, this will sound totally crazy…"

"Slow down. Start with your name and location."

"Oh yeah, I'm Tony Vassallo, I work private security for Senator Winkowski, I'm at his home in Falls Church right now, sir, excuse me a moment…"

As Cap Olsen heard the voice in his ear telling a third party he was already talking to the FBI, he mentally checked through what he knew about Senator Winkowski: wealthy, colorful, womanizer, business interests in food and beverages, immortalist in orientation, probably had enemies on various fronts, which would account for the private security.

"Sir, the Senator is dead, that's the bottom line, it happened too fast, really…" There was a catch in Tony Vassallo's voice. "We couldn't do anything, and the crazy thing is… it has to be bees. Bees killed him. And killed him bad, sir, real real bad, it's a real mess, really horrible…"

"Tony, take it easy, you're saying bees? Bees killed him? That's pretty hard to believe."

"I know it, but that's the way it was. We saw it. I mean we saw the end of it, on the screen. Thing is, the Senator had us employed on a twenty-four hour surveillance, but it was a floater actually in the bedroom, at this time of night, 'cause the Senator… Anyway, the floater alerted us and put up the video, and it was bees, pretty obviously, got through all the warning systems of course, and they was just about done, they was into the brain, sir, through the eyes, and I can't describe to you…" The voice broke off.

Cap closed his eyes for a moment. *Jesus,* he thought. Adrenaline kicked in and when he opened his eyes he began to function in Director of Internal Security mode.

"Tony, listen, what you're saying is the Senator is dead and the brain is unrecoverable, right?"

"Yes sir."

"Did you notify any paramedics?"

"As a matter of fact, no. Didn't think they could do anything."

"Good thinking. Anyone else in the house?"

"My partner. And there's a daughter visiting for a few days. Angeline, her name."

"Has she seen the body?"

"No sir. We haven't disturbed her. She's still sleeping, so far as we know."

"Okay, Tony, here's what you do. Stay out of the crime scene, lock the door on it if you can, keep the daughter out. I'll have a team on its way in a couple of minutes. The FBI has jurisdiction on this, understood? Nobody else gets into that room. Keep this line open and we'll keep talking with you. Anything else I should know right now?"

"I guess that's it."

Cap transferred the call back to Headquarters and told the duty agent what had to be done; adding that he wanted to hear from the response team when they had seen the body. "And do a full background on this Tony Vassallo."

Christ Almighty, Cap thought, after he'd cut off the call.

"Did I hear that right?" Alan Connacher said. "Bees killed someone?"

Cap looked up. He had half-forgotten about Alan, half-forgotten where he was. He was, of course, in Alan's den. Alan was sitting in his chair, his face registering curiosity and shock. He said to Alan, "Unless that guy was on the mother of all bad trips and was hallucinating… But I don't think so."

"A senator?"

"I shouldn't be telling you this stuff, but what the hell. Yeah. Winkowski. A Republican, but he supports most of the government's policies."

"How was it done?"

"In through the eyes. Brain thoroughly messed up. No hope of recovery."

Alan said nothing, his expression concentrated.

"Is this it, Alan?" Cap said quietly. "The start of a new era? These little shits resorting to full-blown terrorist attacks? Monkeys no longer enough?"

"You think it was youth? Mickelburgers?"

"Who else? You think a jealous lover did this? Business rivals? And why go to the trouble of using bees? Can you imagine what you'd need to do to bring this off? This was an attack against the government, a demonstration of power."

Alan said nothing.

Cap heard a beep, another high priority call. He winced. What the hell now?

"Go ahead."

"Director, this is Brad Phillips at the Field Office. I thought I ought to tell you. Headquarters said you were still working…"

"I never stop, Brad."

"Yeah, I guess. Well sir, we got kind of a strange call. This was from Michelle Smith, she's number two to Susan Schwartz at the PMA, and she's on our rapid response protection system… Anyway, our system clocks her saying, 'Help FBI', and then the record has her saying, 'There's bees in here, all around me, I don't usually—' and then something that sounds like a little cough, or a gasp, and then nothing. We turn up the volume to see what's going on, and sure enough, there's the background drone of bees, and something else, sort of a whirring sound, like an eggbeater or something… Sir?"

Cap Olsen felt shock reverberating down through his body.

This cannot be happening, he told himself.

He squeezed his eyes shut for a moment, forced energy back into his limbs. "Brad?"

"Yes sir."

"Did you send a response team yet?"

"Just a single agent."

"You'll need more than that. Crime scene guys, everybody. Send your best people. I think you're going to find a body, and you won't be able to resuscitate. Seal everything up tight and get back to me when you have any news."

"Got it."

Cap Olsen closed his eyes again. He was beginning to feel a slow-burning anger: these attacks were impossible; bees didn't have these capabilities; the whole point of bees, their public acceptance, was that they were harmless, in emergencies using only a safe form of short-term anesthetic. Their firmware made any other form of aggression impossible.

Even law enforcement bees, which sometimes used a longer-term anesthetic, could do no more than immobilize the trouble-makers. But killing people! Scooping out the brains! It just couldn't happen.

And suppose these things were rogue bees, contraband bees, imported from some dubious jurisdiction... Well then MAIMCOM, the military, were supposed to shoot them down! That was the point of the MAIMKEY! Unlicensed bees couldn't survive on the street for more than a minute or two.

In fact, if these attacks were part of a major offensive against public figures, then what he was in the middle of might be an attack by a foreign power, not a youth protest at all.

Jesus Christ, what a nightmare.

He started speaking again, opening the line back to Headquarters. "Get on to our Secret Service liaison, and tell them we have logged two, that's right, two probable attacks on public figures using bees, and they should be on maximum alert, bee defenses fully deployed. Make sure they understand this is a threat from bees with apparently unrestricted capabilities. Okay? And genie, I want to speak with the MAIMCOM commander, General Anderson."

As he was waiting for the General's genie to wake him up and get him on the line, Cap Olsen was thinking: if these rogue bees have somehow got hold of the MAIMKEY, then surely we can shut down all the legitimate bees of all known agencies and let MAIMCOM destroy whatever is still out there.

In his ear, his genie's voice said, "Director Olsen, General Anderson is not responding to his genie's wake-up request."

Cap felt a chill in his stomach. *Jesus God, not another one.*

"Does the General have any military backup at his home?"

"Nothing shows up in the official telcom record. Second-in-command is General Lee Ponting, but he is at a different address. Only the General's wife, Louise Anderson is listed at the General's address."

"Wake her up. I need to talk to her."

Did they not sleep together? Cap wondered. Well, that wasn't uncommon these days in the senior community. Or maybe the General would turn out to be okay...

Remembering again where he was, Cap raised his eyes and looked around. Alan had disappeared.

Suddenly his mind started down a new path. If this was a youth op, not an attack by a foreign power, then Alan was a target.

He himself was a target.

FBI personnel in general were targets. FBI personnel were targets whatever the hell this was, youth op or enemy invasion.

So what was he going to do if bees attacked, here and now? Nothing. There was no defense.

A woman's voice said, "Mr. Olsen? Is something wrong?"

"Oh, Mrs. Anderson, no, we hope not, but we need to talk with your husband. It's very important. Mrs. Anderson, is your husband there in the room with you?"

"No. He likes to sleep early, and I was out at the opera."

"Does he sleep in a room nearby?"

"Yes. I can wake him if you like."

"Mrs. Anderson... I don't know how to say this... there have been several reports of attacks on public figures... And your husband is currently not responding to his genie... Do you have anyone else in the house? Anyone who could check on your husband for you?"

"No, Mr. Olsen, I don't. But if anything has happened to him, I want to know about it." There was a background rustling, sounds of movement.. "He was asleep when I came back from the opera, so I didn't disturb him. Anyway, I'll... Oh, Lord help us... Oh my God..."

There was a muffled sound like a scream rising from the back of the throat, then a jarring sound, the thump of a heavy weight hitting the ground.

Shit, Cap thought, clenching his fists. I had to do that, Mrs. Anderson. No choice.

He summoned up Headquarters again: "We need another response team. Suspected bee attack, General Clem Anderson. Address per the record. Same instructions as last time. Also a situation brief for MAIMCOM command HQ. They may maintain a vital signs monitor on the General, in which case they already know. If our guys meet up with the military, they should make a strong claim for jurisdiction. The General's home is not classed as military territory. Also put out a maximum alert and mobilization, we need guys on the ground everywhere. And you'd better wake the Secretary. He can decide whether to tell the President."

Cap looked around, panic and fury growing at the back of his mind. *Where the hell is Alan?*

Because the best defense they had, Cap realized suddenly, the only defense they had, was never to run into the things at all. Just get in the car and drive. Bees wouldn't try tracking a motor vehicle.

He didn't like running, and he probably wasn't at risk himself, here, because the bees would be on a single mission, with a single target; but for Alan's sake they should go.

Maybe Alan had realized that already and was long gone.

Cap Olsen looked around. There was the door to the main hall through which they had come, and there was a pair of glass doors on the other side leading probably to a porch or conservatory. He should try one or other and start shouting.

But he hesitated, his mind scrambling through the possibilities. Suppose they were too late. Suppose there were bees out there now. Was there anything he could do?

As Cap stood frozen in thought, desperately chasing through bee references in his training, his briefings, he began to close in on something. *There was a way.* He had come across it somewhere. Then he had it: a course at Quantico, a couple of years ago. Extreme bees. What they could do if the enemy bypassed all the firmware, all the controls, used souped-up technology. What they could do and what you could do in response. Extreme survival strategies for an attack by extreme bees.

Something to do with water…

CHAPTER 9

W hen Alan Connacher heard Cap Olsen reacting to the third bee attack, he got up and went quickly and quietly through the glass doors to his sun-room. The sun-room looked out on the gardens at the rear of his home, now lighting up as he stepped into the room. A spiral elevator went down to the basement level, where he had his exercise pool and gym.

He told his car to drive out of the garage and wait by the front door, engine running, and then he spoke his daughter's name.

In the couple of seconds it took for her to respond, he found his mind going back to Trudie as he had left her a couple of hours before. He had been late getting to her party, but had not managed to avoid the beautiful nano-biologist, who had turned out to be not very beautiful, and not really a nano-biologist. But he had done his duty and talked with her: and had then stayed on for a drink with his daughter afterwards. Trudie had given off a post-party glow, relaxed and confident, and it had felt as though the difficulties in their relationship were gradually receding.

Trudie said, "Dad? You still up?"

Alan came abruptly back to the present. "Sweetheart, this is very urgent. Where is the Senator?"

"Andy? Gone to bed. Quite a while ago. I think he's getting old."

"Trudie, I want you to listen carefully and do what I tell you. Don't argue with me, please. And don't ask me how I know this, and don't tell anyone where you heard this. Bees, you heard me, *bees*, are attacking public figures, government figures. Now listen, wake up Andy, get your car out and both of you, *both* of you, okay, get in the car and drive. Just get away from the house. Have you got that?"

There was a slight pause, and then his daughter said in a small voice, "You're serious."

"Absolutely. Do it now. Go!"

"But Dad, what about – "

"Trudie! Are you moving?"

"I'm moving!"

"Move faster! Don't think about anything else! Just go! I'm cutting off now so you can talk to your car and concentrate. Love you, sweetheart."

Alan stood still for a moment, picturing his daughter, the stubborn look in her eye, hoping that for once she would trust him.

Then he saw the bees, a faint iridescence, moving in a wave across the floor. He jumped towards the door into the den, opened his mouth to shout.

Cap Olsen came tumbling through it before he got there, bullish head tucked down into his broad shoulders, like a rugby player heading into a scrum.

"Back!" Alan shouted, putting one hand on Cap's shoulder and pointing at the floor with the other. "My car!"

Cap shrugged him off and grabbed a handful of Alan's shirt. "No! Too late! Where's your pool?"

Alan froze for a moment, contrary thoughts racing. He didn't like abandoning the hope of escape, but he could see that Cap was right: the bees wouldn't let them climb in a car and go, even if they didn't yet know enough to attack.

The bees swarmed up over both of them, settling densely over exposed skin, their hands and faces. Alan shook his head instinctively, as thick gauze seemed to cut off the light. He could still see Cap beside him, but his face looked blurred, wolfish.

"Pool!" Cap shouted again, wrenching hard at Alan's shirt.

Seeing Cap pinching his nose between finger and thumb, Alan did the same and stumbled through the gauze-shrouded gloom to the spiral elevator, Cap clinging and pushing all at the same time. Alan launched himself on to the moving treads and slithered down two at a time, Cap piggy-back above and behind him, both of them hanging on to the rail.

The bees already knew this was his home, Alan thought: they would have confirmed that before showing themselves.

So now they were deciding which one of the two males was Alan Connacher.

How long would that take? Ten seconds?

The pool was only three steps from the base of the spiral elevator. Alan scrabbled to get his balance and launched himself at the water, Cap releasing his grip on his clothing and following behind. Just before he hit the surface, Alan felt a sharp stinging on his hands. What was that? He felt the splash and surge as Cap went in beside him.

Alan flailed with his legs and arms to get his whole body below the water: if he could get all the bees off him, they would at least be forced to re-group, give him a few extra seconds. But he hadn't drawn breath since the bees had swarmed around his face, and his lungs were crying out for fresh air.

It's hopeless anyway, he thought. His hands were burning, which meant the bees had injected something. He was already feeling woozy. Dead or alive, he'd float to the surface, and the bees would find a way to his brain. Cap had driven him to this place and into the water for nothing. In any case, he had to have air. He relaxed and turned to let his face emerge from the water.

Then he felt Cap Olsen's heavy weight closing on him from above, forcing him down. He struggled weakly. Didn't Cap understand? He had no chance. He might as well at least take a dying breath.

Cap's arms were around him and he was aware of Cap's legs moving, pumping, pushing both of them deeper into the water. He felt a bump as they hit the bottom, four feet down. Precious bubbles of air escaped from his straining lungs.

He wanted desperately to draw breath. A wave of panic was descending on him. Cap was somehow keeping the pressure on him, stopping him from moving. Cap was drowning him, killing him. He was ready for death, but not like this, please.

He fought for a couple of seconds, but his strength was disappearing fast. Cap was superhuman, holding him, pressing him down. Then he felt something hard-edged on his chest, a jarring weight.

Cap was standing on him.

He could feel the imprint of his shoes, knew that Cap had got his upper body out of the water, had generated the weight to crush him, hold him down.

Alan could only make small protesting movements of his head. Why? Why do this? Why kill him? He had to breathe. And then, with his last bit of conscious intelligence, he understood. He understood Cap's plan. And he understood that it might work.

Using all his remaining willpower, he opened his mouth and breathed in water.

CHAPTER 10

HOAX OR HORROR?

The image is grainy, the cinematography not exactly Oscar quality, but the content is brutal, nauseating: a man's eyes being destroyed, pulverized by a swarm of tiny creatures; MAIMs, bees, robots, whatever you want to call them. And not just any man: the features, before the bees get to work, seem to be those of Congressman Abraham Tillett, Chair of the House Sub-committee monitoring MAIMs, defender of the PMA policies that resulted in the death of Rose Mickelburger, the mentally ill girl who thought she was pregnant and fell off a roof.

He is lying in bed, apparently unconscious, as the bees begin to work. His surroundings can be observed with reasonable clarity. And yes, the African carved figure on a pedestal by the bed-head, and the Yale graduation picture on the wall behind that, are both features of the real Mr. Tillett's bedroom, according to the only family member we were able to contact this morning, a niece living in Mr. Tillett's home state of Indiana.

The video segment was contained on a memory capsule delivered by robot messenger to the Post's offices early this morning, marked for my attention. There is no indication who sent it; and every indication that the anonymity is deliberate and unbreakable. And here's the kicker: the capsule also contained a list of twenty-six names, famous public figures all, with the chilling little notation, dead, against each one.

A spectacularly unpleasant wind-up, I thought, by some half-deranged youth with a grievance. A Rose Mickelburger relative. Sad but not real. That's what I thought until I did my job and started phoning around.

An FBI spokeswoman said she had no information on bee attacks against public figures. Congressman Tillett's staff were evasive, or nervous, or themselves in the dark; and no, there was no way I could talk to the Congressman at the moment. That's when I tracked down the niece in Indiana, and asked non-leading questions about the Congressman's Washington home, which she remembered from childhood visits. When she had recalled there was a carved figure, African-looking, in the bedroom, I excerpted the image from the video and showed it to her. She claimed to recognize it.

So all African carvings look much the same, right? I began working through the names on the list. When I'd done six and got nothing but a lot more nervous evasions, I got an intern to help me and we went through the rest of the names. In not a single case did we succeed in getting a word, an image, a connection. Of course, they're famous, they're busy. After a while we started saying we understood there had been a serious accident, and could they confirm that the Senator, the Director, the Undersecretary, was still alive? Well no, despite empty reassurances, they couldn't. There was some acknowledgment of cancelled public appearances, but it was all diary changes, minor ailments, sudden trips. Has the Senator, the Director, the Undersecretary, been attacked by bees? What? Are you crazy?

The Post will not be publishing the list of names just yet. But if you're out there, Congressman Tillett, please call in. The intern and I would like to get some sleep tonight.

Reporter: *Sheryl Kempinski*
Washington Post 18.10

◇◇◇

President Christine Diaz held up her copy of the Washington Post download. "Director Olsen, it strikes me that if you impound this capsule from this reporter, you're confirming her worst fears, and from then on she'll treat everything we do or say as a cover-up."

Cap Olsen closed his eyes for a second. He had never in his life felt so exhausted. Since managing the extraction of Alan Connacher's body from his exercise pool with the help of one of the members of his hand-picked team, and delivering it himself to the FBI suite at the Washington Hospital Center, he had gone from one crime scene to another, one meeting to another, creating policy on the hoof, bludgeoned every few minutes by news of another death, another attack; agreeing with his boss, FBI Secretary Stephen Cox, that containment was the only possible short-term response, and issuing instructions to FBI personnel, and personnel of other agencies, to make it aggressively clear to witnesses, and their own response teams, what the consequences of leaking information would be; and passing through a state of driven hyperactivity into a state of intense fatigue. He dozed for an hour, involuntarily, after lunch, and then threw himself back into the fray, trying to maintain his vigor as the event continued to snowball in size and impact.

Miraculously, they had kept the lid on it, the bereaved and the chance witnesses, the domestics, the aides, and the security guards, themselves so stunned, so uncomprehending, that they chose not to defy authority and tell their crazy story to the media or post their experiences onto public forums.

He himself had told nobody, beyond the colleague he had summoned, about the bee attack he had experienced at Alan's place: and he was aware that if Alan's name was on the list of twenty-six names given to the *Post* by the killer, then Alan's death would be validated, made public, and he could develop his own plans; but he was too exhausted to see exactly where that led.

Cap forced himself to concentrate on the President's remark. "Ma'am, I think we can persuade Ms. Kempinski to hand over the memory capsule voluntarily, and to report the matter that way. Especially if we have your authority."

President Diaz turned her bright blue eyes on him, and he was aware of the power of her gravitas, her mildly-accusatory stillness, that sucked in the unwary, unsettled even the boldest campaigners. She wasn't the oldest person in the room, but she seemed, with her white hair, her apple-smooth cheeks, her comfortable figure, timeless, dependable, a permanent fixture in the life of the nation.

Cap had also been impressed by the occasional flash of steel beneath the benevolent surface. The second female to be elected president, now in the middle of her second term, she gave no sign that she had feminized the office or, indeed, the Oval Office; but then the décor had probably been done by her husband. The only distinctive touches were the portraits of famous women on the walls, and the densely packed family photo-gallery on the table behind her desk. Rumor had it that, like President Kennedy, she kept toys in a drawer, even though her great-grandchildren numbered only two, and were not known to be frequent visitors.

The events of last night were surely the most testing of her presidency. She herself, and a handful of others, had not been vulnerable to attack: the Secret Service maintained systems, at the White House and several other environments, that prevented the ingress of bees. But the attacks nevertheless felt personal: the ruling elite had been brutally assaulted in its own private space; any of them might have been chosen; and all of them were still vulnerable if the attacks should resume.

Cap realized that the President was talking. "I don't want you using my authority, Director Olsen. That could be inflammatory. But you have my permission to make a tactful request." The blue eyes flashed around the semi-circle of faces. "That won't solve our problem, however. We all know what that problem is. At some point in the next few days, probably sooner rather than later, word of these events is going to leak out to the general public, and we'll face an outcry that may border on panic. That's especially true if there are more attacks in the meanwhile. In fact if there are more attacks, say tonight, we'll be accused of providing no warning, no defense. What do you say about that, General?"

Cap struggled to follow the debate that followed. General Lee Ponting, who had taken over command of MAIMCOM in the early hours of the morning, suggested briefing the top one thousand administrators and politicians in Washington, so that they could take evasive action.

Don Lester, Washington Police Chief, said that this might create the very panic they were trying to avoid. Cap roused himself and put in a comment in support of that view.

"Are we all agreed," the President said, moving on, "that this is domestic terrorism? I should tell you that that is the view of the Chairman of the Joint Chiefs and the CIA."

No-one dissented. The debate shifted first to the issue of which activist group might be responsible, and then to the issue of the methodology used.

"My understanding, General," the President said, "was that rogue bees, foreign bees, would be quickly identified by MAIMCOM and destroyed. So what went wrong?"

As Cap studied the General, he had the impression, common in the military, and in the FBI for that matter, of a man with a mission: that sharpness in grooming and uniform, that dedicated light in the eye. The General didn't possess the clean-cut hero look, being jowly and overweight, and looking a good percentage of his 82 years; but in all aspects of bearing and self-presentation, he radiated the air of a man who took himself seriously.

"Our defenses depend, Ma'am, on a security protocol which goes by the name of MAIMKEY. This is a five kilobit key which changes daily and is issued by NSA to all licensed bees in the country, and needless to say, such a key cannot be broken. As you correctly point out, MAIMCOM detection systems challenge bee swarms wherever they operate, and any swarms not in possession of a valid MAIMKEY are in theory destroyed. I think we can rule out the idea that these killer swarms evaded our MAIMCOM friend-or-foe challenges. That's simply not possible. So I'm afraid we have to consider the idea that the MAIMKEY was somehow leaked, either from NSA, or more likely from one or other of the agencies operating bees. I'm going to have to ask my colleagues in these agencies to assist in the broadest possible investigation."

Cap and the others nodded.

"Okay," the President said, "let's work on this with every resource we've got. We need to know how a safe and trusted asset turned deadly.

I'm not standing down bees for the moment, but I warn you that may be coming, especially if we don't get answers, and most obviously if anything like this happens again. I assume there is a lot to analyze and learn from crime scene forensics. I want to be kept up to date on that. By the way, weren't there some spent bees at the crime scenes?"

"Yes, Ma'am," Cap said. "Chief Lester and I agreed the FBI would examine those at our Quantico facility. I believe there were 13 at last count."

General Ponting sat up, body language combative. "Madame President, I would urge most strongly that you authorize the transfer of these spent bees to MAIMCOM. We are responsible for bee security, and we have better facilities than anyone for examining them."

The President said, "What are we likely to learn from these bees?"

"Very little," General Ponting said. "Under almost all circumstances of failure, bees manage to zeroize themselves. But there might be an exception. We might also get some kind of a clue from zeroized bees. Zeroized memory can sometimes be recovered, if you have the right equipment. Which makes it very important that the lab work is done by us. At a more conventional level, we might find traces of a chemical payload, and those chemicals might be tracked to a supplier."

"I'm going to make a Solomon-like dispensation here. MAIMCOM gets half. Okay, gentlemen?"

"Madame President, it's important that MAIMCOM gets all the bees, at least in the first instance."

"I've made a decision, General."

"Yes, Ma'am."

"I expect you to hand over the bees without delay, Director Olsen."

"Yes, Ma'am." Cap wanted to ask, *Is he getting six or seven?* but he held his tongue.

"Which leaves us with this cover-up," the President continued. "I don't want to get deep into a cover-up. Cover-ups end badly. So Mr. Olsen, you will negotiate with the Washington Post. My job will be to jump in at some point and address the nation and try and calm things down. Any questions?"

Cap and his colleagues were silent.

"Then I think that does it for now. Please keep closely in touch."

CHAPTER 11

T he building looked more like a factory unit at the wrong end of town than a morgue. Trudie stared at it through a haze of confused emotion, turned half in anger to her younger son, Jason: she should never have agreed to this, would never get through it; how was she expected to be calm, rational, look at a body, when that body was… The tears welled up.

Jason, in fact, was already out of the car, moving towards the little entrance porch at the side of the building. A police agent of some kind, a bulky man in plain clothes, was standing outside, watching them closely.

Oh God oh God, Trudie thought, fighting down the tears. This was so impossible. So completely beyond anything she could cope with. If she'd been playing this scene in a movie, she could have been a little bit dignified, at least. She could have cried the right amount, could have kept control. But this ugly, ridiculous, reality…

She jabbed at the button and the car door retracted and she got out. The hot sticky air invaded her as thoroughly as a swarm of bees and she immediately felt faint.

Damn him, damn him, she thought, staggering towards the porch: why did he let this happen, why didn't he save himself, why didn't he just *go*, escape, instead of wasting time calling her? She was okay! So was Andy! All of that was unnecessary!

Jason had explained to the agent-guy who they were, but they had to go through an ID check anyway, and then they found themselves in a dismal corridor with some kind of outdated rubber on the floor that squeaked under her high heels.

No, there was no point trying to rescue anything here: she would collapse or throw a fit or whatever, and they could carry her out and make jokes and say what the hell they liked. She wasn't Trudie Lightfoot any more; she was an unconnected mess, a blob of pain.

She must have stumbled. She found Jason holding her arm.

"Come on, Mom. You can do this."

And of course just before he died the poor man had accused her of being too busy, of putting up defenses; and after the party they'd talked, understood each other a little better. Suddenly she was shaking with fury. This was the man who was going to rejuvenate everybody, put an end to these prematurely broken relationships. And then he'd gotten himself killed! Damn him! Damn him!

"Come on, Mom. In here."

Trudie felt the air turn cold. She looked around in disbelief. No big cabinets full of bodies. More like a prison cell, shutting up the souls of the deceased. Cold, penetrating to the bone. And stainless steel benches, racked up, with… her heart seemed to leap in her chest and then stop… one body. Just one body. Or something in a silvery bag.

Two people in sealed suits were flanking the body in the bag, pulling at the zip. Jason was holding her, she couldn't run, she couldn't just fall down.

Dad. Oh God, Dad. Why did you allow this?

There was some kind of black covering over the eyes. At least… She couldn't have borne it, seeing the eyes gone. But the shiny black… It made him look more dead, like a man invaded by some strange machine. So this was it. The moment she had dreaded. The tears welled up again.

Somebody was asking a question. She nodded. That's what she did in movies: she just nodded. Up went the zip and her father was gone. She blinked, turned away.

She raised her head, to the men in suits, the men at the door, tried to smile as she went through.

Back in the car she sat lifeless as Jason told the car where to go.

Home again, of course. A drink. Some pointless rituals, work, getting through the day. Getting through eternity, her father's bequest.

"Mom? You okay?"

She turned her head to look at her son. He had that dissatisfied look. Almost the accusing, hard-done-by look. She turned back and looked out of the window ahead. The pacifying reply stuck in her throat. No, I'm not okay, Jason. I'm really not okay.

"Mom?"

"My father is dead!" she said harshly. "Is that likely to make me okay?"

"I was wondering…"

"Jason, sweetheart, it was kind of you to come and you were right to make me do it, but please don't ask how I feel just yet."

"No, okay, but what I was wondering… I mean I know how tough this is, but I was just wondering… if everything seemed normal back there?"

"Normal? Jason, it was a nightmare, a scene from hell."

"Yeah, I know, but those guys, those FBI guys… I mean, did you notice anything… anything peculiar?"

"Did I *notice* anything…" She glanced again at her son. He was looking out at the passing roadway, an intent, concentrated look on his face. Did he feel no grief? she wondered; did his grandfather mean so little? "Sweetheart, what the hell are you talking about?"

"I thought you might have noticed something. That smell, maybe."

"What smell?"

"Okay, Mom." Jason gave a half laugh. "Forget it. I know what you're going to tell me. I can be a little weird sometimes."

Trudie stared at her son. You can be more than a little weird, Jason. You can be very weird. You can be positively strange.

CHAPTER 12

W hen Alan Connacher began to recover consciousness, he was so pleasantly sedated, designer molecules anticipating and controlling his panic and pain, and so comfortably supported, the clinical pod in which he was immersed managing his bodily functions, that he couldn't be bothered to exert his normal powers of thought. He remembered his name and several details of his life and family, but he didn't try to string them together into a coherent story about where he was or how he had got there. He drifted comfortably along in a haze of memory and fantasy, unworried by the past or the future.

An image of himself underwater, unable to breath, teased the edges of his mental world, and although he knew it was important, and threatening, he didn't allow his agreeable journey through the sunny uplands of his mind to be diverted.

A clinician stood beside his pod, face blurred, and told him about two phases during which his life had been in suspension, heart stopped, respiration stopped; and assured him that no brain damage had occurred, and that he would be back to normal in a couple of days. Alan didn't care about the next couple of days, and didn't want to know about his flirtations with death, although it crossed his mind that the white-coated clinician, the room beyond, the floaters moving around above him, and the containing vessel which he could sense enclosing his body, were all hallucinations, part of some post-death limbo, phantoms from a state of being he had left behind.

Another clinician told him that he was doing well and that the change in medication, the phasing-in of real-time programming to his micro-screen glasses, would start soon, bringing him slowly back to reality. Alan didn't pay much attention to that, not believing that reality was of much interest, but gradually the coloring of his thoughts began to change, turning darker, acquiring emotional context. Past and future began to separate. He found himself probing at disturbing memories: bees smothering him, water covering him; panic and pain still contained, but confusion, worry, now disturbing his mental world. The images appearing on his glasses included newspaper reports of his own death, and for a time he persuaded himself that they were true, reassurance that he was beyond the messy, painful complications of life.

Cap Olsen came to visit him. The only thing that he could remember about Cap was that he had been in the water with him when he couldn't breathe, and had either killed him or saved his life, the distinction not important.

Cap told him that his daughter Trudie had identified his body, that he was officially dead, but the only response that conjured up in Alan's mind was a picture of a little girl on the beach at Cape Cod.

On his second visit, Cap told him that the medics would soon withdraw medication, and that Alan would have to get a grip on his situation because there was urgent planning to be done.

"Do you understand that, besides you, *twenty-five people* were attacked by bees and killed? Do you understand that there's a national crisis?"

Alan, now moved from the resuscitation pod to a bed, stared at Cap and tried to work this out. Was he supposed to make contact with the twenty-five dead people? What about?

Hours or perhaps a day after that, he was aware of a headache gathering, a new immediacy in his surroundings. The newscasts fed to his glasses began to seem as though they could be real, part of a world to which he must adjust. It occurred to him that he was, in fact, alive, and that he had survived some cataclysm in which other people, congressmen and senators amongst them, had died.

He began to see Trudie, his daughter, not as a little girl, but as a grown woman, and he was nagged, angered, by a mental picture of her identifying a body. His body. He saw her peering at his face, shocked, in tears. And he began to struggle in his mind with the circumstances of that. Why had she had to do that? Why had Cap

Olsen organized his death? And shouldn't he get up out of bed and start finding some answers?

◇◇◇

It was evening when Cap came again, according to the clock in the room. Alan's mind was on fire: he had got up at last, legs weak, head spinning, and taken a shower in the cubicle and looked unsuccessfully for clothes; shrugging the hospital gown back on, he had tried the door, which had brought a nurse technician, and somebody looking suspiciously like a guard, who together had bundled him back into bed. He had been feeling increasingly faint and was half-relieved: but during the last couple of hours he had thrown off the remains of his lethargy and worked furiously at reconstructing everything that preceded the attack by bees, the nightmare in the water.

He ignored Cap's serious, distracted expression.

"You saved my life," he said flatly. "By drowning me in my pool."

Cap looked at him and gave a small nod.

"And then you killed me again so that I'd be a realistic corpse."

"We briefly suspended heart-beat and breathing. Not really death."

"You couldn't have asked me first? Whether I wanted to put my family through this?"

"You weren't sufficiently recovered. I took a decision."

"Why? Why the charade? Why pretend I'm dead?"

"Shall we start at the beginning?" Cap said.

Alan stared at Cap Olsen. He felt his anger dissipating; he knew that without Olsen, his death would have been permanent and non-recoverable, half his brain missing. "Does my daughter still think I'm dead? Does everyone think I'm dead?"

"My team knows you're here, alive. The clinicians, obviously. The nurses. But basically they're FBI."

"Is that where I am? Some FBI hospital somewhere?"

"You're in a small secure wing of a civilian hospital inside the Beltway. But it's purpose built and effectively it's FBI. Mainly, of course, it's to provide high tech care for FBI personnel and anyone the FBI wants to protect. The security is very good."

"So I discovered."

"We can't have you wandering around, Alan. You're dead. I hope, after we've discussed all this, that you'll want to stay dead."

"Do you realize what Trudie, my son, my grandkids…"

"I'm sorry about all that. No doubt one day, when all this is behind us, you'll straighten that out. But meanwhile, do *you* realize just what's going out there? What sort of a national crisis this is?"

Alan took a deep breath and dropped his gaze to his hands, resting on the white sheet. "Maybe I don't. Not yet. It doesn't really seem credible."

"Exactly. It isn't credible. It's horror film crazy. Everyone is in shock, not just your kids and grandkids. Everyone from the President on down. Although I must say the President has provided good leadership so far."

"Trudie's husband didn't get hurt, did he?"

"As far as I know, Senator Lightfoot is okay. Alan, you've got to move on, refocus. Your kids are going to survive. Have you seen the communiqué from this bastard?"

From his shift of expression, the clenched jaw muscles, Alan could see that this was what was preoccupying Cap.

"What bastard?"

Cap gave him an exasperated glance and threw up a hand. "The bastard who did this! Killed our politicians and officials! Tried to kill you and me!"

"You mean it was one guy? I didn't watch a newscast this afternoon."

"It's all over the place. Kronos, he calls himself. I'm told that Kronos was a Greek god who killed his father to gain power, and then killed his children as well. Nice sort of a guy. Anyway, this Kronos has issued a communiqué, it was in the *Washington Post* this afternoon, telling us how to re-arrange our political institutions for his benefit."

"So it wasn't the Mickelburger people?"

"Who knows? Is it really one person or a group? I think that Kronos is probably a group, and if the group isn't the Mickelburger lot, then it's another bunch of old-style protesters who've got fed up with non-violence."

Alan's memory, increasingly clear, suddenly put into his mind the conversation with Cap, long ago, in his den, before the bees attacked.

"So that's why you killed me off."

Cap stared at him challengingly.

77

"This rejuvenation idea of yours," Alan said. "Now that I'm conveniently dead, you think that I can rejuvenate myself and go to work as your agent. You think nobody will make the connection."

"I'm glad to see your brain has recovered its usual speed and brilliance."

"It's a ridiculous idea. It was a ridiculous idea when you first brought it up, and it's still a ridiculous idea."

"Why?"

Alan was silent. His headache was getting worse. "Because I'm a scientist," he burst out, "not some kind of spy fiction hero. I don't have a clue about undercover work. And you haven't exactly earned my gratitude by telling my family and the world that I'm dead."

"Would you rather this Kronos character thinks you're still alive?"

Alan looked away, his thoughts veering onto new paths.

"You've got the perfect cover," Cap went on. "I wish I had that kind of cover."

"Wait a minute," Alan said. "You're saying this guy thinks I'm dead? That he believes the news stories? Why should he? The bees should have put in a report, mission failure, that kind of thing. He ought to know they didn't get me."

"Well he doesn't. Your name was on the original list of 26 dead sent to the *Washington Post* before any public announcements were made."

"You're sure?"

"Of course I'm sure."

"And your name?"

"No. But there's no evidence that I was targeted. My wife saw nothing."

"So why doesn't he know that I'm alive?"

"I'd have to check with our analysts." Cap was getting that irritated look. "Maybe the bees told him that you were dead. Maybe these guys were simply in a hurry and fouled up. Does it matter?"

Alan shook his head, letting it go. "Have you been able to estimate how many swarms were involved?"

"No. Total time between first and last killings, and the geographical distribution, suggest at least four. But it could have been a different swarm every time."

"Where was I in the sequence?"

"Towards the end, certainly. Maybe one of the last. Obviously we don't always have an exact time of death."

Alan nodded slowly. His mental acuity was declining, as fatigue, his aching eyes, began to overwhelm him.

Cap, watching him, said suspiciously, "What are you thinking?"

"Nothing." Alan felt his head and shoulders drooping.

"Don't decide yet about the rejuvenation. Think it over. I'll bring a couple of people with me and we'll talk through your objections. Just remember that this Kronos guy is out there, trying to destroy our morale, our government, everything. If ever we needed information, any kind of information, it's now."

Alan made an effort. "But if I'm not the guy to go looking for that…"

"We think you'll do okay. We'll train you, we'll be behind you."

"To find a guy like this?" Alan spread his hands helplessly. "Someone the whole world is looking for?"

"Look, Alan, old-fashioned police work, luck, actions by the public, technology, may all be more important than someone like you: but even if you only have a ten per cent chance, even if you only have a *one* per cent chance, it's still worth it. Because my job description says I've got to do everything, think of everything. And I'd like to hang on to my job description."

◇◇◇

Alan slept, and when he woke in the early morning, he felt rested. His headache had gone. He lay in bed and watched the little insect-like machines, SAIMs, cleaning every corner of his room.

His mind roamed around the conversation with Cap Olsen. It was true beyond denial: his daughter, his family, believed that he was dead. With the exception of Cap Olsen and his team, he had ceased to exist. His resentment lingered, but beyond that, beyond the fear of complete isolation, a small seed of interest in his new situation was taking root.

Cap was right about one thing: it was a relief if this Kronos entity believed him dead. Somewhere in his mind he had been expecting further attacks. That now seemed unlikely. But the question remained: why did Kronos believe he was dead? At the end of the mission to kill him, when the bees had returned to the hive from which they had come, what had prevented them from downloading an account of the mission and its failure?

Perhaps, Alan thought, the bees didn't belong to Kronos, but had been hijacked from some public body, the FBI, the PMA. In that case, to cover up that fact, they had probably been returned to the agency from which they had been taken; which left much more opportunity for error, for not receiving a full mission report.

He was aware of the agency codes and the MAIMKEY protocol which made hijacking difficult, and of the behavioral controls which would have prevented them from killing humans, but at least this theory solved the mystery of why the bees had not been zapped by the military. He also found it comforting: it allowed him to believe that Kronos really didn't know he was alive.

◇◇◇

He slept for another hour. When he woke up he took a shower and asked for some breakfast. While he ate, he caught up with the news to which Cap Olsen had referred. He found the Kronos communiqué in a *Washington Post* article:

> *Death is what you fear, isn't it? You fear death because you are old and you are close to it, you live in its shadow, cheating it daily; and because you avoid it only by stealing your lives from others, from those who will never be born, and from the young, who will never accede to wealth and power; guilt drives your fear.*
>
> *So I have brought death into the heart of your establishment, to your leaders and legislators, your cheaters and dissemblers, and I have written in blood on your self-admiring faces. Now you know what death is like; now you can be afraid of it in earnest. Ask not for whom the bell tolls, you of the empowered elite; it tolls for thee.*
>
> *Can you avoid your fate? If you gather together and make wise decisions, you can. Your Congress must enact an amendment to the constitution, restricting the vote to those under the age of 70. This will restore democracy to America, and make the young electable. This must be ratified before the mid-term election in November. You must incentivize death,*

making childbirth-rights heritable: any person over the age of 90 choosing euthanasia may leave a childbirth-right to his or her descendants. This legislation must be passed before the mid-term election in November.

Those attempting to prevent the passage of these measures will be marked for death; those advancing them will be spared.

Senior citizens, go to work and dismantle your gerontocracy!

Well, Alan thought, after reading it through twice, it's literate, ambitious, rational, and although there was no chance of Congress responding to a terrorist threat, there was a political plausibility about the measures demanded that suggested the author was intensely serious about his role, his potential leadership. This guy wasn't going to give up and go away. He might even generate a real following. In other words, he might be extremely dangerous.

He finished his breakfast and sat thinking. He would be totally out of his depth going after this man, even if he succeeded in rejuvenating himself. So what was he going to tell Olsen? Find somebody else?

CHAPTER 13

"Ask me another one, uncle Zeb," Sam said.

Jason had been upset and irritated, on arriving at his mother's house, to find Zeb already there; Zeb always managed to seem so relaxed and friendly, giving him the big cheesy grin, playing happily with Sam; whereas in the past their relationship had been far from happy. But now he could see that Zeb might be useful. He stood up.

"Would you look after Sam for a moment? I've got to collect some stuff."

"Sure, no problem," Zeb said. "You ready for a tough one, Sam?"

"Not a very *very* tough one, uncle Zeb."

Jason went out into the hall and stopped for a moment to listen. He could hear his mother's voice floating up from down below, instructing workers or robots. He walked quickly down the corridor and got aboard the elevator and rode down to the basement, where there was a gym and a couple of rooms used for storage. He and Zeb still had a few boxes of ancient possessions here, and some kit for use in the gym. Jason found an apparel bag with a sporting logo and checked that it was empty. He got back aboard the elevator and rode up to the fourth floor, where his mother had a bedroom and dressing room and media room.

He was expecting to find someone here, a maid or personal assistant of his mother's, and his original plan had been to use Sam as a distraction, engaging their attentions while he sneaked into his mother's closet. But Sam was unpredictable, reporting tales of everyone's doings unasked, and after arriving at his mother's house, Jason decided he would be better off on his own.

As it happened, the media room was closed, but as Jason moved past the wall of stills from his mother's movies, the portraits by famous photographers, he heard the sound of doleful singing from within the connected suite of rooms. Conchita. He stopped and drew breath. Should he hang around downstairs and try again later? There was no guarantee that would work. Conchita's hours seemed very flexible, and she lived on the top floor.

Jason moved on around the corner and knocked on the open door of the bedroom and looked inside. "Conchita?"

The singing stopped. Conchita, a middle-aged woman in a pale blue uniform, turned from polishing a mirror on one of his mother's vanity units and gave him a measured glance, unsurprised, it seemed, to find him visiting his mother's bedroom. Always cool and phlegmatic, Jason was never sure what was going on in her mind.

"Thees robot no good, Mr. Jason," she said, pointing to a machine standing against the wall. "I put him away. I tell him what I think. Know a few treecks, is all. Don't do a good job. Polishing all wrong."

"Well, yeah," Jason said. "You would do better, for sure."

"Your mother coming?"

"No, no. Actually, Conchita, I wanted to take a look through my mother's clothes. Planning a gift, you know? I wanted to check colors. I won't be a moment."

Conchita gave him a shrug and an inscrutable look and went back to polishing. Jason went on through the arched door to the dressing room and began quickly to check through the large walk-in closets, containing hundreds of his mother's outfits. He had little idea how these were organized, but he discovered after a moment that dresses, suits, outdoor coats were segregated and even subdivided by season. He had a clear image in his mind of the coat she had worn to view his grandfather's body: it was wool, a somber grey, a silvery cross thread, a weave like tweed. His work checking fabric orders had sharpened his awareness of fabric styles, and he had a good visual memory. He found it after a couple of minutes. Sure enough, there were a dozen others of equivalent weight. It was very unlikely, he thought, that she had worn this one again.

He glanced behind him and then took it quickly off the hanger and folded it and put it in the apparel bag. He hoped that Conchita wouldn't notice the new bulges in the bag.

On his way out, he said, "Better not tell my mother I was here, Conchita. You know, the gift: I want it to be a surprise."

Conchita shrugged as though this kind of thing was family business, nothing to do with her, and Jason turned and made his way back to the elevator.

A few minutes later he had said goodbye to his mother and Zeb and he and Sam were walking back to Georgetown, the apparel bag swinging at his side.

◇◇◇

It was the visit by the sales manager that set his boss, Trevor Northwich going. Northwich must have felt he had been in some way criticized, because he got into one of his aggressive moods, his tone barking sharp, with a pretend veneer of jocularity:

"Your kid legal, Jason?"

Jason gave him a brief glance and nodded.

"You're sure?"

"What do you mean, am I sure," said Jason, keeping his gaze averted.

"Maybe there's lots of them out there, illegals, maybe you doomers have got a real scam going, maybe you're covering up for each other."

Northwich was referring to the news out yesterday that another illegal child had been discovered. This was a two-year-old girl in Lubbock, Texas, who had fallen seriously ill, and whose mother had been forced to take her to a clinic, where the normal ID check had revealed her illegal status. Jason had followed the case with interest. The first case, very similar, had involved a mother in Madison, Wisconsin, who had taken her three-year-old to Minnesota to see a sick relative, and had been discovered by bee checks as an illegal. In both cases the children had no provenance, had appeared out of the blue. How had the mother avoided the bee checks, which Sam and all children had to endure?

"It doesn't work like that, Mr. Northwich," Jason mumbled, continuing to watch the work dockets on the screen.

"No, you got that right, it don't work like that. We give you kids the right to have what children this country can cope with, and you kids keep to the rules. That's the way it works. You got any objection to that?"

In spite of himself, Jason felt the dangerous stirrings of anger. "No, sir," he muttered. "Why should I?"

"You want to change the system? Well we can change the system too."

Jason gritted his teeth, said nothing.

"You know what I'm saying?"

"No sir."

"Why do we give childbirth rights to young people? Eh? What do you think, Jason? Because you make better parents? Because you've got the resources to bring up kids? Eh?"

"Maybe because bringing up kids is hard work, Mr. Northwich."

"That's right. Bringing up kids is hard work. And it needs time and resources. And you know who's best placed to provide the time and resources and the hard work in this day and age? Old people. That's right. Old people. Old people who ain't going to die the way they used to and who will live to see the kids grow up. Old people who are stable and got some experience of life. I bet you didn't think of it like that before. Why do we have lotteries and give away childbirth rights to young people and only young people?"

Jason stayed quiet.

"Habit. Habit pure and simple. And maybe to keep the peace. Stop these Kronos guys from trying to tear us apart. Well that can change. If you're going to try and tear us apart anyway. If you don't keep up your share of the bargain. That can change. Eh? What do you say?"

Jason knew that if stayed in the room with Northwich he was going to put his fist straight into his prominent, too-white, teeth. He pointed at the screen, muttered something about robots and got out through the door to the factory. He clattered down the stairs, and turned back out of sight of the office and stood still, breathing hard, clenching and unclenching his fists, glad he had managed to escape, but wondering how he would get through the rest of the day; or indeed the rest of the week.

This, of course, was what had happened to his predecessors: they'd finally lost patience with Northwich and quit. Told him what they thought of him and walked out. For a moment he indulged the idea of doing the same, then he took a deep breath and held it and forced himself to calm down. Somehow, he had to hang on. If not for his sake, then for Sam's.

◇◇◇

The lab to which he had taken the coat got in touch a couple of days later and Jason went by after work and picked it up.

He collected Sam and took him home and made supper before settling down with a roll-out screen and pointer.

There were, as he had thought, thousands of molecules listed, all of them substances deposited on the coat at one time or another. The lab had provided the chemical composition, but Jason had to run software and access data banks to determine names and uses of the compounds. Then he had to group these by type.

He excluded all the biotic molecules. Of the remainder, most were components of skin-care, make-up, cleansers, foodstuffs, or random pollutants picked up out-of-doors. Molecules present in very small quantities, sometimes one or two only, ranged over everything from paint to rare metals to industrial catalysts to drugs like LSD and cocaine. Of special interest to Jason was a small group of molecules which had medical or pharmacological uses.

He went through these one by one, tapping with his pointer on the screen and bringing up a full description of origins and current applications. After an hour of reading and cross-checking, he had narrowed the field to just two. Anything that was detectable to the weak human olfactory sense, he decided, would have left at least several hundred molecules on his mother's coat; that eliminated a few of the more exotic compounds. After that, he discriminated on the basis of plausibility: what might have been used in treating his grandfather that was consonant with his instinctive sense of less than simple death?

The two that interested him most were, first, a blood additive used to slow certain oxidation processes during periods of suspended blood circulation; and second, a constituent of a nutrient bath used to maintain muscular viability during induced or post-accidental death.

He realized, with half-guilty excitement, that both of these substances, if deposited on his mother's coat during the identification of his grandfather's body, indicated efforts, probably ongoing, to preserve his grandfather's life, indicated, in other words, that his grandfather's state of death might have been recoverable.

Jason sat back from the screen and looked across to where Sam was playing with a robot. The girl at the lab had been right: he was cute. Whatever his family thought, Jason had never regretted the financial burden he had imposed on himself by bypassing the lottery and paying the full market rate for childbirth rights. He remembered collecting him from the vicarium, a tiny baby born, like most children, to a machine, the genome cleansed, every gene a perfect copy, 60% of them drawn at random from his own genome, the other forty percent drawn at random from a multiracial database: a beautiful specimen of human life. He had loved him from the moment he had taken him in his arms. His black hair, when it grew, and something in his features, seemed Asian, but his own genes were clearly apparent. Sam dominated his life from then on. Jason was registered as the sole parent, which meant he could lose his child if he couldn't fulfill his obligations. He wasn't going to allow that to happen.

He returned his gaze to the screen, determined to be careful and prepared. If the government wanted everybody to think that his grandfather was dead, while secretly keeping him alive, then something important was going on; presumably something to do with the hunt for Kronos. That meant the stakes were high. He was venturing into dangerous territory. On the other hand, if he could figure it out, he would have something valuable to offer his own side.

He settled down to work. He was making a lot of guesses. Somehow he had to get hold of these two suspect substances in a form that he could smell. If he recognized the smell, he had at least the beginnings of a story. Otherwise, he could and should forget it.

CHAPTER 14

A t times, Kronos thought that he was going to blow his cover. Impatience and exhilaration raged inside him. In meetings, at lunch, in the street, he wanted to tear off the mask and shout, "I did it! I'm the one! Look at me and grovel, punks!"

The *New York Times* called it 'the defining event of the century', and 'a new paradigm of evil' and was joined by other news media, commenting, theorizing, reporting. Everyone he met was wrapped up in the story, most of them shocked and worried, a few of them, the younger ones, of course, willing to acknowledge an element of *schadenfreude*, even a cautious approval, underneath the horror of the violence; but all of them fascinated, however much repelled by the pictures that found their way onto the news screens.

As the days went by, his secret burned a deeper and deeper hole in his psyche. He was frantic to enroll someone, instruct someone, conspire with someone, rejoice with someone. Was ever a revolutionary so alone? he wondered. Was ever a man who has electrified the globe so compressed within his own tiny space?

He could talk to Merko, but Merko was his problem, not his partner. At work, he had to sink himself into the pretenses and habits of his job. But in his own world, at home, he had opened up a ravenous need for action or the company of those, like himself, who had gone beyond the normal boundaries and exiled themselves from normal thoughts and satisfactions. On the streets, riding the metro, he found himself catching sight of a young, pliable face, and coming dangerously close to reaching out a hand, putting a proposition: join me and bring your friends and we can drive these bastards out of power.

Already, the jagged, electric excitement of kicking the collective Washington elite in the balls had faded and been replaced by a nagging worry that the momentum could be lost if he didn't follow up with further action; in particular, making good on his reckless boast that those in Congress opposing his demand for constitutional change would suffer. But he could hit the ruling elite again, and again, he thought, and without an organization to channel the response, direct the revolution, he would lose. Youth would lose. As in the ridiculous conspiracy theory he kept hearing: according to this, the Pentagon had done the killings and dreamed up Kronos to justify a crackdown on youth. Such a theory might make his so-called doomer generation feel better about themselves, might increase resentment of the one-niner regime; but he, the real Kronos, would be nowhere, airbrushed out of existence.

Kronos started to drop by his girlfriend Valerie's place, usually late in the evening, to get the latest news from her PMA office.

Internal investigators were hard at work, going through the bee management systems, talking with employees, particularly younger employees. Kronos wanted to know what sort of questions they were asking, what connections they were making with the killings. Valerie wasn't sure, although she had heard that MAIMKEY and the landline link from NSA was one of the things under scrutiny. There was a lot of gossip in her department about the discoveries of illegal children in Madison and Lubbock, but this didn't seem to be the main focus of the investigators.

Valerie didn't ask him what he had done with the data she had stolen for him, but he could see it was on her mind, gnawing away at her. She hadn't yet been interviewed by the investigators: she was a little too old, a little too senior, and too remote from technical work, to be on their primary list; but Kronos assumed she would be interviewed in the end. He was worried that she would react badly: a clever interrogator might attack her weaknesses and get an admission of something, if not the whole story.

He had already been interviewed by the FBI. The questions were straightforward, but they included an enquiry about what he was doing on the night of the bees. He had thought about that in advance and he had an answer ready. It was lucky that Merko had blinded the devices recording registration numbers at the car parks where they had parked their trucks, because they also wanted to confirm the registration numbers of the vehicles he drove.

Kronos found himself oddly satisfied, even excited, by the interview. It wasn't the excitement of killing, but the obverse, the excitement of knowing that he was prey, but unidentified prey; the excitement of eluding the hunters.

He felt himself becoming reckless, light-headed, in the aftermath, and he tried to rein himself back, take more care. But he knew he couldn't mark time, he had to come up with a new plan. When Merko told him that the Washington PMA bee protocols had changed, thus stalling any immediate attempt to stage a new attack, he felt his frustration flaring up to dangerous levels.

"You've got to do it all again, Val," he told her one evening, in a light, bantering tone, after listening to her stories of growing tension and suspicion at work.

She stared at him, uncomprehending. "What?"

Let it go, he told himself.

"They've changed," he said. "Can you believe it? All those frigging codes and protocols. Junked. And we never got to use them."

"But I thought…"

"Thought what?"

"The kids in Lubbock and Madison… the illegals… I thought maybe…"

"Old stuff, Val. Nothing to do with us."

"Then who…?"

"God knows. Some group like the Mars Three Resistance maybe?"

"So I did all that for nothing." There was puzzlement, a trace of bitterness, in her voice.

"Isn't that good? Doesn't that make you happy?"

"Happy?"

He reached out and nudged her jaw. "You're not in the frame. Nothing can be traced back to you."

Her expression was distant. "I thought there was going to be a baby… babies… I wanted to hold them."

"So do it again."

She stared at him, uncomprehending. "Even with this Kronos stuff?"

"Even more so with this Kronos stuff." Kronos could sense his tone hardening, his deepest ambitions and feelings riding up towards the surface.

"What are you saying?" she said, intent on his face. "What are you trying to say to me?"

"I'm saying we've got to hang in there."

"Why are you looking at me like that?"

"I'm not looking at you like that."

"You're looking at me as though I've let you down. What more do you want? What more do you want from me?"

"Hey, take it easy."

Valerie began to cry. He watched her coldly.

"I can never do enough for you," she said, wiping at the tears. "I know it's not your fault, you have this great mission, you're always thinking about that, so why should you spare me? I don't want much, but... those people, those investigators, might find out what I've done, that's my career gone, my life over... For nothing? I get caught because *some other people*, some other *group*, had a scam going? And you just look at me as though... as though I've *failed*."

"Hey, Val, Val." He took her arm. She was trembling. He guided her to the couch, sat her down, stood in front of her. "It wasn't for nothing, Val. What you did. I lied."

She looked up at him, suddenly still.

"I am Kronos." It slipped out easily, and he felt a moment of satisfaction, of stature, and then instant regret. *Back away now.*

She blinked a couple of times, and then shock drained the color from her face.

"But... You couldn't..." she said, her voice not much more than a croak.

"You did well, Val. Really well. You made it all possible. One day the youth movement will build a shrine, give you proper recognition."

"Oh God." Her tears were little desperate sobs.

Kronos watched her. "So, will you do it again?"

"Again?" She looked at him, choking on her tears. "Are you crazy?"

"They've changed the codes, Val."

"They'll catch me! What good is that going to do?"

"All the same, will you do it?"

After a long time, her voice mired in misery, she said, "I have to believe in what I'm doing. I don't believe in... killing."

"But will you do it? For me?"

"I wouldn't succeed," she said in a flat, lifeless tone, "I wouldn't manage it."

He turned away and crossed to the kitchen and got a stinger from the bar, two parts brandy, one part white crème de menthe, chilled. It was more or less the expected conclusion, the Valerie he knew. He went back to the sitting room and sat down beside her and gave her the glass.

"Time to relax, sweetheart. I think you'd succeed, but you're right, of course. There's no point taking the risk. And that stuff about Kronos was a tease. My God, you should have seen your face."

Valerie looked at him as though he had slapped her, then turned away and nodded slowly, wiped at her tears. A moment later she put down her glass and went to fix her face.

She knows, Kronos thought; she had seen the truth and she wasn't going to let it go. Which was good. She hadn't fallen over herself with admiration, but she'd taken it aboard without a total collapse.

What was bad was that he'd indulged a dangerous whim, a stupid bit of posturing, just to feed that yawning hole in his psyche. Val wasn't going to get the new protocols, whether or not she volunteered; it was much too dangerous. And meanwhile, he'd added to her stress, made her more vulnerable under interrogation, given her a huge secret to worry over.

And then suddenly his mind sheared away, back to what Valerie had thrown up earlier in the conversation. *The illegal kids in Lubbock and Madison.*

Why had he never thought about this? It was, of course, M3R who had put together the program to smuggle in babies and hide them out in various locations, with various foster-mothers, around the country. And now a couple of them had come to light. But the point was, there should be lots of them. Surely the program had been running since way back, when he'd had connections with these people. He had definitely had the impression of successful placements in lots of places. Which added up to lots of PMA offices penetrated by activists. Because that was the way it was done, bee systems tweaked to make these particular babies invisible. And most of these activists, from the decaying, demoralized, increasingly irrelevant, Mars Three Resistance, were probably still in place.

He jumped up and began walking in circles around the dining table, cursing himself. He had been procrastinating, not keeping pace with events.

Now he could see where his nationwide operation was coming from, maybe where his cadres, his followers were coming from. Now he could see what he had to do: he had to get back in contact with those earnest new activists from the Rose Mickelburger Faction. They might be a bunch of amateurs, but that wasn't all bad: they were ripe for strong leadership, and they had access to a network of people who might give him what he needed.

He gave the high-backed dining chairs an affectionate tap and headed for the door, calling out to Valerie as he went.

CHAPTER 15

As Alan entered his machine and swung himself down into the coffin-like enclosure, he hoped his face didn't register the fear gnawing at his gut. He wished he could do this like the monkeys, unconscious and ignorant; but 85 kilos of human being was not so easily put in place as 10 kilos of monkey. He was naked, clean-shaven from head to foot, and as he lay back amidst the multiple-textured prosthetics, he felt vulnerable and exposed, aware that these greedy probes and molecular invaders were going to wash and suck and absorb him down to a bare essence of bone and nerve before cleaning and upgrading and rebuilding him afresh.

He had dreamed of this great moment: but as an observer, not the leading player; bringing youth to others, before finally accepting the benefits for himself. And he had dreamed of it before those benefits, or the right of the old to re-acquire them, had been thrown into question, and all sections of society began to ask: was it fair to compete so directly with the young?

Spiderman, attacking him here in his labs, didn't think so. Would Sam, his only great-grandson, grow up to think the same? That rejuvenated oldsters were like aliens intruding on their rightful space?

Part of him remained fascinated by what he was doing. Perhaps, in other remote parts of the world, humans had already been rejuvenated; there were rumors, certainly; but here in the United States he was one of the first, perhaps the first. He was the person who would prove whether it was possible to become young again, what it felt like. Even if he was destroyed, driven mad, nothing could entirely remove the satisfaction of discovery.

It was bad luck, fate, that all of that was now overshadowed by the planning, the mission for which he was being prepared. Instead of fulfilling his dream, he was a pawn in a deadly conflict.

Cap had decided that as well as enrolling as a graduate student at Georgetown University, he should join the new program recently inaugurated by the President, under which a few carefully-screened young people were given part-time internships in the White House. Cap believed that having regular access to the White House would be of significant interest to the dissident groups. Since the President was more or less untouchable by bees, Kronos would surely have ambitions to mount some other kind of attack, and with his access and technical skills, who could be better than the new Alan?

So as well as being young, and a student, Alan thought, he now had to look plausible as a presidential assassin.

Alan could feel body-temperature liquids seeping along the base of his spine. A few more moments and he would have been identity-checked, examined from top to bottom, blood-tested, and the pre-determined master-program, the Procedure, would have been downloaded into all processors; only then would he be taken over by invading molecules, rendered unconscious, engulfed in fluids behind sealed doors.

Machines of the future would have prep chambers and soothing music and a pleasant descent into unconsciousness, and then delivery mechanisms to take the patient into the processing chamber. But this was a humble prototype: it was do-it-yourself; crawl in and crawl back out when consciousness returned. Which might be as much of a shock, perhaps, as being born in the first place.

Roger Enquist and several of his FBI colleagues would maintain a vigil out there in the lab; but there was almost nothing for them to do; no way for them to revive a failed bundle of nerve and brain fibers if things went wrong. Either he crawled back out at the end of the week, alive and well, and young, or they could bury him for real.

Alan's imagination failed him when he tried to anticipate this moment. What would it be like? It was simplistic to imagine he would feel in all respects wonderful. More likely he would feel terrible. It had taken the monkeys a week of physiotherapy before they seemed in control of their new bodies.

He would spend that week immersed in other forms of learning as well. His new identity, his name, the details of his life. The culture and habits of youth. His hair would grow back into a bristly crew-cut, but it would be black, not red. His nose would have a new profile. The bone of his cheeks and jaw would be enhanced beyond the shape determined by his genes, giving his face a heavier look. His eyes would be brown, not blue.

The genetic changes, which included several not associated with appearance, were a gamble. Some involved fixing bad genes, some were functional. He had modeled them, studied them, and as far as he could tell there should be no impact, no tendency for his existing skeletal and nerve tissue to reject, or be rejected by, the new genetic form; but he couldn't be absolutely sure. It was, in fact, the thing that worried him the most, the untested factor; but he could see no way out.

The changes were necessary to generate a new genome which was separable from his old genome when DNA identity checks were applied. He and Roger between them had hammered out the changes needed, and Cap was using a high-level link with the ID database director to get the new record inserted in the database, listing him as a 29-year-old born in Alton, New Hampshire.

Cap chose Alton because it was rural, slow-changing and because Alan mentioned spending summer vacations, as a boy, on a farm nearby. Cap suggested that his alter ego had grown up on just such a farm, and been educated largely at home because of a childhood illness. That would excuse his ignorance of some of the finer points of modern youth culture, while giving him a childhood based at least partly on fact. Farm life hadn't changed a great deal in fifty years.

Lying in the coffin, waiting to be anaesthetized and engulfed in fluids, Alan's mind drifted back to the Alton farm: sun-drenched fields, birches in woodland groves, wooden gates, harvesting machinery, and barns, one barn in particular. He baulked and mentally veered away, returned to the present. He knew what had happened in that barn when he was nine years old, he knew that his younger brother had died; but he never let himself think about it. He wished he hadn't mentioned Alton to Cap; he had encumbered himself, in his new identity, with a childhood he wanted to forget. But perhaps, when he came out of the machine renewed and young, he would be purged of all that; he would be starting again, without parents, without history.

He closed his eyes and bunched his fists. He was trembling as the probes snaked across his body and delivered him at last into unconsciousness.

CHAPTER 16

G eneral Lee Ponting normally enjoyed walking the corridors and rings of the Pentagon: customs and courtesies prohibited saluting, but the four stars on his uniform ensured that he got the attention of people who mattered; colonels jumped, majors might even fawn.

But today he hardly noticed the colonels and majors, his pit-bull determination blunted by the over-riding sense of crisis; a crisis centering on his own newly-bestowed command. As he penetrated the upper reaches of the E-ring, he was still reviewing what he had learned, what he should report.

It had been a ferocious few days at MAIMCOM. The organization had exploded in a frenzy of post mortem investigations, as the four thousand plus employees realized that they, or their cousins at NSA, were perceived by the world at large to have screwed up, failed to protect their leaders against attacks by unregistered bees.

As the new incumbent, Ponting was shielded from some of the blame, but as second-in-command at the time of the attacks, he was also deeply involved in the collective soul-searching. Instead of trying to direct the investigations, which erupted spontaneously and which included simulations in the control center, painstaking trawls through all of the data captured on the night of the killings, brainstorming sessions with bee contractors and firmware designers, Ponting spent his time interviewing his staff at every level, probing for weaknesses, doubts, lack of commitment, dishonesty. Where he could he brought in the younger rather than the older staff-member for questioning, and he didn't hold back from establishing a courts-martial atmosphere, with his own new deputy commander present, the questions sharp and aggressive. Although a system failure was possible, more likely at NSA than MAIMCOM, the General already suspected that betrayal, a youth cell within the military, or simply a disaffected individual, was going to turn out to be the ultimate cause of the MAIMKEY circumvention.

What exactly he was going to report of all this was the matter preoccupying him as he proceeded through final ID checks to the office of the Army Chief, which was distinguished by soothing abstract art on the walls and a view of Arlington National Cemetery. Other invitees were gathering as though by a process of lucky coincidence, stopping by without aides, horseholders, or briefing documents, exchanging friendly words and first-name greetings, uniforms weighed down by stars and medals. Before sitting down at the conference table, the generals allowed the floaters to check for surveillance, and the Army Chief, General James La Salle Jr., closed the shades on the windows.

General La Salle took the seat at the head of the table and the others sat down without regard to rank. There were eleven of them and they were all men.

"Gentlemen, good to see you," La Salle said. "Terry, Brad, Lee, thanks for coming across from the boondocks. Sandy sends his apologies but he's tied up with the SecDef this afternoon. Anyway, looks to me like we got a pretty convincing quorum."

There were murmurs of agreement around the table.

"You all know why we're here. We're here because of *cosa nostra*. We're here because as well-meaning conspirators we might have got caught with our pants down."

"Easy, Jim," said the Navy Chief, "None of us wanted to be conspirators. In fact I'm not sure I'd use that word."

"Okay, but the point is, there's a guy out there using bees to kill people. Bees that for some reason we can't zap. And we're all asking ourselves the same thing. Did we get penetrated? Did someone find out about BEEKEEP and figure out a way to use it against us?"

There was an outbreak of quick comment, from an exasperated, "There's no connection, Jim," through to several worried remarks suggesting that the majority shared in General La Salle's concerns.

La Salle cut in after a moment. "Lee, you've got the worst job in the military right now, what can you tell us?"

As he had listened and picked up the tone of the meeting, General Ponting had been making some mental adjustments to his briefing. He leaned forward and rested his clasped hands on the table. "Obviously we're in lessons learned mode at MAIMCOM at the moment. There's a bunch of stuff going on, and I can update you all as we get results through. My thinking on the penetration of BEEKEEP by extremists is that it's extremely unlikely. I've been delving as hard as I can over the last few days into the state of the MAIMCOM organization, and there's absolutely no sign of a breakdown of the chain of command, loss of military discipline, slack procedures, pockets of dissent, that kind of thing. Nothing to make me think that a subversive group could take control of MAIMCOM systems and program bee missions. So I don't see that a knowledge of BEEKEEP would be of any use."

General Ponting realized that in making this claim he had set aside his own doubts about the ultimate integrity of MAIMCOM; but he believed that what he had said was broadly true.

An Air Force general asked him where he thought the failure had occurred.

"NSA is a more porous organization than MAIMCOM, Frank. My money would be on a leak of the MAIMKEY out of NSA, together with bees from India."

"Do we have a beekeeper at NSA at the moment?" a general down the table said.

That led to a few minutes discussion about the half dozen civilians with knowledge of BEEKEEP, one of whom, it turned out, was at NSA, although not as director; and what to do about them. It was agreed that one-on-one meetings were needed to debrief them about possible leaks and keep them onside, and the generals parlayed over who should talk with whom. La Salle said he would talk with the guy at NSA. Ponting himself volunteered to talk with a former DepSecDef with whom he had maintained a cordial link.

"Okay, where do we stand?" General La Salle said at last. "Should we broaden this out and look at fundamental issues? We all know that BEEKEEP was created by the last president in the wake of the Guam crisis. We needed to be able to weaponize all of our domestic bee systems and centralize command of that, just in case. But does that still apply?"

"I think it does, Jim," Ponting said. "Maybe more than ever. And I think this Kronos business proves the point."

Several others spoke up, and Ponting was relieved that for the most part they shared his point of view.

"Okay," La Salle said, "let's get back to the reason we're here: whether *our thing* has been penetrated by this freak. We'll get more information in due course, from the beekeeper civilians, and from Lee's investigations at MAIMCOM. But I'd like to jump ahead and get a quick tally of how we think we should proceed, should we get a negative outcome. How many feel that we should tell the President?"

"Tell the President what?" one of the generals asked.

"A full briefing on the origins and capabilities of BEEKEEP."

La Salle waited sharp-eyed for the response. General Ponting kept his hand down, but he noted, with disappointment, and a trace of anger, that a number of hands were going up.

"Thank you, gentlemen," La Salle said. "Of course we would take a sounding on this again; but at the moment it appears we favor telling the President, if our suspicions of BEEKEEP grow severe. Let's hope it doesn't come to that."

◇◇◇

The day after his expedition to the Pentagon, General Ponting received a message from his Director of Technical Services, Colonel Melvin Reznichek, telling him that some tentative conclusions had been reached on the spent bees provided by the FBI.

Reznichek was an army colonel from the Corps of Engineers; a man in his seventies with a soft, owl-like face and wide-open eyes that looked permanently surprised. Ponting's duties as second-in-command had brought him frequently in contact with Reznichek, and he had no doubts that he was technically competent and a dedicated soldier and loyal to MAIMCOM. He had not found it necessary to submit Reznichek to an interrogation-style interview. But Ponting was aware that the business of analyzing the spent bees from the Kronos killings, which Reznichek had managed with a small, mature team, was uniquely challenging. Reznichek was only now assembling tiny fragments of data into some possible conclusions. Ponting had been aware for several days of the trend of the data, and when Reznichek called, he jumped up from his desk and trotted down five flights of stairs rather than endure the whims and uncertainties of an elevator.

"What?" Ponting said as he closed the door of Reznichek's cluttered office.

"Assuming the bees from the different crime scenes are essentially from the same source, we have quite a strong result."

"PMA origin?"

"Yes."

Ponting nodded and sat down on a metal chair, his breathing slowing towards normal. It was the news he had been hoping not to hear.

"How strong is strong?"

"There are a lot of factors. I'm guessing. Fifty-fifty?"

"Any of those factors things I'd understand?"

"Most of the data suggesting PMA protocol come from one bee. If that bee is anomalous in some way, we haven't got much of a case."

"Okay. Supposing that bee is not anomalous?"

Reznichek gave his owl-like blink. "Let's say three to one in favor."

Ponting chose his words carefully. Reznichek was not inside the loop on BEEKEEP, which made this delicate territory. "Assuming for the moment that all these bees are PMA bees, and that they did the killings, is there anything in the data you extracted to suggest how they overcame the firmware controls on behavior?"

"Sorry, General, not even close. If anything like that could survive the zeroizing process, we wouldn't have a very secure piece of technology. Thousands of dead bees end up in the hands of hot-shot hackers every year. If they could extract anything useful, and believe me, they've tried, then we'd all be in deep trouble."

The General nodded. This was the reply he had expected. "Okay. Anything else about these bees I ought to know about?"

"Nothing that we've so far deciphered. We'll keep working on it."

General Ponting stood up, his mind busy. He turned around, placed his hands on the back of the chair and leaned towards Reznichek. "Colonel, this information, every facet of it, is SCI."

"Understood, General."

"Not only is the case unproven, but if civilians get to think that ordinary bees might attack them, we'll have a serious security problem."

"Agreed."

On top of which, the General thought, his colleagues in BEEKEEP might take it in to their heads to tell the President. And those like him who concerned themselves with national security wouldn't be at all happy about that.

"How many on your team, Colonel?"

Reznichek did some mental counting. "Five."

"All with SCI status?"

"Yes sir."

"I'd like you to remind them of the status of this investigation."

"I'll take that for action, General."

Ponting frowned and dropped his gaze. He had some experience of controlling the flow of information. That stuff in Iraq, all those years ago. He didn't think back on it if he could help it. The fallout had been bad: a busted marriage, alienated kids. But he'd learned a few lessons out of that. Sometimes you had to talk to people, one on one, spell things out. Never assume.

Of course he'd done a lot of interviewing within MAIMCOM already, maybe even personnel from this same team of analysts, but that had been different. That had been prodding, sparring, looking for disloyalty, bad attitude, guilt. This time he'd be doing what he'd done in Iraq: getting the guys onside, on message, making sure they knew about the little ways that things slipped out; and trying to spot the vulnerable individual. This was about keeping stuff in, not looking for stuff that had got out.

He looked up. "I'd also like to speak with them as a group and individually," he said. "Set that up for me, Colonel."

CHAPTER 17

K ronos had a sense of suppressed excitement as he settled down to speak with Kate Nakamoto on a telcom link. It was late at night, the safest time for undisturbed contact. He had spent a couple of days preparing for this, thinking it through. He couldn't be sure that she was the leader of the Rose Mickelburger Faction, but his gut feeling told him she was the one: willful, driven, a lover of risk, and a believer in the insurrectionary power of youth. In fact, a person not unlike himself.

There was a problem, of course: the couple of occasions on which they had met, she had irritated the hell out of him. Her planning was garbage, her attitude to males apparently that they were expendable muscle. But things would be different this time around. He was Kronos. Even Kate Nakamoto would have to defer to that.

Merko had set him up with a system monitor which would disguise his voice and appearance; and knowing Merko as he did, he was confident that Kate would be unable to break that down, even if she got her best comms guys working on it. That gave him another advantage: he knew who she was, but she would know nothing, except that he was Kronos.

Assuming she believed that. Kate hadn't survived this long without being able to defend herself. She had an instinctive resistance to bullshit.

When Kate's flat, oriental features appeared on his screen, her expression, as he had guessed, was impatient, suspicious. She looked as though she was studying the doctored image of himself that he was sending and finding it less than impressive.

"Thanks for taking this call," Kronos said in neutral tones.

"You going to tell me who you are?"

"Kronos."

Kate's eyes narrowed and she held a look of sharp concentration for a couple of seconds, staring at his image, and then irritation broke up the stillness and she gave a half toss of her head. "Oh yeah. And I'm the goddess Aphrodite."

"Kate, I assume you're by yourself in a secure location?" Kronos had told her this was necessary when booking the call with her telcom genie.

She acknowledged this with a slight lifting of the head.

"I want you to look at some video. We'll discuss this when you've seen it." Kronos touched a display pad on his desk and saw in the corner of his monitor that the video was running. He concentrated on Kate's face. She watched at first with reluctance and then with more attention. What was interesting was that where the bee attack became graphic, most people, including Merko, would look horrified and sick; whereas Kate went cold and concentrated, her eyes hooded, her brain clearly working.

When the sequence had run, Kronos said, "Did you follow the media coverage of the killings, Kate?"

"Of course."

"So you'll know that that footage was never shown."

"Which tells me one of two things."

Kronos waited.

"Either you are Kronos, or maybe an associate of Kronos. Or else… you're the feds. You acquired that video, impounded it, made a deal with the media… and withheld it from public release."

"And now I'm trying to entrap you into damaging admissions, names of your associates, and so forth."

"Always assuming I had any such damaging admissions to make, yeah, that would be the procedure. Or you might be trying to recruit me into something more devious."

"So, which is it?"

"How the hell should I know? My telcom genie is not giving me an ID or an origin for this call, so you've fixed the system somehow. I guess the face I'm looking at is not your real face, either, right?"

"Right."

"So it looks like you've got a credibility problem."

Kronos felt momentarily irritated, but he controlled it. This was typical Kate. "What you don't know, Kate, because of course I'm not going to reveal my identity, is that we've met before. A few years ago. I used to have some involvement in M3R. I can't tell you more than that, but the point is, I was aware of you and where you were headed. I remember who you hung out with, Myra Dunkley and Joe Gonzalez, for example."

"And now you've taken your story to the FBI."

"Now I've formed my own cell and turned myself into Kronos. And I want to explore the possibility of working with you and your organization."

"Which is?"

"My guess is that you're the driving force behind the Rose Mickelburger Faction."

Kate kept a straight face, but Kronos thought he saw a momentary glint of something, probably alarm, in her eyes. "Sorry," she said, her mouth turning obstinate, "you're going to have to do more to convince me. And of course I totally deny the RMF connection."

"What do you need?"

"I don't know. Maybe I'm just going to end this conversation right here."

"Before you do, Kate, think about this. If I'm not Kronos, you're in deep trouble. You and maybe your whole organization is compromised. The feds have made a remarkable breakthrough. They can pick you up now or later, but either way, it's all over. If you want to sleep at nights, you'd better let me persuade you that I'm Kronos."

Kate stared angrily out of the screen. "Is this some kind of threat?"

"Kate, listen to me: I've got an operation planned, a nationwide operation, that could take us to a new level. Your stuff is good, you're doing great, but, let's face it, it's marginal. You're not going to change the world. Whereas with me, you could. That's what's at stake here. That's what I want you to think about."

Kate kept her head still, but her eyes, blinking rapidly, mirrored the thoughts chasing around in her brain. "So how are you going to persuade me?" she said at last.

Kronos watched her a moment longer, turning things over in his mind. "I have a girlfriend," he said. "Someone who took risks and got some important information for me. Unfortunately she found out who I am."

"And?"

"She'll have an accident. A fatal accident. What I could do, I could tell you her name, and where and when she'll have the accident. I think you'd agree, that's not something the feds would be authorized to do."

Kate's eyes had widened.

"Think about it," Kronos said. "I'll call you tomorrow."

CHAPTER 18

T he reassuring voice said, "Vital signs stable. Molecular systems at neutral. Native heart re-starts… *now*. Heart rate normal. Three minutes to fluid withdrawal. Blood pressure normal. Vital signs stable. Two minutes and fifty seconds to fluid withdrawal…"

Cap Olsen said, "Why do I keep thinking of those old Frankenstein movies?"

Roger Enquist was on his feet, studying the data screens that occupied one wall of the lab. "You think he's going to stagger out of there, wild-eyed, and start attacking people?"

"All I know is it's weird. One of the great moments in the history of mankind, and there's only two of us here to open the champagne."

Cap could feel his own heart beating fast, as he sat at the lab table, a pile of briefing papers in front of him, and waited for the new Alan Connacher to emerge… walking, crawling, he didn't know how… from the machine beside him.

A lot was riding on this. The FBI and other agencies had done thousands of interviews and checks across D.C., and got nowhere. None of his younger agents, operating across the country, some of them nominally in touch with youth organizations, had got anything to report, apart from a general upsurge in radical activity. However implausible, Alan and the Rose Mickelburger connection was his best hope.

"One minute and ten seconds to fluid withdrawal."

He had briefed the President, a few days ago, one on one. Cap had thought long and hard before taking that step: if Alan produced nothing, and even Cap conceded this was probable, the FBI, and Cap

Olsen in particular, would come out of it a loser, especially if details of the operation leaked out; but he wanted to get the new Alan into the President's special intern program, no questions asked, and he decided also that on balance he would look better in the President's eyes for making a bold attempt, even one that failed. The President had promised the nation that the security services would find Kronos: she expected radical initiatives.

"Twenty seconds to fluid withdrawal."

Cap exchanged a glance with Enquist and got to his feet. The machine itself seemed expectant, alert. Little sounds, deep within, the clicking of a thousand tiny servers, were concentrated, final.

"Everything okay?" Cap said, aware of the banality.

Enquist turned away from the displays, shrugged. "Does he like chocolate?"

"What?"

"Doughnuts. I bought chocolate." Enquist waved at the bag on the table.

"Ah."

"I thought he might be hungry."

"Yeah. Maybe." Cap couldn't imagine that Alan would be hungry, but he couldn't imagine anything at all about his thoughts, mood, feelings, as he came out of the machine.

The reassuring voice said, "Fluid withdrawal successful. Vital signs stable. Breathing started. Breathing normal. Vital signs stable. Muscles energized. Probes withdrawn in ten seconds."

As Cap waited, the tension grew and settled over the small room like a heavy cloak. It was hard to breathe.

"Subject is conscious. Vital signs stable. Sensory data normal. Probes withdrawn."

What now? Cap thought. Will he just lie there and think about things for a while? Should we knock and say hello?

But faintly, from inside the machine, they heard, "The procedure is complete, Dr. Connacher. Please be careful. Muscle tone is poor. Exit tunnel is to your left."

Cap stood still, clenching and unclenching his fists. Enquist had found Alan's robe and was holding it ready. The seconds passed in claustrophobic silence, as they strained their ears listening for human sounds.

From the three-foot high portal in the face of the machine a naked human foot appeared; then another. Cap grunted in release of tension and instinctively reached out a hand. The feet came up, moved forward, dropped down again, and the figure of a man appeared, sitting, hunched forward, bald and naked, but clearly alive, eyes blinking, head turning.

The fact that this human figure was visibly not Alan Connacher, being almost boyishly young, and of a subtly different cast of feature, was not quite the surprise that Cap Olsen had anticipated: it was a conjuring trick, certainly, but one he had been told about in advance; his emotions ran quickly beyond awe to relief, to a sudden flood of belief in their project. Say hi to a new, bespoke model FBI agent.

Enquist moved forward and took hold of the new man's arm and offered the robe. The man remained sitting on the lip of the portal, looking up blankly at Enquist.

"Alan?" Enquist said.

"Or if you're not Alan," Cap said gruffly, "we want our money back."

The man looked up at Cap now, as though trying to make sense of that remark. Then he reached down with his hands and pushed up and tried to stand. Cap instinctively jumped towards him, Enquist on the other side. The man got it all wrong, lost balance, tumbled forward, Cap and Enquist grabbing at him, cushioning the fall.

"Oh Jesus," Cap said, kneeling beside him, "paramedic time again. Come on, let's get this guy over to therapy."

CHAPTER 19

V alerie hadn't seen much of Kronos in the last few days, but that just made it worse. Ever since he had told her who he was, she had been living in a state of mental panic. She never thought of believing his later denials. She had seen the truth on his face: the flash of ego, the glow of pride; as though the door of a furnace had slipped aside for a brief moment, revealing the molten fires within.

She thought that now at least her love would die, and she would recover her wiser, lonelier, self: but as time passed, she was humiliated to find that it didn't; it was different, more than ever like a destructive fever, but it hung on, strangling her will, her self-belief. Whatever kind of a monster he was, however mad, she found herself arguing, there was also something idealistic there, a cause channeling all that egotism and violence; and he had trusted her, still trusted her, to help him. She hated what he had done, but she half-understood it; even was in awe of it. She had no thought of betraying him. She still gave way to his love-making, swallowing her fear in total surrender.

But when she thought of her own contribution, so innocent, so well-intentioned, to the deaths of twenty-six decent, high-achieving citizens, one of them actually known to her parents, she felt she could scream. She went through her work day sick to her stomach, unable to concentrate, unable to eat, struggling desperately to survive through meetings and deflect the well-meaning enquiries of colleagues. Her career at the PMA had turned sour anyway, particularly after the sad death of Rose Mickelburger in Syracuse had made the agency seem more than ever repressive and ugly; and now it was a nightmare. In the evenings she struggled with panic, seeing herself an accessory, arrested, everyone she knew horrified, her life over.

This was when it was worse without him: at least if he was there, she had a focus, someone to be frightened of, someone who could, perhaps, miraculously change everything, convince her it wasn't true; even though she knew it was.

One evening, going home to her parents to escape the lonely pressures, she nearly broke down and told them everything. They were semi-retired, in their early seventies, comparatively rich. Her father did some consultancy work for a bank; her mother taught Russian classes. They were one-niners themselves; members of the establishment; not powerful enough, nor senior enough, to be chosen as victims by Kronos; but the right age, the right social group.

That discouraged her, held her back at the last moment. Also their character: her parents had never shown much love when she was growing up; always busy, delegating to hired help. They were kind, interested in her career, apparently glad to see her when she visited them, but lacking some vital involvement. Their involvement had been with each other.

Valerie was half-aware that this had given her low self-esteem and made her vulnerable to someone controlling like Kronos. She had never introduced them; Kronos wanted their relationship to remain a secret. If she told them now, they would be appalled, and would certainly demand she go to the police.

But she did assent to a suggestion which her parents, noticing her fatigue and her distress, made to her by telcom link the next morning: come to the Adirondacks for the weekend: the fall colors are beautiful.

Her parents had a few acres on the eastern side of the park with a cottage, a guest cottage, and stables; and although she felt her status there was much the same as any other guest, she enjoyed the peace and quiet, the mountain trails. She drove up in her own car, ready to come home early if her guilt and mental anguish got out of hand.

When she reached the mountains and valleys, the wooded banks shot through with orange and red, the light was fading, but the beauty, instead of raising her spirits, brought her close to tears. These sights, these places, were things she would never be able to appreciate properly again; they were contaminated by the anxiety and despair deep in her soul.

She managed a weary politeness with her mother and father, relieved to find she was the only guest, and could therefore opt for the guest cottage, on the grounds of not disturbing them with her comings and goings. But the guest cottage, when she was settled in there after supper, was lonely, seemed to proclaim the absence of real warmth in her family.

In the morning, after a familiar, troubled, night, wrestling with hopeless plans of escape, she got up, half-stupefied with fatigue, and tried to engage with the day in front of her. Her parents kept horses, and she decided to go for a ride. She chose a docile chestnut gelding called Charade, and the stable-boy helped her to saddle up.

She rode down towards the lake, waded a shallow stream, and cantered across open meadows, a couple of boathouses visible to her right. The sun glinted behind the trees, began to disperse the mist. Nicely shaken up, she dismounted to pass through a gate, and then began the climb into the mountains.

As the views opened up, she felt taken out of herself, able to relax a little, enjoy the golden splendor of the maples and birches; then her brain took advantage, said, Okay, you're detached, you've got a new perspective, so... *what are you going to do?*

Wearily, she let the debate start again. Plan one. Leave Washington. Plan two. Get herself arrested. Plan three. Fall off the side of a mountain. The thought made her cringe and close her eyes, sensing that her life had collapsed to the point where such things became possible, almost welcome.

She started suddenly and raised her head and turned to look behind her. A big-tired electric quad bike, the modern substitute for a horse, was in sight and closing, its motor silent, but its tires kicking small stones onto the escarpment below, creating the sound that had startled her.

Valerie had passed a small group of riders down by the lake, and a couple of quad bikes soon afterwards, but for the last few miles she had felt on her own. Her heart rate jumped. Charade tossed his head and became skittish. She reined him back and turned him full circle at the side of the trail, to let the quad bike go by. As she swung round, she noticed a silver-edged blur against the background of the trees. Out here? she thought. Impossible.

The quad bike stopped instead of going by and the driver got off. She almost screamed. Of course it was possible: the lord of the bees had arrived.

"Hey Val, how's it going?"

She couldn't breathe. In her mind loomed the thought that at the moment she had thought about betraying him, hey presto, here he was.

"You okay? You look like you've seen a ghost."

Charade, picking up her terror, was beginning to shuffle nervously. She leaned forward and stroked his neck and muttered comforting words, hoping they would calm her down as well.

"What are you doing here?" she said at last. It sounded harsh, stressed, but it was the only question in her head.

Kronos grinned. "Not bad, huh? I drove up overnight, caught some sleep on the way, and been chasing you for an hour or so. Isn't this great?" He waved at the mountain scenery. "I just love this place. Listen, I've got a nice bottle of wine, some salmon sandwiches… I thought we could have a real nice day."

Valerie gave him brief little glances, her mind as skittish as her horse. The bees, he must have found her by tracking her with bees. Did he have bees of his own? Obviously. Could they avoid detection by the MAIMCOM umbrella? Evidently they could, out here in the wild, if they used tree cover. Was he going to kill her with bees? Because it was certain that he was going to kill her, one way or another. She saw that with absolute clarity. So now, for the last time: *what was she going to do?*

"Val? You okay?"

"It's… it's a big surprise. Why didn't you tell me?"

Kronos shrugged. "Thought it would be fun to just show up. Didn't know I could make it until the last minute." He took a couple of paces towards her. "It is going to be fun, isn't it, Val?"

"Yeah. Sure."

"Why don't you call your folks and tell them you'll be gone for the day?"

Valerie immediately understood the meaning of that. When he'd killed her, he didn't want anybody finding the body. Not for a few hours at least, after which resuscitation would be impossible.

"You know my parents. They probably won't notice if I come home or not. I'll call them later."

Kronos gave her his mildly-frustrated look. "Do me a favor and talk to them, Val. Just in case they've got something planned. But don't tell them I'm here, okay? Etiquette says I should call by and see them, and I really don't have time for that."

Valerie had one brief regretful thought: did this man, whom she had loved, really think she was this stupid? And then terror overwhelmed her and she kicked Charade in the ribs and urged him forward up the trail. He was ready to go, and his hooves sent small stones flying as he leaped forward into a gallop. Valerie hung on tight and shouted to her telcom genie:

"My parents. Emergency. Quick. Mom? Dad? Are you there? Mom? Please, whatever you're doing, listen to me."

She heard nothing. Then her telcom genie said, "I'm sorry, Valerie, the up-link is dead. We have heavy interference. I'll keep trying."

She heard herself half-scream in despair. The bees. She had read that somewhere. Bees could jam telcom links to stop terrorists from communicating or detonating bombs.

Okay, she was going to die. She knew that was likely. But she didn't want to die for nothing, in a state of guilt. Any loyalty she might have had to Kronos had suddenly gone. She wanted to tell someone who he was. But how?

Charade was still pounding up the trail, snorting with effort. She could feel the heat of his body penetrating her jeans. She didn't dare look back, but she knew that Kronos was behind her. The big wheels of his quad bike would have no problems on this kind of ground. Her only hope was to find a minor track through the trees that would be too narrow for the bike.

Instead of that, the trail suddenly opened up on her right. She was on the edge of a ravine. The ground sloped steeply away from the edge of the trail, smooth rock and scrub, to a watercourse fifty feet below. She caught her breath and concentrated on holding Charade to the trail.

Then she saw the bees. They weren't hiding now, they were a small black swarm, and they were bunched around the eyes of her horse. She couldn't be sure if they attacked, but almost at once Charade reared and stumbled and twisted into the ravine. It was over in a second. She felt her horse scrambling and twisting, then she was thrown off and flew into nothingness.

◇◇◇

The world came back at last and she knew that was bad. Death was now the only option. She felt burning, probing fire all over her body, but no intense pain. Adrenaline shock. She opened her eyes unwillingly. A blue sky, a familiar landscape around her, like a postcard from afar. No meaning for her. Please let me go, let me sleep.

But Kronos was there. Her malign god, her fate. Of course. The coup de grace. She closed her eyes again.

"I need a favor, Val."

She half-opened her eyes. He had approached, holding a water bottle. She sighed, moved her head a fraction, as though by that little movement she might escape from him.

"I'm truly sorry, Val. This isn't what I wanted. Can you speak?"

Why should I speak? she thought. But she moved her lips apart. Moved her tongue. There was blood in her mouth. From where? She swallowed. "Yes."

"You see, we can't leave it like this. I need a favor."

She closed her eyes.

"This can be tough on you, Val. Or it can be easy. Let's make it easy."

She opened her eyes. He was squatting now, close beside her, holding the water bottle. His expression was pained, even caring. She couldn't make sense of anything at all in her life. She had never had children. She had chosen this man. What was she doing here, in this place? What had brought her to this?

"I'm going to die," she said. Her mouth had dried.

"Yes," he said.

"My horse?"

"Broke his neck. It was quick, Val, but…. like I said… this whole thing sucks."

She said nothing, a depth of sadness washing over her.

"Val, I need you to leave a message for your parents. Just a few words."

"So they won't come looking."

"Yeah."

She felt anger, but it was distant, out of her reach. "Why should I?"

"Val, okay, I've used you, I'm the agent of your death, but… I am Kronos. I'm doing what has to be done in our society. I don't think you want to destroy me."

"I wasn't going to."

"I know. But it was risky, Val. You could have been questioned. You could have said something. You could have said something without knowing what you'd said. I'm truly sorry."

"One more thing for me to do," she said.

"One more thing."

"And that's enough. That's the end."

"That's the end."

"How stupid I was."

"You were great. I mean that. You were great."

She relaxed, felt herself dozing. Kronos nudged her.

"My genie?" she said.

"Functional."

"Telcom message for my parents," she said.

"Yes, Valerie," her genie said.

"Tell them I'm going to visit some friends. Probably be gone most of the day."

"Yes, Valerie."

"And then you'll be off-line," Kronos said.

"And then I'll be off-line."

"Yes, Valerie."

"Okay?" She opened her eyes.

Kronos nodded. His expression was intense, serious. His eyes glittered. He's got what he wants, she thought; everything from me that he wants.

He reached out and put the bottle of water to her lips.

CHAPTER 20

Kronos studied his wall-screen for the nuances of Kate's expression: yes, she now believed he was Kronos; she had confirmed Valerie's death and drawn the obvious conclusion; and yes, she was a little bit scared of him. No, that wasn't quite right. She was looking at him with a certain calculated intensity: jealousy, perhaps, at his empowerment, his status; maybe a hint of respect.

But there wasn't much respect in the way she spoke: "I want a fair share of input into this. Don't give me the 'Kronos rules the world' crap. You need what I can provide."

"And what's that?"

"An organization, at a guess. Manpower."

"Actually, something more specific."

"Tell me."

"Some ground rules first." Kronos was feeling the familiar buzz of irritation. This girl really knew how to rub him up the wrong way. "This is a Kronos operation. I make the rules, communiqués are in my name. I'm the franchisor, you're the franchisee. You're in this for the good of the cause, not to get your name in the history books. If you don't like that, walk away now. No hard feelings."

"You know," Kate said, her eyes bright with a kind of coquettish willfulness, "I'm looking at this face on my screen, this doctored face, and I've got to say it's full of ego. Here's a guy who's really off on his own trip. Is that the real you?"

"Yes. That's the real me. I'm an egotistical bastard, and I have no interest in anything except power. To put it another way, I'm a politician. Like I say, if you don't like it, get out now."

"You need what I've got, Kronos, otherwise you wouldn't be taking this risk. You'll deal like anyone else."

Kronos was getting increasingly angry. "No I won't. I can be nice if I want to be, I can even listen to what people say, but I only work on the basis that I'm in charge. If you opt in, you and your people will take orders from me. So what's it to be?"

Kate's face on the screen was mulish for a second or two, then softened, became more teasing than challenging. "Just testing. But you'd better be good, Kronos, because I'm not dumb, and I don't like it when ego-driven males get it wrong. Okay? Now tell me what this is about."

Kronos breathed in and out a couple of times, let his heart rate subside. "Illegal children."

"Excuse me?"

"I take it you're no longer denying that you are the Rose Mickelburger Faction?"

"Yeah, I'll take credit for that."

"I'm also assuming that you call the shots."

"Pretty much."

"And of course you were a senior figure in the Mars Three Resistance."

"Okay. Mars Three. Illegal children. That girl you killed, Valerie Thompson, she worked for the PMA, right? The information you got from her was PMA information. Oh my God."

"What?"

"You used PMA bees."

"Now you know why I need to trust you, Kate."

"And you want... you want the Mars Three network. You want the agents who have penetrated PMA offices... and who have access to the local bee management systems. You're planning a nationwide operation."

"You were right back there. You're not dumb."

Kate's expression was intense, almost radiant. "How many fossilized one-niners are you planning to kill this time around?"

"As many as we can, Kate, as many as we can. Carefully selected, of course. But we need to ramp it up and take it across the country."

Kate went quiet for a moment, her face turned aside, serious, engaged in thought. A couple of times she gave a probing glance back at her screen, weighing him up: but she seemed immediately to have understood and embraced his proposal.

"So, what are you telling me, Kate? Are you in or not?"

"Are you crazy? Stupid question. Of course you're crazy. Yeah, I'm in."

"Good."

"Just do me a favor, Kronos."

"What's that?"

"Don't ask me to be your girlfriend. I'd like to keep living for a while."

PART TWO: DOOMERS

CHAPTER 21

Alan Connacher got out of the auto-cab and stood balanced on the balls of his feet, getting his bearings. It was nine o'clock in the evening in Adams Morgan: bustling, ethnic, lit up by shop fronts and traffic; an area he knew well. In the old days he had come here occasionally with his wife, to eat in one of the neighborhood's unfussy restaurants; and when they ran out of uncontentious things to say to each other, there had usually been some useful distraction in the bright vitality around them.

That memory, of Adams Morgan thirty years ago, brought home to him the perilous novelty of his situation now. He wasn't supposed to remember things from such a remote era; he wasn't alive then. He was twenty-nine years old and his name was Doug Edie, and he was a graduate student, albeit unmatriculated, at George Washington University. He knew that Milwaukee was a group of post-techno-head pop musicians, not a city, and he knew how to dance the dragonfly.

The truth was, he thought, as he began to move, he had trouble walking, let alone dancing the dragonfly. The extra energy, the spring in his new body, was wonderful up to a point; and it was surprising how quickly he had adapted to the new muscle dynamics, like an athlete adapting to a change in altitude, or a change of racket; but old habits still caught him out. The training environment set up by Cap and the doctors had included a real-time picture of himself on wall screens, so that he could get used to his new body image and correct the defensive posture and cautious movements of old age; but in new situations he tended to revert, slowing down and dropping his head, and sometimes he would over-compensate, prancing around on the balls of his feet like a ballet dancer.

Concentrating now on the easy, arrogant gait of the young, he strolled amongst the late shoppers, the diners-out, the tourists, the students hanging out, trying to think of the young faces as *us* and the old faces as *them*. Fall had arrived and Washington was getting back to business. It was his first major excursion outside Cap's secret training environment. He was beginning to notice that young people looked at him with friendly, unveiled interest, but the middle-aged and the one-niners shuttered their expression, sliding away from eye contact, occasionally revealing a trace of suspicion or even hostility.

This was as it should be, he told himself: it meant that no-one was questioning his portrayal of youth, and that in turn meant success: but it made him uneasy, not only to lose the trust of his peer group, but also to realize that he had probably behaved in the same way, reacting to the young as a threat; might still behave in that way, if his concentration lapsed.

Did I ever look at Yinghua like that? he wondered, as he passed a group of one-niners emerging from a restaurant, and caught the wave of unthinking censure in their eyes. For a moment he sought sanctuary in the past, remembering the happy six months during which he and Yinghua had conducted their affair, their secret rendezvous around Washington, their deep and absorbing discussions. No, he was sure he'd never seen here through prejudiced eyes: but it was nevertheless the polarization between young and old that had been destructive in the end.

His strolling took him gradually in the direction he wanted to go: onto Columbia, then back down Champlain. There were fewer people here, less light. The building he sought was close to the sidewalk, industrial, brick arches around the windows, the whole façade blank, painted over, crouching in shadow. A small entrance porch and a couple of steps, a knot of young people clustered there, laughing, teasing each other. High above the porch hung a row of illuminated icons: a transparent cube with CUBECHESS written in several colors from corner to opposite corner; a pool table; a beer logo; a guitar.

Alan stopped, his limbs suddenly rigid, new muscles locking up. He wasn't going to survive this: his cover story would vanish, his training desert him. How had this happened, this absurd mismatch of task and ability? He took a deep breath and thought about Kronos, killing his contemporaries, pushing for the violent breakdown of American society.

I wanted to do this, he thought. I wanted to be young again. So here I am: just follow it through.

Holding his head up, he crossed the road and entered the porch. The knot of youngsters glanced at him, passive, unsuspicious, too wrapped up in their own world to give him more than the briefest check. Inside there was an attempt at a magic grotto entrance: he had to bend and maneuver around a tunnel, colored light pulsing, allow a cobweb mist to tickle his skin and extract cells for DNA, and choose an exit from a three-way split of the tunnel. Suddenly he was in a high-ceilinged room with three gateways and counters beside them and a trompe l'œil 3D projection of the counters sloping up the wall ahead at 45 degrees. Alan saw his new self, young, still alien, hanging out of the wall at a crazy angle, and for a moment he was disoriented, unable to work out what this meant.

There was a kid behind the counter with a weak floppy moustache who looked no more than fifteen. He was watching a hidden screen.

"How you doing, Doug?"

Alan made an effort, kept his head up, gave his attention to the kid. "Good." He was relieved, in fact, that the DNA had successfully produced his new identity. It was something they had tried a few times, with no failures, but this time it was for real. The nightmare was that some rogue cell would contain the old DNA and would call up, "Alan Connacher, 89 years old." That would be the end of his mission right there.

The kid had a cocky, smartass attitude, and Alan, still distracted by the displaced image of the room, struggled to understand the payment process. At last he realized what the kid was saying and instructed his telcom genie to pay fifty dollars to the club's account.

The kid watched his hidden screen. "That's done. Have a good evening, Doug."

"You too," Alan said lamely, and pushed through the barrier, his slanted image moving towards him instead of away from him, so that he blended with it as he passed through into the club.

He was in a big space, a onetime warehouse, he supposed, the iron rafters visible above, with decks at several levels built up from the ground, giving railed-off areas above, and cubicle interiors below; everywhere broken up into smaller spaces by pillars and umbrellas of colored light in Tiffany-style designs, shifting, exploding like fireworks, generating sounds and music, a kind of design in progress. Through this camouflage of light, Alan noted that the structures and furnishings were basic: plastic tables and chairs, bare floors, scaffolding and wood for the upper decks.

It felt temporary: a warehouse on a short lease, decorated and disguised with the cheap technology of light and illusion, managed by floater. And of course it *was* temporary: the university student age-group was due to plummet in a few years, as the stringent population controls began to affect the final years of school. The merrymaking here was like a wake for a vanishing era.

One thing for sure: rejuvenated people like him would not be giving these places a new lease of life.

A band of tension tightening across his forehead, Alan blundered through flashing barriers, heading for what looked like a bar built beneath the top level of decking. At the end of the concourse was a dance floor, another illusion swelling and compressing the dancers into grotesques. Music pounded as he drew nearer. Were they dancing the dragonfly? It was hard to tell from the exaggerated movements of the grotesques, but it didn't look like it. Maybe Cap's research was out of date, the dragonfly yesterday's fashion.

The bar turned out to be staffed by humans, not robots, mostly girls barely out of their teens.

"Hey, how are you tonight?" one of the girls said brightly.

Alan was going to order a scotch, and then changed his mind: young people probably didn't drink scotch. He ordered a beer instead. The transaction this time was straightforward. He took his glass across to a table and sat down. There were several groups socializing at tables nearby. As he sipped at his beer, he tried to eavesdrop. A group of four youngsters, three boys and a girl, were mimicking their professors, and laughing boisterously, before deciding on a suitable form of punishment for their inadequacies, post-revolution.

His beer was half gone when a girl exuding energy and purpose startled him by sitting down at his table.

"Do you want your D&R match-ups active during the evening, Doug?" she said.

Alan felt his face go blank, his jaw slacken momentarily. "What?" he said, trying to pretend that he had been distracted by the conversation at the nearby table.

The girl repeated her question.

Alan had no idea what D&R match-ups were. He cursed Cap's team for leaving another gaping hole in his briefing.

"The thing is," he said, forcing a half-smile and hoping he looked stupid, "I'm new in town. Got here late."

"Okay." The girl, who was overweight but who radiated goodwill, seemed pleased that he had provided such clear-cut information. "Where're you from?"

"New Hampshire. And Bangor University."

"But you joined the program, right? I mean Bangor would have your data?"

"Well…"

"Bangor can't be that much off the map. D&Rs are *everywhere*."

"Well…"

"You don't know what I'm talking about, do you?" The girl leaned forward with a peal of laughter and put a hand on his arm.

"I had some health problems," Alan improvised. "I didn't spend much time with the Bangor student body."

"O-*kay*… Wow, I've heard it all today. Well, D&Rs are dating and recreational match-ups. All the kids use them. It's basically analysis of your DNA for personality dimensions, combined with some self-assessment responses. I can get your data together here and now, if you like. We would normally set you up with two to three dozen match-ups in the Washington area, and then if you don't want to organize formal meetings, you can work on a chance basis when you go to places like this. You might think the odds are against you, but it's surprising how often you find you've got a soul-mate, here, there, wherever…"

"It sounds great," Alan said, trying to look positive, while inwardly recoiling. He thought briefly of his daughter, Trudie, trying to fix him up with suitable dates, and how bad he was at dealing with that. If anything was going to give him away, it would be a series of dates with naïve youngsters, expecting him to behave like them. "Can I take a rain-check for today? I wanted to watch some cubechess, but I'm too tired to hang around for long."

"Sure. When you're ready, talk to anyone in student counseling. And welcome to Washington. It's a really exciting town."

"Thank you."

The girl jumped up and bustled off, waving at somebody behind the bar.

Alan let the air out of his lungs, felt his posture slumping. Had he got away with that? Or was the girl running off to her colleagues to tell them that a very strange student was let loose amongst them?

He swallowed some more beer. He felt as though he was in a bad dream: young again, strong again, his deepest desires fulfilled; but thrown into a world he couldn't understand, couldn't join; a permanent outsider.

Tomorrow morning, unless some disaster intervened, he had to show up at the White House and begin his tenure as an intern. That would crank the risks up to a new level. To judge by results so far, Cap's briefing wasn't likely to help much. The young lived in a different world. Amongst themselves, at least, they spoke a different language. For how long would he be able to fake membership of such a closed society?

He finished the beer and stood up and left the bar, head up, shoulders back. He began to ascend the short, open staircases leading from deck to deck. Pool was being played on one of the mezzanine areas, there was another bar, a snack service on a terrace overlooking the concourse below, and the top decks were taken up by cubechess.

Alan had taken a crash course in cubechess from an FBI enthusiast. Although mainly played by the young, because of their brainwave control skills, acquired in childhood, plenty of older people had worked on the technology and become competitive. Limits to success were largely mental, not physical, and the game was popular with the disabled.

Strictly speaking, it was not a computer game, or an electronic game: it could be played in any three dimensional space, with real pieces, moved by hand. Technology was used to speed it up, monitor and penalize player error, and display the pieces within a virtual transparent cube, usually a meter high.

The cube was divided into 512 boxes, each about five inches along a side, distinguished from each other by shades of grey and shades of violet, which changed slightly with viewing angle, giving an enhanced stereoscopic effect. Each player had two sets of pieces, or icons, red and yellow for one player, blue and white for the other, lined up at the start on opposite faces of the cube. The icons had similar names and abilities to chess pieces, but queens became barons, and one king became a queen of the complimentary color. Players made two moves at once, one icon of each color, usually every three seconds. Taking an opponent's icon involved targeting it in two dimensions, with two icons. Both king and queen had to be checked or targeted simultaneously to win the game.

Technology also allowed the players to see the game from the viewpoint of any icon: personal sensors tracked eye and body movements and delivered a stereoscopic display to the player's glasses. Most players chose to follow the action from the viewpoint of the king or queen or a combination of the two. Players in the heat of battle would turn and duck and weave as they got involved in defending their key icons.

Alan and Cap supposed that this was where Peter Johnson had learned to follow and control two things at once: cubechess meant attacking with two icons at once, and defending in the same way.

Alan had learned to move the icons around with brainwave sensor control, but he remained a long way from being able to play a game.

The two cubechess displays on the top deck had swivel chairs and control panels fit for an aircraft pilot on each side of the cube, and a surrounding circle of plastic chairs for enthusiasts and team mates. The top deck also had the in-vogue decoration of hybrid plants that grew like climbers, then mutated into a fixed, plasticized form, with programmable features. These pseudo-plants had grown up the railings and into the rafters, and been programmed so that bands of color rose slowly up the stems, giving them an illusory sense of continued growth. Alan didn't like them, but at least they enclosed the space with some color and texture.

Both cubes were in use, intent players at each of the four stations, heads twisting and jerking like demented puppets, hands hovering at the console, occasional sound effects signaling an illegal move.

Alan hovered in the background for a few minutes, pretending to watch both games, and then found a chair a little away from the half a dozen fans clustered around the cubes. He watched for over an hour. He thought he had identified one of the players, a Georgetown University associate professor of physics called Jay Kirilenko, a possible contact of Peter Johnson, according to Cap Olsen. Alan felt faintly encouraged by that: he had at least got within range of the people he was supposed to study. But as he continued to watch the group at the table he felt his confidence slipping away. He was blending in with youth; nobody was looking at him as though he was an outsider; but he was still a million miles away from impersonating a neophyte revolutionary; a million miles away from gaining the confidence of people like Kirilenko, with their self-protective habits and rituals; especially if they felt themselves under threat.

He got up suddenly and began to make his way back down the decks.

CHAPTER 22

Perhaps it was the apartment, a down-at-heel studio with garish furnishings, or the huge expenditure of nervous energy over the last few days, or the realization that now he was truly alone, cut off from every aspect of his previous life; but when Alan returned to his new home after his visit to the Adams Morgan club, he felt himself sliding rapidly downhill into a depressive episode.

He knew the signs: lethargy, failing belief in his plans and prospects, a weight inside his head.

The faded orange stripe on the sofa irritated him. The fresh fruit delivery had failed to include the items he preferred, and the auto-chef produced a meal he could barely force himself to consume.

The bed was just a bed, without micro-massage or other refinements, and although he felt deeply tired, he couldn't sleep. The soundproofing wasn't good, and he could hear a penetrating whine: a motor somewhere, endlessly pumping air.

In the end his brain took him where he didn't want to go: back towards his own youth, his real youth, which began to resonate in his mind unavoidably, brought close by the young lives he had encountered that evening.

His head was suddenly full of defensive attitudes and guilty denials which he had long since put aside, but which had been part of his teenage years: it was not his fault if his mother was still unhappy, not his fault that his parents had been unable to work out their problems, his brilliant career would resolve everything, he would show everyone, he would atone for his mistake…

And on he went, back into his boyhood, as though completely entrapped now by the sadistic pressure of self-examination, to that day that shouldn't have happened; to that event he had struggled to redefine, wipe from the record, ever since.

Such a cloudless, carefree day, at the start; all the excitement of those New Hampshire summers, hitching rides on farm machinery, bowling in the woods on an old concrete bowling alley, swinging on the thick rope in the huge barn, from a loft on one side to a loft on the other, letting go the rope and rolling in the hay. He was nine years old. Innocent and free. For the last time.

Of course he knew that his six-year-old brother was getting worse. Duchene muscular dystrophy. He didn't know that term then, but he knew that his brother had a disease and that it was serious and that he would die young and that his parents were very unhappy.

So unhappy that sometimes they didn't seem to notice that they had another son who was perfectly okay and doing well. And of course he did resent that, and sometimes he even resented the brother himself, for taking up so much of his parents' time and making them argue.

But on this occasion he wanted to help. He really had tried to do something to make his parents happy and make his little brother happy. He really had.

Gary fell over a lot and had trouble moving around and Alan thought it would be really good to give him a swing on the rope in the barn. He was strong and he could hold on to Gary and Gary would think it was great and be really excited and tell Mom and Dad that Alan had given him a good time. Gary had watched him swinging a couple of times and said he wanted to do it but Mom and Dad said it was too dangerous, but of course it wouldn't be dangerous if he was holding on to Gary and kept him safe.

And he was looking after Gary one afternoon when Mom was busy and Dad had to go to Boston for something and it was a perfect chance.

"Come on, Gary: you want to swing on the rope?"

Oh yeah, oh yeah.

The terrible thing was he couldn't decide later whether he hadn't *known* it was risky, hadn't *known* something bad could happen, but had gone ahead anyway. The kick of the wily unconscious. Because Gary was making it difficult for everyone. Because their family wasn't normal.

But as he remembered it he had wanted Gary to enjoy it. He had practiced a couple of times, with gentle swings, holding Gary tight round the waist. Gary gripped the rope himself, and he said it hurt a little, but he was really excited, he really wanted to do it, fly through the air just like Alan.

And so they had flown, from the loft to the loft, but as they came up the far side, Gary's fingers slipped, and Alan couldn't hold him, and he had hit his head on the edge of the loft and fallen six feet to the dirt floor.

Everything went hard and blank in Alan's mind, as he swung backwards and forwards and stared at his brother, motionless on the floor, thinking there must be a way to change this, I can go back, start again, I didn't mean this. He let go the rope at last and bent down and touched Gary's body gently, and then screamed his name in both agony and anger, and started running home to call his mother.

When he told his story in court, the coroner ruled that it was an accident. But Alan didn't think they would all have come to court looking so serious if they thought it was an accident. They knew he was a murderer. They all thought he was a murderer. Even his parents thought he was a murderer. He had killed his little brother out of jealousy. That's what they all thought. And now he was responsible for everything: for his brother's disease, his brother's death, the collapse of the family. He was the demonic seed, the emblem of bad fortune.

His parents couldn't handle it: instead of looking after their clever son, the son they had left, they argued more and more and then broke up.

He was a murderer, a brother-murderer, like in the bible, and he had ruined his parents' lives.

He went into medicine and biology first as a form of atonement, then with conviction. He helped promote the cause of genome cleansing, the removal of genetic defects from fertilized eggs before implanting in the womb, the achievement that brought to an end the era of genetically-transmitted diseases.

But he still felt like a murderer.

Gradually the pain and guilt dulled, as he managed them into a remote corner of his brain. At last he entered the field of life extension, and began to dream of a new life, a second chance, restored youth, never quite connecting that with the now-distant memories in the corner of his brain.

And the absurdity of it is, he thought now, lying awake on the uncomfortable bed, sweating and wrestling with tears as the long-buried events came alive in his head, the irony of it is that returning to a youthful state was entirely the wrong way to go. Instead of banishing the trauma forever, he had brought it all back.

He fell into a troubled sleep soon after four o'clock in the morning, and woke up an hour later in the midst of a bad dream.

He got up and took a shower and dressed, and paced around the little apartment, staring at the furniture and the gadgets, all of it coldly unfamiliar, feeling absolutely disconnected from his present incarnation.

Returning to the bathroom, he stared at his face in the mirror: that was the most unfamiliar sight of them all. He pulled his lips back in a smile, pushed at his nose, ran a hand through his stubbly dark hair. For the first time since he had staggered out of the machine in his labs, he understood the enormity of what he had achieved, and the enormity of the consequences. He really had jumped into the unknown, broken all links with his ongoing life. And it hadn't been anything like he had thought. He hadn't escaped from his past, his real past; he hadn't gained relief from the rigors of age, the threat of death. He had become a lost soul. He had stepped into a nightmare.

He left the bathroom and stopped still. He realized he was close to breaking down. That couldn't happen. However lost he was, he would preserve some shred of dignity, at least. If he died, he died, but there were certain things he was supposed to do, and he could try and do them, albeit on his own terms, within his own capacity.

He sat down on the sofa and waited for his breathing to slow. The first thing he had to do was get a message to Cap Olsen. He wouldn't be going to the White House this morning. In fact, he wouldn't be going at all. Ever. He didn't suppose that Cap would be pleased, or would agree the change, but after his experiences last night, he saw it as the wrong move. In any case, he didn't think he could carry it off. It was a risk too far.

The second thing he had to do was get in touch with Yinghua.

◇◇◇

The staff cafeteria at the new Mitsuoka Artificial Intelligence building at Georgetown University was on the south and east face of the fifth floor solarium, with a view of the top of the Washington Monument. It was a big area with lots of comfortable subdivided spaces for food or coffee breaks. Alan had been there a few times and he knew the procedure for getting a visitor pass.

He arrived at MAI reception in the middle of the morning, footsore after walking the streets for hours in new shoes, too unsettled to stay cooped up in the claustrophobic apartment. The documentation fabricated by Cap's team and held in remote database archives survived interrogation by the appropriately non-human scrutineers at the desk, and visitor status was given to his DNA ID.

He went up to the fifth floor cafeteria and bought a cup of coffee and found a secluded spot back from the windows where he could watch the entrance. Of course he didn't know Yinghua's teaching schedule this semester, but most days, he remembered, she liked to come in here for a coffee or a light lunch, and more often than not, being absorbed in her work and not by nature gregarious, she would be alone.

He waited in a state of nervous agitation, seeing new angles, new pitfalls, every few seconds. Who could he safely say he knew, without getting tangled up in unraveling chains of deceit? Her former lover, his grandson Jason? Her current boyfriend, Trudie's stepson Russell? Safer not.

Hardest of all would be remembering who he was himself, if something she said triggered memories, emotions.

He risked a quick visit to the men's room, returned and got another cup of coffee. They were into the lunch period now and more people were arriving, as classes finished, administrators took a break. And at last he saw her. He watched intently, the hand on his coffee cup frozen. She was dressed, as usual, in a quiet feminine style: dark blue woolen dress with a split hem falling just below the knee; a cream blouse with pale blue birds in a Chinese-style print; hair falling in straight silky lines to her shoulders.

She was moving through the food display areas, choosing the small varied items she liked. Suddenly she turned and said something to the man behind her. Were they together? If so, this was probably the end of the road.

She exchanged several remarks with the man, who was much older, Alan noticed, but when she had assembled her tray and went to sit down, she was alone.

He felt gripped by indecision, all his reasoning suddenly void: but as he watched her, lit up by the window behind her, taking a plastic sheet from her bag and beginning to read, lecture notes perhaps, or student project material, he began to feel the steady calm of her personality penetrating his own. His mind took him back to days, nights, when just being with her was a source of contentment and peace.

It suddenly seemed that this was an obvious and beneficial thing to do, restart, if he could, this empowering relationship; something, moreover, to be done quickly, before someone else sat at her table. He stopped a couple of feet away and waited for her to look up. She did after a moment, her face cool, but a familiar sharp curiosity in her eyes.

He gave a half bow. "Excuse me. Are you Ma Yinghua?"

She blinked at him a couple of times. "Yes?"

"I wonder… if you'd mind…"

He stopped speaking, but her gaze remained steadily on him for a few seconds, and then her eyes narrowed slightly, expressing a kind of puzzlement. "Do I know you?"

Alan felt mild shock. But it was perhaps something in his attitude, some expression of remembered intimacy, that had generated that remark, rather than recognition of his features.

"No. No, I don't think so. My name is…" He stalled for a moment, admonished himself, started again. "My name is Doug Edie."

"I am Ma Yinghua." She put out her hand suddenly, and Alan, a little surprised, reached out his own and shook it.

"It's a great honor," he muttered. "I am familiar with your work."

"Are you one of my students?"

"No. No, actually, I'm George Washington. Via Bangor, Maine." He gave a little smile. "Would you possibly… I mean, would you have any time to…"

She looked at him a moment longer, and then moved a little further towards the window and waved at the chair diagonally opposite.

Alan's heart was beating fast. He wasn't sure he was handling this as well as he had hoped, yet Yinghua was trusting, apparently intrigued by him, willing to talk.

More than he had anticipated, he was overwhelmed by her presence, by the emotions stirred up. He could hardly take his eyes off her, in love again with her delicate, porcelain-clear features, searching also for the familiar markers, the little widening of the mouth, the raising of the jaw, that gave away her feelings.

He took a deep breath and sat down, looking away from her, trying to remember his role.

"You're doing research?" Yinghua prompted.

His gaze returned to her face, stayed caught there too long. "Yeah." His head jerked nervously. "Actually, my field is bio-science," he said, words suddenly spilling out, "genetic determination of cognitive processes, that kind of thing. Language structures comes in there, of course. I'm fascinated that you seem to have solved the problems relating to… cultural context in translation. That is, I understand you have created a method of encoding cultural elements for a wide variety of sub-cultures in English and Chinese, and filtering your translations in real time through these to get an appropriately flavored… I'm sorry if I'm mangling your ideas here. I'm kind of nervous, meeting you like this."

Yinghua smiled. "It's okay. You're right about the sub-cultures, in essence."

As she talked, Alan had the luxury of watching her closely, remembering the fine detail, the sharpness of her mind, the grace and beauty of her manner.

He managed to hold up his side of the conversation, his interest in Yinghua's work having continued even after their relationship had ended. She seemed intrigued by some of his comments. Maybe, he told himself, relaxing a little, maybe I'm going to get away with this.

"Yinghua," he said at last. "May I call you Yinghua?"

"Sure."

"I don't really know how to say this. You're kind of an amazing person. Would you want to get together some time? Maybe have dinner or something?"

Yinghua's mouth tightened slightly and her eyes glazed over. Alan knew those signs: withdrawal. He had jumped ahead too far. Or maybe these approaches were usually validated by the D&Rs he had learned about.

"I'm sorry," he said. "I got a bit carried away. You have your own life, obviously."

"If you're suggesting what I think you're suggesting, Doug… Don't you think I'm a little old?"

"In other words, I'm a little young."

"How old are you?"

"Twenty-nine."

"I'm forty-one."

"Does it matter? Really?"

"Because we're all going to live forever?"

"Something like that."

"Age still matters." Yinghua dropped her eyes. Alan wondered if he was right in detecting a trace of bitterness.

At any rate, he knew her too well to argue. "I respect your feelings, of course, Yinghua. And maybe I'm not suggesting exactly what you think I'm suggesting. Would you allow me to come and chat with you again some lunch-time?"

He held his breath. She raised her eyes and watched him for a moment, composed, silent, that suggestion of puzzlement still present.

She thinks there's something familiar about me, he thought, and she can't track it down.

At last she nodded. "Yes," she said simply.

Alan felt a rush of relief, as though his life had been forfeit and was now reprieved. He got up quickly. Yinghua wouldn't like displays of emotion.

"Thank you," he said. "It's been a great pleasure meeting you."

He gave a small respectful bow and walked away. When he was safely out of the building, he punched the air and muttered, "Yes!" between his teeth. He wasn't sure, now, that his preparatory thinking had charted any realistic benefits or outcomes; but the thought of seeing her again was like a protective talisman, giving him hope and keeping him sane.

CHAPTER 23

J ason extracted the two tiny phials from the mailer and held them up to the light, one by one. One hundred and twenty-six dollars-worth. This had better work. Otherwise he had wasted time and money, made a fool of himself, for nothing. If his mother got to hear of it, she'd say he was more than a little weird; she'd say he was from another planet.

He unscrewed the cap of the first and dabbed the liquid on a tissue and sniffed cautiously. It seemed vaguely familiar, clinical, hospital-like, but not distinctive. He tried the second. To his relief, the smell was immediately evocative, taking him back to the makeshift morgue, his mother's histrionics, his thoughts and feelings at the time.

Jason sealed the phials and put them in his medicine cabinet, out of Sam's reach, his mind active, calculating. There was no doubt about it, this was the distinctive smell he had noted hovering over his grandfather's body. A chemical that shouldn't have been there unless there were ongoing efforts to sustain his body for resuscitation. A definite indicator that his grandfather could still be alive.

Doing what?

It was during the next hour, while he was thinking about his grandfather's work, his business, his labs, that he suddenly made the final connection. Of course. That was why the FBI had taken over the building: not because it was part of a crime scene, but because something was going on there. Rejuvenation, in fact. Alan Connacher had rejuvenated someone; and most probably, he had rejuvenated himself. Because Alan Connacher was dead. The perfect cover. It all added up.

He began to picture his grandfather, young, somehow disguised, inhabiting the city, going around, living a life. Would he be tempted back to his old haunts? Would he be irresistibly drawn to his lab building, to his old home? Would he want to see his daughter, Trudie? Or would he be afraid of giving himself away?

◇◇◇

"I'm not frightened of bees. Not really. They're my friends. But sometimes, if they jump out at me…" Sam waved his arms in big circles. "I could scream."

"Could you?" Yinghua said.

"Yeah. I could. But I'm not frightened, really."

"Not like me, then."

"Are you frightened of bees?"

"Yes, Sam, I'm very frightened of bees."

"Why? They won't hurt you. Daddy says they can't hurt you."

"I'm sure he's right."

Jason was glad that Sam, at least, was playing his part, talking innocently to Yinghua, giving some weight to his assertion that Sam wanted to see her again.

It was Sunday afternoon in the park, a warm October day, seniors strolling, some teenagers throwing a football, but small children almost absent. Jason watched Sam with proprietorial care. It was not unknown for children to be swooped upon, stolen, in broad daylight, even though such abductions were never successful in the long run.

He also kept an eye on Yinghua. Seeing her had stirred emotions which he had thought dead and buried. Yinghua had fallen for Sam, and then she had fallen for his grandfather, and he had just been nobody. Yinghua might have tried to mitigate the damage but her efforts to make him feel better had if anything made it all worse.

The bitterness he felt settled mainly on his grandfather: Alan had betrayed him over Yinghua, had failed to help with Sam until it was too late, had preferred Zeb. His grandfather had let him down, if he really looked at things realistically, ever since his mother had come to Washington. Now he was threatening the whole youth movement. Well, one form of betrayal begets another. What could he do? He was just trying to strike a balance; protect himself and his beliefs.

"I guess my granddad's death hit you pretty hard," Jason said.

Yinghua looked at him sharply.

"I mean," Jason stumbled on, "I know you weren't together long, but…"

Yinghua looked away, followed Sam with her eyes, as he chased a grasshopper. "He was a good man," she said at last.

"Yes."

"I have no sympathy with that kind of youth action."

"No. All the same, maybe now, if you meet somebody…"

She was looking at him again, eyes cool. "Meet somebody?"

"Well…" He shrugged. "Maybe it would be a good time. Kind of a new start."

"Or a bad time."

"Yeah."

"Death is a reminder. Now all I think about is…" Yinghua's voice tailed away, and she stared at the park, and Sam.

"Did you meet someone though?"

She gave him another sharp glance. Maybe he was pushing it too much. He looked away. She was silent for a moment.

"No, I didn't meet anyone," she said. "But what I appreciate, Jason, is the chance to meet Sam. I'd be happy if you brought him to see me again."

"That might get easier," he said, unable to keep some measure of self-pity out of his voice. "My boss at work, Trevor Northwich, put me on the second shift."

"Which means? You'll have trouble looking after Sam?"

"It means I'll have to quit the job. Which is what he wants."

"Why? I thought you were doing okay."

"I was doing okay." He took a breath and stared across the grass at Sam. "But Northwich's age finally caught up with him. They're bringing in a new manager. So he wants my job instead. He knows I can't look after Sam working the second shift, but he insisted. Even though Dave was ready to do it. I took Sam with me to see the owner of the company, but he wouldn't help."

"I'm really sorry, Jason."

"Yeah, well, it's one of those things. The problem is, there aren't any jobs out there, unless you know someone."

"I can look after Sam now and then, if it helps."

"Sure, thanks," he said, nodding. "Sam likes to see you."

And maybe one day, he thought, you'll tell me that you've found a new young man.

CHAPTER 24

A lan got a message from Cap Olsen late in the afternoon: a
lucky sighting indicated that Peter Johnson, Spiderman, was
in Washington. Cap had been grumpy about his decision to
withdraw from the White House intern program, but on the whole
had taken it better than he expected. Now Cap wanted him to canvass
the targeted venues in the hope of spotting Johnson and his entourage.
There was no cubechess scheduled at Adams Morgan, so Cap suggested
he concentrate on the others.

Alan had spent the previous evening visiting several of these: most
promising was a huge sports bar not far from Catholic University
offering 48 kinds of beer and 3D displays showing live or recorded
games. He had watched a lacrosse game featuring Johnson's Baltimore
team, with Johnson himself playing, and had fallen into conversation
with some young people at the next table, workers rather than students,
the Kronos killings the main topic of conversation. He had bought a
round of drinks and told them he hoped to see them again. They had
evidently accepted him as a bona fide student and he had been relieved
by that. This evening he would start there.

He walked up to Chinatown and ate Chinese at a small restaurant
he had visited a couple of times with Yinghua. He looked around
hopefully, but there was no sign of her tonight. He took a cab back to
the apartment and watched a couple of news broadcasts: the President
had supplied more detail on her initiatives for bringing youngsters into
politics, and a debate was raging about the idea of trading a life for a
life; bequeathing childbearing rights when volunteering for euthanasia.
A few seniors were in favor; but for the most part they were opposed,

frightened of being pressured into suicide. Nothing in this, he decided, was going to have much effect on Kronos.

He took a shower. As he was toweling down, he noticed a small bruise on his thigh. He had a vague memory of bumping into something at the apartment. There was no pain, no apparent effect on mobility. He made a note to keep an eye on it, but it wasn't something that he felt he should worry about. In every other way he was fine: physically, at least; depressive inertia still lingered, but he hoped he was working through it.

He got to the sports tavern soon after eight. He looked around for his friends from the day before, but saw none of them. He decided against patrolling through the bar areas and the bowling lanes downstairs: as a newcomer he could do that once, but a second time would look odd; and some device somewhere could easily be tracking and analyzing the behavior of the clientele.

He sat down within sight of a 3D display and ordered a beer. He watched a soccer game haphazardly, trying to keep tabs on people coming and going around him. There was no sign of Johnson. After an hour he got up to go to the washroom, using the opportunity to survey a couple of other bar areas. Coming back, he suddenly saw a face he knew, at a table not far from his own. Kate Nakamoto. One of the Johns Hopkins medical team who used to come across regularly to his labs to help with the nano-level processing. He checked his stride, hesitated. Immediately on top of recognition came anger: if this was Johnson's territory, maybe Kate was the insider, the one who'd betrayed the functioning of his lab.

He hesitated and then made a reckless decision. Kate had already noticed him, he thought, had caught his eye when he went by, seen him check. He veered back now, and crossed to her table, forcing aside his anger, using it to drive his courage.

"Excuse me, but am I right? You're Kate Nakamoto?"

"Yeah. Do I know you?"

There was a trace of suspicion in her voice, but nothing, it seemed, beyond the uncertainties of dealing with a stranger. She was a woman in her early thirties, Japanese origins apparent, her face not structured for beauty, her manner brisk and artless, as though she accepted her lack of appeal, in any case had no time for games of attraction or seduction.

"You probably won't remember," he said. "I did a bit of lab work in the summer at Life Extension Sciences."

"Oh boy. Another refugee from the one-niner dream palace." She gave him another look. "Nope. Sorry. Don't recognize you."

"You wouldn't. I wasn't there much."

"How come you know my name?"

That was a good question. Alan realized that he could stumble at the first hurdle if he didn't think fast. "As a matter of fact… I was thinking of applying to Johns Hopkins. Research degree. I sort of took note of you guys. There was, let's see, you and Ken Taylor, you'd know Ken, I guess, and Liz Fogarty. Couple of others, right? I was going to ask you guys lots of stuff, then I changed my mind and applied to George Washington." Alan spread his hands apologetically. "I'm Doug Edie, by the way."

"Well… Glad to know you. I'm sorry, I was usually pretty busy on my visits over there. Doing my little bit for immortality." The sarcasm was obvious.

"Oh sure. No problem."

"And now you're at George Washington?"

"As of next semester. I've hooked up with Professor Baillie, who's a real one-niner, practically old enough to remember the Civil War, but he seems okay. We're looking at some research projects."

Baillie was a contact Cap Olsen had arranged and Alan had talked with him the day before.

"Rejuvenation?"

"Oh God, no. To be honest, I'm not much interested in fixing up old people. Certainly not rejuvenation. I mean, nothing against you people, and I'm not saying Dr. Connacher deserved what happened to him, but… well, I just don't think it's what we need right now. Old guys getting young again. I thought the guy who got in and killed his monkeys was, well, making the right point. But hey, I'm probably out of line."

Alan raised his hands defensively and made as though to step back. Had he gone too far? Been too obvious? Kate was looking at him closely, her attention engaged, but her judgment of him unclear.

Alan was aware of a couple of other faces turned his way, as Kate's companions at the table became aware of the conversation. He was about to conclude that he had pushed it as far as he could, and that withdrawal was the safe option, when Kate said: "Actually, Doug, we're not unreceptive to that point of view. Why don't you join us?"

Alan did his best to look shy and doubtful. "Well, sure, I'd like that." He glanced across to where he had been sitting. "My friends didn't show yet. But if you're, you know..."

"It's okay. Sit down. Bring your drink."

Alan brought over the remains of his beer and sat down beside Kate. Her companions gave their first names and he smiled and nodded and said hi. He decided he should consolidate his identity by talking research issues with her, and by mentioning a couple of the things he'd done during his brief time at Life Extension Sciences. His involvement with research and development at all levels of his business enabled him to pick plausible examples for Doug Edie to talk about; and he also found he was able to infiltrate into his remarks the dissident views about age-related medicine that would hopefully gain the approval of his youthful listeners.

He was gradually gaining confidence in his role, the phraseology and opinions of the young beginning to appear spontaneously in his speech. To be perceived as young was the real ticket to acceptance: he could see that clearly now. It was like a badge proclaiming cultural or religious origins, but in some ways stronger; nobody who was young could truly identify with the old; the old were an obsolete species, struggling to overcome their deficiencies and protect themselves from the legitimate new wave. That was the way they were perceived. No wonder Cap had trouble recruiting young agents to work against their own age-group. The young might respect their grandparents, sometimes, but it was a biological impossibility for them to see the old, the eighties plus, as a just repository of power and wealth.

As he chatted, Alan kept an eye out for Peter Johnson. Was he right in thinking there might be a link between Johnson and Nakamoto? His doubts were resolved about twenty minutes later, when a tall, athletic man with pale brown skin and a brooding manner appeared at the table and stood there for a moment unsmiling, eyes darting, settling on Alan briefly, returning to Kate as though with a question.

Alan felt a crawling in his stomach, antagonism and fear mixed. This was clearly the lacrosse player, Peter Johnson, the man who had invaded his labs: and instead of strangling him, he had to keep his face blank and innocent.

Or get up and go.

Reckless instinct took over again. He got up and held out his hand to Johnson.

"Hi. Aren't you Peter Johnson? I saw your game the other day."

Johnson seemed taken aback. Alan guessed he wasn't a big enough star to get recognized very often. But he allowed his hand to be shaken, and offered a hint of an apologetic frown. "We lost," he said.

"Not your fault," Alan said. "You made some nice moves."

Johnson shrugged.

Alan waved his hand at Johnson and Nakamoto. "This is kind of weird," he said. "Do you guys know each other? I butted in on Kate because I recognized her from Life Extension Sciences, now I find I'm saying hello to a sports star." He began to laugh. "DC, eh? Listen, I'd better get going. It was real nice meeting you guys."

As he turned to go, Kate said, "Come back and see us some time."

Alan stopped and smiled. "Really? Do you mean that?"

"Sure. We're here quite often. Do you play cubechess, by the way?"

Alan made a face. "Missed out on it as a kid. But I love to watch. Do you guys play?"

"Peter is quite good," Kate said with an ambiguous smile at Johnson.

"Really? As well as lacrosse?" Alan made himself give Johnson an admiring look. "Hey, that's cool."

"There's a club match tomorrow. Come and watch, if you've nothing better to do." She named the venue beyond the beltway that he had visited the previous day.

Alan glanced quickly at Johnson, who nodded vaguely. Who was the leader here? Alan wondered. He said to Kate, "I will. That'd be fun."

On his way out, he noticed one of his acquaintances from the previous day, watching a basketball game. Alan felt exhausted from the stress of maintaining his pretense of youth, but he forced himself to stop and chat with him for a few minutes. This would register with the Johnson group, probably, and add to his credibility.

When he was finally out in the open, walking away from the tavern, he felt momentarily light-hearted: it might all blow up in his face, but it seemed that, more by luck than judgment, he had made a start.

◇◇◇

He got several hours of good sleep that night, but in the morning, after getting up and showering, he noticed that the bruise on his thigh was a little bigger. He also discovered another one on his ankle. He dressed and tried to put this information out of his mind, but his brain went on processing anyway. He poured himself a cup of coffee and allowed the results of the processing slowly, reluctantly, into consciousness.

These were not bruises acquired in the usual way. Internal bleeding was the likely cause. No symptoms of this kind had been recorded during any of the monkey trials. So probably the changes in genetic code introduced to give him a new identity and a new appearance were implicated. Treatment with molecular machines would be straightforward, as long as the condition wasn't progressive: if lesions spread to the heart or lungs he'd die quickly. He'd survive that as well, as long as he got to hospital within a few hours, but he'd told Cap not to watch him, to leave him alone, and he had a feeling that Cap was sticking to that. So if he died in the night, he might be in trouble.

He didn't mention the bruises when he reported in to Cap.

At lunchtime, he found himself back at the cafeteria in the Matsuoka building, watching hopefully for the arrival of Yinghua. He felt relief and an unexpected intrusion of doubt when she finally appeared, wending her way through the food displays. He joined the queue behind her, threw a couple of dishes at random on his tray, and managed to show up at her table a moment after she sat down.

When she looked up at him, he forgot to speak, so intent was he on reading her expression; which was not unfriendly, but remained quizzical, as though she was remembering the puzzling features of their last encounter.

"Doug Edie," he said at last. "Do you remember me?"

"Of course."

"Uh… I got some lunch. Would you mind if I…?"

"Would I mind if you what?" she said with a faint teasing smile.

"Joined you."

"You can join me, Doug." She said the words in a very serious tone, but the smile hadn't entirely left her face.

He put his tray on the table and sat down.

Yinghua poked at a bowl with a bread stick, watching him from the corner of her eye, but saying nothing.

Alan suddenly felt the ground shifting beneath him: what he was doing was, of course, completely unfair, completely selfish. Depression and the frightening novelty of his situation had driven him to seek out her company, but he should have known better. If he really loved her, he thought, he would leave her alone, not draw her into the risks and uncertainties of his new life.

He coughed and focused his eyes on his food, noticing with surprise that he had picked up a bowl of chili and a bowl of tiramisu, neither of which he particularly liked. At last he raised his eyes. She was still waiting, it seemed, for him to begin.

"I wanted to apologize for intruding on your privacy the other day," he said. "It was rude of me."

She looked at him calmly, her faint smile still in place. "Then why did you do it?"

He drew in his lips. "You must know, Yinghua, that you're an attractive woman, and that your work is very interesting. But that's no excuse. I behaved in a boorish way, and I promise you it won't happen again."

She nodded a couple of times.

"In fact, I really shouldn't have cornered you into lunch." He moved to get up. "You're busy, and you probably have better things to do."

She reached out and put a pacifying hand on his arm. "I wasn't offended, Doug. Surprised a little, maybe. But I found you quite a sincere person. Why don't you stay and tell me a little about yourself."

He hesitated. Perhaps it would be simpler, and more polite, to maintain a friendly interest, and then disappear quietly out of her life.

He bowed his head. "There isn't much to say about me, Yinghua. I'm basically boring. But I'd be honored if you'd talk to me about your own career. How you came to be fluent in Chinese, for example. Because your first language is English, right?" He reached out and began taking his food off the tray.

Yinghua watched him and then nodded slowly. "I learned Mandarin from my grandfather."

"Who was a native speaker? An immigrant from China?"

"My grandmother and my grandfather arrived together. As a couple. China was in a period of rapid growth, increasing prosperity, but it was very corrupt, not much freedom. So they got out, went to Canada, came here after a few years. Settled in New Jersey."

He prompted her and listened to her familiar story, eating his chili without tasting it. She became animated and absorbed, giving him a sharp glance once or twice, when his prompts or comments, about the breakup of her father's marriage to an Italian American, her determination to go and live with her grandfather, became a little too prescient.

"You loved your grandfather?"

"Yes. Of course. He treated me like a real person with valid interests and ideas. He never talked down to me. He was steady and wise. And when he suggested I take a Chinese name, I was very happy with the idea."

"You weren't christened Yinghua?"

"Oh no. Can you imagine? An Italian American mother? No, I'm not going to tell you the name I had, because I came to hate it. It was so... commonplace. My grandfather consulted a fortune teller and suggested Yinghua."

"What does it mean?"

"It depends on the intonation. The simplest meaning might by Cherry Blossom, but when I say it like this, *Yinghua*, it can mean English and Chinese, which I think is rather appropriate. So that's what I chose. You see, I owe a lot to my grandfather. He knew a lot, he'd been through a lot. I think through him I picked up this respect for ancestors which most Chinese have."

"You don't see a lot of that nowadays. Here in America, anyway."

Yinghua fixed her gaze on him. "No. Ancestors, if they're still alive, are the enemy."

"You don't subscribe to that?"

"No. How could I? My grandparents are dead now, they just missed out on longevity, but they're still important to me. You have to respect the generations above you."

Alan said lightly, "I can see I'm not going to be able to recruit you into the radical youth movement."

"Is that what you were hoping, Doug?"

"No, absolutely not. I'm much too simple-minded for politics."

They talked a little longer, mostly about her work. When he'd finished his lunch, he got up to go. He thought he detected a wistful sadness in her expression when he repeated his apologies and said goodbye, but she made no reference to meeting again. His heart was heavy when he left the building and began walking back to his apartment. He'd done the right thing, no doubt about that; but he felt like Cortez, burning his boats so as to concentrate on the conquest ahead. Now he was truly on his own.

CHAPTER 25

It became apparent to him, after attending the cubechess match with Kate and her immediate circle, that Kate's interest in him was not related to his political views, nor to the possible usefulness of his connections, nor to his scientific knowledge; she was thinking of bed.

The lack of obvious beauty, it seemed, didn't indicate a lack of interest in sex, if anything the reverse. Unless he was reading youth culture wrong, she was sending strong signals, not just at him, but at several other males who crossed her path, signals suggesting she was available, more or less without preamble, as long as the sex was on her terms. There was a spark in her eye, a challenge: are you good enough for me? Can you handle the pace? Once or twice as she was talking to him, making a point, she leaned forward and touched him briefly on the thigh; it seemed natural, but the look in her eye made the message clear.

Alan also had to modify his views on her attractiveness. Although her face was certainly not beautiful, her mouth was lively, full, expressive, and her body had a dancer's fluidity.

Her personality added to her appeal: direct, teasing, subversive, she came across as her own woman, giving way to no-one. The more he watched her interacting with the group, with Peter Johnson, the more he came to believe that she was the leader, certainly of this particular cell, perhaps of something wider.

Kate's interest in him, the barely concealed invitation, placed him in a situation of acute discomfort. His old brain was not accustomed to adventurous sex. And now that the initial shock and fear of failure had moderated, and his depression had retreated, the dishonesty of his position began to bother him. Okay, these youngsters had attacked his lab and killed his monkeys, or one of them had, but as he spent time with them and picked up their grievances and frustrations, he could see that they were taking risks for something they believed in. Whereas he was the privileged one-niner sent amongst them to betray them.

But this was undoubtedly his big opportunity: if he was going to find out anything useful, he needed to pursue a relationship with Kate.

There was another problem: the bruising on his body had grown. The original bruises were larger and more colorful, and bruising was beginning on his chest and one bicep. He wasn't yet feeling pain, but sudden movements created a burning sense within the bruising. On top of that, his body hair and pubic hair were only half re-grown, something else requiring explanation if he should be required to take off all his clothes. He talked with Cap Olsen and agreed that he should return to hospital for a couple of days of treatment.

◇◇◇

Cap and his sidekick Roger Enquist came by on the second evening, after Alan had graduated from the recovery pod and done some gentle physio and eaten a steak.

Alan's first thought was that they looked old: healthy and well-preserved, but old. He wasn't sure why this surprised and irritated him. Mixing with young people and seeing himself in the mirror had already, it seemed, shifted his viewpoint.

He made an effort to get on Cap's wavelength, and submitted to a detailed debriefing.

"Kate Nakamoto," Cap said at last, articulating the name as though trying to gauge its weight. "Certainly high on our list... especially since we learned of Peter Johnson's link with Johns Hopkins... but with restricted surveillance we hadn't placed her close to Johnson at a social level. You're saying you think she organized the monkey-killing gig?"

Alan struggled to put aside his new allegiances. "There's something... dangerous about her. I get the feeling she doesn't care what risks she takes. Even Johnson looks a little uneasy in her company, as though he's wondering what she's going to demand next. She carries the authority in the group. I would say she's the most likely originator of big bold stunts like the one against me."

"Roger?" Cap said. "What have you got on background?"

"She's smart, that's number one. Looking at educational records, she was outstanding at school, and that was in spite of what looks like a difficult home. Japanese father who seems to have stayed away from people, family or otherwise, working nights mostly, maintaining heavy machinery, and a mother who went the other way, smothered her kids with her problems, and was institutionalized a couple of times. Kate ran away from home at 15 to live with a boyfriend. That didn't last, but she survived, ploughed her way easily through the educational system, ending up, as we know, as a researcher at Johns Hopkins, specializing in intelligent molecules. The usual political activism, demos, Fair Deal for Youth, no arrests, no street violence. Could she be one of the original creators of the Mars Three Resistance? She's kind of young, but it's possible. We have no firm data on where she was during the month or so of the sit-in at the old Mars Three Habitat. As for Rose Mickelburger, well, it's a good fit. We get the sense that Johns Hopkins might be a nodal point of the Mickelburgers. Someone on the teaching staff is recruiting from the student body, disseminating cells to other parts of the country. Nakamoto plays cubechess, by the way, not to the highest competitive standard, but enough to get her into the tournaments and conventions which we are supposing provided the meeting places for the original M3R. Johnson was presumably recruited via some cubechess connection, although from what you say, he is merely a foot soldier, not a leader. Which is probably what you'd expect of someone undertaking a dangerous mission. The oddity is that he has identifiable connections with people as high up the organization as Nakamoto. A little careless, that. Assuming she really is at the top level."

"For what it's worth," Alan said, "during the time I've spent with them, she hasn't said word one about the Rose Mickelburger Faction, the need for extreme action, that kind of thing. But then I'm still an outsider."

"Kronos?" Cap asked. Cap had raised the Kronos name several times already. He was obviously frustrated that Alan had picked up no clear references to Kronos as a diversionary front for the Mickelburgers, or even as a front for some rival organization.

"No."

Cap gave an irritated grunt.

"If anyone young mentions Kronos," Alan said, "and they do, quite often, then it's like he's a kind of genius, out there, who got lucky and pulled off a brilliant coup. Or else Kronos is a front for the military, the government."

"Jesus, that's annoying," Cap said. "Have they lost their minds?"

"The point is, nobody seems to know anything about him, not even people like Kate Nakamoto and Peter Johnson. Or if they do, they're not telling."

"I can't believe he hasn't left a trail somewhere," said Cap Olsen, his brow deeply furrowed. "How could he bring off something this big on his own?"

"Nothing come out of forensic police work?" Alan said.

Cap looked at Enquist.

"We've done thousands of interviews," Enquist said, "and basically got nowhere. Ditto the other agencies."

"What is MAIMCOM saying?"

"Nothing," Cap said disgustedly. "They're blaming NSA for a lapse in security. NSA is saying there's no way that the MAIMKEY could have got out. Deadlock. The truth is Alan, you're still our best shot. Don't take crazy risks, but keep on digging. We've got the midterm elections in just over four weeks. I have the feeling that if Kronos is going to try another stunt, he'll aim for just before or just after that."

◇◇◇

Alan was returned to his apartment late at night, after Cap's team had reconnoitered the surrounding neighborhood, and he managed a few hours' sleep. When he got up, and checked his body for bruising in the familiar mirror, he felt his orientation, his mental processes, slide back towards youth. His old life, his life as an old man, worrying about his business and his workers, the competition, the bottom line, the hostility of the young, the paradox of an indeterminate lifespan, seemed further away than ever.

Even his sense of his family was fading; he no longer felt like a grandfather. His grandchildren certainly wouldn't approve of what he was doing. To them he was already dead, and maybe he should take the equivalent position; let them go. His daughter would be fine, his son in California also had a solid life, good connections. Let them live, free of a problematic entanglement. While he started again as a young man.

Alan finished dressing and went through to the kitchen, blinking back sudden emotion. His situation was impossible, perhaps; too much for the old brain to manage. But he had to carry on, pursue the mission, embrace youth; there was no other choice.

At midday, he took a deep breath and put Yinghua out of his thoughts and asked his telcom genie for Kate Nakamoto.

"What took you so long?" she said. "I was beginning to think you were gay."

Alan covered his awkwardness with a laugh. "I had to go back to Boston for a couple of days."

"Listen, I've got a seminar assembling around me. Make me an offer."

"I was thinking of coming to Baltimore to watch Peter's game today. I thought you might join me."

"I hate sports. Especially lacrosse. Call me when the game is over. I'll show you a bit of Baltimore."

"Done."

Kate cut the link, leaving Alan shaking his head and wondering whether he could push himself hard enough to keep pace with her.

◇◇◇

The bit of Baltimore that Kate most wanted to show him was her own apartment, a sparely-furnished, metallic, open-plan space in a regenerated area of the city near the docks; but she took him first on a little tour of the neighborhood, which was upscale modern, and they stopped at a bistro for a late supper.

"This is incredible," Alan said when they finally arrived at the apartment, and walked around and looked out of the big windows at the lights of the city. Privately, he found it a little weird, but he knew that the style, usually called techno, in which intelligent materials and intelligent lighting combined to produce decorative effects in a constant state of flux, was popular with the affluent young. Kate had chosen a cool, steely, embodiment of the style, with murals in blue, grey, silver, shaping themselves, fluorescing, condensing, dripping, dying in contracting pools of light. Alan found the shifting, fractal-like effects both distracting and pretentious, but the advantage, he acknowledged, was that every wall in the apartment could be re-programmed, the decorative ambiance totally

155

changed, by having a short conversation with the software.

"Did you write it yourself?" he said.

"Just a few bits. Otherwise it's the usual crap. There's a nice feature in the bedroom, though. I'll show you later. What do you want to inhale or drink or swallow?"

"Alcohol. Brandy?"

"Only got generic."

"That's fine."

"Two brandy," Kate said, crossing to her bar, and picking up the glasses which dropped down after a brief moment. "I used to use a lot of drugs when I was a kid," she said, turning back with the glasses, "but after a while I thought, do I really need this stuff? Am I such a feeble personality? Is it such a great experience? All three in the negative. More to the point, what the hell am I doing to my brain?" She handed Alan a glass.

Alan saluted her with it and took a sip. "I was never really into drugs. But I was out of school a lot as a kid, and I got used to doing my own thing. Drugs just didn't figure."

Kate stretched out on a couch and put her glass on the floor.

"What about sex? Do much of that?"

"As a kid? Not really."

"Later?"

Alan sat down on the floor in front of a stuffed chair, legs stretched out in front of him, his gaze on Kate. He shrugged. "Some."

"I guess I'm kind of an addict. Which annoys me sometimes. Kind of like drugs. Do I really need this stuff? Is it such a great experience? But at least, as far as I know, it doesn't do anything bad to the brain."

"The brain, no, probably not."

"You're not leaping all over me, Doug," Kate said, turning her head and giving him a look.

"I get the feeling that you'll tell me when."

"And how would I do that?"

"I don't know, but I'll recognize it when it happens."

Kate slid off the couch and crawled over to him and ran a finger down the intelligent zip of his shirt front.

"Is it happening now?"

Alan laughed. "I think it might be."

"Actually this is *me* leaping all over *you*. Sorry, bad habit. I love male bodies. Have to get at them." Kate was pulling his shirt out of his trousers, running her hands up his chest and easing the shirt off his shoulders. Something about her openness and guilelessness took away the romance from the situation, eased Alan's guilt. He shrugged his arms out of his shirt.

"Yeah, nice, I like it." She smoothed her flat palms over his chest, then rolled on her back and flung out her arms. "Hey, come on, catch up here. I'm not too bad myself."

Alan played along. He eased the chair back and turned so that his head rested sidelong on his hand, his elbow on the floor, his gaze close to the low-tech tee-shirt, swirled black like her hair, swelling invitingly beside him. "Confident, uh?"

"I'm always confident."

Pretending more shyness and naivety than he felt, Alan pulled at the bottom of the tee-shirt and peeked underneath.

Bored by that, Kate sat up and pulled off the tee-shirt. "Da-daa!" she said, raising her arms above her head and jiggling her torso.

"I see why you're confident," Alan said.

The sex began, a roller-coaster ride for Alan, Kate having new ideas every few minutes, constantly teasing him, challenging him to hold it back while she experimented with sensual enhancement, until he lost patience and overcame her with sheer weight and brought things to an end, worrying immediately afterwards that he had relapsed into old-style patterns of male dominance and sent a false cultural signal.

Kate, while not having given him the comfort of orgasmic squeals, seemed happy enough, lying beside him on the rug, a faint smile on her face, giving his body analytic attention, running a finger around the muscles of his leg and upwards. She stopped at the pubic hair.

"I thought I was seeing this. Gee, Doug, you didn't."

"Yeah. I shaved it. But I couldn't get used to it. So…"

"I'm good with pubic hair. But you'll have to let it grow some more."

"You're the first stylist I'll call."

Kate stretched and rolled away from him. Alan gave a little sigh of relief.

Kate said, "How come we never made it to the bedroom? My God, you must have been a horny bastard. Come on, let's go lie on something more comfortable."

Kate got up and recharged the glasses and led the way to the second main room of the apartment. She put her glass on the bedside cabinet and disappeared into the bathroom for a couple of minutes. Alan lay down on the bed and studied the décor. It reflected the first room's bloodless emphasis on style and form, although the drapes had, at this moment at least, half a dozen large red poppies superimposed on the steely fabric, and the bedspread was softer-colored, with thin yellow stripes.

Kate emerged from the bathroom, still naked, and threw herself down beside him. Alan had half-thought he might get kicked out after the sex, because Kate had satisfied her curiosity and her sexual instincts, or perhaps, in the latter case, because she hadn't; he wasn't sure what she thought of his performance. But now, if not warm, if not intimate, she seemed a little more relaxed. The next sex, following after a little idle chat, a few sips of brandy, was less energetic, sloppier, more friendly; just bodies joined together in undemanding exploration, sleepily wending their way to orgasm.

The bed, it turned out, had some clever sensors built in: Alan became aware that the walls, even the ceiling, were providing a visual commentary on their activity, murals growing into peaks, colors intensifying, as they moved and bonded, exploding into fireworks at the moment of climax, somehow unifying and intensifying the pleasure.

"Seen that kind of thing before?" Kate said.

Alan shook his head.

"Oh Doug, where you been?"

"Not with you, obviously."

"You want to do a little trip?"

"A trip? As in…?"

"As in a visit somewhere."

"Now?"

"It's only what, a little after midnight. You tired already?"

"I'll survive. Where to?"

"It's a surprise."

◇◇◇

Kate took him down to the basement car park and got in her car first and programmed the destination and then let him in. She shaded the windows and left the internal lights on so that he couldn't see where they were going. Instead of conversing, she put on some music. Alan braced himself for incomprehensible modernist pop, which would expose his cultural ignorance. To his startled surprise, it was Vivaldi.

"The Seasons?" he said after a moment.

"Smartass," Kate said.

The journey took about twenty minutes. When the car had parked itself, Kate cleared the windows. Alan got a shock: they were just outside the perimeter of his own office building in Wheaton Science Park. He sensed immediately that some kind of test was in progress, and he forced himself to go carefully, relax.

When Kate didn't comment, he said, keeping his voice neutral, "Old times, uh? You been back since Connacher died?"

He turned to look at her. She was watching him closely, and he thought he saw a faint smile of relief pulling at her full mouth. "Uh-uh. I never left any work materials here. You?"

"No. Likewise."

"Where exactly did you work?" Her voice was mildly frustrated. "It's bugging me. I *notice* good-looking men."

"I wasn't here very often, and sometimes I was moving around, and sometimes I'd settle for a while in a corner. Okay, let me give you a for instance. Take the elevator down from the main lobby, through lab decontamination, then down the half-stairs to the main work area there, okay? There's a space in under the half-stairs for gofers like me, and a couple of times I'd be in there. Sometimes I'd be a couple of floors down dealing with the experimental arkanes. It's almost wholly automated, but occasionally somebody has to go in and check and maybe see why an arkane died. That's the kind of job they'd give me."

"I'm surprised you noticed me."

"I was motivated. I was looking out for the Johns Hopkins people. I just never got around to introducing myself."

"Yeah, okay Doug." Kate stared through the window at the building, ripples of warning light ascending the intelligent face in waves. "Sorry if I seem paranoid, but… well… let's just say I'm made that way."

"I had the impression you let it all out."

"No, I don't. Don't let that fool you." Kate was silent for a moment. "The other reason I brought you here was because I heard they'd closed this place up tight, Justice Department, FBI, whatever, and I wanted to take a look. You hear anything about that?"

"No."

"I'd suggest we get out and look around, but do we want to be on record as intruding on the building's perimeter space at one o-clock in the morning? I guess not."

"We're young, after all. And ex-inhabitants."

"Right. All the wrong signals. Anyway, I think we can see the place is sealed up good. It looks about as welcoming as Folsom." She paused. "Why would they do that?"

"Good question. Looking for something to connect Connacher with Kronos? Why he was chosen?"

"I suppose so. But how long does that take?"

"I don't know. Could be, with the business kaput, they're just guarding the place: preventing demos and break-ins and people like us from trashing the place."

"What makes you think the business is kaput?"

Alan turned his head to look at her. "Because I watch business news. You obviously don't."

Kate accepted that, nodded her head a couple of times. "I guess you're right. I guess the business side wasn't my first interest. Although I could see he wasn't exactly selling a lot of rejuvenation treatments." She smiled thinly. "Doug, I'm going to call it a day. Where do you live?"

"Foggy Bottom."

"Okay. I'm going to put you in a cab."

Kate spoke a few words to her telcom genie and then drove him back to Wheaton center. The auto-cab was waiting. Alan made to get out of the car.

Kate wrapped a hand around his arm. "Doug, you're a good sport. You said I let it all out, and in some ways I do. I don't pretend to be something I'm not. I sleep with a lot of men. But that doesn't mean I give up on the good ones. Call me, uh?"

He held her gaze for a moment. "Sure. I enjoyed it." He thought about kissing her, but decided against. He opened the door and got out of the car.

CHAPTER 26

K ronos chose an evening midweek to get his truck to drive him up to Merko's apartment. The signs were bad: He'd tried calling a couple of times, but Merko's telcom genie was refusing to connect him. He told the genie to warn Merko that he was coming, and that they needed to talk.

He felt the usual rage burning inside him, the usual deep resentment of Merko's importance. Ah, if only Merko had been a true revolutionary, a man serving the cause of youth! A brother-in-arms, instead of a fucked-up loony! How much that would mean to him now...

He walked the hallway to Merko's apartment and pressed the buzzer. The door opened. Kronos found himself looking at two young men, one tall, one short, wearing identical white roll-necks, with a glistening, shimmering golden sphere emblazoned on the chest. His immediate thought was that they were fresh from some super-hero fan convention, geeks who liked to dress up in their hero's costume: then he noticed that apart from some ding-dong floating spheres, and a model of an inter-galactic spaceship, Merko's apartment was barren, almost clean; even the snake habitats had gone. He remembered that Merko had been talking recently about some cult he might join, not unusual that, for Merko, hardly worthy of notice: but it seemed he should have paid more attention, because here in front of him were Merko's guardians and instructors, senior cult members no less. He didn't know whether to laugh or cry. He settled on a friendly grin.

"Don't tell me," he said, pointing at the golden sphere, "Cosmarians."

The two looked at each other and nodded.

"Hey, good to meet you," Kronos said. "Merko said you guys had been helping him out."

"Merko's gone out," the tall one said.

"Really? Do you know when he'll be back?"

The two men shook their heads. "No," the short one said.

"Gee, that's a shame. Hey, maybe this is a chance to get to know each other a little. I've been a friend of Merk for quite a while. Could you guys spare me a few minutes?"

The two exchanged another glance.

"We don't think so," the short one said.

"Sir, we know who you are," the tall one said.

"You know who I am?" For a brief instant, Kronos saw everything collapsing. He'd have to kill these two clowns and then there'd be a massive investigation centered right on Merko.

"Merko's put all that behind him. All that dark energy."

Kronos stared at them. "Excuse me, guys, but what are we talking about here?"

"Merko won't need to get anything from you from now on," the short one said.

"Like what exactly?"

The two men looked at each other. "Drugs," the tall one said.

"Dark energy, we call it. Drugs and alcohol and promiscuous sex."

Partly from relief, Kronos suddenly began to chuckle. He shook his head ruefully. "Merko told you I was a drug dealer?"

The two men stared at him. The tall one put his hand on the door. "So you'll understand…"

Kronos held up a hand. "Listen, guys, excuse me, but you don't know Merko that well, do you? I mean, a couple of weeks or less? See, Merko, well, he has some problems. Probably you figured that out. Like, if I'm a drug dealer, then probably I've got some drugs to sell, right? Search me." Kronos held up his arms. "I'm serious. Search me."

The two men exchanged a glance but didn't move.

Kronos lowered his arms. "Maybe I should introduce myself properly. I'm a voluntary social worker, and I work with a few clients in this neighborhood. Merko is one of them. Merko is a genius, of course, but very unstable. Did you know he'd been institutionalized a couple of times? Paranoid schizophrenia. Not a really bad case, of course, otherwise his genome wouldn't have made the cut, but symptoms like his still appear from time to time, as you probably know. You allow room for the inventive genius, and sometimes it goes a little wrong."

Kronos saw the doubt on their faces. "Maybe you guys wouldn't mind telling me your names."

"Deck," the tall guy said at last.

"Moss," the short guy said.

Kronos leaned forward politely and shook their hands. "Deck, Moss, glad to know you. I don't want you to think I disapprove of your approach, as a matter of fact I think it would be great for Merko to be a part of your organization, it could be just what he needs. But like I say, if you've got a few minutes, I think it could be helpful for both of us."

Deck and Moss looked at each other one last time, and then Deck waved him inside.

When Kronos emerged an hour later, his head vibrating with Cosmarian precepts and principles, he was saying to himself, "Merko, you're going to pay for this."

◇◇◇

The call from Merko came twenty-four hours later, after ten o'clock in the evening. It wasn't very coherent.

"What did you do to them?" he kept screaming.

Kronos calmed him down a little and said: "I told them you were a pretty disturbed character, Merk. Which I've got to say is not an exaggeration."

"You always have to destroy everything? Kill, break, destroy?" Kronos could hear that Merko had now broken down in tears.

"Hey, take it easy. I'll come on over."

"Yeah, you'd better. You-know-who want to see me."

"What?"

But Merko had closed the link.

Kronos told his telcom genie to get him an auto-cab, and grabbed a leather jacket. Merko let him into his apartment and then turned away, wandering distracted, near comatose, around his denuded sitting-space as though surveying the ruins of his life.

Kronos watched him and then said, "Jesus, Merko, come on, I did you a favor. You didn't believe that stuff, did you? Souls wandering through the cosmos, avoiding all the dark energy?"

Merko didn't look at him. "They were my friends. And yes, I did believe that stuff. I still do."

"You're kidding yourself, Merko. You're too smart for that. Maybe you'd *like* to believe that stuff, maybe you'd *like* to believe there are inter-galactic beings who will take charge of your life and wipe out the past, but fundamentally, you know that's garbage. I'm the inter-galactic being in your life, Merko. I'm in charge. And if you play your cards right, I'll make you one of the heroes of the revolution. Do you realize what's going on out there?"

Merko stopped in front of Kronos and stared at him. His thin body, his hands, his fingers, were jerking, alive. He spoke with sudden passion. "Yes! Every fucking old guy is trying to find us and kill us!"

"We've got 'em riled, Merko. Don't you see the importance of that? We've got them showing their teeth, their real intentions. And youth won't stand for that. Youth will rise! We're a success, Merko. A magnificent success."

Merko slowly crumpled and dropped down on the coach, his head down. The jerky movements of his limbs turned to trembling. "Jesus, I'm so scared," he muttered.

Kronos noticed that his thin frame had lost flesh: especially without the chameleon jacket, ribs and shoulders had sharpened.

"Okay, tell me. Who's after you?"

"NSA."

"Merko, you were always telling me NSA were after you, but they never were, were they?"

"They are this time. They sent me a message."

"I thought you told me you'd made yourself disappear off the records."

"This was a personal message. Some guy who remembers me. I guess NSA are going nuts trying to figure out how the MAIMKEY daily code got out, and this guy remembers me as knowing the systems better than anyone else, so he's appealed for help! They want me to help find me!"

Kronos closed his eyes for a moment. It was almost laughable, but not quite. "So he just sent a message out into cyberspace and it found you?"

Merko nodded slowly, head slumped down again.

"Show me."

Merko raised his head and nodded at the empty shelves.

"By telcom?"

Merko shook his head.

"Get it to me, Merko. Maybe you're imagining it."

Merko went on shaking his head.

"How long ago?"

"A few days."

"A few days?"

"Three? Four?"

Kronos clenched his fists. "Would this guy know that you've removed yourself from the employee records?"

Merko blinked at him. "Why would he?"

"I'm asking."

"He's not the big honcho in the department. I doubt if he'd have access to the records."

"Then you've got nothing to worry about, have you, Merko? You send him a message back saying, sorry, I've been having psychotic breakdowns, my brain is not what it was, can't remember anything about MAIMKEY, and at the moment I'm a Cosmarian monk."

Merko looked up with doubt, but also a trace of hope in his eyes.

"It's plausible, isn't it?" Kronos said.

Merko nodded slowly, rhythmically, like he was listening to music. "I guess."

Kronos jumped up. "Listen, Merko, I want to get you back fighting fit, all this behind you. We'll get you some processors, good gear, brain wave stuff, all the stuff you're used to. Maybe a couple of snakes. I'll come by the next couple of evenings and over the weekend and we'll tune it all up. The youth movement needs you, old buddy, and you need them. It's your destiny." Kronos pointed his finger at Merko. "Don't try and back away from destiny. It doesn't work."

Merko looked at him, unhappy, uncertain, suffering deep in his eyes. But Kronos noticed that he'd stopped trembling.

CHAPTER 27

After their first coupling, Alan found himself having sex with Kate quite a lot. She was clearly very busy, traveling a lot at weekends, but she made time to see him, usually late at night. She came to his apartment once and made fun of the décor: "Doug. Come on. Yuk." He felt himself slipping more and more into youth ways of thinking, and half-consciously concealing this in his reports to Cap Olsen. He tried not to think of Yinghua.

One night he was propped up on pillows on Kate's bed, the mural fireworks past, Kate sitting cross-legged and naked at the foot of the bed, eating a slice of pizza from the box. She seemed less rushed, more reflective than usual, not yet ready to kick him out.

"I guess you never killed anyone, huh?" Kate said.

Alan took a moment to register what she had said. He stared at her then gave his head a little shake. "No."

"Think you could?"

"No."

"Even for a cause? Something you believed in?"

"I doubt it. I suppose it depends on circumstances, depends on the cause. What are you thinking of?" Alan was wary now, more alert.

Instead of answering directly, Kate put aside the pizza box and studied him intently. "I guess you never really told me where you stand on youth issues, Doug. Suddenly I find I want to know."

"Why?"

"No reason. Except I live and breathe this stuff and okay, sex may come first, but you can't ignore the rest of life forever. Not if you've got a brain in your head, which I think you have."

Alan could see that Kate's question was an important turning point, a test of his youthful credentials, but he was relieved more than worried; almost as though Doug Edie's point of view had been gathering inside him, waiting to be released.

"Actually, yeah, I think about this stuff a lot myself."

"So what's your take on it? Youth versus age."

Alan took his time, spoke slowly. "First, I guess we're agreed that the current social-political model is flawed."

"The old have acquired a lock on money and power. I guess that's a flaw. I guess that's quite a big flaw."

"But we'll all be old one day, and the young will just be a decorative fringe. Maybe we could transition to that without society imploding, and maybe we could wrest power from the one-niner generation without a civil war. But there's a bigger flaw, in my opinion. It's the behavioral, evolutionary problem of old brains. No matter how much you re-program old brains, nurture them with rejuvenated bodies, they're still old brains. They're stamped with the developmental limitations, the outdated assumptions, of the childhood that produced them. They will never respond to new geopolitical conditions, new intellectual frameworks, in the way that the newly-minted, explosively-developing brain can do. And so they're inadequate vehicles to take our species into the future, with all the future's unknown challenges. From a Darwinian perspective, they're a poor and compromised piece of kit, and I don't frankly see how you're going to change that."

Kate was still staring at him, her eyes fixed, glowing. "Except by getting rid of them."

Alan breathed in. "Are you ready for the enormity of that?"

"It's the way the world used to work, Doug. Remember? People died."

"In a functioning humane society, there's a world of difference between helping people live when they are pre-ordained to die, and helping people die when they might otherwise live. It's the difference between the Hippocratic oath and the guillotine."

"But you don't call it the guillotine. You've got to get back to the concept of a limited lifespan. Maybe religion can help. I don't know. But to get back to your main point, Doug, you called it like it is and there's no getting round it. The old brains will get increasingly decadent, and ultimately the species will not survive. We've got a guy at JH, Jeff

Savage, he's written a lot about this, and he's not all that young, either. Do you know him?"

Alan tried to look uncertain, but the name was new to him.

"Of course," Kate said, "he's not saying anything the one-niners want to know, so he doesn't get much air-time, but he's very persuasive. Species survival is the ultimate issue, and the 'un-refreshed brains' as he calls them, won't cut it."

"To be fair," Alan said, "there are those who say that age and long life bring compensating benefits: wisdom, a greater stake in your own life and the lives of others and therefore greater caution, and so on, qualities that should make us less likely to destroy the planet."

"Yeah, and we all know how benevolent the one-niners are when it comes to anything that threatens their personal survival. I don't buy it."

"Neither do I. Age tends to mean less flexibility, less adaptability. It's the young who sign up to the new waves in understanding and knowledge. It's the young who sacrifice themselves for what they perceive to be the public good."

"Exactly." Kate pushed her fists into the bed and leaned forward. "And here's where I get on my hobby horse. Because you know something, Doug? We're the last of the young generations. The Last! The birth rate is currently at about one tenth of what it was when we were born. In twenty years' time, the percentage of the population under thirty will be down to something incredibly small, like three or four per cent. Three per cent! As you said, just a decorative fringe, a curiosity. And the attention lavished on those poor kids is probably going to turn them a bit nuts. There's no way they'll have a flourishing culture. They'll be just another tiny, demoralized minority, valued, no doubt, by sentimental parents and grandparents, but without influence. Today, okay, youth has no political power, but at least we have influence, we're still numerous enough to have an impact, start a revolution. Tomorrow we'll be gone. Which is why we've got to do something before it's too late."

"I go along with all that," Alan said, and paused.

"But what?"

"I just don't see what your revolutionary program is going to be. Or how it can work. The old have to die. That's the bottom line. If you're going to get back to old levels of breeding, the young a potent, even dominant force, the old have to die. Otherwise we destroy the planet. So you're talking about organized killing on an industrial scale. More the holocaust than the guillotine. I don't see how you can preserve a functioning society under those conditions. We'll descend into barbarism. Even though the alternative, as you say, is that our species is doomed."

"Nobody said this was going to be easy, Doug. You've got to win hearts and minds. How do you convince people they're going to have to die for the good of the species? I don't know."

"Especially just after they've realized they *don't* have to die."

"Especially just after that. But you've got to try. I mentioned religions. Maybe we'll need them again. Convincing people that when you die you don't really die is a clever trick, but the successful religions managed it. Maybe we'll have to present death as a challenge. You don't know when it's going to happen, and for a few lucky ones it may not happen at all. Maybe the clear idea that a death means a birth. Maybe we'll have to go back to ageing. Legislate against life extension technologies. Act like we did against our friend Connacher."

Kate broke eye contact and looked down. Alan thought he should ask the obvious question. "We?"

Kate shook her head dismissively. "Youth. Activists. Whatever. The point is we have to find a way to make death acceptable."

"Again, I agree with you in principle. I just think it's going to be tough. And you know what worries me? Suppose we mount a revolution, seize power... because that's what it's going to take, isn't it? That's the only way we're going to make the old face up to the truth about species survival..."

"Yeah. That's the only way."

"Suppose we seize power. Go back to natural patterns of breeding. Persuade the old to make the ultimate sacrifice. And then what happens? We begin to get old ourselves. Not our bodies, but our brains, our chronologies. Pretty soon we have to think about dying. We don't like that and we begin to wonder if it's really necessary. The technologies for revitalizing and re-educating the brain have moved on and we think it's different now, the species will be okay, we don't need to die. We keep political power in our hands and go back to restricted breeding and immortality and we're back in the same old trap."

"But we mustn't keep political power in our hands, that's the whole point, that's what the revolution will be about. Power must remain, constitutionally, in the hands of the young."

"Is that possible?"

"Why not? It's just a matter of voting age. The same thing Kronos was talking about. Only he didn't go far enough. You'd need a voting age below fifty."

Alan was silent for a moment. The mention of Kronos had slightly disturbed the flow of his Doug Edie thoughts. Kronos was still a multiply-charged name, evoking his FBI mission and a cluster of buried emotions. To be safe, he knew, he had to pre-empt all that with a blanket halo of approval and respect.

"Okay," he said at last. "But you're disenfranchising a lot of people. Maybe two-thirds of voters? How would you sustain that? You might need some kind of a police state."

"We've *got* some kind of a police state. We're under the tender care and attention of bees. Remember? The one-niners use the bee infrastructure to control breeding. We'd have to use it to control them."

Alan switched gear, allowed his voice to lighten up. "Of course we'd be kind. Much kinder than they are."

"Of course we would. Seriously, Doug, it may not be pretty, but what else can we do? You said it yourself, Jeff Savage and others have elaborated the theory with some very convincing studies: we're talking about saving the species; saving the species from terminal decadence and decline."

"Not to mention voting out the Democrats."

"Cynic." Kate crawled up the bed and lay beside him and put her hand on his chest. "Why do I get the feeling that you're about to volunteer your services?"

"Maybe because I'm about to volunteer my services."

"What if I told you that… I have some connections with activists."

"I wouldn't be hugely surprised."

"Why not?"

"After what we've been saying? No, in fact, it's more your personality. You're obviously a force. Original, independent, determined. And not just in bed."

Although her face was below him, turned aside, the lighting shadowed, Alan could tell she liked that assessment.

"Suppose I found something for you to do," she said at last.

"I'd rather not kill somebody."

"Really? What a disappointment. Okay, something easier."

"Yeah. Okay. I think I would like to be committed."

"You know what you're saying?"

"I know what I'm saying."

Another pause.

"Okay. Just don't blame me."

"If what?"

She rolled over onto him, legs apart. "If you get screwed."

CHAPTER 28

" Doug?" his telcom genie said politely.

"Yeah?"

"Miss Ma Yinghua would like to talk with you."

He was lying splayed out on the couch at his apartment, tired and physically relaxed after a game of squash.

He jerked himself into an upright position on the couch. "Ma Yinghua?"

"That's correct."

A dozen thoughts chased through his head. His abortive contact with Yinghua seemed a long time ago, a foolish aberration. Of course she had his name and his George Washington connection, so she wouldn't have found it hard to speak to his genie. But it was entirely unexpected. He stayed frozen for several seconds, heart rate high, trying to see the implications.

"Okay," he said suddenly, deciding it was better to be friendly than otherwise. "I'll talk with her."

"Doug?" Yinghua's voice said.

"This is a surprise," he said, keeping his voice level.

"I thought you'd probably forgotten about me." Did her voice sound faintly aggrieved?

"No. Of course not. I'm an admirer of yours." he said.

"Can we go to video?" Yinghua said.

Alan checked his state of dress, his immediate surroundings. "Okay."

His genie took that as a yes. Almost immediately Yinghua's face appeared on the wall screen in place of the newscast he had been watching. She looked calm and serious, her classical bone structure nicely caught by the camera. Behind her he recognized an abstract sculpture in stainless steel that placed her at home.

"I have a favor to ask you," Yinghua said, "and I thought it would help if we could see each other. I don't want to press you if you have doubts."

Yes, that was typical Yinghua: self-contained, not interested in anything less than a genuine response; and probably not understanding that her own pretty face on the screen would make a genuine response more likely.

Alan waved a hand, indicating the space around and behind him. "Sorry about the apartment," he said.

"I understand. You have what you need."

"What's the favor?"

She gave him a measured look. "I need an escort. Once only. I need someone whom I can trust, and someone whom I can explain the reasons to frankly. I'm not sure why, but I believe I can do that with you."

He thought quickly. Was there a downside? She'd said once only, very specifically, and usually she meant what she said. It could be a way of broadening his base, his background cover. As long as he kept the old emotions out of it. "Okay."

Yinghua hesitated, dropped her eyes, made an effort. "You've heard of Trudie Connacher? The Senator's wife?"

An electric shock went through Alan. He kept his expression frozen. "Trudie Connacher," he said stupidly.

"Used to be a movie star."

"Oh yeah. Okay. I know her. I mean I've heard of her."

"She's a big Washington socialite. I've known her for a while. I go to her parties sometimes."

He kept his face neutral. "You want me to go with you to one of these parties?" No, he thought, as soon as he'd spoken. That's impossible. I have to get out of that.

"There's more, I'm afraid, Doug." She tried a moment of coquetry, smiling, tilting her head. "This is what I have to try and explain. You won't know, of course, that as well as my job at Georgetown University, I do some work for… well, let's call it a Chinese think tank. In fact, really nobody at all knows about that. I'll have to ask you to treat this as very confidential."

"Are you telling me you're a spy?"

"No, no, no. We don't work that way. This is a private contract. I wouldn't do it, but let me just say that... it's of some assistance to my father and my grandfather's relatives in China. By giving this institution some reports, some information... none of it secret information of course... well... the Party will be more inclined to view them in a friendly light. It's not very easy to explain without knowing Chinese culture. Nothing is in any way contrary to the interests of the United States."

Yinghua was looking flustered. He remembered her brief disappearances, and he remembered what Jason had said about her.

"Now you have that look again," Yinghua said.

Alan spread his hands. "Sorry. Keep talking."

Yinghua averted her eyes, breathed in. "This isn't very easy for me to say... but... the Senator has a son, Trudie's step-son, called Russell. Russell is... well, he's a bit maladjusted. I didn't know that. Trudie didn't tell me. I thought he was a bit of a playboy, lots of girlfriends, easy come easy go, plenty of money, but basically... good-natured. I needed some information about congressional procedures. Russell offered to help. I thought he was just being friendly. I'm quite a lot older than him, and, you know, what would a playboy see in me? I offered him a fee, to make sure he understood the situation. We had a couple of visits to Congress, the Senate, where of course he has access, and everything seemed fine. He was quite attentive when I was round at Trudie's, but I didn't think anything of it. Trudie thought we were somehow an item, but I just laughed when she mentioned it. Anyway... he invited me to dinner one time and I put him off by having a drink with him. He made a couple of... a couple of... suggestions over the drinks, and I... I just didn't like the feel of it, so I walked out on him. With lots of apologies, of course, big day ahead, and so on... but... anyway, he started hitting on me after that, whenever I was round at his house... and... I mean, I guess I could cope with that stuff normally, but... he made me uneasy. He's very egotistical. It was like he couldn't take anyone saying no to him. Nothing happened. I don't suppose he's dangerous or anything. But it got to the point where I figured I'd better not go round to Trudie's any more, and I didn't like that. So... so... and this is where it gets really unfair, I suppose… I thought if I could show up at Trudie's with, you know, a *guy*… somebody Trudie and others could think was *my guy*… well, I thought that would deal with the problem before it got any worse."

Alan's thoughts were spinning off in several directions. Trudie had told him about Yinghua's relationship with Russell, and he was stupidly relieved to hear that it was, apparently, one-sided. But he knew he couldn't take the risk of going to one of Trudie's parties and meeting not only Trudie herself but others from his past and distant life.

He also knew he couldn't turn down Yinghua's appeal for help: he had used her to steady himself at the beginning of his mission; and the chance of helping her back, and seeing off Russell at the same time, and seeing his daughter…

"I can see I'm asking too much," Yinghua said quietly.

"When's the party?"

"Tomorrow night."

Alan thought quickly. He had nothing arranged with Kate. "Okay. You got yourself an escort."

Yinghua gave a little bow, her expression serious. "I'll pick you up at nine," she said.

◇◇◇

Yinghua looked lovely in loose-fitting silk.

"Stay close to me for a while, do you mind?" Yinghua said as they moved into the ballroom. "This is going to work best if we look like a couple."

"Why would I dump the prettiest girl in the room?"

She gave a little smile at that, but she seemed nervous.

Doug Edie, as Alan increasingly felt himself to be, looked around for people he might have known in his old life, and felt a buzz of excitement. Trudie had always been good at bringing in a younger element, and although the healthy sixty-year-old look was dominant, and included those whose real age was close to one hundred, there were some young faces in the crowd. Remembering how his old self had perceived these youngsters as both different and suspect, Doug now had the disorienting feeling of seeing them as his own group.

It didn't take long for Trudie to come over and say hi to Yinghua. Doug looked at her as though she was a ghost. He hadn't anticipated how odd it would seem that she was carrying on her party hostess role exactly as before, when her father was nominally dead, when his own world had changed so completely.

Yinghua introduced him, and Trudie turned to him with a smile, but behind the smile Doug was surprised to see a hint of hostility.

"I hope you know, Doug," Trudie said, taking hold of Yinghua's arm with both hands, "how lucky you are to be invited out by this very special person. She doesn't bother much with social dating. Are you at GU?"

"George Washington. And I know what you mean. I had to work on her."

"So you two have known each other for a while?" Trudie was looking from Yinghua to him and Doug recognized the signs: she was trying to figure out the nature of the link. At the same time she continued to hold on to Yinghua, as though hoping to keep her out of his clutches.

"A few weeks," Yinghua said. Perhaps needing to counter Trudie's possessive hold on her arm, she reached out and put a hand lightly on his shoulder. "Of course I tried to pretend I was far too busy to bother with a graduate student," she smiled, "but fortunately he had a secret weapon. He knows almost as much about sub-text proto languages as I do."

"Really," Trudie said, her smile widening, but her eyes registering increasing dismay. "Is that your main field of study, Doug?"

"Yinghua is exaggerating. I hit the texts to try and impress her. In fact I'm a nano-biologist."

Trudie's face suddenly softened, lost focus. "Like my father," she said, her voice husky. "I suppose you've heard of him. Alan Connacher." It didn't sound like a question: more like a lament, an invocation.

Doug hadn't seen this coming, and Trudie's emotion took him aback. "Yes, of course. I'm... I'm very sorry about what happened."

Trudie let go of Yinghua and turned her head. "I keep thinking I'm going to get used to it, come to terms, but I don't. I just get angry. Him, of all people. The leading figure in rejuvenation. Which should make our lives better, shouldn't it? It's so barbaric."

Doug stared at this ghost-like figure from his past and felt a shudder go through him. This was the person he loved, now more like a mother than a daughter. He wanted to reach out and hold her, comfort her, tell her that Alan Connacher was alive. "I worked for him briefly, during the summer," he blurted out, remembering this recently-added feature of Doug Edie's biography. "He was... definitely a smart guy. That Kronos thing should never have happened."

Trudie looked at him with a trace more sympathy. "I'm glad to hear a young person say that, Doug. I've got so sick of all this Kronos stuff. I have to lose my father because of some wicked political stunt, and on top of that I have to find my way through this *minefield* of intergenerational conflict, which is destroying our society. Here in Washington, here in this *room*... well, we won't get into that." Trudie made an effort, reached out again to Yinghua. "Yinghua is one of the few I can count on. You were fond of my father, weren't you, honey? Why can't the young and the old just *get along*?"

"Mostly they do," Yinghua said. Doug noticed for the first time that she too was showing signs of distress.

"Speaking of the young," Trudie said, standing a little straighter and glancing around the room, "does Russell know...?" She glanced briefly at Doug, something of her earlier disapproval returning. "I mean, is he ready for this?"

"Ready for what?" Yinghua said, recovering her poise.

"Honey, you know how he feels about you. Doug, I'm sorry if I'm being crass and motherly, but Russell is my stepson, and I just don't want any unnecessary..."

"Trudie, there is nothing between Russell and me. Honestly."

"But sweetheart, you've been sort of... together... and I thought..."

"I needed his help with something. There was never anything romantic."

"Okay. Who am I? I'm not even the mother. I guess I was hoping. You would have been good for him."

"That's sweet of you. Is he here?"

"Oh yeah." Trudie glanced around. "I've seen him somewhere." She leaned towards Yinghua. "Be *political*, sweetheart, as I know you will."

"Oh sure. Not that it's necessary, really."

Doug was beginning to see that Yinghua had brought him as much to educate Trudie as to discourage Russell. If Trudie was promoting the relationship as a stabilizing influence on Russell, it would be doubly awkward for Yinghua.

Trudie gave Yinghua a little pat and moved on without a further glance at Doug. Doug exchanged a look and a little nod of understanding with Yinghua. They picked up drinks from an attentive robot waiter and moved further into the crowd. Even here, Doug thought, where everyone was pre-selected for achievement and charm, and where civilized manners were expected, there was, as he had foreseen, a sense that they, the young, were invisible, even undesirable. Doug had an early encounter with a loud, florid man, somewhat drunk, who thought he was offering insightful views on education.

"Tell me this," he kept saying. "You're a graduate student, okay, tell me this: you have all kinds of financial help, all the time in the world, wonderful institutions, but you're not taking advantage. Standards are down. Young people are seriously deficient in educational achievement. Spend most of their time protesting. Taking drugs. Complaining about being marginalized. I don't get it. Tell me this: why should society support a bunch of people who won't show some appreciation, do the work, try and contribute?"

Doug said, irritated, "Your characterization of education is false. The institutions may be wonderful, at least in a historical sense, but the teaching is lousy."

"Excuse me?"

"Do you think the real education policy is to produce brilliant, trained, minds? The real education policy today, for the young, is to sidetrack brilliant minds, put them out to grass. Because you don't want the young challenging you for your jobs."

Doug felt Yinghua putting a hand on his arm.

The florid man got redder and began laughing. "Well that's a nice theory, son, tell you what, I'm going to be watching my back, just in case you brilliant minds get yourselves back on track, ha, ha, ha."

There were a couple of exceptions, guests who seemed to enjoy the company of the young; but Doug noticed that they tended to be male and to address most of their remarks to Yinghua.

Doug kept an eye out for his grandsons: Jason was unlikely to be at a party like this, but Zeb liked to network with the movers and shakers. He was just beginning to wonder whether he too had stayed away when he saw him, working his charm on a couple of seniors whom Doug didn't recognize. Again he felt a momentary slippage back towards Alan, a sense that he should be taking Zeb aside and getting a run-down of his life, making up for the failures he had no doubt displayed when contact was easy; but a little later, when the age-related flow of the party brought them together, he had got control of himself and was firmly in character as Doug.

"You look gorgeous, Yinghua," Zeb said, giving her a kiss. "Who's the lucky guy?"

"The lucky guy is Doug Edie," Doug said, shaking hands with Zeb.

"He used to work for your granddad," Yinghua said. "So I found out tonight."

"Oh really? Good for you. With an imprimatur like that, you can't go wrong." Zeb gave Yinghua a knowing look and she dropped her gaze. "Seriously though," Zeb said, turning back to Doug, "we miss him. We miss him a lot. He was a client of mine, as well as being my granddad, and I loved the guy. What the hell kind of a world do we live in?"

Doug didn't wait to get choked up, said immediately, "Unfortunately, a world in which the young are in decline."

"So should we all be revolutionaries?" Zeb said with a trace of irony.

"Oh please," Yinghua said. "We should all be peacemakers."

Zeb was looking around at the predominantly old partygoers with the beginnings of a grin. "This would be a good place to get our act together, though. Suicide bomb, anyone? You could take out half the cabinet."

"Zeb."

"You're right. Mom would ban me if she heard me saying things like that. And luckily for us, if say Doug here was a secret Kronos type and was packing some serious weaponry, he wouldn't get through the security systems. But it makes me a little worried sometimes. Young and old still mix freely in lots of places, and some crazy kid could decide to kill us all."

"Let's hope it doesn't come to that," Doug said.

Yinghua said, changing the subject, "Did you know Valerie, Zeb?"

"Oh Jesus, yeah, poor kid, wasn't that terrible? Yeah, I met her a couple of times, and Mom knew her, of course, although I don't think she's been to a party here for a while. Maybe Russell knew her better than we did. Anyway, talk about lousy luck. I couldn't believe it."

"What happened?" Doug said. He had a vague memory of a Valerie in his daughter's circle, but he couldn't remember anything about her.

"Freak accident, eh, Yinghua? Fell off her horse?"

"Yes. She was staying with her parents in the Adirondacks, went for an early morning ride, and her horse must have slipped and gone off the edge of a mountain trail. Horse and rider both dead. Really awful, like you say."

"They didn't find her?" Doug said.

"Her parents thought she was riding over to see some friends. They didn't start the search until the afternoon. By the time they got to her, it was too late to bring her back."

"Mom was cut up about it," Zeb said. "'Everybody's dying,' she said."

"She was a nice person," Yinghua said. "Quiet, but dedicated. Like you, Zeb, I met her a couple of times. She was doing pretty well in the PMA, I heard. I had the feeling she had some questions about what the PMA were doing, especially after Rose Mickelburger, but she was trying to use the agency to help young girls cope with childlessness. It was a real shame."

The conversation turned to other things, but Doug found the story of Valerie's death continuing to reverberate at the back of his mind. There was a connection here he should be making: something he had thought about, deduced, long ago, before his new life had begun; something to do with Kronos.

Whatever it was, it related more to Alan than to Doug, seemed to threaten an emotional conflict he didn't want, and he gradually let it go.

When at last they made the rendezvous with Russell, the encounter failed to generate the anticipated bad feeling. Perhaps forewarned, Russell had provided himself with a female companion, a girl from Tennessee, daughter of a congresswoman, with southern belle aspirations. She was vacuous but attractive, and seemed taken with Russell. Doug was introduced, the girl was introduced, superficial chatter followed. Russell, who could be boorish, and liked the conversation to revolve around him, was holding himself in check, preferring the guise of a happy man enjoying the company of his pretty companion.

Once or twice, when Yinghua touched Doug's arm or his shoulder with familiar intimacy, Doug saw a glint of something less pleasant in Russell's eyes; but this was quickly smothered, and didn't disturb the flow of conversation.

Yinghua said later the meeting had been useful, a success; to Doug it was a fascinating, if disruptive, mixture of memory and loss and sentiment, in which Russell had featured hardly at all.

CHAPTER 29

"Just going down to the gym," Jason told his mother.

He had caught her at a good moment, drinking morning coffee with Conchita and the cook, planning the day's activities. There was no-one else around.

Jason went down to the basement by the back stairs, got aboard the elevator and went up to the fourth floor. The doorways to his mother's media room and bedroom were closed but unlocked, and he moved quickly through to his mother's dressing room, identified the closet he wanted, and opened the apparel bag and took out the grey and silver coat. He hesitated a moment, trying to recall exactly where it had been on the rack, decided that a minor error wouldn't be noticed, and hung it between coats of a similar weight and color. He picked up the apparel bag and walked back to the elevator.

He returned the apparel bag to the gym and lingered there a few minutes. He was relieved that he had got rid of the coat at last, When he went up to the first floor, his mother had gone from the kitchen area. He found her in the family room, talking to her telcom genie.

"Jason, sweetheart," she said vaguely, "are you going to stay for a few minutes? Did you get yourself a cup of coffee?"

Jason, as usual, couldn't determine whether or not this was an invitation. "I guess you're busy, right?"

"I try to be busy because there's so much to do, but sometimes it doesn't work. Sometimes they shoot other people's scenes. Where's my favorite grandson?"

"At school, Mom."

"Oh really?"

"It's a weekday."

"They all seem like weekdays to me. Darling, if you're going to stay, why don't you sit down? You look worried and it's making me nervous."

Jason had just about decided that he would have a cup of coffee, but he followed his mother's suggestion and sat down instead. He was waiting for the obvious question: if it's a weekday, why aren't you at work?

"I'm not absolutely right in the head, if you want to know the truth." His mother tugged at her hair. "I think I just agreed that Conchita could take a holiday."

"You had a party last night?" Jason said.

She nodded. "You should have come. We had lots of young people. Zeb was there. Russell was there. Even Yinghua."

"Yinghua?"

"It won't upset you now to know that Yinghua brought a new guy with her? No of course it won't. That was long ago, wasn't it, sweetheart? Kind of an odd character, I thought. I wonder how they got together."

Jason was sitting up straight, watching his mother intently. "I think... she may have said something about that. Do you remember his name?"

Trudie frowned. Jason held his breath.

"Doug something. Garden of Eden comes to mind. Doug Eden? No, Doug Edie. I'm pretty sure that was it. Names are important to me, as you know. Anyway... I guess he was smart enough, because Yinghua said so, but there was something just a little bit creepy about him. We were talking about your late grandfather, and I was getting a little emotional, as I do, and I could tell he was getting all blocked up too, as though he wanted to fall on me and have a good cry. How strange is that? A guy I've never met before in my life?"

◇◇◇

Jason spent a day mulling over the conversation with his mother, but he knew from the start that there was no real doubt: he'd been gifted a result as if by magic. This young visitor to his mother's party, this new friend of Yinghua was his grandfather, rejuvenated. He didn't even need to follow up and check DNA; it was self-evident. Everything had come out exactly as he had imagined.

But he hesitated before taking the next step. A whole weight of complications seemed to descend on him. He couldn't just take his bombshell piece of intelligence into an office of the Youth Employment Network and ask for a job. He had to find his way through to the people who might be directly affected by his grandfather's activities, and hope that they had influence over the youth organizations. He had already begun to hang around the local Fair Deal for Youth activity center, volunteering as a gofer for odd jobs, hoping to make contact with people who had links to the genuine activists. He had been an occasional contributor for some time, but now he tried to consolidate, build himself a bona fide reputation for commitment.

He spent hours in the information meta-world, staring at a roll-out screen and muttering his way through interrogations of all kinds of databases, looking for traces of Doug Edie's activities. He was mildly surprised at the extent of the information, the school photos, the early career, all of it, he presumed, diligently invented and planted by the FBI. Only the recent stuff, the George Washington registration, the visitor pass for the Mitsuoka building at GU, and a few other minor data-points generated by life in Washington were genuine, he supposed; and they tended to confirm, had confirmation been needed, that Doug Edie was Alan Connacher. None of it told him who, besides Yinghua, Doug Edie was spending time with; what activist group he might have joined. And none of it helped him perceive his grandfather as a dangerous threat to the cause of youth, a man who must be stopped.

He went into Sam's room and stared down at his son, sleeping peacefully. Or not so peacefully. Even as he watched, Sam stirred, pursed his lips, mumbled something, turned over, and Jason felt that these small echoes of troubled thoughts were deep down and far away, unreachable; that his son was lost in his own world, remote from his own difficult dilemmas. But of course what he did, what he decided, depended on his son. It was for his son more than himself that he wanted a job. It was because his son took precedence over his grandfather, even over his mother, that he had come this far in his desperate quest. And for the sake of his son, he shouldn't weaken now.

He wasn't accustomed to kissing his son, Sam thought it girly, but he bent over and placed his lips briefly on his son's cheek; then he stood up and left the room and closed the door.

CHAPTER 30

Doug managed to sleep late on the morning after the party, but when he finally dragged himself out of bed his head was pounding, and he couldn't think what his plans and purposes were for the day ahead.

As he got out of the shower he noticed a small discolored patch of skin on his thigh. He examined it more closely and cursed to himself. The bruising was back. It seemed like a bad omen. The last thing he wanted was another visit to the FBI hospital, another grilling by Cap Olsen, another reminder that he was caught in the machinery of espionage, dependent for his very existence, his Doug Edie identity, on Cap and his team.

He was getting used to Doug Edie. He felt that if he was free to live his own life, Doug Edie's life, the life of a young man, he would do all right. Not alongside Kate Nakamoto and her group, that was a value-swing too far; but alongside ordinary youth, people trying to survive and think their way around the repressive weight of one-niner dominance.

Ideally, alongside Yinghua.

He pulled on a shirt and went through to the kitchen and snagged a cup of coffee from the machine. He sat down on the orange couch and stared at the coffee, willing the pounding in his head to subside.

It was Yinghua, of course, who was the disturbing force, even more than the bruise on his leg, even more than Kate Nakamoto. Much as he hated spying on Kate, concealing his real life, he could see the point: Kronos was a threatening, destructive force, and he had signed up for a mission. The problem was, he no longer truly believed that Kate was going to lead him to Kronos, and if that was the case, she shouldn't have to suffer the repressive power of the FBI.

Could he somehow prove that Kate, even if connected to the Rose Mickelburger Faction, had no link to Kronos? And if so, did that mean he was free, or would Cap rein him back in, keep him locked up somewhere for his own good?

How could he prove that Kate had no link to Kronos? Perhaps he could show that her current activities were quite different from Kronos-style killings. And extract a promise from Cap to leave her alone.

Dream on.

But if Yinghua…

Doug took a sip of coffee and sighed.

The Yinghua dimension had become more complicated and he didn't know what to make of it. How significant was her link with the Chinese government? Why hadn't she mentioned it when they were together? What were her feelings for Doug Edie?

She had dropped him off the previous evening with expressions of thanks, but without any sense that the terms of engagement had changed. He had wanted to take her in his arms, but her body language offered no encouragement for that. In retrospect, that seemed fortunate. It would still be a very bad idea to go any further with Yinghua, for her sake as well as his own.

"Tell me what happens with Russell," he had said.

She had nodded solemnly. And that was it. Probably the right outcome, but one that left him feeling alone, deprived of life's deeper essentials.

His telcom genie, using simple biometrics to determine his mood, said quietly: "Excuse me, Doug."

"Yeah."

"You have Ma Yinghua on video."

For a moment, Doug thought his imagination was playing tricks on him; his genie really was a genie, conjuring his thoughts to life.

"Really?"

"Yes. Ma Yinghua."

Doug shook himself, felt the tingle of adrenaline. He ran a hand through his short hair, checked his clothing. "Okay."

Yinghua looked business-like in her office at the Georgetown MAI building. "May I talk with you, Doug?"

"Sure. How are you today?"

Yinghua said nothing for a moment. "In fact, I'm a bit confused."

"How so?"

"Well, for a start, I find I'm not making this call for the reason I thought I was making this call."

"Explain."

"I thought I was just going to thank you for last night. But in fact… I just wanted to see you… see your image…"

Doug stared at her face, which obligingly moved into close-up. He could see doubt and worry and also a surprised, dawning, awareness. He said nothing. They looked at each other for a time in comfortable silence. It was a moment Doug would remember later.

"What's your schedule?" he said at last.

"I have seminars this morning."

"Can I join you for lunch?"

Yinghua gave a sigh, as though resigned to losing some inner battle. She smiled weakly. "I guess you'd better."

◇◇◇

Yinghua didn't change her mind, didn't hold back: she acknowledged, almost as soon as they were settled in a corner of the Matsuoka cafeteria, that she felt an affinity between them that she didn't want to suppress. After that big admission, she relaxed: and as their talk roamed over familiar topics, they began to reproduce the shorthand of their old relationship. Yinghua didn't mention Alan Connacher, but her laugh, her quick jumps to mutually held opinions, her look of rapt concentration, were increasingly like the Yinghua whom Doug remembered. She seemed to recognize, and take on trust, that here was an Alan Connacher equivalent, to whom she could respond at the deepest level. Love began to flow between them like water flowing back into dry channels.

After the lunch, Alan started walking, recklessly fast, east towards Foggy Bottom, part of his mind singing, but the expression on his face a deeply-etched frown. He came to the Oak Hill Cemetery and jumped down from level to level of terraced gravestones, jockeyed with the fast-moving convoys of traffic on the Rock Creek Parkway, and pulled his way up through the brush on the other side, landing scratched and disheveled on Massachusetts Avenue.

He was barely aware of his physical condition: the pain was inside. He knew he couldn't get into a serious relationship with Yinghua. He would never be able to sustain his fraudulent Doug Edie identity with her, had already felt it getting thin and transparent. Yinghua deserved the truth, Yinghua would intuitively discern the truth. And what could he tell her? Nothing. His life and identity were in hock to Cap Olsen. And in any case there was no way he was going to involve her in the risks surrounding his undercover role.

He gave up the walking and asked his telcom genie for an auto-cab. One appeared almost immediately and he climbed in, settled back and stared blankly at the embassies lining the road. There was no escape route. Even if Yinghua was not herself in hock to the Chinese bureaucracy, and even if she was willing to leave her Washington career and friends, he, Doug, would never get loose from the web of obligations which had caught him and which held him fast. He clenched his fists in frustration. For a second time he was going to have to withdraw from Yinghua, a woman he loved; and this second betrayal was founded in his own weakness and stupidity.

◇◇◇

It was the same kid behind the counter, with the same floppy moustache and the same smartass attitude. Doug hadn't been back to Adams Morgan since his first nervous excursion as a newly-made youth, an age ago, a character-change ago.

Doug paid the admission and walked through the leaning image of himself, merging with it, transporting himself abruptly into the busy, multi-level, colorful world beyond, like a child in a fairy tale discovering a magic portal. He paused for a second to get his bearings, then headed for the stairs, leftwards and down the central atrium.

Kate had told him to be here by eight, and he was a few minutes early. He walked up to the top level and checked the cubechess players: one cube was in use, but he didn't recognize those involved. Kate had said that Peter Johnson had a match tonight, and Doug wondered if it could be with Jay Kirilenko, the Georgetown University physicist; this was Kirilenko's territory. If so, neither player had arrived.

He went down a level to a bar with a view across the central space and ordered a whiskey. He tried to concentrate on the evening ahead, but he kept returning to the lunch with Yinghua. He had got what he had briefly dreamed of, Yinghua's trust, perhaps the return of her love, and he had at once been torn away from her, plunged into deepest conflict.

He stared at his whisky, the glass held tight in his hand. Worst of all was the sticky tentacle that tied him to Kate, a woman for whom he abruptly felt revulsion rather than sympathy.

He drained the whisky glass and got up and got a refill. The girl behind the bar gave him a glance and he remembered that on his first visit he had decided that the young didn't drink whisky. Probably true, but it seemed they kept it in stock anyway. He shrugged and sat down and stared at the concourse below. No sign of the players, or Kate.

He knew what he had to do. He had to tell Yinghua that he was bad news, not the person she thought he was, and free her to carry on with her life. And he had to deal with Kate and her group. Prove that they were just another arm of activist youth, nothing to do with Kronos. Then maybe Cap would let him go, God knew where, but at least out of the line of fire, somewhere where he couldn't hurt Yinghua, somewhere…

He slowed, his self-lacerating vision fading. Somewhere where he could tell her the truth?

You don't get it, do you? he thought bitterly. You're not a normal man. You're a grotesque, a misfit, a chimera. You have no options. Zero.

"It may never happen, Doug," a voice said.

Doug turned his head sharply. Kate was standing beside the table, swinging a small brown purse. He tried to abort the dismay and irritation he could feel swelling up inside him, managed a grunt and a pantomime look of surprise.

"That was pretty sneaky," he said, getting to his feet. "You want a drink?"

"I'll get it. What are you having?"

"I'm okay."

Kate came back with something pale in a tumbler. If she spotted the whisky in his own glass, it didn't seem to bother her. "Gee, Doug, I thought you'd be dancing your heart out down there."

"Later."

"Let me warn you about something. There's going to be a few of us gathered for this cubechess match, and at some point we're going to do some talking. Negotiating, if you like. That would be a good time to go dancing."

Doug felt gripped, suddenly, by his earlier, self-destructive mood, and by his distaste for this person and what they had done together. It was the time to take risks, get a resolution. He leaned towards her and said quietly, "Who the hell are you, anyway? You're all over the place like a whirling dervish, everything shrouded in mystery, and it's beginning to get to me."

Kate looked at him with a tight smile tinged with satisfaction. "My my, you're aggressive this evening. What kind of people have you been mixing with?"

Doug was taken aback by the penetration of this comment. He remembered that he had hinted to Kate that he had a date with another woman. He seized on a digression: "The usual. One-niner idiots. Smug bastards. I met this guy who gave me his views on education. Wanted to know why young guys like me didn't do better at school, with all the wonderful facilities we have. I told him that education, university education, was crap. That it was purposely that way. That people like him didn't want bright youngsters competing for their jobs."

"I imagine he saw the truth of that."

"If you guys keep a database on people like that, I'll give you his name."

"A database on people like that would be everybody over the age of fifty-five."

"Just trying to help. I feel like I should be doing something."

"And I said I'd get you something to do."

"Did you mean that?"

"Yes."

"When?"

"Soon."

Doug leant towards her again. "And who would I be working for? Apart from you."

Kate toyed with her drink. "Does it matter?"

"Yes, of course it matters."

"Who do you think?"

"Mars Three? Or some kind of offshoot?"

"You're not far wrong. Think more in terms of an offshoot. We happen to think Mars Three has got the strategy wrong. You're not going to win the fight against the mighty establishment by staging polite little demonstrations. Nor even by smuggling in illegal babies."

"Okay." Doug sat back, twiddled with his glass. "I go along with that."

"What worries me about you, Doug, is that you seem a little sensitive in the matter of killing people."

He looked up. Kate was giving him a steady, appraising look, eyebrows raised, a faint smile.

"What I said was I'd have trouble killing someone in cold blood."

"That isn't quite what you said, but okay."

"Is that what you want me to do?"

"Oh no. I don't want to lose you just yet."

"Killing has to be very very necessary. Am I wrong?"

"You can't go into this fight on the basis of decency and right and wrong. You have to go into it to win."

Watching Kate, Doug felt his deepest hopes crumbling. He wanted Kate and her group to be marginal, organizers of demonstrations and protests, merely fantasist fighters and terrorists. He wanted to show that she and Johnson and Kirilenko were on the fringes, unlikely allies of Kronos, and therefore of no interest to Cap in his efforts to track Kronos down. He also wanted to escape the undoubted power of Kate, her ability to suck him in and mobilize the youthful aspirations of Doug Edie.

But the Kate in front of him didn't seem like a poseur, a fantasist. Maybe she dramatized her role, exaggerated, liked to shock, but there was something steely, determined there as well. And of course there was no avoiding the connection with Peter Johnson, the connection with his own former workplace.

"So you're prepared to kill people?" he said. "Innocent people? You personally?"

"If I have to."

"What about monkeys?"

Her eyes narrowed and she sipped at her drink. "Yeah, I thought you might put that together. That wasn't me, of course, who climbed the Connacher building."

"You organized it."

Kate cocked her head on one side. There was pride in her eyes. "Formally speaking, Doug, that wasn't me either. I know nothing about it."

"So we'll just have to congratulate certain unidentified members of the Rose Mickelburger Faction."

"And then forget that we talked about it."

"Understood." Doug raised his glass and swallowed a slug of whisky. He was struggling to keep Alan Connacher out of this. Alan, remembering his dead monkeys, the invasion of his territory, might have wanted to seize the self-satisfied woman beside him by the throat. But this was Doug Edie business, and Doug managed to deflect Alan's anger into a holding space: that was for another time, another life.

What counted now was Doug's life: and for Doug, the only remaining hope was that the Mickelburgers were less potent than they might appear.

"As far as I recall," he said, "the Mickelburgers didn't kill anybody yet. Although they threatened to kill anybody who went ahead with the rejuvenation treatment. Was that the real policy?"

"You're pushing it, Doug."

"The strategic issue is an important one, wouldn't you say?"

"Like I told you, we'll do whatever it takes to win. The rejuvenation issue is kind of off the agenda for the moment, for obvious reasons. So maybe we, whoever we are, are going in a different direction."

"Okay," Doug said, picking up his glass, "I'll shut up."

A different direction, he thought. That wasn't a lot of help. It was possible that the Mickelburgers were going to retreat from violence, but nothing in Kate's attitude or remarks gave that much credibility. He was going to have to hang around, bury himself again in Kate's world, in order to find out.

Which meant finally and truly forgetting about Yinghua.

Kate finished her drink and stood up. "Come and watch the cubechess, Doug. Should be a good match. Pete's taking on Jay Kirilenko, who will probably win. Let's hope that doesn't apply to our negotiations."

"See you on the dance floor later."

"Assuming we're all still alive."

Kate gave him an enigmatic wave of the hand, and started up the stairs to the next level.

◇◇◇

Peter Johnson was struggling: hunched forward in the big pilot's chair, eyes manic, sweat flowing down his cheeks from under the sensor cap, his green and blue icons were being driven to the corners of the cubechess cube by the relentless, clever, harrying of Kirilenko's attack. Watching him, Doug could sense that he had the competitive drive and grasp of strategy of the natural sportsman, but that he couldn't match the sheer brainpower of Kirilenko. This was the third game and he'd lost the first two.

Kate was sitting at a table on Kirilenko's side of the cube, and during the intervals between games, which could be as long as fifteen or twenty minutes, she and Kirilenko were plunged deep in conspiratorial discussion, which to the outsider might pass as a coaching and strategy session. Doug could see it was not so much more serious as more partisan than that: the tension between the two was palpable. Doug wondered that Kirilenko was able to get up and play cubechess after the intense exchanges of the intervals.

Peter Johnson had his own table and his own team of supporters or advisers, but he seemed only fitfully interested in talking tactics, his gaze shifting frequently across to Kate and Kirilenko. A couple of times he got up and walked around in frustration, his athlete's body seemingly constrained by inactivity.

When the third game ended, and Johnson removed the sensor cap with a weary swipe and stood up, Doug waved at him and pointed at the tall glass of beer he had bought and placed on the table in front of him. He was sitting at an empty table on the outer ring of spectators, but Johnson saw him and waved back, and after a few moments sitting with his team, he got up and came across.

"Got to hand it to that guy," he said, sitting down; "he makes me look like a, like a…"

"Like a lacrosse player?" Doug said.

Johnson gave a reluctant grin. "Yeah. Something like that. Here's to you." He raised the glass and took a long draught.

One of the ironies for Doug was that the screaming, cold-blooded intruder whom Alan had faced and somehow seen off, a youngster who had at first aroused Doug's deepest antipathy, had turned out to be someone he could relate to, not obviously evil.

But he killed my monkeys, he sometimes reminded himself.

Wrong. He killed Alan Connacher's monkeys. He attacked the enemy. He did what he had to do.

"Is Kate winning?" Doug said, tilting his head towards Kirilenko's table.

Johnson had said little since sitting down with Doug, his attention still on the negotiations. He shrugged, stared at his glass. "He's a throwback, that guy. He doesn't get it. But she'll win. She has to: he's kind of a key access point."

Doug realized at once that Johnson had given away something important. He risked a quick glance at him, but the bright nervy eyes had shifted away, back towards Kate; probably Johnson was unaware that in all operational matters Doug was still outside the loop.

Doug followed his gaze and saw that at Kate's table things had suddenly entered a new phase. Kirilenko had settled back, his face abstracted and stubborn, as though the meeting was over. Kate's lips were pressed together and her eyes flashed furiously. The woman next to Kirilenko was nodding uneasily. Kate said something to her but she didn't respond. Kate glanced upwards, as though praying for strength, gave her companions a withering glance, and stood up. She looked around, spotted Johnson, and strode across, swinging her purse.

"Stupid son of a bitch," she said, sitting down at the table.

"He didn't go for it?" Johnson said.

"He hasn't got the courage to go for anything. He talks about his non-violent principles, but it's just an excuse. Fuck him. We'll get his people anyway. They're swinging my way and he knows it. Kirilenko is finished."

"So what do we do?"

"Finish the damn match. We're supposed to be cubechess players."

"And then?"

"I'll talk to our friend. We'll put together a serious recruitment package. Kirilenko is going to look like the outdated fossil he really is."

Johnson nodded and got up and went back to his group.

Kate looked brightly at Doug. "What were we saying about dancing?"

CHAPTER 31

D oug Edie backed the Ford pickup into the loading bay, his body twisted around to watch out of the rear window. The truck glided to a stop and he turned forward and told the truck's genie to hold and wait. He opened the cab door. It was spotting with rain but the loading area was covered with a fixed canopy and the tarmac was dry. He jumped out and slammed the door and strode across to the driver entrance, confident in his new body's resilient and supple movement. It seemed a long time ago that he had floundered about, unable to manage his new muscles, and even longer since he had moved with the caution and restrictedness of age.

Ten minutes later, having followed the routines which Kate had described, he had a large wooden box in the back of the truck.

He piloted back to the exit, where cameras and sensors on robot arms examined his truck from top and bottom. He gripped the wheel, tension flowing into his arms. Kate had not suggested there would be any problem at this stage of operations, but then again, if everything was guaranteed safe and easy, why use Doug Edie? The light turned green at last. He felt a surge of relief and accelerated forward and joined the northbound traffic. The truck had route and destination pre-programmed. He said, "Syracuse," and the truck said, "Yes, Doug," and took control. He moved the seat back and took his hands off the wheel and tried to work the tension out of his limbs. Even in convoys moving at 110 miles per hour, it was going to be a long drive.

He spent the next hour thinking about the warehouse operation, checking the surrounding traffic, and persuading himself to relax. He turned a couple of times and stared out of the back window at the body of the truck. The light rain was streaking the box with droplets of water. It was about three foot square and two foot high. Kate had told him nothing about the payload, and he hadn't asked.

He hadn't told Cap about this trip. Cap would want all the details, might try some kind of surveillance. He wanted to be free to make his own judgment. He was still dreaming of escape, that was the problem. Still imagining there was a life for him, somewhere, somehow. He tried not to think of Yinghua, the expressions of pain and confusion and distrust that must have crossed her face when he made his bumbling attempts at extricating himself from their newfound togetherness on a voice-only telcom link. What on earth had she thought of him?

Something else gnawed at him: his first and original betrayal of her trust. Not that it had seemed like a betrayal... it had seemed necessary, necessary for her... but still, the fact was he had broken off the relationship, just as he had broken it off now... Was there a hidden pathology there, an emotional dysfunction? Was he incapable of long-term commitment, at the deepest level? Because of his brother... the secret knowledge that he was guilty and unworthy, a murderer, a fraud, someone rejected by his own parents?

He had not slept well for several nights: and after staring at the road for another half hour, he fell into a troubled sleep.

◇◇◇

When he woke up, he looked out of the window, saw green hills and rolling mist, and asked the truck for a location update. Approaching Binghamton, the truck told him.

Doug sat up and made an effort to concentrate. His best guess was that Kate and her group were following his progress by satellite or high-altitude floater. There would also be a listening device in the cab of the truck, maybe a camera as well. These would be recording, not broadcasting live, but it meant that his behavior would be reviewed later.

He was nearly three hours into the trip and in need of a battery change and a meal. He chose a service exit. A minute later the truck moved out of the convoy and began to slow. He drove first to a restaurant. He had driven out of the rain, but the misty air felt cold. He stretched and pretended to check the load, while examining exactly how it was positioned in the bed of the truck.

He ate a hamburger and drank coffee. He was walking back to his truck when he was surprised by bands of black dancing in front of his eyes. Bees. He stopped.

ID CHECK, the bees signaled.

He nodded, mildly irritated. The bees enveloped him with their usual delicacy. He carried on walking. After a few seconds, they rose above him, disappeared, and finally reappeared in front of him in black letters:

THANK YOU, MR EDIE.

He inclined his head in an ironic salute. PMA bees, he assumed, although if they had identified themselves, he had missed it; law enforcement bees more or less limited themselves to felons and suspected felons.

He got into the truck and drove on to the big roofed space where vehicle service was in progress. He saw an empty bay, drove up to the barrier, and got down from the cab. He told the robot to make a full battery replacement and check the oils and fluids. The robot turned to the battery compartments at the base of the truck's side panel and began work.

He took the floaters he had prepared out of his pocket and dropped them into the corner of the truck beneath the rear window of the cab. His assumption was that there were no cameras outside in the payload part of the truck. The floaters needed about ten seconds to scan opposing faces of the box, exchanging low level radiation and building a picture of the interior. He walked around and checked the windscreen and then retrieved the floaters. He bent down and pretended to check the tires; at the same time, he took the control screen from his pocket and noted the result of the scan. A warning beep sounded close beside him: the vehicle service was nearly done.

He went round to where the robot was closing up the side panel of the truck and authorized payment. As the final, longer, beep sounded, and the barrier in front of the truck began to rise, he ran to the cab, got up behind the wheel, and drove out before the barrier chided him for keeping the next customer waiting.

He pondered the ghostly image he had seen on his screen for the next few miles. There seemed no doubt that his cargo consisted of a communications dish of some kind, probably a satellite communications dish, to judge by the size. There was nothing immediately alarming about that: satellite dishes had recreational uses as well as various industrial uses. But the fact that the dish had been sourced from an industrial complex near Baltimore, rather than locally, and that he was driving it up in person, suggested that it might have unusual capabilities.

Was there some connection here with Kronos? Did Kronos need this kind of gear to manage his bee attacks? Was he transporting vital equipment to an activist group in Syracuse, helping to set up a new round of one-niner killings? His Alan Connacher memories had mostly faded, but he couldn't help remembering the horrors of a bee attack, of dying.

Doug suddenly had a picture of Alan lying in hospital in a pleasantly relaxed state, speculating about the bees which had attacked him, probing at some anomaly. Something to do with what Cap had told him. He didn't remember the detail, but he remembered the conclusion: the bees that attacked him were not Kronos's bees; they were somehow hijacked by Kronos; they were the bees of some public authority, police or PMA, with their firmware overridden, turned into killers.

Did that have any importance? Yes. It meant that Kronos didn't need bees, he needed the means by which bees, probably airborne bees, could be contacted and abducted. He needed wireless communication: perhaps from a ground-based dish, or more likely from a satellite; in which case the ground-based dish could be a secure way of linking up to a satellite network.

Was the box behind him a mobile control center, to be used in some future Kronos operation?

Doug's mind began to fizz with ideas, as he tried to connect the dots, Kate with Kronos, Kronos with Syracuse. He was getting way ahead of himself, of course: Kate's organization, the Rose Mickelburger Faction, had its own operations, and maybe her people needed communications dishes to keep in touch. But the reference she had made, after her argument with Kirilenko, to "her friend", and the "serious recruitment package", had reverberated in his mind: she was getting into something much bigger than her usual small-scale gigs, and what could that be but Kronos?

He thought about the other item he was due to deliver to Kate's associate in Syracuse, a small memory tab attached to the back of his shirt. That could also be Kronos-linked: Kate had certainly given careful instructions about retrieving it and swallowing it if he came under suspicion and scrutiny, particularly from the national police agencies.

That thought neatly coincided with a loud beeping inside the cab of the truck. He looked up and saw a Highway Patrol floater hovering a few feet from the windscreen, flashing red. He stared at it as though it might be a figment of his imagination. Then he cursed and told the truck to leave the convoy and follow the floater.

A couple of miles later he was nestled up against the crash barrier behind a patrol car. Dark thoughts occupied his mind as he watched the patrolman, a tall and broad figure with a walking gait about as smooth as one of Dr. Frankenstein's creations, advance towards him. Did this have some connection with the ID check at the service station? PMA data were not supposed to be referable to law enforcement except in a clear case of illegal status; but this looked too convenient.

Doug lowered the window. He was hoping to see a young face. He was out of luck: the guy was into one-niner territory, his features craggy and a little dumb. He looked like he wasn't a great fan of young drivers.

The patrolman held up the usual grey box. "Get your John Thomas please."

Doug put his fingers in the box until it beeped. The patrolman stared at the back of the equipment as though the information on offer was profoundly uninteresting.

"Doug Edie," he said. "Graduate student." He looked up and studied Doug's face. "This your truck?"

Doug realized that the patrolman, unless he was really very slow, already knew the answer to that question. "Belongs to a friend. Guy called Jake Bariclough. I can spell that for you."

"Where you headed, you and this truck?" The tone was patronizing.

"Syracuse. Jake is a student there. Then across to New Hampshire."

The other man pursed his lips and studied the screen with a frown. "What's in the box?"

"Don't know."

"Shall we take a look?"

"I don't have the authority for that."

"Me, I got the authority for that." The patrolman turned and motioned at Doug. "Hell now, I'm sure you want to know."

"No, I don't."

"Well *I* want to know."

"I'm afraid I can't let you open the box."

"Excuse me?"

"Unless, of course, you've got a search warrant?"

"I don't need a search warrant, son. You're driving someone else's truck with a mysterious box in the back. I got probable cause."

"That's not the way I understand it, patrol officer."

"Son, you're behind the times." Against the scream of passing convoys, the patrolman had to raise his voice, and it weakened rather than strengthened the confident menace he was trying to project. "You youngsters are organized trouble-makers. Probable cause is baked into the cake."

Doug was seething with anger. Since turning young, the one-niner attitude had got to him more and more. He kept his voice steady: "If I heard you right, you're saying you've got probable cause because I'm young. I shouldn't have much trouble finding a lawyer who can shoot that one down on constitutional grounds."

The patrolman kept his expression bored. "Way to go, kid. Think you're real smart. Are you going to feel smart when I take you and your truck into custody?"

"You can't do that. You have no grounds for arrest." He realized he should be apologizing to this dumb cop rather than provoking him, but his anger was still getting the better of him.

The patrolman looked as though he was trying to decide between the forced-search option and the arrest option, and was enjoying the prospect of either one. Then he turned as though distracted and covered one ear with his hand. He mumbled a few words which Doug didn't catch and listened again.

He turned back to Doug. "Ain't that a bummer?" he said, pitching his voice above the convoy noise. "Just when you're having fun. Somebody blows up on the northbound. Watch yourself, Mr. Edie. Next time you won't be so lucky."

The patrolman gave him a self-satisfied, pitying, look, and went back to his cruiser.

Doug took a quick gasp of breath and watched him go, relieved but still angry. Kate will not be proud of me, he thought, when she plays that back; nor was he proud of himself. He had yet to adapt to the constant one-niner harassment and let it wash over him. He barked an instruction at his truck and settled back as it joined a northbound convoy.

◇◇◇

The industrial landscape of Syracuse seemed misplaced amidst the green hills and the lakes. His truck took him to a large mall on the western side of the city with a view of a railroad line. The building from which Rose Mickelburger had fallen to her death, Kate had explained, would in other circumstances have been worth a visit: it was nowadays a shrine for the young, the abandoned playground wheel onto which she had fallen always covered with bouquets of flowers; but for that reason it was shunned by the real activists, and even driving by, Kate said, would be too dangerous. Nevertheless, she implied, the city was a significant reference point for many young people, and whatever they did there had an enhanced value.

He took over the driving in the parking lot and found a space a little removed from other vehicles, facing the entrance to Macy's. As he settled back and waited for the contact, he found himself thinking again of the cubechess match between Kirilenko and Peter Johnson. What was it that Kate Nakamoto wanted, and had failed to get, from Jay Kirilenko? Intelligence? Personnel? A particular brand of activist? And how might that relate to Kronos?

It seemed almost certain, from Cap's briefing and Kate's passing mention of non-violent principles, that Kirilenko was a founder member of the Mars Three Resistance. M3R was a solid, longstanding organization, widespread and secretive. Most of their demos and sabotage efforts had been directed at the PMA and their policies: the compulsory pregnancy tests, birth restrictions, and child rights auctions so hated by the doomers. It was widely rumored that M3R had sponsored and assisted the mothers whose illegal adopted children had come to light in Wisconsin and Texas, but this had never been acknowledged by the organization.

Suddenly intrigued by this latter possibility, Doug began to review the implications. What did the existence of these illegal children imply? Primarily, that the parents had somehow managed to avoid the PMA bee checks. Here was a convergence point. Kronos might have used PMA bees in his attacks. Mars Three might have found a way of countering PMA bee activity, at least in certain localities. Was this significant?

Another memory sprang into life. At Trudie's party, Zeb and Yinghua had talked of the death of an acquaintance of theirs, a woman who had held a senior position at the Washington office of the PMA. It was in the environs of Washington, of course, that he and others had been attacked by bees. Was that just a coincidence? Or another convergence point?

Below the conscious level, he had been keeping an eye on comings and goings around him. A couple of cars had pulled in to spaces not far away, another had gone. To the left of the main entrance, a young woman in overalls had been supervising the robot bugs which were cleaning a giant screen displaying the day's bargains. He became aware now that she had recalled her bugs and packed them away in a satchel and was moving in his direction. She was a little above average height and overweight; definitely not glamorous; but her round face had character and glowed with serious intent.

She zigzagged amongst the cars. When she reached his truck, she held up a plastic sign at the passenger side window. He pushed the button to lower it.

"Hi," she said with brisk authority. "Can I interest you in my cleaning services? I'm good."

"Thank you," he said, digging the prescribed response out of his memory, "but I'm very clean at the moment."

She gave a quick nod. "Wait about five minutes and then join me at the jewelry counter."

"What about the load?"

"It's covered."

She continued to zigzag amongst the cars, and he saw her make another approach to a driver. At last she reached a battered red Ford and stripped off her overalls and threw them together with her satchel in the trunk. She stood up and glanced around and went into the mall.

He waited a few minutes and followed her into Macy's. It took him another couple of minutes to find the jewelry counter, but she was there, engrossed in the display. She looked up and gave a lively smile and waved him close. For reasons not clear to him, here in Macy's a different relationship was to be exhibited.

"Hey, you made it," she said, warm and bright. "Take a look. I think I found the perfect thing." She was pointing at a pearl necklace with a price tag over five thousand dollars.

"It's nice," he said, wondering just how far he was expected to go to stay in character. "Can we afford it?"

"No, but it's a big occasion."

"We'll save up."

"I knew you'd like it. Come on, let's get coffee and cheesecake."

"Okay."

She took his arm in a light but possessive touch and guided him through the store.

"I know your name is Doug, and the truck verifies you. My name is Naomi. You don't need my ID, in fact I would object if you tried to take it. What kind of cheesecake do you want?"

"Blueberry."

"Go to the restroom and retrieve the memory tab. I assume you've got the memory tab?"

"Yes."

"I'll be at a table over there. There's no surveillance here or in the restroom. Unless, of course, you see floaters."

"Okay."

He moved off in the direction of the restroom sign. Naomi, it seemed, was a force of nature. He felt reassured by that: more chance of her communicating with him, less chance of things going wrong. In the restroom, he used a stall to extract the memory tab from the inside of his shirt, and then freshened up. Back at the restaurant court, he found that Naomi had already acquired cheesecake and coffee and was sitting at a table waiting for him. She gave him a probing look and then another quick smile. He glanced around but saw no possible source of surveillance, human or otherwise, and Naomi gave a confirming nod. He sat down and put the memory tab carefully amongst the condiments.

Naomi picked it up and rubbed it between her fingers. "Do you know what's on it?" she said.

He shook his head. "I don't want to know what's on it."

"Sure you do." She took a pair of glasses out of the side pocket of her smock-like jacket and put the tab in the slot. He guessed that her DNA would already have made the content readable.

"I assume it's some kind of recruitment tool," he said. "To get the attention of the people we're trying to sign up."

"So you do know what's on it." She put the glasses on and tapped a finger on the lens.

"Not really."

Naomi had evidently got pictures and sound from the glasses, and she was becoming absorbed. "Eat your cheesecake," she said, waving vaguely at his plate. "I just want to get a quick feel of this."

"No problem. Take your time."

"It's so important that this is, above all, *believable*..."

"Sure."

He picked up his fork and worked slowly away at the cheesecake. Naomi reached out a couple of times and took a sip of coffee, but her expression, what he could see of it, was intense and focused. Occasionally she grimaced, as though in pain. After ten minutes, she tapped on the lens and took off the glasses and put them in her pocket. She looked momentarily stunned. Then she cast her eyes around carefully and picked up her fork.

"Jesus," she said. "That was... dramatic. I'm in shock." She glanced at him. "This is a big policy swing... this will change everything. If we do it. If it works. If we can recruit the people we need."

"Can you?"

Naomi's round face showed a flickering of intense passion. "If we go for it, yes, we've got to. It would be *so* important to lock in Syracuse. Think of the symbolic importance."

He risked a guess. "Of bees? Retaliating for Rose Mickelburger?"

She gave him a sharp look. "You do know what's on the tab."

He shrugged and tried to look nonchalant. "It's pretty obvious that bees will be involved, given that..."

"Given that what?"

"Given that there's only been one form of action in recent times that's really had an impact."

Her gaze was more intent. "Does Kate know you know?"

"Probably. If not, I'll tell her. If she doesn't tell me the whole story first."

Naomi closed her eyes and grimaced in mock pain. "So tell me this. Is it right? Do you approve?"

He took his time. The curious thing, he thought later, was that he wasn't planning how best to lie. He was trying to determine what he really believed. Naomi jumped in before he could begin:

"I went with Kate's group," she said, "because I thought we weren't getting anywhere. How much of an impact are you going to make when you finally say: 'Look at us. We brought up all these illegal kids and you never noticed.' I mean, it's hardly earth-shattering. Whereas this thing with... It's brutal, but if it works? If we finally break through?" She fixed him with her bright eyes.

He nodded, dropping his gaze, noting but ignoring the information she had revealed. "Kate is always asking me why I don't want to kill people. And it's true I don't. And probably most of us don't. But at the end of the day you have to assess the possibility of reforms without violence. Are we going to get the things we need, a new child policy, a new voting policy, freedom from authoritarian controls, without violent revolutionary action? Probably not, because the *ancien régime* is so deeply entrenched. Most of the one-niners don't even see there's a problem."

"I'll take that as a yes."

He gave a little sigh and a nod.

Naomi began eating her cheesecake. "I'm supposed to give you a tab with a response and an up-to-date assessment. Can you wait around until the evening?"

"Sure."

"Good." Naomi finished her cheesecake and stood up. "I'm going to leave you, Doug. Tell your truck to bring you to the Englewood Lounge around seven." She gave him a bright, almost flirtatious smile. "We can have some supper before you go."

He sat over his coffee for a few minutes after she had gone, gripped by a claustrophobic sense of inertia. Was this someone else he was going to betray, or someone he could turn to for help, if he went on the run as the doomed Doug Edie? He still felt himself in limbo, not certain where his core personality belonged, where his true allegiances were.

He now had a good idea of what Kronos, with the help of the Rose Mickelburger Faction, was planning to do, and how he was planning to do it. He could even see a possible way of stopping him. More by luck than skill or judgment he had acquired the kind of information that Cap Olsen was looking for. But he had no idea at all what he was going to do with it.

CHAPTER 32

Kate said, her expression darkening, "Something you're not going to like."

Kronos watched Kate's face on the screen and felt an uneasy premonition. "Tell me."

"This is not entirely my fault."

"Of course not."

Kate paused, dropped her gaze. "Someone I took a liking to recently. About my age, a little younger. Very smart. I thought he was promising. Okay, good-looking too. But mainly… smart. A guy called Doug Edie."

The name rang a small bell in Kronos's mind, but he didn't at once track it down. "Go on."

"Without telling him anything significant, I let him in on a couple of small things. Let him hang out with us." She looked up. "You're *really* not going to like this."

"Just keep going."

"I guess you remember Alan Connacher. I believe you tried to kill him."

Kronos felt a stab of alarm. "Tried?"

"Tried. Maybe didn't succeed?"

Kronos said nothing.

"You're aware, of course, that the FBI took over Connacher's labs and offices after the bee attacks. Supposedly because it was a crime scene. Well, try this on for size. The FBI took over Connacher's labs so that Connacher, who somehow must have survived whatever efforts you made to kill him, could rejuvenate himself, and start a new life as Doug Edie."

"What?"

"Startling, isn't it?"

"What makes you think this?"

"Some guy figured it out. We don't yet know who this is, or how he, or she, got on to it, but we figure he has to be an employee, or ex-employee, of the Connacher operation."

"And how and why did they come to you?"

"I don't know. Because of our hit on Connacher's monkeys? Because they thought we were a link with you? Take your pick. As for the how, the spade work was done by a paralegal who does stuff for the Washington Fair Deal for Youth. And you know what we had to agree to provide in exchange for the information? A job."

"A job?"

"Right."

"So when this informant signs on for the job, we're going to know who he is, aren't we?"

"We are. But since we've got the information we need, we're not in a hurry about that. It'll take a few weeks."

Kronos's mind was racing. If this was true, it was seriously bad news. A bee attack failure. Alan Connacher alive.

But why hadn't Merko told him the Connacher bee attack had failed?

Because Merko, in spite of being so smart, or maybe because of being so smart, could sometimes be very stupid. Maybe he flipped swarms that ran late straight back to the PMA without getting a report. Maybe he thought the result would be obvious. And in the case of Connacher, apparently, it wasn't obvious at all.

Kronos felt anger and frustration ripping through him. He struggled to contain it. "Let's go back to the beginning here. Yes of course we mounted the usual attack mission against Connacher. Unless we aborted it for some reason, but that's unlikely. Connacher must have got lucky. Incredibly lucky. Are you absolutely sure about this?"

Kate had been watching him, head on one side, still perky. "It adds up. Doug Edie had half-grown pubic hair when I first got to know him. I fell for the line that he'd shaved it."

"You've slept with him?"

"A few times."

"Jesus, Kate. I thought you were a professional."

"I am a professional. It's the way I operate."

"Yeah, okay, and you think this guy is Alan Connacher. I mean, does he *look* like Alan Connacher?"

"No, he doesn't look like Connacher. That would have been a giveaway, wouldn't it? They would have had to fix that when they rejuvenated him."

Kronos was beginning to remember now. Doug Edie. The guy at the party with Yinghua. Short black hair, strong, youthful. A rejuvenated Alan Connacher? Absolutely unbelievable.

"So the FBI masterminded all this in order to infiltrate him into your group. How did they track you down?"

"That's the question, isn't it? I wish I could tell you. We're beginning to think we must have left a clue or two behind, after the Connacher operation, but we don't know what."

Kronos thought for a moment. "What's the next move? We need definite proof, right?"

"I'm convinced. A number of reasons, but to me it's a done deal. However, I'll get you DNA if you want. Maybe you can think of a way of getting Connacher's DNA and doing a match. There'll be a couple of minor differences, hair color and so on, but otherwise you'll see a match."

Kronos drew breath. "He has to be eliminated, of course."

"Hey, whoa, we thought you'd go at it like that. In fact, you're lucky I'm telling you all this. It wasn't the unanimous view of our leadership, that you should know. I said you did. Don't let me down here. If you kill Doug Edie, the FBI will move in and harass us to death. They may not have anything they can stick on us, but they can make life real difficult. You understand? That's no good for any of us."

"I can kill him and make it look like an accident."

"I'm sure you can, but that's not the point. The Feds are only leaving us alone because they think they have a source inside our group who's giving them good information. *Sabe?* Remove the source and they have no good reason for not jumping on top of us."

"Okay." Kronos saw the point. Kate, of course, didn't know the situation at his end, didn't know the personal risks he was facing, but hers was the stronger imperative. "Maybe there's an opportunity here. We can use this Doug Edie to feed misinformation to the FBI."

"Now you're talking," Kate said, nodding her head. "We've already laid out some groundwork on that. We think we can turn this into a positive."

Kronos frowned. This was hardly a positive. When he finally cancelled the link with Kate, he got up and paced around his apartment for twenty minutes. He still found Kate's story hard to believe. Alan had no special defenses against bees, he knew that for sure.

And there was a body. Trudie, he remembered, had done the identification routine, and had been suitably shaken up. Of course the medics could have induced a death-equivalent state, which would fool anybody, but the eyes were a giveaway. Except that some morticians would re-build the eyes for cosmetic purposes. Or the eyes might have been covered. He should ask Trudie some time. Or maybe not.

Because the evidence he couldn't ignore was Doug Edie. The more he thought about Doug Edie, revived his memories of the party, the more he could see the possibility of it all. Yes, the face was different, the hair was different, the voice was different, but even at the time he had felt something familiar: hand gestures, perhaps, the intensity of the gaze, the sense of mental power.

But the real clue was Yinghua, the way he looked at her. Connacher had never gotten over Yinghua. He was crazy, of course, to come to a party like that, but Yinghua made it plausible. The idiot had somehow encouraged or allowed Yinghua back into his life. Did Yinghua know who he was? It would not be in Connacher's interests, surely, for her to know. Had she guessed? Possible, but unlikely.

Kronos got himself a cup of coffee and sat down again at his desk.

He had put Connacher's name on the original list, of course, because he was a danger. He was just too smart. There were things he could put together. Valerie's death now being one of them. So far, it seemed, he hadn't made any of these connections. But every day he left him alive was a risk.

◇◇◇

"Can you believe this, sweetheart?" Trudie said, rolling her eyes. "Jason is into cross-dressing."

"Oh yeah?" Kronos was collecting a cup of coffee in the family room, and his mind was elsewhere. Not only was he worried about

Connacher, but there were now just six days to the midterm election, six days to Platinum Sting.

"Really, he gets more and more peculiar," Trudie said. "He came round in the morning the other day. I mean, it didn't strike me at the time, but I thought he had a job to go to."

He sat down with his coffee, his attention suddenly focused. "You're saying he's lost his job? I never see him."

"I'm saying he's peculiar. He took one of my coats. Didn't ask, of course, just sneaked in and borrowed it. Is that peculiar or what? I said he's into cross-dressing, but if you're a *normal* cross-dresser you'd take a dress, wouldn't you? No, he takes a formal, outdoor, lightweight, silver-grey, *coat*."

Trudie, sitting at the other end of the couch, put down her coffee cup and raised her hands in a gesture of despair.

"When was this?"

"Yesterday. I was looking for something to wear and I found it in the wrong place on the rack." Trudie turned towards him defensively. "Not that I'm obsessive-compulsive, but okay, you know me, sweetheart, I like things in order. Of course I blamed Conchita. She said, 'No, no, I never,' all upset, then later she said, 'Oh, Meez Trudie, I know what happen, he take it one day, your son, Jason, he pretend he need to study the colors, you know, for a geeft, but he had theez bag and he must have take it...' And guess what? I believe her. My own son borrows a coat and then doesn't have enough sense to get it back in the right place on the rack."

He still didn't see where this was going, but the tingle of interest had grown. "Anything special about the coat? Anything different about it when you got it back?"

"I can tell you this much, it was the coat I wore when I had to go and identify my father. You remember? Nightmare of a day. I've kind of erased it from my mind. Jason was there, though. I suppose I should give him that. He offered some support. But then taking the coat... I don't know. Is that ghoulish, or what?"

He was now very interested. I should have gone with you myself, he told himself. At the time, it had seemed like a bad idea. And he had been so pumped up, he didn't think he could have survived the funereal pace of such an expedition. But he should have gone. He had obviously missed something important.

"Did Jason... say anything... maybe about the body? About the eyes? Any peculiar remarks?"

Trudie seemed to recoil.

"Hey, I'm sorry if this is still difficult."

She was silent. "I'd forgotten this," she said at last. "He did say something peculiar, afterwards, in the car. He asked me if I'd noticed the smell."

"The smell?"

"The smell of the body..." Trudie suddenly got to her feet. "No, no, I can't go through all that. That was the worst day of my life." She turned to him and spread her hands, suddenly emotional, her voice rising in a wail: "But what the hell did that boy want with my coat?"

He excused himself soon afterwards and told his car to drive home. His mind was buzzing.

Jason. Another unbelievable thing in this unbelievable business. Jason had guessed there was something not quite right about the body, something to do with the smell. He had got hold of Trudie's coat and done some analysis and made a clever guess.

It was Jason who had got to know the paralegal at Fair Deal for Youth; Jason who needed a job.

He'd always been sneaky, Kronos thought, but surely nothing like this: betraying his own grandfather. Jesus, he wouldn't have thought he had it in him.

He paced up and down in his office, trying to figure out the lie of the land. Of course what Jason had done was useful, very useful. But Kronos could see all kinds of dangerous developments from here. A friendless loser, without a job, sitting around at home, brooding on what he'd done to his grandfather, what he'd done to his mother, maybe running short of money, maybe figuring he was failing his son... None of it was reassuring. He might have a spasm of conscience, do something crazy. He might talk. He might look for his grandfather, seek forgiveness or some damn thing.

Kronos sighed. Just when he needed every moment to monitor Platinum Sting, it seemed he was going to have to go to work.

CHAPTER 33

Kate took him to a diner up near the Beltway. The clientele was young and transient and the food Greek, served in big portions without pretensions. There was too much coming and going, too much chatter, too much noise from the adjoining kitchen, to which guests were taken to inspect the dishes, for Doug to have much conversation with Kate or get a feel of her mood; but if anything she seemed over-excited, volatile, and by the end of the meal, after imbibing more than her share of a bottle of wine, drunk.

Returning to her car, Kate clung on to him as though he might have been thinking of escape; and once inside she instructed the car to take them home without offering him an alternative.

During the twenty-minute drive the music was Gershwin's Rhapsody in Blue and Kate became amorous, which involved a lot of rubbing against him and feeling around under his clothes. Doug wasn't sure how to deal with her hyped-up mood, or what it meant. He tried to play along.

In the apartment, the techno-décor seemed less cool, reds and browns draining into the swirling mix. Kate swirled a little herself, kicking off her shoes and ridding herself of her silk top and pulling it around behind her like a kite.

She startled him by sneaking around behind him and jumping suddenly onto his back, arms around his neck, legs around his waist. He grunted, held his balance.

"Ride 'em, cowboy. Take it away, big guy," Kate hissed provocatively.

He walked with as much dignity as he could into the bedroom, feeling as though one of his lab monkeys, grown a lot bigger, was riding him and attacking him. She slithered off him when he got to the bed, pulling at his clothes, removing her own. She seemed to want him to be rough, and he used his weight and strength to subdue her. Her teeth closed playfully on a piece of his neck as she drove herself and him to orgasm. The walls and ceilings tried to romanticize their struggle with images of their bodies in plunging vessels, storm-tossed seas, fading to blazing sunsets, but the effect was confused, like himself.

"What was that about?" he said.

Kate was lying flat, at least momentarily drained of energy. "What, you don't like my sexy bad-girl routine?"

"Is that what it was?"

Kate said nothing for a moment, then sat up. She got off the bed and foraged around, picking up garments. She moved towards the bathroom, turned back. "Do you want some coffee? I've got some serious stuff I want to talk with you about." She disappeared into the bathroom.

Doug rolled off the bed, found his jeans and work shirt and put them on. He touched his neck where Kate had nipped him and adjusted the collar. He went into the front room and ordered coffee. He wasn't sure what to make of her mood. She hadn't been quite so demonstrative before. Was there real anger behind it? Possessiveness? She didn't like him having a girlfriend in Boston? None of that seemed quite right.

When Kate joined him, she looked brisk and business-like, her sallow-skinned face scrubbed clean of makeup. Her eyes were evasive, as though she suspected he was going to ask more questions about her sexual performance. She took the coffee and drank some and settled down in a lotus position on the floor and put the mug beside her.

"Okay, bottom line, Doug, you ready for the big time?"

He settled down on the edge of a stuffed chair and leaned forwards, elbows on his thighs, hands clasped. "I'm still committed, if that's what you mean."

Kate's eyes fixed on him at last. "I think you've guessed we've got something going on with Kronos, right?"

Doug was startled. He hadn't expected her to be quite so direct. He dropped his gaze and opened the palms of his hands in acknowledgment. "I thought it would explain the buzz. Anyway, you kind of hinted at it."

"It's true. I was careless. So what do you think about it?"

"Depends what it is."

"It's a joint venture. Whatever Kronos says about it, we're equal partners."

"In what?"

"The same as before. Only a bit bigger."

"You've met him? You know who he is?"

"No. He's not that trusting. But I know I'm dealing with the right guy."

"Wow." Doug's mind was racing. Maybe this explained her over-excited mood: she saw this move to bring him inside the loop as a big risk, a big gamble. So maybe this was his moment to make his confession. Whatever she thought about it, she would appreciate being told. And she would see that he had some value. Potentially he was a big propaganda coup, although he hated the idea of that.

Kronos, on the other hand, had tried to kill him once, and might decide he wanted to finish the job. Would Kate protect him? Did she really have the status to do that?

And could he really, conceivably, go along with another killing spree by Kronos, even if he accepted the rightness of the cause?

"So, what do you think?" Kate said.

"I told you I wasn't good at killing people."

"You don't have to kill people. That's what Kronos does."

"What *do* I have to do?"

"Be available. Run errands. Provide backup. The same kind of stuff as Syracuse."

"What's the timescale?"

"I can't tell you that. Stuff you don't need to know, you don't. But I think I can say that we have a couple of weeks to lay down what you might call infrastructure."

Doug felt momentarily relieved: two weeks took them past the election date, provided some room for maneuver. He covered this thought with a frown.

"Well?" Kate said.

"We're all going to end up outlaws, right?"

"Doug, this is so big, we might just end up as proper revolutionaries at last."

Doug pretended to give that some thought. He sensed that the moment to reveal himself had passed. He might still do it, but it really did mean burning his boats. It meant debriefings, revealing everything he knew. And even that might not stem the wrath of these people, who hated everything that he had stood for in his old life.

He took a deep breath. "Okay. I can be an errand boy."

Kate reached out and punched him lightly on the calf. "Good going. Now I'm going to kick you out. I've had a big day. By the way, don't say anything to the others, okay? You just moved up a grade in terms of status and briefings. But keep in touch with me."

Doug nodded and stood up. He gave Kate a final glance. She looked immersed in her own thoughts and plans. He said goodbye and made his way down to the street.

He tried to get the new information from Kate in perspective: Yes, the Kronos operation was real. While he had merely suspected it, he had felt it was something he could withhold from Cap's team. Now the weight of his responsibility deepened. To say nothing was another way of endorsing the lethal bee attacks. But at least he had also learned another new fact: Kronos's operation wasn't going to go forward on election day, just five days away, which was the date he was afraid they would choose; instead, it seemed they needed another two weeks to prepare. He had a little more time to work out which side he was going to betray.

As he got into a cab, he felt his life had truly passed into some untenable region where basic human processes sputtered and died.

CHAPTER 34

CC Is he never ever coming back, Grandma?" Sam asked.

Trudie had just handed him a milkshake, because a milkshake, she thought, was okay, she might be out of date with kids, but she'd never heard anything against milkshakes, and he had taken a dutiful sip and then raised the glass with both hands and put it on the kitchen counter.

Never ever coming back. How could she answer that?

Trudie felt, above all, a helpless anger. A sense of the world unraveling, unfairly. And where was the support here? Andy was off campaigning, of course, and she could never insist he came home, not for this, not after all that she'd said about Jason, not when it was suicide, when it was, in a way, *Jason's fault...* and cook was off, and Conchita was flapping around, 'Oh Meez Trudie, Oh Meez Trudie.'

And then a question like that.

No, he's never coming back, Sam, that's what it means, *death,* it means that *my* father is never coming back either.

She felt emotion swelling in her, but she wasn't going to hug him and hold him again, there'd been a lot of that already, and Sam was beginning to look frightened of her. Poor sweet Sam, how could he understand that this repeat shock, this hammer blow, had flattened her into a state of complete dysfunction.

"They're still working on it, sweetheart. Trying to find out where he is."

"Is he dead?"

Trudie took the glass from the counter and squatted down beside him. "Drink your milkshake, honey."

"I don't want it."

Trudie was struck by a haunting remembrance; herself, fantasizing about a situation in which Sam, for some reason left alone, abandoned, would come and live in her household, where he would thrive and flourish and develop great qualities and be an ornament to her family, the envy of her childless friends. She hadn't wished it, she really hadn't, it was just a fantasy, and she would never, conceivably, wish any ill to befall her own son, Jason, who had never glistered, never shone, had taken the wrong path at times, but who remained her own son… No, she hadn't wished it, but it had seemed, that stupid little fantasy, somehow right, somehow the best thing for Sam… And now, of course, now that he was here, an emblem of misfortune, it seemed desperately, desperately wrong.

"I know what dead is, Grandma."

"We don't want to think things like that, Sam, until we know."

"It said on the news he was dead. They said he was your son and he was dead."

Trudie stood up and put the milkshake back on the counter. What she needed was a drink of her own, a tiny little milkshake with some gin in it. With a lot of gin in it. She wasn't quite sure how she was still on her feet, with that thing in her brain, the thing that every mother dreads, the loss of the child. She was on autopilot, battering forwards blindly, ever since she had heard the news.

What she needed to blot out was the thought that had come a moment later, a much more terrifying thought: *suppose it was Zeb who got killed?*

Of course Jason mattered. Of course she was devastated. She had lost a son! And the awfulness of that seemed to fill her head with moaning and wailing. But the moaning and wailing didn't quite obliterate the guilty glow at the back of her mind: *it wasn't Zeb. Zeb is okay.*

"How did you work the screens, honey?"

"Oh I know the codes, Grandma. Zeb taught me."

Trudie sighed.

"So he's never ever coming back, is he?" Sam's voice was soft, his head bent.

"I'm so sorry, honey," Trudie said, putting a hand down on his rich black hair.

"Can I go home?" Sam said.

"This is your home now."

"Grandma, you see..." Sam was looking earnestly up at her, as though he knew that what he was about to say was not quite right, but would all the same be understood: "You see, I don't like it here. Not forever, I mean."

"You'll have everything you want, sweetheart."

"I want to go home, Grandma."

"Sam, listen, sweetheart... With your father... with your father gone, there's nobody to look after you at home. Do you understand?"

"Yinghua could look after me."

"What?"

"Yinghua likes me, Grandma. Really."

"We all like you, sweetheart. We *love* you. And your place is here with us."

"But Yinghua wouldn't mind, Grandma. I know she wouldn't." Sam's voice had a persuasive, hopeful lilt. "And I could stay at home."

"Sam..." Trudie began, and then stopped. It was no use railing at this and railing at that, she didn't have the strength. And it was no use expecting a five-year-old boy to be rational. Yinghua was not exactly someone who was unwelcome in her home. It didn't appear to be working out with Russell, but that might change. And what she, Trudie, needed at the moment was some help, before she lost it completely. She had a show to do tomorrow and a party at the weekend and it was midterm *elections,* for Christ's sake. She couldn't go on canceling stuff forever.

She squatted down beside Sam. "Sweetheart, would you like Yinghua to come round? So that you can talk with her?"

Sam nodded.

"I'm not sure that she'd be free to look after you full time, but well, you can ask her, okay?"

"Okay."

Trudie stood up and told her telcom genie she wanted to speak to Ma Yinghua.

CHAPTER 35

oug pretended that his wanderings around the Watergate, and then stage by stage up towards the north-west, were random, driven by restlessness, or perhaps the search for a late night snack. He walked through mall areas, stopped to read menus, exchanged words with his genie, disappeared impulsively through back exits. He walked, rode the metro, jumped in a robot cab. He hoped to lose his followers, or what he'd begun to suspect were his followers, without them knowing that he had done so deliberately. It was slow work. It took him almost an hour to reach the small Cantonese restaurant on U, familiar to him from intense, secret, happy rendezvous with Yinghua in days gone by.

All the while, he was speculating about the origins of her message. *Please come to the Shanghai Quest on U tonight. There's something important I ought to tell you about. I'll wait for you. MY.* It was already evening when his telcom genie gave him the message. It had been a frustrating day. Jason's suicide had crawled into every corner of his thoughts, leaving him less able than ever to plan his future. There seemed to be unwritten messages here, messages about his family, messages about the way he had spent his own life. It was another brotherly death, not his fault, perhaps, but sad and unnecessary, shaking loose some of the old guilt.

Doug walked the area in front of the Shanghai Quest for a couple of minutes, studying the faces of everyone he passed. He had a last-minute onset of doubt. If Yinghua said it was important, then it was important, he was certain of that; and he desperately wanted to see her; but all the things that made the meeting dangerous, for him and for her, remained in place. In particular, would he ever return to his difficult life after spending time with the person he loved?

He hovered a moment longer before accepting that he didn't have the strength to turn away. He slipped in through the door of the restaurant. Despite the late hour, it was still busy. Chinatown itself had disappeared several decades ago, but there were more Chinese than ever in Washington, and Chinese food had proliferated all over the city. Lou Lam, the proprietor, had a good front-of-house style, and had developed loyal customers, like Yinghua. He was on hand with menus and a smile soon after Doug entered. Doug wanted to give him a warm greeting, but remembered that to Lou he was now a stranger, and a youthful stranger at that. He gave Yinghua's name. Lou responded with a bow of acknowledgment, turned, hand raised, and led the way through the restaurant.

The décor was very traditional, green silk panels on the walls, lanterns, small dining areas with screens, lighting low and warm. Yinghua, looking almost doll-like, was seated in a quiet corner, reading an illuminated plastic download. Lou, fussing around one of his favorite customers, made sure that her guest, Doug, was comfortably seated, poured him some fresh tea, bowed again, withdrew.

Yinghua had put aside her document. They looked at each other.

Yinghua's eyes were steady, dark, not giving away much, but not, Doug decided, hostile. He knew before she spoke that she would say nothing about how long she had been waiting, what means he had used to get here, when he had received her message; Yinghua had no use for conversational clutter and complaints.

"This isn't flippant, Doug," she said. Then with a faint smile: "This isn't some emotional woman chasing after you."

"I didn't think it was."

"How are you?"

"Torn up. As usual."

"Explain."

Doug pursed his lips, dropped his gaze. He saw chopsticks, a bowl, a delicate porcelain cup, spread out on the white tablecloth. "No," he said. "There wouldn't be much point." He raised his eyes. "But if there's anything I can do for you, Yinghua, I will try my very best."

Yinghua looked at him for a moment and then nodded, as though accepting that he remained withdrawn from her. She composed herself.

"As a matter of fact," she said slowly, "what I have to say is more about you. Shall I order something for you?"

Lou had returned and was hovering.

"Something I can pick at?" Doug said. "Some dim sum? I'm not very hungry."

Yinghua spoke briefly with Lou in English. When Lou had gone, she said, "You remember, I'm sure, meeting Trudie Connacher?"

Doug nodded warily.

"You've heard about the death of her son, Jason?"

"Yes. Very sad." Doug had half-forgotten about Yinghua's affair with Jason, so much had he been living in the present. He scanned her face for signs of distress.

"I don't know what you're going to think of me, Doug, after the misunderstanding with Russell; you're going to think I set out to catch anyone related to Trudie; but I once had a relationship with Jason."

"Okay."

"It might be truer to say I had a relationship with his son. Jason had a cute kid and I was… well, I was mesmerized. Repressed maternal feelings, I suppose. Poor Jason, it really wasn't fair on him. He wasn't someone I was ever going to love. Anyway, I loved Sam, and I think… I think Sam loved me. This afternoon I got a call from Trudie. Trudie, as you can imagine, is pretty shaken up. First her father and now this. She says that Sam is asking for me and she thinks I can maybe help the kid adjust to the shock, so I went straight over."

A waiter stopped by their table with a bottle of white wine and two glasses. Yinghua tasted the wine. Doug was now deeply absorbed in her story and he waited impatiently.

"To be honest with you," Yinghua continued, "Sam is doing better than she is. Trudie is falling apart, and Sam is calm. You'd think Sam would be crying his heart out. Of course kids are deceptive. I don't think Sam really understands what has happened to his father, or even what death really is. But what concerns him at the moment is how and where he's going to live."

Yinghua's lower lip quivered, and for a moment she covered her face with her hands. She took a drink from her wine glass.

Doug felt a similar twinge of emotion. He could picture Sam's expression, stoic, uncomprehending.

"Anyway," Yinghua said, "I spent a couple of hours with Sam. We had a good talk. He tells me things, he always has. And something he finally told me... well, I'm not sure I understand it, but I thought you ought to know."

"Okay."

"This stuff came out bit by bit, and I'm going to try and put it in order, because that might help make sense of it."

Doug nodded, took a sip of wine.

"First you should know that Jason and Sam came to see me a few weeks ago, soon after I met you. Jason seemed to want to know if I had any new relationships. I was a little surprised about that. I thought he was okay with things, I thought he'd moved on. Anyway, I didn't tell him about you, of course, what was there to say?"

Doug grunted.

"So now Sam, this evening, tells me these things: that his dad has been acting crazy for the last few days, moaning to himself, losing his temper with bees, terrified of telcom calls, completely losing track of what he's doing or what Sam is doing... and that he keeps mumbling this name, 'Doug Easy', at his screen, or his genie, like it was some magic formula... and here Sam gets kind of nervous and starts whispering and I have to lean close and put my arm around him, and he says I have to promise not to tell anyone, and I do that... And then when he asks his dad the next day what it means, this 'Doug Easy' person, his dad goes nuts and tells him never ever to talk about it."

Yinghua paused. Doug was concentrating hard. "Anything else?"

"That's all I could learn."

"Did he say who he thinks this Doug Easy is?"

"I think he may see a connection with what has happened to his father. But in truth, I don't think he has any idea who Doug Easy is."

"What did you tell him?"

"About Doug Easy? Nothing. I told him he had done the right thing to tell me his story, and that I would look into it, but that at the moment it should be our secret."

Doug nodded. "Good. Will he be okay?"

"Trudie seems to want me to be involved, so I'm going to make sure he's okay."

"Thanks," Doug said.

Yinghua seemed to pick up something in his voice. She stared at him questioningly for a moment. Sam is nothing to do with you, she seemed to be saying, so why thank me?

Doug moved on. "Tell me what your own conclusions are. What is the link between Jason and me?"

Yinghua lowered her gaze, appeared to concentrate. "I'm guessing that Jason found out about you from his mother. I could ask her, but I thought I wouldn't do that just yet. The point is, Trudie likes to gossip. She might have told him. Also, and it seems cruel to say this now, but Trudie didn't have an awful lot of time for her second-born. I know Jason was aware of that, and it affected him. So she might not have cared very much if she hurt him, telling him about you. And if his personality was in some measure vulnerable, damaged... I don't know. I suppose my conclusion is that he was finding out about you, maybe contacting people, maybe with some kind of jealous intent. I mean, if it was benign, what he was doing, why get so upset with Sam for eavesdropping? I can't honestly believe he was that jealous of me, especially now, over a year later, but anyway... I thought you ought to know."

Doug glanced around at the clock on the wall. It was nearly half past ten. Was the conclusion clear-cut? No, but it was a possibility. A strong possibility. Because of the way Kate was behaving. The people following him around, who were not FBI, he thought now, but Mickelburgers. The way she had kept him away from Peter, whose volatile temperament could not be trusted, and who might have tried to deal with him violently. The information she had recklessly given him about Kronos. Kate knew. Everything pointed to that.

And Jason's death was an indicator as well.

It was weird, unthinkable, but Jason must have ferreted around in the way he had always done, must somehow have guessed at the rejuvenation, been gifted the information about Doug Edie and Yinghua from his mother, and then... what? Betrayed him to his youth activist connections. Why? Did he hate his grandfather that much? Or was this purely to do with money? A job? Status? Keeping himself viable in the eyes of Sam... And had he then been filled with remorse and killed himself? Or had he been killed by his new colleagues...

He felt numb with shock, inclined to see it as his own failure more than Jason's. Unless he was making the wrong connections.

No. Kate knew. She knew not just that he was suspect, uncommitted; she knew the whole story; she knew he was Alan Connacher; she knew he was linked to the FBI. That's why she had let slip such a critical piece of information. Or misinformation. Letting him guess about Kronos was nothing compared to the crucial matter of when the Kronos operation was going to take place. She would never have let a newcomer like him know something like that. Kronos would have killed her for such carelessness. So she was feeding him false information. He should have seen that from the beginning.

Which had to mean that the operation was taking place sooner: perhaps on election day, in line with Kronos's original threats.

He recoiled from a further thought. If, as he had briefly thought of doing, he had confessed to Kate that he was Alan Connacher, and that he was no longer relaying anything to the FBI, she would have seen his usefulness evaporating in front of her eyes. He would probably be dead.

Yinghua was watching him quietly.

"I'm sorry," he said. "You can't imagine how important this is. You have probably saved my life."

A waiter arrived and spread dishes on the table. Yinghua had a brief conversation with him, pointing at a couple of things. The waiter poured more wine and withdrew.

"Try this," Yinghua said, indicating a steamed bun. "I think you need to eat something."

He picked one up and took a bite. He had no idea what he was eating, but he nodded to show it was fine.

"Yinghua," he said slowly, "suppose I told you that Kronos had formed an alliance with the Rose Mickelburger Faction, and that they were going to kill a lot more people. One-niners, of course. That this time they will try and get doomers out on the streets and generate a real revolution. What would you think about that?"

She watched him for a moment, as though weighing what he had said, and satisfying herself that he was properly attending to his needs. "I would think that they ought to be stopped, as long as that can be done without killing them in exchange."

"But the injustices are real, are they not? We are doomers, and we are in the right."

"Doug, if you start killing people you may never stop. That applies particularly to doomers killing one-niners. If you give them, us, a tribal sanction to start, it may end with bloodletting on a huge scale and the complete destruction of our society. And no, I don't think that's a benefit."

He stared at Yinghua's gentle face, wishing profoundly that he could end the pretense and tell her who he was. And perhaps he could. Because surely the farce was over. He was no further use to Cap. And he was certainly finished amongst the Mickelburgers. The only question was how he could resolve his multiple loyalties, limit the damage to himself and others. Would he damage Yinghua if he told her the truth?

He continued mechanically eating his bun. Yinghua would want him to give his energies to stopping Kronos. It seemed like a regression, back to his one-niner origins, but wasn't that what he was going to have to do? She was surely right that an orgy of violence would solve nothing. And if he drew Yinghua with him, into the fight, wouldn't that too be what she would want?

He checked the clock again. Ten-fifty. If he was going to work with Cap on a strategy to defeat Kronos, he was going to have to start now, tonight.

At last he fixed his gaze on Yinghua and said: "Do you remember telling me that you were once in love with a much older man?"

She nodded gravely.

"Was it Alan Connacher?"

She looked only mildly surprised. "I thought you might have guessed that. Zeb gave it away, didn't he?"

"And you were... you were truly in love?"

"Yes."

Doug felt suddenly scared. He reached for his glass and swallowed some wine. How would she react? How would he react himself? He leaned forward, feeling emotion swamping his words. "Yinghua... if I told you that Alan Connacher had somehow avoided death and that he had got involved in... in the struggle against youth terrorism, against Kronos... that he was conscripted by the FBI and penetrated the Rose Mickelburger Faction... that he became very confused and didn't know where his loyalties lay… would you still love him?"

Yinghua stared at him, eyes blinking. "Of course," she said at last.

Doug felt his composure breaking down, his eyes stinging.

"And if," he said, his words blurting out unevenly, "Alan Connacher, to do this work, rejuvenated himself, and turned himself into… into someone else…"

Yinghua stared at him, eyes wide, still. "Are you saying…?"

"Yes."

"You?"

"Yes."

"Oh my God."

Yinghua pulled back, continued to stare at him, breathing fast.

"Yinghua…"

"The two of you? Together?"

"I'm Alan Connacher. I think I'm still Alan Connacher. But in being young, living young… I may have changed a little."

Yinghua gave something between a gasp and a laugh. Her face had gone pale. She stood up suddenly. "I'm… I'm…" she said, not looking at him. "It's okay. I'll be back." She turned and disappeared towards the back of the restaurant.

Doug half rose in his seat himself, then settled back. Nothing he could do. He cursed himself for not foreseeing the impact of his news.

He seemed to wait forever. Yinghua looked calm when she returned. She sat down, met his gaze, put her hand on his. "It's okay. Just the world shifting on its axis. I'll get used to it."

He clung to her hand. "You never guessed?"

"Nowhere close."

"And?"

She shrugged, waited a moment. "I'm in shock. First that Alan Connacher is alive. Alive! My God, do you know how I felt when he died? Even though we were… not together… And even though… I had been hurt… And now you say that he is… you. I mean, it's impossible. I can't get a grip on it. But at the same time it's like… It's like when translation software starts working and the words suddenly begin to make sense. It's like something implicit has finally revealed itself. Why didn't you tell me before?"

"You know why. It would put you at risk and it would put me at risk. I only tell you now because I think it's all over. I think Jason found out who I was. I don't know how he did it, but it would be in line with his personality. He always liked to get into family secrets. He must have given my identity away, to some youth activist, presumably, who passed it on to the Mickelburgers. And then I guess he realized what he'd done and he couldn't live with it."

Yinghua was quiet, her thoughts turning inward. At last she looked up at him, her eyes deep pools, glistening. Her voice was shaky. "Eat some more food," she said with a half laugh, indicating the dishes.

Doug leaned forward and took her hand again. "Yinghua, I've missed you every moment since we… since you and I… since you and Alan… parted."

"Yes, that parting…" Yinghua looked away, gave a tiny shrug. "That wasn't my doing."

"You were young and I was… high-profile old. I just thought I would ruin your life."

"I know what you thought."

"You told Doug Edie that you understood why I had to… let you go."

"That was in confidence to Doug."

"Doug gave me permission to quote you."

"It's still pretty sneaky of you to use it as an exculpatory device." Her expression was serious.

"I love you, Yinghua." Doug took a deep, unsteady breath. "And if it seemed like the right thing before to give you up, then I'm quite sure it was the wrong thing to approach you secretly as Doug Edie. I'm sorry."

She looked back into his eyes, a trace puzzled. "Your life had completely changed, you were in danger, why wouldn't you turn to me? I would want you to do that. It's just that I didn't know…"

"The thing that kept me going was the hope that you'd approve… of what I was doing… but you couldn't know. You couldn't share it. I had to be Doug Edie, not Alan Connacher. I had to try and think like a youth activist. I had to sleep with this crazy Mickelburger woman to get her to trust me. I turned to you out of weakness, because I needed something steady to cling onto, but that was wrong, because I couldn't offer you anything, and I still can't offer you anything. If I ever go back to being Alan Connacher, then I'm a sitting duck for terrorists, and if

I stay as Doug Edie, then I'm a non-person, a fugitive."

Yinghua studied him for a moment. "You missed out one thing."

"What's that?"

"You're dying, surely. A terminal disease."

Doug looked at her, then smiled faintly. "As a matter of fact, the rejuvenation is imperfect. If untreated, I would probably die in a few months."

"There you are. It's the full romantic package. You're stitching me up. Eat some of this food."

Yinghua cocked her head and gave him a look. Doug obediently picked up a spring roll. Yinghua chose a shrimp dumpling. For a couple of moments they ate in silence. Doug looked around at the clock. It was nearly eleven.

"Listen, Yinghua," he said, "I hate to have to do this, but if Jason has betrayed me, there's follow-up to be done, immediately. I need you to come with me to the FBI."

He saw something immediately in Yinghua's eyes: a flinching, a doubt.

"Is that a problem?" he said.

The eyes fluttered with uncertainty.

"You don't want to collaborate with the old guys?"

She shook her head. "Alan... or do I call you Doug?"

"Better stick with Doug."

"Doug... you've unwrapped the layers of your existence... and thank God you did... but I have some things to tell you too, things to be explained... but not now. What I must tell you is that my Chinese... friends usually know what I do, and if I was seen to be talking with the FBI, it would be awkward. Actually, it would be more than awkward."

She looked at him, a trace of fear in her eyes, hoping for understanding.

"Yinghua, the team handling me is extremely restricted, extremely secure. I can't be sure of anything, but I do believe they have exercised proper controls. They know the extent to which the FBI is penetrated at lower levels. My contact, Cap Olsen, talks to his boss, the Secretary of the FBI, and to the President, and that's about it."

Yinghua nodded slowly.

"I need you to talk with them because there's a lot riding on this, and they'll want to analyze your information for themselves. They'll want to assess your credibility. They might believe me, especially when I give them the other stuff I've been withholding, but they'll see me as the guy at the sharp end, whose nerve can break, whose judgment is skewed, and whom they probably think has crossed over."

Yinghua nodded some more, eyes downcast.

"Of course we'll meet at a safe house, not FBI HQ. And of course the FBI can provide protection for you later."

"No, no, no. No protection."

"Okay." Doug leaned forward, looked into her eyes. "Yinghua, if you tell me to do this on my own, I will. Nothing further said."

Yinghua squeezed his hand, took an unsteady breath. "No. Of course I'm coming with you."

Doug looked at her a moment longer and then drew back. "Cap Olsen," he said.

"Yes sir," his ever-vigilant telcom genie replied.

PART THREE: PLATINUM STING

CHAPTER 36

Kronos was groggy: it was four thirty-five in the morning and his telcom genie had just woken him up from a deep sleep. Urgent message from Kate, his genie said: she would be on the secure link round about five; stand by.

Kronos rolled out of bed and stood under a needle-sharp shower for a couple of minutes. He put on a robe and stumbled through to his office. He wasn't panicking, but he didn't like the feel of this. Ever since taking out Jason, he had felt a morbid, unfamiliar sense that he had done the wrong thing. It had been a miserable task, no thrill of the chase there, no kick from exercising power. He had talked to the kid, confirmed that he was falling apart, and done what he had to do; but it had felt mean. Maybe he'd done the kid a favor, who knew: the problem was the family was in upheaval, and he never liked that. Sam was a dangerous floater, maybe sharper about his dad than he had figured; Yinghua was on the scene, which was quite unexpected; and everything had degenerated into uncertainty.

It was particularly irritating because everything else was going right. They had eleven cells, from De Moines to Fresno, confirmed armed and ready, bar a couple of bits of equipment which should be in place by tomorrow. Even Merko was playing ball.

Kate's features came up on screen about ten minutes late. Kronos was now fully awake, hopping with impatience. Kate looked wild, distracted, but very alive, as though hooked on a new drug.

"Listen up, Kronos. This'll be short. We're under attack. FBI pigs jumped all over us. I'm okay, had a tip-off."

"Where are you?"

"Never mind. I'm out of the city. Just got clear. Just as well we had emergency planning. Also, I did it."

"Did what?"

"What I had to do, Kronos, what I had to do."

"What?" Kronos said with irritation.

"You'll find out."

"What?" Kronos shouted.

"Don't get excited, it's going to be okay."

Kronos clenched his fists, closed his eyes briefly. "Who did they hit, the Feds?"

"Not you, Kronos, just us, a few of us, not got a final list yet, but guess what, I think it was those of us known to Doug Edie. Surprised?"

"What, he found out?"

"Must have."

"Found out that we knew about him?"

"Must have."

"Shit. *Fuck.* How did that happen?"

"How should I know? He didn't talk to us in advance. All I know is a bunch of us got hit, and we're the ones he knows."

"Who escaped?"

"Me and another one."

"So it's out? The whole thing? The false date?"

"I don't know, do I, Kronos? Probably."

"Jesus Christ, Kate…"

"It's not my fault, my Lord."

"They're going to search and interrogate. The ones they nailed. Right? What will they learn?"

"Not much."

"Cell leaders? Locations?"

"No. I did what I had to do."

"What are you telling me, for fuck's sake?"

"You'll find out."

"Kate, so help me…"

"*I'm on the run, I'm escaping, don't you understand?* I don't have time to tell stories."

Kate's face registered her intensity: her eyes glittered, her cheeks were red. She looked as though she might spontaneously ignite.

"Who knew about the misinformation?" he said.

"Only me."

"Are you leveling here?"

"Yes! Back off, you greasy pimp! I am in the front line here, taking the hit!"

"Okay, okay. Okay, Kate. Let's just keep this together."

"I'm risking my ass to tell you these things!"

"I know. You did good."

"Damn right."

"We're still going to do this, Kate."

"We'd better."

Kronos drew breath. His head was reeling. "Where are you headed?"

"North."

"Keep the vehicle sealed and don't get out."

"I'm not dumb."

"Where is Doug Edie?"

"Don't know. Our system got busted."

"No ideas?"

"Let's talk again."

"Keep the faith, Kate."

"Shalom, my Lord."

The link went down. Kronos stared at the screen a moment longer, then swung away, his face hardening. One thing was clear: he'd better get rid of that Frankenstein, that abortion, that unnatural machine-progeny, Doug Edie; or he'd never breathe another satisfied breath.

But where was he?

CHAPTER 37

C ap Olsen stood in the softly-carpeted space in front of the long display screens and struggled to make sense of what he was seeing. At intervals his vision blurred and he swayed on his feet. It was after six in the morning and he had managed only an hour of sleep. After the rancorous meeting with Doug Edie and his girlfriend, he had plunged into a frenzy of activity: mobilizing his team, waking up lawyers, arguing legalities, obtaining warrants; even as his colleagues were liaising with the Field Office and getting personnel briefed and on the streets.

The escape of Kate Nakamoto and Peter Johnson had pitched him out of his brief stuporous slumber and into a boiling rage. They'd been tipped off, obviously; by his own FBI. He had known the risks, but he was still incensed at the betrayal. And he knew that there was little hope of finding the person or persons responsible. The move against the Rose Mickelburger Faction had involved eighty or ninety personnel directly and a lot more indirectly; which meant the whole of Headquarters and the Field Office knew about it. And despite his own views on the matter, the organization contained a lot of doomers. As he was fond of saying, you might as well put Fair Deal for Youth straight on the briefing list.

He found himself wondering: had he been right to take Doug at face value and jump into this mess? Doug's genie had replayed several conversations between Doug and Kate, and another with a girl called Naomi in Syracuse, and in the heat of the moment he had decided they were okay. Telcom recordings were notoriously easy to fake and would never stand up in court, but Cap couldn't believe that Doug was that far gone. It had happened like he said: yes, he had been carried away with doomer attitudes and injustices; but once it was clear his cover was blown, he had reset his allegiances to stop the horror-show of another Kronos operation. It was maddening, and the debriefing still had a ways to go, but in the meanwhile it was surely a no-brainer to jump on Kate and her pals while they still believed that they were in control of the Doug Edie situation.

He was conscious of a hand on his arm: he had swayed off balance. He straightened and blinked rapidly to bring the screen in focus. He was in the resource section at the core of FBI HQ, in an area where the outcomes of bee missions were monitored on a big display.

"Where's Baltimore on this thing?" he said suddenly.

A technician beside him, features old enough to be reassuring, said, "It's okay, Mr. Olsen, we're watching that for you. The Nakamoto and Kirilenko apartments are up there, sir." He pointed to the top of the display.

"She killed him," Cap said, reminding himself, still half-disbelieving.

"Yes sir. Intelligent bomblet. Blew the back of his head off. Like the monkeys at the Connacher building."

"How did she…" he said and stopped.

"How did she…?"

Cap tried to think. "He let her in, poor bastard."

"Yes sir."

"We needed him. He was a…"

"Yes sir."

Cap closed his eyes and quickly opened them again. Jesus. Kirilenko might have given them something: operatives, areas, cities. First Nakamoto and Johnson, and now this: This was the worst disaster of the night.

He remembered at last what he was doing here, standing in front of this display: he was hoping for some sign that bees had picked up Kate Nakamoto's scent since leaving Kirilenko's apartment. Traffic data from vehicle control systems gave a good indication of vehicles in the area at the time; but finding those vehicles and getting access was a Herculean task, even for the several dozen swarms of bees which were out there working on it.

He realized that to his companion, the supportive technician, he had so far sounded at best distracted, at worst senile or drunk. He tried to phrase a sensible question and articulate clearly:

"The latest on Nakamoto would be…?"

"No luck, sir."

"Nothing, uh?"

"I'd have to say we've lost her. But of course there's now a nationwide alert, and that will go out to the PMA and local police as well. Bees are on her case."

Cap nodded. His eyelids were drooping again. He turned and gave the man a pat on the arm and started navigating his way out of the display area, trying not to bump into anyone. He took the elevator to the basement and decided on a swim rather than a shower, hoping the gentle exercise would revive him. A keen agent was plowing through the moving waters of the exercise pool, but the main pool was deserted. He changed and flopped into the warm water and realized after a few strokes that he was losing energy rather than gaining it. He wanted to roll on his back and relax and let the pressure and the problems go away. He swam on, only half aware that he was losing speed, letting his head drop. Turn over, he told himself. Now there was water in his mouth and he was spreading out flat, dipping into sleep. Dream images of drowning merged suddenly with a vision of himself being forced down into the water by a heavy and vengeful Doug Edie; a repeat of his own attack, but now he was the victim, bees menacing above, no option but to give in, let Doug Edie destroy him…

His alarm reflexes cut in suddenly, pushing him back to the surface in an outburst of spluttering and flailing limbs. He reached for the rail and hauled himself out of the water and lay for a while, coughing. The vision of Doug Edie still hovered. His telcom genie told him that emergency help was on the way. Hating to be caught helpless, he staggered to his feet. When the paramedics ran in, bristling with equipment, he told them he was fine. They ignored that, laid him down, checked him over, and installed him in the basement sick bay, loaded down with sensors, and covered with a blanket. Cap felt aggrieved and foolish for a few minutes and then gratefully fell asleep.

CHAPTER 38

Doug woke up to selfish contentment: Yinghua was close beside him, still sleeping, her arm protectively across his chest; and the room around him, although showing wall-patterning and furnishings that were bland and impersonal, was flooded with daylight and seemed like a cozy refuge against the hostile world.

He lay still for a few minutes, allowing his recollections of the previous night to accumulate unexamined. He knew those recollections contained elements that would fire him into disturbed and active life, so he let them go; turning his head instead to study Yinghua's face beside him on the pillow.

At length her eyes opened; and he was rewarded with a faint smile of recognition, as she took in his presence alongside her. She shifted closer to him, rested her head below his.

"Why black hair?" she said sleepily.

"To be the same as you?" he offered.

"Liar."

"Does it matter that I'm different in these ways?"

"Yes. It's very confusing. I get used to you as Doug Edie. I quite liked Doug Edie. He wasn't Alan Connacher, of course, not as smart, I thought, not as mature…"

"Too young for you, in fact."

"Much too young. But I liked him. You. Then I find out that he *is* Alan Connacher. Or so you tell me. It's very very confusing."

Yinghua sighed, snuggled into his chest.

"If we get through this," Doug said slowly, "which we will, I'll do the rejuvenation procedure again, and revert to pure Alan Connacher."

"Suppose by then I've fallen in love with Doug Edie?"

"You won't. He's too immature."

"But he's better looking."

"How do you know? You never saw me young."

"I can guess. I can look at simulations."

"I can't stay as Doug Edie. I'll die."

"Keep the black hair, that's all I ask."

"This is a ridiculous conversation."

She stirred, raised her head. "At least let me call you Alan."

Doug slid down in the bed and began kissing Yinghua urgently.

"You are *so young,* aren't you?" she said, and began kissing him back.

A little later, as they lay wrapped in each other's arms, she said, "What's the time?"

Doug said, "My genie says it's eight eleven."

"Does your genie happen to know where we are?"

"North-east DC."

"I've got to go home and get changed and go to work."

"It's Saturday."

"I work Saturdays."

"You're saying this was a one night stand?" Doug tried to sound flippant, but he heard the tightness in his voice.

Yinghua moved back and looked into his eyes. "Are you saying you need me here?"

"What I *am* saying," Doug said defensively, "is that maybe we should talk to Cap Olsen about security. I'm not sure what's safe for you at this moment."

"Did any one of those Rose Mickelburger people you were mixing with know about me?

"No. As far as I'm aware... No."

"So I'm probably safer at home than I am with you."

Doug frowned, looked away. Yinghua reached out and gently smoothed his brow.

"Sweetheart, I explained before, there are... complications. It's better for me to follow my routines, stay within the normal framework."

"Your Chinese friends?"

She nodded.

Doug hesitated a moment and then jumped in. "Yinghua, have these people threatened your relatives in China?"

Yinghua's eyes widened in surprise and then she looked away. After a moment she said, "It's not as simple as that. Nothing like that has ever been mentioned. But the reverse, yes. That I will be bringing benefits to my relatives and the people of China. The trouble is, I know them. I spent a couple of years in China as a student. I got to know my cousins and great aunts. I was naïve of course, more enamored of Chinese culture than I am now. Of course it's a prosperous country today, but there is still political repression. Things are still done in a traditional way, through family. I got involved. And once you're involved… it's very hard to get out."

"You think that, if you tried to get out… your relatives would suffer. You haven't been threatened, but you believe they would suffer."

"I know they would. They wouldn't be arrested or tortured or anything, but they would lose privileges. Lose status. It's like that, I'm afraid. It's a burden I have to carry."

"And they watch you all the time?"

"I don't know about all the time. Maybe I get paranoid sometimes. But they see me as an asset. They see me as someone holding secrets about them. Even though I rarely meet them, you understand. If they thought I was here, talking to the FBI… they'd probably think I was giving up their secrets."

Doug kissed Yinghua on the nose and cheek and untangled himself and swung around to the side of the bed. His worries about Yinghua's safety had led him down a new path. Russell. It was a crazy idea, perhaps, but if Russell was Kronos, then he represented an acute threat to Yinghua's security as well as his own. Russell knew Yinghua, knew of the link with Doug Edie, and would also therefore know that Doug Edie was Alan Connacher. He might see Yinghua as a way of getting to Doug Edie, or as a target in her own right. Was this, in fact, the reason for trying to kill Alan Connacher in the first place? Had he been jealous of Alan's affair with Yinghua?

He turned back to Yinghua. "Will you have some breakfast before you go? There's one more thing I want to ask you."

"Okay."

Doug went to the shower aware that the brief interlude of shared contentment had gone. It was back to reality. He dressed in yesterday's clothes and went through to the apartment's living area. It was clinical and modern, with a big sideboard service system at the back, a stocked refrigerator, and a utility area for processing dirty tableware and for personalized cooking.

Doug studied the menu and ordered orange juice, blueberry muffins, and coffee for two. He found cutlery and put knives and spoons and plates on the table. The orange juice was delivered to the sideboard windows in a small plastic jug, tumblers separate; the muffins came in a warm basket with a faux linen wrapping; and the coffee appeared in a temperature-controlled beaker in the drinks section. He found coffee cups and added them to the table. He put the muffins on the table and added butter from the refrigerator. The FBI, he reflected, didn't run to the advanced species of household robot. It would be surprising if they did; anything up from a cleaning robot being a luxury appliance for the few.

As he waited for Yinghua, he suddenly felt an acute sense of anxiety and guilt wash over him. Surprised, he pulled out a chair and sat down. He leaned forward and put his head in his hands. Images from the previous day and night jumped into his mind. What the hell was he doing? Had he really abandoned his new friends, turned over all the names he knew, switched back to the oppressive one-niner regime? Just because he'd been found out?

Yinghua appeared in the room. He raised his head with an effort and stared at her, seeing a young beautiful face that he loved, but also someone complicit in his switch of loyalties, his multiple betrayals. She stopped and looked at him, her expression changing towards surprise and concern. She came around the table and squatted beside him and put a hand on his leg. He looked down at her and slowly put his hand on top of hers. Some of the tension across his shoulders seemed to fade. He drew breath but didn't speak.

"What's the matter?" she said.

"I just... I don't know. I guess I'm not as young as I look. I suddenly couldn't understand..."

"Delayed shock," Yinghua said, giving his hand a gentle squeeze. "Too much happening too fast. Come on, eat something."

He sat still. "Did I do the right thing? Turning in all those kids?"

"They're not innocent, sweetheart. They're old enough to know what they're doing. What else could you do? The priority now is to stop Kronos."

Doug took a deep breath and nodded slowly. He still felt flat, cast adrift from the contentment of waking up with Yinghua, but he knew that she was right. It didn't quite assuage the guilt, but he slowly felt his energy and sense of direction recovering.

He stood up at last and went mechanically about the business of pouring orange juice, serving the muffins. For a few moments they ate in silence. The food seemed to give him strength, settle his thoughts. He remembered that Yinghua had spoken of leaving, and that he needed to ask her something. Russell, the dark horse in the Senator's family. Bit by bit he recovered his focus, his sense of urgency. There was a lot he was going to have to work through, justify for himself, but in the meantime, Yinghua was right: there was no point in switching sides unless the outcome was defeat for the forces that Kronos was trying to unleash.

He started at a tangent. Did Yinghua remember the death of Valerie Thomson? Did she know Valerie held a responsible, senior-level post at the PMA? She did, so Doug digressed to explain his theory about Kronos using PMA bees. It was territory he hadn't gone into with Cap; there had been no time. As he had expected, Yinghua immediately grasped his arguments, and made a couple of pointed observations; but she acknowledged it was a plausible idea.

At last Yinghua said, "I think I see where you're going with this, but tell me."

He got up and poured coffee. "Valerie was the source of the technical data you would need to take control of PMA bees. Which raises the possibility... I know this is crazy, I just want to rule it out... the very faint possibility that Russell is Kronos. He got the PMA data he needed from her."

Yinghua stopped with a cup half way to her mouth and stared at him. "Are you serious?"

"Here's something else. Am I really an obvious choice of target for Kronos? I know I'm fairly well known, I know there's the rejuvenation thing, but still... I think I'm the only scientist or entrepreneur on the list. Could there be another reason for killing me? I've tried to think of a personal reason, and the only thing I've come up with is that he was jealous of my affair with you."

Yinghua slowly took a sip of coffee and put the cup down. "You're saying, then, that Valerie's death wasn't an accident. Kronos, or Russell, killed her because she knew too much."

"Right. I don't know how it was done, but that's a detail."

"And he put you on his hit list because of a personal thing… a jealous hatred of Alan Connacher… even though he was going to bring extra attention on the family."

"I know. I actually think the personal thing is not enough. There has to be something else. But I can't think what. So maybe it's nonsense. It has to be nonsense."

"This may upset you… don't take it hard, but… you know what? If I was looking for a Kronos in your family, I'd pick Zeb."

It was Doug's turn to freeze, hold still, and then slowly return his coffee cup to the saucer. "What?"

"We're just speculating, right? I'm not saying it's plausible. But I noticed something odd when we were at the party. Do you remember that Zeb said that Russell knew Valerie better than he did? In fact that wasn't true. I happen to know it was Zeb who had a clandestine link with Valerie, not Russell. I know someone who saw them together, and they were intimate."

Doug felt the way Yinghua must have felt the previous evening: the world moving in the heavens. He recovered his balance with a denial: "But Zeb is… I mean Zeb is a normal kind of guy. I've worked with him. We get on. He's okay. Zeb a killer? I just don't believe it."

"I didn't say it was likely. Just more likely than Russell. Don't misunderstand me, Alan; I'm not making any claims for Russell. Russell is pretty creepy. But he hasn't got the ego, the organized malevolence, the two-facedness, of a Kronos."

"And Zeb has?"

"Again, I would only say this to you because of what's at stake here, but Zeb… Zeb is a fake. Yes, he's charming, and amusing, and even likeable, but it's hollow. What's on the other side of the mask, I don't know. But just occasionally I feel something implacable, something hugely ambitious."

"Sweetheart," Doug said, still giddy, still shutting out the possibility, "I know you're a lot more gifted than me when it comes to people, but I just can't see it. Kronos is not just an ambitious terrorist, he's a real psychopath, or he is if he's the person who killed Valerie Thomson, and me, his grandfather, and maybe…"

"Jason?"

"It's not credible. It's just not believable."

"You opened this can of worms."

"But not to dig out Zeb."

"I'm just saying, you opened it because you thought Russell might be the kind of psychopath you're describing. I'm telling you that Zeb is a better fit. You can take it or leave it. But I think Trudie would agree with me."

"What?" Doug held up a hand, as though to ward off another blow.

"She loves him unreasonably, but I get the feeling that she knows he's not a good person."

"Trudie? Thinks her own son is…"

"How old was Zeb when Trudie moved to Washington?"

"About twenty-two, twenty-three?"

"How much did you see of him when he was growing up?"

Doug sat back, took a deep breath of air. "Not much. Okay, yes, I was too deep in my own career. I went to California a couple of times. But Trudie was… well, she was pretty deep in her career too."

"Maybe she didn't encourage your visits?"

Doug could see where this was going. Trudie, the daughter he loved, going into movies, a couple of marriages, children, escaping his orbit, becoming gradually more remote, more wrapped up in her own world.

"Maybe," he said, head cast down.

"Did you ever think there was something she might be hiding?"

"Zeb?"

"Some scandals, incidents, difficulties at school…?"

Doug felt as though he was being flayed, beaten down like a guilty child. "There were some rumors. I never took them seriously. I still don't take them seriously."

"What kind of rumors?"

"Cruelty. Animals. And… Jason. Things he did to Jason. But… but… he never pretended he was a wonderful older brother. It was just a childish… phase…"

"Alan…" Yinghua reached out a hand towards him. "Do you want to do this? Do you want to go on with this?"

"Yes. Of course."

"Because there's more."

Doug looked at Yinghua, half smiled, gave her hand a squeeze.

Yinghua sat back. "Is there more coffee?"

Doug got up and filled her cup from the beaker.

"Zeb's money," Yinghua said.

"What about it?" Doug said, sitting down.

"You know where it came from?"

"From his grandfather. The other grandfather."

"You know how he died?"

"He was killed. A robbery. At his home. They never caught…" Doug stopped. His eyes searched the table for something to distract him. A cold weight was gathering in his stomach. "It isn't possible. It just isn't possible."

"Maybe not. I'm not the prosecuting attorney. I just think I ought to tell you that… Trudie thinks her son may have been responsible. She hasn't said so in so many words, but I get that feeling."

Doug stared blankly at Yinghua. "Why didn't she talk to me about these things? Why didn't she give me some idea?"

"Isn't it obvious? She loves you and respects you and you're the last person she wants to know."

"Maybe it's my fault. I sort of lost touch with her. I was too busy."

"It wasn't your fault. She was determined you were not going to know about Zeb. She was so happy that you two were working together."

Doug thought about work sessions with Zeb: Zeb cheerful, entertaining, apparently solicitous of his grandfather's career and welfare.

"A fake?"

"I hope I'm wrong."

"And you reckon Russell is out of contention?"

Yinghua looked at him as though trying to penetrate his mood, his distress. "Alan, considering what's at stake, you've got to pursue both possibilities. There's low odds on both, but what you tell me about Valerie and PMA bees has got me scared. I trust your judgment on things like that. Get Cap Olsen in on this. Do the follow-up. Just don't leave out Zeb, that's all I'm telling you. Beneath the surface charm, Zeb is a scary guy. Believe me on that."

Doug nodded unhappily, his eyes on the table in front of him. He didn't want to pursue these ideas about Zeb, which made him sick to his stomach, seemed to carve up every remaining illusion of family life. He would do it for Yinghua's sake, out of respect for her; and because the consequences were so huge and dangerous; but not right away, his brain was telling him; let him first step back, reflect, see whether something in the broader situation didn't rule out Zeb right from first principles.

"Sweetheart, I've got to go." Yinghua was standing, hand on his shoulder.

He looked up. "I wish you didn't."

"I'm a liability. Especially when you guys get down to your next session of strategic planning."

Doug got up from the table. "Yinghua, this stuff we've been saying... If Kronos is Zeb or Russell, he knows about you... Maybe the Mickelburgers don't know about you, but Kronos would do... He would also know that you're in contact with Doug Edie. It's not safe for you out there."

"We're talking about a very low-odds possibility."

"I don't care how low odds it is. Okay, I don't think it's Zeb, but if you find Zeb scary, then for God's sake act frightened. If you're easy to find, at home or at work, they, whether it's Zeb or Russell, could grab you, demand to know where I am, use you as a hostage, whatever."

"I thought Cap said he was going to move you to a safer place this morning."

"What difference does that make?"

"If you don't tell me, I won't know where you are."

"Is that supposed to make me feel better? You're in the hands of a maniac, and you can't tell him what he wants to know?"

Yinghua sighed. "Sweetheart..."

Doug reached out and rested his hands on Yinghua's shoulders. "Listen to me a second. Forget my theories and obsessions and blind spots and think about this for yourself. Is there any possibility, any possibility at all, that Zeb is Kronos?"

Yinghua took her time, raised her eyes at last. "Yes."

"Then you can't leave this place without FBI protection."

"Is Cap going to go along with that?"

"Cap had better go along with that."

Yinghua moved against him and they hugged for a moment. When she pulled back, Doug saw that her eyes were moist.

"I'll go to the bedroom," she said, "and start talking with people."

Doug followed her half way, watched her disappear. Turning back into the room, alone with his burden of guilt and uncertainty, he suddenly bunched his fists and mouthed curses at the ceiling.

CHAPTER 39

K ronos struck pay dirt soon after ten. He had spoken with Kate again, and her FBI source had given him the addresses of six FBI safe houses, and he had monitored them with a suite of Merko's special software, which hacked into PMA overhead surveillance data. Privacy constraints as usual meant that the data didn't resolve individual identities, but he could watch comings and goings.

Now the software signaled that someone, probably male, had entered one of the six safe houses, an apartment building in north-east DC. Nearly a third of the people he had tracked had come or gone from this building. He set the system to track this figure backwards to point of origin, and watched the speeded-up result on the main screen display: the man flew on dancing feet around a couple of blocks to a parked unmarked vehicle, disappeared into the vehicle, and the vehicle then tore backwards through Washington streets, going south and west, and finally going down a ramp into a very familiar building on 9th and Pennsylvania: FBI Headquarters.

Kronos felt a quickening of the pulse. He had already done preparatory work on the six buildings, and he now ordered a download of architect's plans of the north-east apartment block. Some instinct made him return his attention to this building and watch for a few more minutes. Sure enough, another male; another entry. This one had got out of a taxi, and when he tracked the taxi ride back he got another bull's eye: the Washington Field Office of the FBI.

Once again he felt a kick of excitement, but he made an effort to stay cool: what had he really got? He had a couple of people going from FBI buildings to an FBI safe house. Nothing very unusual about that.

But on this particular morning, with no other FBI traffic showing up on the other safe houses... well, there had to be a good chance he had got what he was looking for. This movement of FBI personnel surely had to do with the unfolding business of the moment: which was the attack on the Rose Mickelburger Faction and the probable hiding of Alan Connacher. There was no question he had to check it out.

He jumped up and went to his bedroom and opened the concealed cupboard. He took out a lightweight bag and threw in a camouflage suit, a few self-targeting bomblets, and a modern handgun, which fired tiny projectiles capable of self-correcting a head-shot by up to five degrees. He sealed the bag and told his car to stand by.

CHAPTER 40

As Doug went through his thesis, point by point, he began to worry that Cap Olsen would suffer a health crisis. Cap hurled himself at the issues with quick, irritated questions, but Doug could see that the FBI director was physically exhausted. Doug hadn't heard about the near-drowning and would have been more worried if he had. Olsen seemed to wrestle with the information about Zeb as though it was a threat to his sanity, rather than a possible breakthrough; and a threat, moreover, for which Doug might be partly responsible.

They were sitting around a coffee table in the apartment, Yinghua calm, saying little, Cap Olsen on the edge of his chair, bullish shoulders thrust forward. Roger Enquist stayed in the background. Doug was restless, standing up from time to time, as he developed a point, appealed to Yinghua for a comment.

He had moved back, mentally, from the material. He could see no way that Kronos and Zeb together made up a believable personality. But he respected Yinghua's intellect, and he was determined that, with her safety ultimately at stake, the possibility would be opened up to investigation.

Cap said at last, his voice a deep dissatisfied growl, "It comes back to this PMA bees thing of yours... Uh? Kronos might have somehow been using PMA bees. But that isn't going to work. There is absolutely no way that PMA bees, or anyone else's legal registered bees, could kill people. I've talked to our experts about this. The security module in all bees just can't be bypassed."

"So you're saying Kronos used rogue bees, illegal bees, homemade or imported?"

"Had to have done."

"So how did Kronos get hold of the up-to-date MAIMKEY?"

"According to General Ponting, they've got some kind of a pipe into the NSA system."

"And what does NSA say about that?"

"Obviously NSA is not happy, but they've allowed the General to interview their staff."

Doug sighed. "Cap, you're looking at two impossible things. One, it's impossible for legal bees to kill people. Two, it's impossible for illegal bees to acquire MAIMKEY and avoid incineration by the MAIMCOM systems. One is just as impossible as the other. We can't say, like Sherlock Holmes, that once we've eliminated the impossible, we're left with the truth: in our case, when we've eliminated the impossible, we have nothing left, no theory at all. So take your pick. Toss a coin. Me, I'm going for PMA bees, because we have other bits of information, like the stuff I got from this Naomi in Syracuse, which suggests that Kronos needs people who have penetrated PMA local offices."

"Yeah, we ran down Naomi," Cap said in exhausted tones. "She wasn't hard to find. She denies everything. She says you faked the recorded conversation."

"And you think that's true?" Doug felt an uneasy spasm of guilt at the thought of Naomi in custody; she was one of those he had least wanted to betray; but there was no way, he had decided, that he could leave her out of his briefing.

Cap gave a disgusted shake of the head. "Okay, okay, let's get on with it. I don't believe in the PMA bees, but I'm not a smartass like you, and I'm not going to argue the point. Let's assume the Thompson woman helped Kronos get PMA information in Washington. Let's assume he somehow killed her by getting her horse to fall off the trail. Or not. It doesn't really matter."

Doug shrugged. "You're agreeing that Zeb is a possible?"

Cap pointed a finger at him. "Let me tell you something. Zeb was on our high priority list. Both your grandsons, the ones in Washington, and also Russell, the Senator's son, were on the list. We identified about a hundred doomers with clear connections to one or other of the Kronos victims. And we talked to them. Standard procedure. Russell, as a matter of fact, we had a couple of reservations about. Uh?" Cap addressed that grunt of interrogation towards Roger Enquist. Roger nodded. "But Zeb… Nope. Nothing. Came across well. Seemed like a guy with nothing to hide."

Doug said, "Yinghua says he's a fake."

Cap glowered at Yinghua for a moment but said nothing.

"Cap, there's a check you could make that might help with this."

"Tell me. Because at the moment I can't get hold of it."

"Forensics at Jason's apartment. You would have had bees check DNA and compile a list of Jason's visitors, right?"

"Right."

"Was Zeb one of those visitors?"

Cap gave Roger a look. Roger took out a screen and began talking quietly.

"You questioning the suicide?" Cap said. "Putting another one down to Zeb?"

"I'm expecting a negative. But the suicide worries me a little. I know Jason had good cause, but he was devoted to Sam, his son. Not to even leave him a message?"

"What's the motive?"

"We think that Jason was the person who betrayed me to Kate's people. So, he knew too much. Zeb saw it as a threat."

"I've seen a lot in my time, God knows, but we're saying this guy killed his grandfather, sorry, both his grandfathers, his girlfriend, and now his brother?"

"Half-brother. And not forgetting the other twenty-five bee victims."

"Zeb's DNA was there," Roger Enquist said, looking up from his screen.

Doug felt an electric shock go through him. He had wanted this test as negative reassurance, not as further indication of something which even Cap found hard to credit. He gave Yinghua a look. She returned his gaze gravely.

"And why the hell *wouldn't* it be there?" Cap said with sudden belligerence. "They're brothers. Half-brothers. This DNA could have been from weeks ago. Didn't they hang out?"

"No," Doug said.

"Not one visit?"

"No. They talked to each other if they met at Trudie's, but they didn't socialize. If Zeb went to Jason's apartment, there had to be a very special reason."

"To kill him."

"I realize it isn't proof. And of course I hope I'm wrong."

"Jesus Christ," Cap growled. "What a mess."

Doug turned to him with impatience. "Look at the upside: I may have a crap family, but you've got a suspect."

"What I've got," Cap shouted, "is a half-assed theory which could tie us up in knots for hours. Midterm elections are in three days! Has that got through to you? We've got three days to come up with a defensive strategy and sell it to the President. We don't need red herrings."

Doug got to his feet, brow furrowed. "If you want to settle this thing, why not put Zeb's DNA through behavioral analysis?"

"I would need probable cause to do that, and I'm not sure that a girlfriend who worked at the PMA gives us probable cause."

"Isn't time to throw away the rule book?"

Cap Olsen caught his breath, gave his head a little shake.

"You may not have probable cause," Doug added, "but you're damn close, surely."

"Roger?" Cap said.

"If you're asking my advice, I'd say, yes, it's worth the risk. But we won't be able to use it to justify the arrest."

"If I want to arrest the bastard, I'll arrest him," Cap said. "Okay. Do it. Keep it off the record."

Roger got out his screen.

"Not that it's going to settle anything," Cap said. "We all know genetics is only half the story."

"With behavior this extreme," Yinghua said, "the genetics is a necessary pre-condition. Given that we know that Zeb was not trained to do these things as a child."

They all stared at her.

"But it's still not proof," Cap said at last.

"No," Yinghua said.

Doug crossed to her and put his hand down and rested it for a moment on her shoulder. His mind was in a state of upheaval. He was deeply shaken by the news that Zeb's DNA was present in

Jason's apartment. It was the first solid piece of fact supporting all the speculation. He knew that whatever emotional denials were shaping themselves in his head, he had to act as though Zeb was now a very plausible candidate for Kronos and he had to see that through. Make Cap see that through.

He realized suddenly that in defending himself against the Zeb possibility, he had ignored the question he had asked himself in regard to Russell: if Zeb was Kronos, why had he tried to kill Alan Connacher? Why was Alan on that prime list of targets? Because he might figure out the Valerie Thomson killing? But that had come later, after the main killings were done, and was perhaps not something Kronos knew he would have to do. And Alan wouldn't have made the connection with PMA bees, and hence with Valerie, if he hadn't been caught up in the failed attempt to kill him.

Because Trudie might give Zeb away, betray his real character? Better then to kill Trudie.

What did Alan know that was unique to him? That demanded his death?

"Here's what we got," Roger said.

Doug stood up straight. Cap turned his head.

"The so-called Q factors working in favor of this behavior, 76%; the so-called R factors working against, 22%. That's for Zeb. The neutral control is strongly divergent: 11% in favor, 83% against."

Doug felt a cold sensation penetrating down to his shoes. "What behavior did you input?" he asked.

"The bee killings material came mostly from the media. For the family stuff I made a brief descriptive summary. The software looks at hundreds of behavioral pre-conditions that are mainly hard-wired. Of course there's a lot of epigenetic stuff that's not covered here."

"Do you have the relative odds?"

Roger looked at his screen. "Zeb is eighty-one times more likely to have committed these crimes than the neutral control."

"That stuff is crap," Cap said.

"It's very ballpark," Enquist agreed. "But it's stood up pretty well to validation studies."

Doug walked around Enquist's chair and stood beside the coffee table. They all waited for him to speak. Even Cap seemed to defer to him. At last he said:

"We've placed him at Jason's apartment. That's a fact. We have strong genetic indicators that he's a psychopath. We have Yinghua's opinion that he's a fake. We have Valerie Thomson. We have the other grandfather. He's my grandson and..."

He broke off. What was he going to say? *And I like him?* He waited for the lump in his throat to subside.

"He's my grandson but we have to ignore all that. I have to ignore all that. Cap, surely you have to treat him as suspect number one. And pick him up now."

Cap Olsen still didn't speak.

Doug glanced at Yinghua. "And how safe are we here? If Zeb thought he had to kill me before, maybe he sees it as a priority now."

Cap Olsen suddenly jumped to his feet. He seemed to be trying to throw off terminal distaste and fatigue. He stepped forward with pugnacious intent. "I'm going to move you, okay? I know, this place is compromised. Your frigging doomer friends in the FBI can probably work out where the safe houses are. So I'll move you!" He swung round on Yinghua. "And you stay with him!"

Doug realized that Cap had included him amongst the dangerous youths, the deceitful enemy, and was shouting at him in an irrational attempt to regain control and confidence.

"Jesus, what a nightmare." Cap was now plowing his way to the door of the apartment as though trying to escape from beneath a dangerous encumbrance. He gestured back towards Doug. "Could you have figured this out, like, a little sooner? Instead of farting around with Kate and Naomi? Could you have given us a shot at mopping things up before midnight minus one?"

Cap turned away, turned back again, pointed at Doug. "But of course we need you. Don't we? We need your mind to work things out for us. Except the biggest thing of all, you don't work out. You were blind! You've got a psychopathic grandson and..."

Cap broke off, turned to Enquist, dropped his voice. "Roger, look after him. We need him. We may not like it, he may be wrong a lot of the time, he may have doubtful loyalties, but we do, we really do need him. Talk to him about anything else he feels he would like to share with us. Don't let him go anywhere. Don't let anyone kill him. I'm going to arrest the grandson. We need him too. We need him under so... much... fucking... constraint that he can't move so much as a toe!" Cap swung back to Doug, his voice rising again. "And I am *not* going to tell any doomers what I am doing. I am *not* going to enlist the help of the FBI machine. I am *not* going to have the backup of all those enthusiastic young agents. Okay? Any questions?"

Cap stopped, waited a second, turned back again, and pointed at Yinghua. "And don't let her go anywhere."

He made a final turn and was gone.

Doug breathed out slowly, exchanged a worried look with Roger Enquist. Was Cap just letting off steam, or was this something worse: was he close to collapse?

CHAPTER 41

W hile his car drove him across the city, Kronos studied the architect's plans of the apartment building in north-east.

It was a recent building in a regeneration area north of McMillan Reservoir, containing thirty-six apartments on six floors. The FBI had picked it, perhaps, because security was state of the art. Access from the street was via a pair of colonnaded porches, which were shown as housing DNA identity check booths. This was familiar technology to Kronos: his own building had retrofitted booths of the same kind. Residents would have fast-track access using visual recognition methods, but all other entrants would leave a confirmed identity on the record: a record maintained off-site, naturally, by the third party security provider. Even if he could talk a resident into letting him in, not easy when visiting service engineers were these days validated with a link back to the service company employer, he would still leave his name on the record, a record that couldn't be destroyed. And that was just as bad as leaving Doug Edie alive.

Kronos was keyed-up, jittery, driven by the excitement of the challenge: but there was too much pressure from the imminent Platinum Sting operation for him to be pleased about what he was seeing on the plans. Not only were these entrance porches visible from the street, they were almost certainly video-monitored. Plus which, the FBI would have some video monitoring of its own, maybe from floaters, maybe from surrounding buildings. Getting out of the car anywhere in the immediate vicinity would be risky.

Even taking his car within surveillance range would be a mistake. Not as bad as leaving DNA behind, but probably it would be identifiable on the surveillance records. This drive across town in managed traffic, on K and then New York Avenue, would leave a vehicle trace, but he would exit the main roads and drive himself the last twenty blocks, which should be sufficient dissociation from the crime scene; or so he hoped. He had to remember to devise a good cover story for the day, just in case.

He concentrated again on the plans. The target building ran along the street, its footprint much like the half dozen row houses it had replaced. The end apartments went deeper back than those in the middle, protecting a paved yard, from which two ramps, one at each end of the yard, ran down to the basement level. The eastern basement contained resident parking, and the western basement housed the building management plant, including sewage recycling and water maintenance and solar power storage and reform. Kronos studied the layout of the eastern basement. Each apartment had a dedicated delivery chute for food and parcels originating here. That meant delivery personnel coming and going. Trucks driving in and out. Chemicals and parts for the industrial plant. There would be a robot of some kind, perhaps a human supervisor in charge. No DNA checks. Security relatively weak. No access, of course, to the apartments and reception areas, except through another portal like the ones from the street. Which would get used only infrequently. Which might even get switched off. Well, probably not. Not with the FBI as a tenant...

His car beeped, and he put the plans aside and grabbed the steering wheel and took the north bound exit. His car guided him a couple of times and got him on Twelfth. The regeneration of these neighborhoods still had some way to go, but he was now passing pockets of new, high-tech homes, or fenced-off work in progress. A couple of blocks from his destination he passed some old housing where sloppy front yards, flaking paint, still prevailed; he saw a small stretch of cracked concrete at the end of the block and he pulled off the road. There was an abandoned pickup beside him, a small, fenced-off, electrical substation just beyond. He drove on a few yards, turned, and parked ready to move off.

The sky was overcast and there was moisture in the air. The temperature outside was 9C. Not a day to hang around on the streets. The neighborhood looked dead. Maybe there were people in these old houses, but they weren't paying any attention to him. That was perfect. He could hang around in his car and nobody would call the cops.

He had come up with a first stage plan during the last minutes of the drive. He opened his case and extracted a small floater about half an inch across. He plugged it into the car's control panel and downloaded current location and target building location and specifications. Referring to the architect's plans again, he described the location of the apartment's windows on the façade of the building. He told the floater what to look for through the window. He named a viewing methodology that should keep the floater invisible. As an afterthought he told the floater to trail a filament on the glass and record sound. Then he ejected the floater and lowered the car window an inch and flicked the floater out into the cold air and watched it disappear as the intelligent camouflage cut in.

He couldn't use a wireless-linked floater to deliver images in real time, because it would be detected; but he could use a mission-directed floater, with no wireless links, and hope it came back with some images that would make sense.

He felt restless as soon as the floater was gone. He got out of the car and stretched and began walking north. Trees had been planted along the sidewalk here, branches bare but cover of a kind; new apartment buildings loomed up, with well-kept forecourts, gardens. Occasional cars moved on the streets. After two blocks he knew he was approaching the street he wanted: he could see the end of the building he had been studying, apartment windows looking towards the street he was on, the access driveway for parking and services just past the building on the left. The windows, at least, were of clear glass: no fancy protective coatings to distort the interiors. He moved cautiously. More of the building came into view. The FBI apartment, he calculated, was the second along on the fifth floor. There seemed nothing to distinguish it from the others. The first of the entrance porches was visible: behind some shrubs and up a couple of steps.

Kronos pulled up close to a young mulberry. He judged he was still outside the surveillance perimeter. He stood for a moment getting the feel of the building, the street in front, the access road behind. He knew already from his surveillance at home that people activity was low. It was now quite late in the morning, most people were at work, food deliveries were largely done, it was a quiet time.

Someone emerged from the porch. A man, very short hair, thick neck, bull-shouldered, pushing quickly forward to the street, obviously in a hurry, talking as he walked. Kronos froze. FBI, he thought. The man turned right, walking away from Kronos, disappearing behind the building on the near corner. Kronos had a flash of inspiration: the guy he had studied, put on a target list; the Director of National Security, Cap Olsen; the guy with whom Alan Connacher had a connection.

Kronos turned and half ran back towards his car. Olsen was getting away, which was a pity, but the odds on Doug Edie being up there in that apartment were suddenly a lot higher. He got back in the car, lowered the window an inch, and waited. There was a small beep, and the floater was there, hovering. He plugged it in and asked for full replay and watched the screen.

The images were disappointing in quality. There was some kind of obstruction inside the window, blinds or lace. But the floater, hunting for faces, had assembled data from every possible angle and had constructed three, which were grainy but clear enough to be recognizable. The first to appear was Yinghua's.

Shit, Kronos thought: how had Yinghua got sucked into this?

The next face was Cap Olsen, caught from several angles, as he turned, moved, presumably made his exit from the apartment. And there, thirdly, was Doug Edie. Kronos stiffened, his hunting instinct alive, seeing not so much the Frankenstein youth, the hateful monster, but rather the target, the goal, the prey. He smiled faintly, nodded to himself. Got you.

There was a fourth individual present, but he remained sitting with his back to the window and the floater only got a partial profile: the other FBI guy. Identity not essential.

He looked back at Yinghua. This was a bummer. Trudie liked Yinghua and she was good with Sam. And she wasn't even old.

Then it struck him: Sam. That was where all this shit was coming from. Sam must have known something about what his father had done. Sam tells Yinghua. Yinghua tells Doug Edie. Doug Edie realizes his cover is blown. Jesus. This *really* was a bummer. But Yinghua couldn't expect to get away with that. It was tough on Trudie, but Yinghua had sold out, joined the oppressors. Too fucking bad.

He ran the sound, not expecting a lot: it came as a surprise when he found himself hearing voices and understanding the words. Then he was listening with rigid intensity, demanding a replay, sorting out the different voices, and realizing that everything had changed.

For a moment he stared out of the window of the car, gripping the wheel, trying to see where the priority was, knowing that every second was conspiring against him. Then he went back to the voices, jumping about, getting lost, getting furious, trying to make sure about this, clarify, convince himself.

Here was the bit, the heart of it. Doug Edie's voice: *We've placed him at Jason's apartment. That's a fact. We have strong genetic indicators that he's a psychopath. We have Yinghua's opinion that he's a fake. We have Valerie Thomson. We have the other grandfather...*

This was crazy. The bastard had got there, okay. But he'd got there by a back route. He'd got there by Jason, by Val, the new stuff. He hadn't seen the obvious thing that was there all along.

So he should still do this. Shouldn't he? Even though Olsen was out there trying to find him and arrest him. Even though Doug Edie seemed to know that he was still a target. He should still do this.

Part of Kronos knew how reckless, even stupid, that was, but he couldn't run. He couldn't just run. He could hit that poisonous nest with his best shot, because there were no constraints any more. He was known. Pride flared momentarily. He was known and he'd make them see what they were up against. Without the smarts, the inside knowledge, of his grandfather, they would fail. And he could still make that happen.

He turned and reached back and rested his index finger on the pad under the rear seat. After a couple of seconds, the seat top moved forward and cantilevered back. If he'd had bees, he was thinking, he could have used them; he could have driven in to the service basement of the apartment building, and released the bees, and to hell with the DNA. But the bee-hives were bulky, and he kept them at his West Virginia hideout.

What he had were micro-missiles. These were usually out in West Virginia too, much too risky keeping them in his car, but these were risky times, and on his last visit to the hideout he'd loaded up a couple: the kind, fortunately, with floater bomblets in the warhead. Bomblets that would seek and destroy, young or old; and with a hole in your brain, Mr. fucking Doug Edie, you were not coming back, not this time, not even with your clever rejuvenation machine.

He took hold of one of the missiles, lifted it from the rack, hefted it in his hand; a cylinder about two inches in diameter and a foot and a half long. He swung forward and fiddled with a connector, plugged it in to the base of the cylinder. His eyes flicked up once, checking that he was still undisturbed, and then he downloaded the details of the FBI apartment he had issued to the floater, and contrived a brief mission statement.

He pulled out the connector and opened the car door. This was still crazy, but he was going to get this sucker as close as he could to the apartment. He couldn't stop military surveillance from registering the attack, but with any luck he would beat the response.

He stuffed the missile under his coat and started running.

CHAPTER 42

Roger Enquist said, "You agree with our guys that Tuesday, election day, is the likely time for Kronos to attack?"

"I didn't hear anything from Kate's people that would contradict that. And it's kind of what he threatened, isn't it? Retaliation for not changing the voting age."

Doug was sitting down now, struggling to concentrate on his conversation with Roger Enquist, but his mind was still resonating with shock from the earlier discussion. If he really had to accept that Zeb was Kronos, then as well as coming to terms with a sharply different version of his family's structure and history, he had also to pursue urgently the bee question: if it was Zeb who had beaten the system, turned PMA bees into killers, how had he done it? And how would his personal knowledge of Zeb help him to analyze the possibilities?

Yinghua had been getting some fresh coffee, and he accepted a cup from her with a distracted nod.

After answering another of Enquist's questions, he said, "Roger, I need you to understand about these illegal children. Cap doesn't seem to have got hold of it."

"Okay. Try me."

Doug forced aside his thoughts of Zeb and hunted for the best way to begin. "The basic point is pretty simple. Two illegal children have turned up so far, right? And they're being treated as freaks, anomalies, with the desperate mothers doing bizarre, but unknown, things to keep them away from bees. Is that correct?"

"More or less."

"Okay. But think about it a moment. What are the chances of these mothers, who are not exactly Nobel laureates, avoiding bee searches month after month, year after year?"

"Well, pretty low. That's why there's only two of them."

"But is there any evidence that they have built bee-proof habitats, or studied the search patterns of bees, or done anything sufficiently proactive to explain their success?"

"I'll do some research, but not as far as I know."

"Then isn't it likely that it is not the *mothers* and their children avoiding the bees, but rather the *bees* who are avoiding the children? Or to be a little more specific, just not identifying them as illegal?"

"Got it. You're saying this is subversion or sabotage of the bee system, at least within a particular PMA region."

"PMA regional offices have local responsibility for managing and maintaining their bee systems. I looked it up. And there are close to eighteen hundred of these regional offices. Each one has their own codes and protocols for contacting and controlling bee swarms."

"So you think two of these regional offices, Madison and Lubbock, have been penetrated by activists and the bee control systems compromised?"

"It's possible, isn't it?"

"I'm not sure. None of the doomer protest groups have claimed responsibility. And there doesn't seem to be much connection between the two cases."

"Suppose this is part of something much bigger. Suppose there are lots of illegal children out there, lots of offices penetrated, and the group responsible, Mars Three Resistance, is waiting until the kids are legally immune from action before claiming responsibility."

Enquist was silent for a moment. "Knowing who you are, I'm guessing this is more than a theory."

Doug nodded. "And it's crucial, because what I'm saying is that Kronos has recruited these people and can potentially take over bees in all the regional offices in which M3R have established a foothold."

"Meaning Kronos-type killings all over the country."

"Exactly. Which would be devastating."

"And we could stop him by shutting down bees run from those offices?"

"You might not need to cancel all missions, but basically that's it."

"But how do we know which offices those are?"

"That's what I want you to work on. You've got two offices where you know illegal kids have been found. Very very cautiously, you've got to set up a team to go through the data from those offices, everything the bees download when they go off on a mission, and find the anomaly. Find out why they're ignoring one child. And then you've got to comb through the data from all other regions and find out which ones contain a similar anomaly. You should end up with a list of offices subverted by M3R. But you've got to do it in a way that doesn't arouse the suspicions of any of these offices, otherwise the M3R people may start to change things or hide things."

"In three days," Enquist said, his expression bleak.

"That's why I'm frustrated. You've got to get going now."

"And what about the fact that PMA bees can't kill people?"

"Like I said before, you take your pick. It's one impossible thing or another. Have you listened to my conversation with Naomi, the girl from Syracuse?"

"I tried. Sort of. It hasn't been easy to concentrate."

"Listen again. She makes it clear that there are lots of undiscovered illegal children out there. Remember also that I delivered a comms dish to her group. If you're running rogue bees you don't need a satellite link. You program a mission while they're still in the hive and off they go. But if you're using PMA bees, you've got to communicate with them while they're flying around: that's how you take them over. That probably means satellite channels. Something else you could do is check on people who booked and used satellite channels during the Washington attacks. Also people booking channels for election day."

"Okay." Enquist looked momentarily tired and defeated. Then he took out his screen. "One thing's for sure. We've got to try every option going."

Doug glanced across at Yinghua. Am I doing the right thing? he wanted to ask her. Unpicking all the well-intentioned efforts of the doomers to right the wrongs so blithely inflicted on them by the arrogant old? Yinghua seemed to understand his doubts, giving him a faint smile and a nod. He smiled back and returned to his earlier problem: Zeb; what did he know that might be helpful? What could he remember of his friends, connections, clients? Had he ever met any of Zeb's friends? Zeb, he began to realize, had kept his personal life hidden. If he had met one of his friends, it had been by accident. Like that time...

Enquist was talking again, and he concentrated for a moment to give him a reply. Then he went back to the picture that had surfaced in his mind. Meeting Zeb one time, purely by chance, in a food court somewhere downtown. Zeb had been with somebody, not a friend exactly, but someone with whom he clearly had a relationship. A nervy, distracted, guy, not much more than a kid, wearing one of those screwball jackets that patterned up in not necessarily relevant ways via a brainwave control link. They had spent a few minutes together, eating a burrito or something. That had been a long time ago, several years, maybe before Zeb had got his Kronos project off the ground; which was why he had allowed it to emerge that the kid was a genius who worked, or had worked, at NSA.

NSA. Suddenly he realized he had the missing link, the thing he had been searching for; the reason for Zeb to kill him in the first place. Zeb had understood, maybe later on, that he had made a mistake in sharing these details about his companion; and that mistake had worried him increasingly. Would his grandfather remember? Would his grandfather make connections? Maybe. His grandfather was smart. So better not take any chances. Better put him on the list.

Only his grandfather wasn't smart. His grandfather hadn't even considered Zeb as a possibility until forced to do so by a younger mind. His grandfather was one of the slow and decadent old.

Doug put that thought aside and concentrated on the immediate consequences. That kid could have devised, implemented, the means by which PMA bees were subverted; or the means by which illegal bees acquired MAIMKEY. That kid might be the clue to the whole thing. So all he had to do was remember his name.

Looking up, he realized that he'd missed Enquist's last remarks. Yinghua was looking at him with an *Are you okay?* expression. Enquist had turned away and was talking on a telcom link. Doug got up and went over to Yinghua and began explaining what he had remembered. Enquist interrupted:

"That was Cap. They haven't located Zeb to arrest him, but his vehicle has left a trace going cross town on K and New York. That isn't exactly a direct route here, but he thinks we should play safe. He's sending bees and an armored car to move us somewhere else."

Enquist was crossing to a floor-standing cupboard in the corner of the room as he spoke. "Meanwhile, we should wear these."

Enquist took packages from the cupboard and tossed one to Yinghua and one to Doug. "Pull the green tab and they open up." Enquist demonstrated by pulling the tab on a third package: a grey padded jacket unfolded. He put on the jacket and reached inside his suit and extracted a gun and put it in the outside pocket of the jacket and swiped the auto-zip. "You'll find a mouthpiece here, and I suggest you use it. Make sure the collar is fully secured. It's the collar that contains the main defensive response."

Doug put on the jacket and watched Yinghua do the same. The collar was thick, bulbous around his neck. "The collar blows up?"

"Yeah. Under attack, the collar will almost instantly create a tough foam over the whole head. That's why you should get the mouthpiece in. The mouthpiece will provide a few minutes of oxygen. That should give you time to open up the foam. The foam weakens after a minute or two."

"What kind of attack?"

"Bombs, bomblets, flying debris."

"Bees?"

"No. If you see bees, detonate the collar with this red tab here, lie face down on the floor, cover your head with your arms, breathe through the mouthpiece. You'll get a few extra minutes. Hopefully time for our bees to get here."

Roger made a quick check of their kit and then waved them to the door. "Cap reckons we'll be safer waiting in the basement garage, so let's go."

Doug was content to follow Enquist's lead. He watched Yinghua grab her purse, and then followed her out the door. Roger motioned to the stairs.

They trotted down six flights and came to the portal which controlled entry from the residents' garage. They pushed through the exit bars and Enquist led them along a pathway to a fire door beside the main car entrance.

"We'll wait here. We've got about - "

There was a distant tinkling crash, and the building seemed to reverberate. They looked at each other.

"Wait here," Enquist said. He pushed open the heavy fire door and disappeared. The door clicked back into place.

As the quiet descended, Doug found himself trembling. Was it possible? This monstrous offspring of his had attacked?

He jumped forward suddenly and turned the handle of the door and pushed. Yinghua called his name and grabbed his arm. He let go of the door and turned and put both hands on Yinghua's arms.

"Sweetheart. I have to know what's happened. Please don't move from here?"

Yinghua's pleading expression didn't change but she gave a faint nod. He swung back and pushed open the door. He was at the bottom of a ramp at the back of the building. Enquist had disappeared. He ran up the ramp, feeling the strength in his legs, and moved more cautiously around the end of the building.

Enquist was crouching low at the front corner of the apartment block, gaining a little cover from the shrubs between him and the street. Doug moved a couple of cautious paces along the side of the building, dropping low himself. He saw a flicker of movement beyond, somewhere on the street.

Enquist suddenly jumped to his feet, both arms outstretched, the gun in his right hand, pointing at the street. His voice was sharp, demanding: "Stop! FBI!"

The words hung in the air for a tense moment, then Enquist fired two quick shots. The response was immediate: a stinging crack, and Enquist was flung back, arms spread, hitting the ground and lying without movement. As he fell, foam exploded from his safety jacket collar, turning into a sphere streaked red with blood. Doug started forward, froze as he comprehended Enquist's fate: then anger seized him and he continued onwards in a crouch, settled on one knee behind the shrubs, moved his head backwards and forwards to pick up a view of the roadway through the leaves and branches.

The man with the gun was still there, about forty feet away, close to the junction of the two streets. He was facing the apartment building, dancing with alert energy, but moving backwards.

It was Zeb.

Doug was mesmerized for an instant, seeing this strange and devilish incarnation of such a familiar figure: then anger washed over him again. He looked across at the body of Enquist, a few feet to his right, at the gun still in his hand. But if Enquist couldn't hit a human target at forty feet, he, with no training, certainly could not. He knew from FBI briefings that the fat gun hanging loosely in Zeb's right hand was an intelligent weapon: something that police forces didn't use because it was too lethal. It turned a wild shot into a head shot; and it destroyed brain tissue in a way that was unrecoverable. He looked around at the bare trees, the grey sky, in the desperate hope of seeing a tell-tale iridescent flash.

Where were the bees that Cap had promised?

He looked back at Zeb. Zeb hadn't yet seen him, seemed now to be losing his patience. His lips moved as he gave some message to his genie. He skipped and half turned. Did he realize from Enquist's intervention, Doug wondered, that his attack on the apartment had failed? Was he still hoping to pick up the trail of Doug Edie?

And then he saw them: they had just announced themselves, high and off to the west:

FBI

Zeb had seen them too: he was turning to run. The bees could almost certainly identify him as the perpetrator, and the gun would free them to act without further intervention, but would they be in time?

Doug stood up to his full height and yelled at the top of his lungs: "You want me?"

Zeb, crossing the north-south street, turned and froze. For a moment they stared at each other, grandfather and grandson. Kronos and the translated Alan Connacher.

Doug held it as long as he could. When Zeb's eyes flickered, he flung himself to the left and flat to the ground, locking his arm around a tree, pulling his head behind it. He just made it. The crack of the shot came as he slithered to a stop. There was a vicious whine of a kind he had never heard. A streak of pain hit the crown of his head. At nearly the same instant he was enveloped by another sharp sound, like a champagne cork inside his head, and then the world went away. He was blind and deaf, cocooned in eerie silence.

It took him a stunned second to realize that his safety collar had exploded and that his head was now buried in foam. He had failed to put in the mouthpiece, and he couldn't breathe.

He held his body rigid and breathless and waited. Would Zeb spare the time for another shot, did he realize the first had failed, or was he now trying to escape?

He was suddenly aware of a chemical taste in his mouth, air moving, somebody turning his shoulders. He expelled all the air in his lungs in a pressured blast and sucked in new air. He rolled away from the person holding him and tore at the softening foam around his eyes. He caught a glimpse of a terrified Yinghua.

"Stay down!" she shouted at him, clawing at him, her words just audible.

He kept low, pulling away lumps of foam, his ears coming free. He heard the approaching whine of a vehicle's tires on the damp roadway beyond the shrubs.

"Get him, get him!" Yinghua shouted at the sky.

He looked up at the sky but saw nothing.

The whine of the vehicle stopped, a car door slammed, a motor surged.

Yinghua fell against him, sobbing.

Doug held her, relief and anger mixed. The bees had saved his life. But he knew from the quality of the silence that Zeb had got away.

CHAPTER 43

The hideout was a miserable shack in hilly country near the border with West Virginia. It was at the back end of farmland controlled anonymously by Zeb, in a wooded valley dank and moldering from the fertilizer-enriched run-off of the farm. In this season of late fall, it was muddy and slippery underfoot and smelled of decay. The shack was hidden by the trees and the dip of the valley, but Zeb had left the blackened boards of the superstructure in place as further camouflage, and insulated with plastic sheeting inside. There was a chemical toilet, well-water, a bowl for washing, a generator, minimal electric heating with a low infra red signature, a camp bed, but most of the shack was taken up with Zeb's bee-hives and guns and other forms of intelligent ordnance.

Merko, guided down the approach track by his truck's genie and Zeb's sat nav coordinates, hated it from the moment of arrival. He clomped around the clearing and sniffed the air and opened up the shack in a state close to panic. Surely the Lord Kronos was joking. There would be spiders and rats and all kinds of crap in there. How would he survive?

What he really deserved, Merko thought, as he poked around inside the shack, was a palace; a harem; an acknowledgment of his worth. Instead he was stuck with this piece of decay, this collection of munitions. It was like a foretaste of prison, a dragging of his soul through incriminating muck. Was this what the gods thought of him?

Merko went back outside and stood by his truck. He looked up at the sky. It was cold, but not raining. The afternoon light was waning. He should take his bag into the shack and try and work things out. How to put on the heating. How to put on the lights. What was he going to eat? There were no food deliveries here, no food prep equipment. He'd have to go miles back down the highway, to the nearest takeaway. And come back in the dark.

Merko got his telcom genie to summon his lord and master Kronos and tell him that he couldn't live out here in this wilderness and what was the reason for doing so, anyway, apart from the usual ritual of humiliating his servant Merko.

And Zeb just sent a message back telling him to shape up; they were all at risk, they all had to make sacrifices.

It was then, as he turned back to the dismal shack, and looked in at the bee-hives stacked at one side, that he thought how easy it would be... the Lord Kronos might be a god, but he wasn't, in reality, invulnerable... the bees could be ready, programmed... Zeb maybe comes by to check on things... comes into the shack... the bees strike. Everything resolved. He, Merko, in any case doomed, gives himself up to the police...

But the gods had powers. Even if he told nobody, he would somehow be betrayed. He would betray himself. Kronos would know, the moment he arrived. It could never happen, the way he was thinking about it. In fact, he should stop thinking.

He went into the shack and put his bag down on the floor. He stood still for a moment feeling the panic build. Then he lay down on the camp bed and closed his eyes tight.

Merko survived for the next two days by listening to some new bands and composers. He worked his way through the pieces punched out on piano rolls by Conlon Nancarrow in the middle of the twentieth century. He set himself some mathematical problems. And he drove around a lot. In fact he lived mostly in his truck. That wasn't the way Zeb would have liked it, but it took Merko an effort of will to spend more than an hour or so at Zeb's camp; as though a malign spirit had taken up residence in the place and was intent on driving him away. When he lay down on the camp bed at night he trembled, partly from cold, partly from terror. The second night he gave it up and lay down on the seat of his truck.

He was visited by bees once: PMA bees. He was almost glad to see them. He knew that since his DNA identity was valid, and he wasn't pregnant, there would be no record kept of his location.

Around noon of the third day he got a call from Zeb. Merko could tell at once that something had happened: Zeb was breathing hard, his voice was jerky, and it sounded like he was mad.

"Listen up, old buddy... got a situation here... Connacher is on to us... me, anyway... tried to take him out, got the fucking timing wrong... We got to move, okay? You listening to me?"

"Yeah, yeah," Marko said, his heart sinking. He didn't tell Zeb that he was driving along in his truck.

"I'm going to dump the car and get on the metro. I want you to load up the bee-hives and a couple of rifles and come and get me at Vienna. Don't waste time, I want you underway in five minutes. Got it?"

"Yeah, yeah. Where we going?"

"Tell you later. Just get started."

Zeb went off-line, and Merko gripped the wheel and nearly screamed out loud. Okay, he was only ten minutes from the shack, but ten minutes delay was going to piss off his lord and master in the extreme. And did he really want to do this? Get into a race with the cops, Zeb firing his rifle out the back of his truck? Crazy stuff like that?

No, he didn't, but there was no choice. He bumped his way down the track as fast as he could take it, ran to and fro to the shack loading the bee-hives and the rifles, swept his personal things into his bag, locked the shack, and took off back down the track.

Metro station, Vienna, he told his truck's genie; maximum speed.

Zeb hadn't told him to avoid the automated convoys, the high speed routes; so that was the way he was going.

Then it struck him again: he had bees in the back of the truck; he could set up a mission... Zeb gets in the truck... the bees attack... and it's all over.

Wedged in a convoy going at 120 miles per hour, Merko dreamed for a few miles about what it would be like if it was all over. Back to his snakes, back to consulting work. Maybe try again with that girl, Jennie. Normal stuff like a few beers and a concert.

Merko sighed, a catch in his throat. Fat frigging chance. Connacher was obviously going to figure it out. So they'd track him back to NSA.

Then everything fell apart. That was if these other people, Kate, the Mickelburgers, didn't get to him first. Because if Zeb was out of it, he couldn't release the Key of Power, could he? That was the point. That was the whole frigging point. The Lord Kronos had to sanction that. He wasn't going to kill all those people. Not again. Leave all that to the gods.

So he could quit thinking about Zeb going down. Quit thinking about doing clever things with bees. Just quit thinking, period.

Merko stared out of the cab of the truck, urging the convoy along. I'm coming, my Lord Kronos; your servant Merko is doing his frigging best.

CHAPTER 44

General Lee Ponting sat with his colleagues in front of the President's desk and listened carefully to the discussion, its tone and content: events were sliding in several dangerous directions, and he wanted to see how Christine Diaz was going to respond.

Cap Olsen had presented a review of the morning's dramatic developments, his voice rough, his fatigue obvious: first there had been the enforced retirement from the field of his undercover agent, now bizarrely revealed to be a rejuvenated Alan Connacher, masquerading as a doomer called Doug Edie; then he had reviewed the intelligence acquired from Edie's penetration of the Rose Mickelburger Faction, and also from members of the RMF now being questioned; and finally, his voice cracking with emotion, the teasing anticlimax, the unmasking of Kronos himself as none other than Alan Connacher's grandson, Zeb. As Ponting listened, he couldn't help reflecting sourly that the apparent good news was actually very bad news indeed: all of the principals in the presumed terrorist plot had escaped, including Kronos himself; which left the threat level higher than ever.

Susan Schwartz described how PMA swarms, as well as swarms from other agencies, had tried to follow and locate the missing key players, so far without any success; their efforts would continue. She also mentioned that a third illegal and undocumented child had shown up in Seattle, where someone, a panicking mother, perhaps, had left a baby girl in a hospital waiting room. Diaz expressed sympathy, but otherwise no great interest was shown, which came as a relief to the General: even if the anomaly of the illegal children was somehow to do with PMA bees and their missions, this was not where they should be focusing their attention; bees in public service were simply untenable as the source of Kronos's killers.

The General had long since removed from his conscious consideration the findings of his Technical Services team, purporting to show that bees used in the original Kronos killings were of PMA origin. At best it had been a weak result, and there had simply been too many sources of error and contamination to take it seriously. He was certain he had been right to suppress data which could confuse and misdirect the counterattack.

"So the indications are that Kronos," the President summarized at last, glancing around, "whom we now know to be Zeb Packer, is trying to extend his reach, prepare a nationwide attack, by extending his reach to other terrorist groups, such as the Rose Mickelburger Faction?"

The General and his colleagues nodded.

"Even though the only source is Alan Connacher, Packer's grandfather, whom it seems the Mickelburgers had identified and were trying to mislead?"

Olsen said gruffly, "Our analysis of his conversations indicates that this only happened at the end of his undercover mission. And we are also getting some minor details corroborated by the doomers we now have in custody."

"And you think that between them these people may have been able to assemble the equipment they need?"

"Yes. Possibly." Olsen seemed to have no energy left to rehearse the arguments. "Bees and hives do get into the country, Ma'am, so, yes... it's possible."

General Ponting moved his gaze away from Olsen's inner struggles and back to the President. Was she up to this challenge? He watched the matronly figure on the other side of the desk, dressed today in red plaid, her straw-colored hair short and straight: her relaxed homely posture was countered only by the intent seriousness of her expression and the sharpness of her gaze. The pressure she was under from now on would be unrelenting. Any attacks by killer bees, on one-niner targets, before the congressional elections, would surely damage her party's showing in the polls, probably losing her the Senate and the House; which would in turn weaken her ability to govern. That wasn't a good outcome at a time of crisis, but the General couldn't resist a certain latent satisfaction: a couple of years down the line, a change of president would be more likely to occur, and the current liberal agenda, which had created a lot of these problems, would be a thing of the past.

The General realized, with a mild sense of irritation, that he was speculating about the benefits of something which he must not allow to happen. There was no question but that a nationwide outburst of doomer violence would be a disaster; especially if the response was in the hands of this woman sitting in front of him. It was his duty as a soldier to give her guidance that helped to prevent the disaster. Apart from anything else, he wouldn't help his own career if MAIMCOM again failed in its primary function.

Christine Diaz had paused for a moment, taking in what she had heard. She now raised her eyes. "I think we should treat this as a Category One threat. We have no choice but to assume the worst. Which brings me to you, General: will your defensive systems work, next time around?"

General Ponting noted the mildly sarcastic tone, but he believed he was ready for this. "I'm not sure that they failed last time around, Madame President. By that I mean that they were subverted, and evidently with great efficiency."

"By whom?"

"We must assume, by conspirators in league with Kronos."

"Working in MAIMCOM?"

Ponting gave a sideways glance towards John Corelli, the Director of NSA.

Corelli took the pass: "Ma'am, General Ponting and I agree that NSA is the more vulnerable territory. We set a high premium on innovative thinking, and as a consequence, we, uh, employ a lot of young people."

"You believe, in short, that certain youthful employees found a way of diverting MAIMKEY down what you call an unauthorized pipe?"

"That seems about the only possibility. The conspirators would need something that looks to the system supervisor like a legitimate extension of the MAIMKEY network."

"But you haven't found actual evidence of this?"

"No Ma'am."

There was a brief pause. Ponting thought Cap Olsen, to his left, might have fallen asleep. He wasn't prepared for the President's next comments:

"Director Corelli, General, ideally I would raise this matter under different circumstances, but I don't have a lot of time, and I'm going to raise it now. It has come to my attention, please don't ask in what manner, that you have been taking young members of NSA staff, sometimes at unsociable hours, to military bases around the Beltway, and interrogating them there for long periods, sometimes in excess of twenty-four hours. Is this true?"

General Ponting looked at Corelli, and Corelli looked back at Ponting. Ponting could read the annoyance, the detachment, in Corelli's eyes.

"Well, gentlemen?"

Ponting decided to speak. "I will take responsibility for this, Madame President. I thought it necessary."

"Has it produced results?"

Ponting felt the stirrings of anger: anger with the line of questioning, anger that he had been unable to crack the conspiracy. "No."

"Was torture used?"

Ponting sucked in his breath. "Torture?"

"If, for example, a congressional committee were to investigate this, would they be expected to find that torture had been used?"

Ponting felt his breath tight in his lungs. "We couldn't be effective without pressure being applied. I would be very surprised if our methods met any sensible definition of torture. We are certainly within Geneva Convention guidelines."

"General, we're not dealing with wild tribesmen in some foreign country. We're not in fact talking about enemy combatants at all. We're dealing with American citizens, young and vulnerable American citizens, and the rule of law, criminal civilian law, will apply. If you're worried about youth being radicalized by Kronos, I suggest you think a little more about the effects of these interrogations of yours, which are likely to radicalize youth just as quickly."

"I have a duty to uncover a conspiracy in which military personnel may be involved."

"These interrogations will cease, General. Is that understood? You are infringing upon constitutional rights, and that isn't going to happen on my watch."

General Ponting lowered his gaze. He was seething.

"Is that understood, General?"

"May I just say this, Madame President? Of course I will obey my Commander-in-Chief, but may I just say this: we are in a dangerous and critical time. You would have been justified in invoking emergency powers from the moment of the first Kronos attack, and my interrogation procedures would certainly have been valid under such powers. I still see them as valid by necessity. If we have further Kronos attacks, with dozens, perhaps hundreds of people killed, you will need to introduce emergency powers, and the military will need to use them, but it will be too late to prevent an alarming slide into a revolutionary situation. It will be too late to worry about radicalizing youth, because it will have already happened."

"I understand your argument, General, but it's specious. You also seem to be saying that you were justified in doing something because I failed to do something. That is insubordination, General."

"Yes Ma'am."

"Your methods haven't worked, they have done damage, and you will cease using them. Now can we move on?"

Lee Ponting felt himself on the precipice of real anger and he had to step back mentally, force control over himself. "Yes Ma'am, of course."

The President swung her gaze away. "I want to address the reality of our current situation. Director Corelli, perhaps you'd bring us up to speed on this. Must we expect that, in whatever jurisdiction these new attacks are planned, our MAIMKEY-based defenses will fail, in the same way they did before?"

Corelli hunched down defensively. "Ma'am, I wish I had a clear answer to give you. Without knowing how the unauthorized pipe was created, it's hard to say what its range might be. I think we should assume that if the Kronos agents are planning widespread attacks, then they have the means to bring them off."

Christine Diaz sat back a little, swung her gaze over the whole group. "Then how are we going to stop them?"

Nobody spoke.

"I suppose we *are* going to stop them?"

Ponting kept his head down. More silence.

"Your opinion, Mr. Olsen, is that they will try and strike on or before the mid-term election?"

Olsen raised his head and blinked a couple of times. "I'm afraid it's the obvious conclusion, Ma'am. But there is no hard evidence."

"I think we should make that assumption. Which gives us three days. General Ponting... you told me once that if all agency bees were stood down, your systems could destroy any bees left flying, MAIMKEY-authorized or not."

Ponting was still seething, but he'd got his breathing back close to normal. "It would take about twelve hours to implement that policy nationwide, Madame President, and of course I will take that for action whenever you request it, but you're surely not considering it as a first-up defensive strategy?"

"It might save lives."

"But then again, it might not. If you stand down bees nationwide, it leaves us vulnerable to all kinds of law-breaking stunts. Kronos doesn't need to kill us with bees, he can kill us with guns. It will also be perceived on all sides as weakness."

President Diaz switched her gaze to Cap Olsen.

Olsen had now forced himself into a state of weary attentiveness. "I would reluctantly have to agree with the General," he said. "Law enforcement, especially in extreme situations, has become dependent on bee deployment."

"Kronos and his supporters would see the standing-down of bees as a major victory," Ponting added. "Probably one of their key objectives. You could be faced with riots, pitched battles, property damage. And there's a strategic problem, Madame President. At what point do you stand down bees? Do you make an announcement? And when do you decide to deploy bees again? Kronos can simply wait us out, start his operation as soon as bees are back."

"So let me ask this," the President said. "Suppose we get an indication that the Kronos operation is under way; somebody reporting a bee attack, for example; how fast can we stand down bees at that point?"

General Ponting spread his hands. "That's entirely a matter for the agencies that run them."

"Susan?"

"My understanding is three to four hours."

"Director Olsen?"

"A complete shutdown, yes, that's about right. But most bees would be out of service in two."

Christine Diaz sighed. "So, General, you're saying it would take you another eight or nine hours to start destroying any bees that are left?"

"I'll review that, Ma'am. You must understand that at present our systems are set up only to destroy bee swarms that fail to respond with the MAIMKEY when challenged. For security reasons, many of the procedures involved are sealed up and automated and split into geographical areas. If we're going to change the protocol so that our systems destroy all bees flying, whether responding with MAIMKEY or not, then we will need to get authorizations at national and local levels and unscramble the systems step by step. If you request me to do so, I can do some of that unscrambling in advance, and I would hope that we could then switch protocols with only a couple of hours' notice."

"Please do that, General. It looks to me, from what you all have said, that we'll have to delay standing down bees until we have clear evidence that an attack has begun, which unfortunately means gambling with a few lives for the greater good. I'll be talking with your military colleagues about what kind of personnel, cyber and human, we can deploy to preserve public order, once bees are stood down, but whatever the answer, I have the feeling that if one-niners start to die horribly from bee attacks, they will not discriminate between good bees and bad bees. The demand to cease all bee operations will be irresistible."

"Even then, Madame President, I would respectfully submit that it would be the wrong thing to do. The loss of public order would be infinitely more serious than the bee attacks."

"I take note of your opinion, General, but in the event of such a disaster, other military experts will be advising on policy. Returning to more immediate options, do we warn those most at risk?"

Nobody spoke. Olsen looked as though he was falling asleep again. Lee Ponting cleared his throat. "Public figures, especially members of Congress, are already aware of what Kronos has threatened to do. The only thing you can tell them is: Don't be easy to find on election day. Stay away from home or office if possible. If there are doomers on your staff, don't tell them where you are... Bees have to find you to kill you."

Diaz looked pained. "Okay, General, I take the point. We'll get out something to that effect." She turned and nodded towards her Chief of Staff, and then returned her gaze to him. "Fortunately the vast majority of young people do not harbor homicidal intentions towards their bosses. Anything else?"

He waited a beat, but again nobody spoke. "There is one more thing I should mention, Madame President. A possible way we might identify and destroy Kronos's bees when they first appear."

John Corelli knew what was coming, but Susan Schwartz and the President looked sharply at him. Even Cap Olsen turned his head. "Go ahead, General," the President said.

"It will take a good deal of effort, and I'll need the cooperation of all agencies running bees, but my preliminary work suggests we can get things in place by Tuesday."

"Are you going to tell us what it involves?"

"It's a little technical, Ma'am, but in essence it means changing the Identification Friend or Foe challenge, or IFF challenge, which MAIMCOM sends out to all airborne bees. At the moment, as you know, we ask only that the swarm responds with the MAIMKEY. If the swarm doesn't have MAIMKEY, we destroy it. Unfortunately, Kronos has managed to supply his swarms with MAIMKEY, which means they can fly around with impunity. However, we think we can extend the required response to include the swarm ID. This ID is unique, and is set by the agency running the swarm. Director Schwartz's PMA, for example, in their various regional offices, assigns an ID to each swarm, and they use this in all their communications with the swarm."

"Susan?" the President said.

"Yes, of course, our swarms all have ID numbers for local use. What you're saying, General, is that you need to have access to these numbers?"

"Yes, and the numbers used by all the other agencies. I know it's a big ask. But Kronos won't be able to access valid ID numbers at short notice, and if we ask his swarms for their agency ID, they won't be able to respond. Or if they do respond, we will check the number supplied and find out whether it is a genuine ID or not. In other words, all swarms without a valid agency ID will be destroyed."

"Are you saying, General," the President said, "that if you can get this system running in time, you can destroy Kronos's swarms as soon as they first appear... before they kill anybody... before we stand down all bees?"

"That's what I'm saying, Madame President."

"Mightn't you have spoken up earlier?"

"It's a big undertaking, and I can't at this point guarantee success."

"Work on it, General. Get it running. You have my full support. I'm sure the PMA and the FBI will cooperate fully." She nodded at Susan Schwartz and Cap Olsen and they nodded back.

"Yes, Ma'am." General Ponting was still feeling bruised at his public mauling by the President, but he was relieved that she at least had the sense to understand and support his proposal. She ought, after all, to be grateful: he was handing her an electoral boost that she didn't really deserve. "I'm sure that, with your approval, the national agencies will release their data. The problem will be the local police departments, of which there are hundreds. It will take a huge effort to solicit and extract the data from all of these, and I don't have the staff. Perhaps you could make an appeal to the Association of Police Commissioners. Ideally they should be able to set up a mechanism for pooling the data and streaming it to MAIMCOM."

Christine Diaz looked across at her Chief of Staff. "We'll work on it, General. Meanwhile, everybody, please give this top priority and stay in touch."

When General Ponting left the White House a few minutes later, he felt slightly more comfortable with his performance overall. Whether or not he was giving an inadequate president the benefit of an operational coup, he had done his duty as a soldier and a patriot. There was no way he could sit back and let Kronos kill the elected representatives of the people. But he had managed to draw the President into the most difficult part of the operation, which could be useful if some kind of snafu developed.

Plus he had kept BEEKEEP out of the picture, for which his colleagues would certainly thank him.

He took a crisp salute from his driver and climbed into the back of the car.

CHAPTER 45

W hen Doug had got his scalp wound dressed, back at the familiar hospital, and taken some enforced rest, it was late afternoon. There was no message, his telcom genie told him, from Cap Olsen. Doug didn't like the feel of that. Surely if the FBI had caught up with Zeb, he would have been told. And surely if the FBI hadn't caught up with Zeb, Cap would understand that urgent work had to be done on strategic planning.

He asked his genie to connect him with Cap Olsen, but his genie reported that Director Olsen was not taking calls.

He got up off the hospital bed and asked for a news update, walking the room and assessing the pain in his head as the stories unfolded. There was nothing about the attack on the apartment, nothing about Enquist's death, nothing about Zeb.

He began to feel frustrated and isolated, reminding him of his early days undercover. He had no status, no authority. He had the face of a youngster, and no way of being taken seriously outside the very small circle of Cap's team. And now that he really needed to speak with Cap, now that he finally had something important to say, it seemed he couldn't do so.

He waved the screen into silence and sat down on the bed, suddenly overcome by memories of the morning. Yinghua at risk. The apartment attacked. Roger Enquist dead. And his grandson, the boy he had known, albeit poorly, inadequately, since birth… this boy had tried, had hoped, had risked all, to kill him.

Doug wasn't sure how he could confront and absorb something as corrupt and destabilizing as this. Jason had betrayed him, but he thought he could understand Jason, his inadequacies, the pressures on him. And Jason had paid the price. Jason was dead. Whereas Zeb was still out there, apparently, making his plans, arranging for the deaths of hundreds of innocent people.

One thing, at least, was clear: he should set aside any guilt he still felt over betraying the youthful cause. Yinghua was right: Kronos, Zeb, was not going to advance that cause, he was going to destroy it. Being his grandson didn't change anything. He had to be stopped.

He asked for the attending physician and got a male nurse. He thought there might be some restraint placed on his departure, at least until Olsen had made an assessment; but apparently not. Olsen's team, who had moved in to analyze and sanitize the apartment attack, and who had sent him here for treatment, had placed no restrictions on his movement. He was free to go.

He dressed and asked his genie for Yinghua, now safely lodged at a new address. She was off-line and had left no instructions, his genie reported. He was disconcerted at that, but he told himself she had simply got fed up with students and faculty asking questions she couldn't, for the moment, answer. He put it to the back of his mind and took a taxi to FBI Headquarters. The desk clerk studied the ID generated by his entry into the building and looked at him doubtfully when he said whom he wanted to see, but she relayed his request.

"Director Olsen is not at his desk, Mr. Edie. He says he will see you tomorrow morning."

Beneath his smoldering anger, Doug felt a trace of real alarm: was Cap losing it? He remembered Cap's outburst as he was leaving the apartment, just before the attack. Had the failure with Zeb, the loss of Enquist, pushed him right over the edge?

He chose his words carefully, aware more than ever of his young, suspicion-generating face. "Could you please tell Director Olsen that I have new and important information, and that it is essential that I see him now, wherever he is."

The woman considered this and then turned away and spoke quietly. She turned back.

"Please wait, Mr. Edie."

He paced in front of the big windows, not in the mood to sit down. After about ten minutes, the desk clerk beckoned.

"You may go up. Director Olsen is now at his desk. Your floater will authorize and guide."

He nodded and followed the floater aboard the elevator. The door of Cap Olsen's office was open. Cap was sitting at his desk. His expression was sour, accusing, but also, Doug thought, haunted: as though he suspected that assassins were lurking in the shadows behind him. He said nothing.

Doug swung the door to behind him, advanced into the room, gave Cap another hard look. "What's going on?" he said.

Cap remained silent but the depth of weariness behind his gaze, which drifted momentarily away and down, gave Doug pause. Instead of launching into strictures and complaints, Doug slowly lowered himself into the soft chair in front of the desk. "First," he said, "I want to say how sorry I am about Roger."

Cap's eyes narrowed slightly in pain and he gave a tiny nod.

"Especially when my own... grandson... was involved." He paused a second and looked up. "I did my best, Cap. I tried to delay him. I wanted... passionately... to bring him down. I still do."

Olsen continued to say nothing.

"I suppose you believe that?"

Olsen breathed in, cleared his throat. "I have no choice but to believe that. If I didn't believe that you wouldn't be here in this room."

"You didn't get him. Obviously."

"No. We didn't get him."

"He...?"

"He got away."

"But... he dumped the car?"

"Yes."

"I've been trying to reconstruct that. How he got to the car before the bees got him. I saw him saying something just before I challenged him. He was telling his car to come for him, is that right? What I heard was his car pulling up beside him. He had only to jump in."

Cap nodded slowly. "That's what the bee report said."

"So... you've no ideas?"

"We think he got aboard the metro. We allowed for that, but of course there's no surveillance in the metro. I mean, there's *really* no surveillance in the metro. And bees operate under these constitutional restraints. That's because we live in a free society." Cap's voice was bitter.

"No leads?"

"No."

"Cap… once again, you may not believe this, but… I want to get this psychopath maybe even more than you do. He's corrupting everything I want my family name to represent."

"Okay." Cap sounded neutral.

"You don't think I'm serious?"

"I didn't say that."

"What, then?"

"You don't like being the grandfather of Kronos. I don't like being the guy who put the grandfather of Kronos on the payroll."

Doug thought about that. "Does anyone need to know?"

"It'll get out. Our friends in the Rose Mickelburger Faction know about it. One day everybody will know about it. And of course I had to tell the President."

"The President?"

"You'd like me to leave her out of this?"

"You had a meeting with her?"

"Me and a couple of others. I got back about an hour ago."

"And you told her, everybody, who I am?"

"I figured I didn't have much choice. Who you are goes to the credibility of your intelligence."

Doug frowned, trying to interpret Cap's expression. "And how did she react?"

"I think she'd rather I'd picked someone a little more, shall we say, neutral. Someone not related by blood to the guy we're after."

"Cap, for God's sake, I didn't know! It wasn't a factor!"

"Really? And there I was thinking that genes went from father to son to grandson."

"If you're saying I'm a psychopath like Zeb, that is completely ridiculous."

Cap raised his eyes and looked at Doug but said nothing.

"Cap, your resentment of me goes deeper than just bad family. It's been there from the beginning. Had we better talk about it? Because there is still some very important work to be done and I need you with me."

"You need me with you. *You need me with you.* That just about says it, doesn't it? You assume that you're the big gun and I've got to run to keep up."

Doug stared at Cap Olsen, startled.

Cap sank back wearily, "Okay, I'm an idiot. I'm also exhausted."

"Is that all it is? You think I'm a smartass and arrogant with no respect for your authority?"

"That's a pretty good summary, and maybe that's the way it started out, but no... no, that isn't all it is."

Doug waited. Cap leaned forward, his elbows resting on his desk, his hands covering the top of his head, his expression registering the inner conflict.

"It's since you've gotten young," Cap burst out suddenly. He stood up and walked half way round his desk and flung his arms out in frustration. "It's like I'm dealing with a damn kid! Who is, yes, a smartass and arrogant with no respect for my authority. And I can't stand it! It bugs the hell out of me!"

"Cap, for God's sake, you know who I am."

"Yeah, I know who you are, but I look at you, and I see what you've become. Young!"

"You're jealous? You want the same?"

"Yes! No! Who knows? I want the power and energy of youth. Who wouldn't? But do I want people like me looking at me in the way that I'm looking at you? With... with..."

"Prejudice?"

"Yes! With prejudice. Because we no longer trust the young. Maybe we never did. Do I want that? Do I want to be in that situation? Maybe not. Probably not. Which ruins everything. Because I believed that rejuvenation was going to... God knows. Save me from ultimate failure."

"It should get better when lots of people are rejuvenated."

"Really? You know what I think?" Cap moved a little further around his desk, pointed a finger at Doug. "I think it will get worse. Because then we'll have three classes of people, right? We'll have the young and the old and the rejuvenants, if we can call them that. And the young will hate the old and the old will hate the young, and *everybody*, young and old, will hate the rejuvenants."

Doug sighed, thinking for a moment of his grand hopes, his obsessive struggle with rejuvenation technology. Was it all a pipe dream?

"At least you know what I've been going through these last few weeks," he said at last.

Cap turned, went slowly back around his desk, looked at him with a trace of sympathy. "Been tough, huh?"

"I've been a non-person. With the young, I'm accepted but a fraud. With you guys, I'm an object of suspicion."

Cap sat down in the desk chair, leaned forward across the desk, watching Doug.

Doug said, "I depend on you for my identity, my purpose, my survival. I have no future. It's been driving me nuts. That's why I got in touch with Yinghua, even though she didn't know who I was. I needed a sympathetic face, someone I could trust."

Cap looked at him for a long moment, as though this idea, Doug as helpless dependent, was filtering around in different areas of his brain.

"You want something?" he said at last. "Coffee? Stronger?"

"Coffee," Doug said. "Thanks."

Cap dragged himself to his feet and went to the machine and came back with two cups. He pushed one across the desk to Doug.

"I've got a lot of faults, Doug," he said, "and I guess one of them is that I'm kind of hard on people. I expect a lot. I expect a lot from myself, tell the truth. But the fact is, when I brought you into this thing, I made a good call. Maybe it didn't work out the way I thought, and maybe it's not nice for both of us that your grandson is the big perp, Kronos himself… But it was a good call. Okay, the pressures were severe, they always are when you're undercover, and you flipped, you went native for a while. Not only did you look like one of them, but as far as we knew, you *were* one of them. That wasn't easy to take. Was I going to tell the President I'd lost you?"

"I wasn't one of them, Cap. I was never one of them. But they were the ones treating me decently, and I began to hate what I was doing to them. Even though they were planning bad things. Anyway, I see how it looks. That and Kronos being my grandson. I apologize for all of it. But I'm back on track and I want very badly to stop this grandson of mine before he reduces us to something like civil war. We've got to learn from this, Cap, we've got to find a way to give the young more of a voice, but for now we're on the same side. And I'll try not to be an arrogant smartass."

"Could you also try not to be a *young* arrogant smartass? No, okay. But if you're going to offer opinions, at least make sure you're right. Civil war I can live with, but what I really don't want is to lose my job."

Cap sipped his coffee and looked pugnacious, but some of the anger and frustration had gone from his face. Doug sensed they had reached a more comfortable place.

"So, this meeting," he said. "Despite my going native and having Kronos's genes in my blood, did the President accept my thesis, that a big terrorist operation is imminent?"

"Yeah, that's pretty much a done deal. But as I say, you'd better be right, for my sake."

"And what's she going to do?"

"She's not going to stand down bees until seniors start dying. And General Ponting thinks he can prevent that from happening."

"How?"

"I hope I've got this right. When MAIMCOM systems send out an IFF, they ask for MAIMKEY, right?"

"Yes."

"But Kronos's swarms have somehow got MAIMKEY, so the General is going to ask them for a swarm ID as well."

"Shit."

"What?"

"It won't work."

"Why not?"

"Kronos's swarms have got perfectly valid IDs."

"How come?"

"Because they've been hijacked from the PMA."

"So you keep saying. But the opinion of all those present, including John Corelli of NSA, is that officially licensed swarms cannot possibly kill people."

"Cap, at the risk of sounding arrogant, that's bullshit. Look, I went through this with Roger, and I think he got the point. It's equally impossible for rogue swarms to acquire MAIMKEY. But of the two impossibles, the evidence favors PMA bees killing people. I mean, a lot."

"So the General, whom I admit is a self-righteous prick, is wrong."

"Probably. At any rate, he's made the wrong decision. Cap, you've got to get me someone who can replace Roger. FBI is fine, as long as he's technically competent, or else PMA, or better both. They've got to investigate the illegal children thing, and they've got to do it in a clandestine way, and they've got to start today. This is really really important."

Cap gave a theatrical sigh. "Okay."

"And there's something else. This is really why I came to see you. I remembered meeting a friend of Zeb's, a couple of years ago, who was at NSA. He could be the key to this whole thing. I don't remember his name, but I think I would recognize him. You need to mobilize someone at NSA so that we can identify him and find out what he was working on."

Cap gave another sigh. He said plaintively, "We were doing so well there for a while."

CHAPTER 46

C ap Olsen had decreed that, with Kronos's identity known, and the Mickelburgers on the run, FBI protection personnel were not required to secure the new safe house. Doug suspected that a swarm of FBI bees might not be too far away, but bees would not record his movements. He could leave the safe house without consequences. He ordered a robot cab and got out a block away from the *Shanghai Quest*. It was just after eight-thirty at night. He went into a couple of stores and mingled with shoppers. He had no sense of anyone paying him any attention. After a few minutes, he walked around the corner and approached the restaurant.

Yinghua had sent him a message to come and meet her Chinese friends, and his mind had been busy with many doubts and concerns: her safety, the exact nature of her links with these people, what place these people had in the very large and widely dispersed firmament of Chinese bureaucratic power; his own options, the likely trade-offs, his personal loyalties.

China was not an enemy of the United States in any recognized military sense. Both countries were signatories to a range of international treaties, including the population and refugee treaties. He wasn't selling out his country by talking to Chinese apparatchiks. But China was the world's dominant economy, and was assumed to have a military advantage as well. The US retained technological superiority in a few key areas, like robotics, but that was slipping and was not sufficient, most observers believed, to tip the balance; which created a certain paranoia in military circles. He wasn't selling out his country by talking, but he was setting himself up to be misunderstood; a further attack on his embattled status.

As he went through the door of the *Shanghai Quest,* he felt his Doug Edie identity embarking on yet another duplicitous excursion, with yet more conflicts of loyalty to be endured. Lou Lam appeared after a moment, smiling, recognizing him, and led him towards the back. As Doug caught sight of Yinghua, apparently calm, several Chinese at her table, he knew that one thing was certain in his strange and uncertain life: he would trust Yinghua, put his faith in her, beyond country, beyond ideology.

The partitioned area of the restaurant in which Yinghua was sitting seemed busy, with several occupied tables near hers. As he approached, an expectant hush spread amongst these tables. Doug noticed that the faces turning towards him with interest were all Chinese. The two Chinese sitting with Yinghua stood up, smiling, bowed and shook hands, and waved him graciously to a seat. They were, Doug judged, a little older than Yinghua but young enough for anti-ageing interventions to preserve some elements of youth. The man had a round face and small, twinkling eyes, and very white teeth; the woman was plain, with flat cheekbones and a strong nose which made her look hard-willed; but her smile seemed genuine.

Yinghua introduced the man as Lin Xiaobao, and the woman as Jiang Sing. Doug mentioned his own name, and they sat down.

"Mr. Doug Edie," Lin said, "we are very pleased, very pleased." He used his hands to suggest he was speaking for the whole community of Chinese, and his voice carried an unctuous authority. "Some food? Of course. Please, let me suggest… let me… excite your palate, uh?" He waved Lou over and gave instructions in Cantonese. "Lou has very nice restaurant, you agree?"

"I do."

"You were here before at Mr. Lou Lam?"

"I was here…" Doug gave Yinghua a quick glance. "…once before."

"Mr. Doug Edie, you very young man. You very good healthy young man." Lin was smiling broadly, showing the white teeth.

Doug inclined his head in acknowledgment. "Thank you."

"Yinghua say you work for United States government." Lin's eyes were suddenly sharp.

"I'm a student," Doug said. "But my loyalty is to the United States government."

"You work for FBI perhaps?"

"I have a good connection with the FBI."

"Mr. Doug Edie, we very interested to know the name of this FBI person."

Doug hesitated. "I have a direct link with the office of the Director of National Security."

"Ah so, ah so," Lin said, nodding.

His companion, Jiang, said quietly, "Mr. Cap Olsen."

"Ah so, Mr. Cap Olsen. Very good connection. You put first loyalty to this person? To United States government?"

"If you mean, am I simply an intermediary between young people, young organizations, and this person then no: I'm not a middleman; I am entirely loyal to the United States government."

"Ah so. Very good. We are very good friends of United States and United States government, Mr. Doug Edie. We want to make sure United States government has necessary information for defeat of terrorists. You share this view, I think?"

Doug nodded. "I do."

"Very good. And now you must relax and try one of these dishes." Lou's waiter was adding several plates to those on the warmer. "Have some words with your lovely friend Yinghua."

Chinese tea and a sparkling white wine were poured. Lin settled back and waved his hands like a director of a theatrical production. Doug glanced at Yinghua: her expression was hard to read, except for a faint, apologetic downturn of the corners of her mouth. He helped himself to a couple of the snacks on offer, dipping them in the sauce provided. Lin was clearly not in a hurry. He seemed settled in for the evening. It occurred to Doug that his relationship with Yinghua was one of the things under scrutiny: these people had leverage over Yinghua through her Chinese relatives; the only leverage they had over him was through Yinghua herself. Should he acknowledge their closeness? Or play it down? Yinghua seemed prepared to acknowledge it: at one point she leaned over and put her hand on his and asked if he was okay. He took that to refer to the gash on his head, and he nodded and said that the hospital was satisfied and had released him a few hours ago.

After a quarter of an hour of idle chat about food and Chinese culture and Washington restaurants, Lin stood up and beckoned authoritatively at somebody at an adjoining table, nodding quickly and with a hint of impatience when that failed to produce an immediate response, indicating the table in front of him with a precise wave of his hand. A young woman with an eager, dedicated look appeared, and Jiang stood up and retreated to another table. Lin gave his big smile and introduced the newcomer as Wang Na and waved at her to sit down. He then sat down himself.

Doug turned to look again at the several tables of Chinese in the partitioned space, and then glanced quickly at Yinghua. She gave a faint nod: yes, these people were all a part of Lin's team. The density of the Chinese presence in Washington was sometimes a matter of half-amused, half-worried, comment in the capital: like it or not, the Chinese were everywhere. It was the first time Doug had felt it so vividly and personally.

"Miss Wang Na very smart girl," Lin said expansively. "Speak, Miss Wang Na."

The girl focused intense green eyes on Doug. "Mr. Lin wish to know if Mr. Doug Edie has information about the bees used by terrorists."

"What kind of information?"

"First, if bees public bees or special private bees."

Doug hesitated for a moment. He looked across the table at Lin. He was aware that he had asked nothing about Lin's official status, which Chinese agencies he might be involved with. He assumed he would be denied this information, or Yinghua would know and tell him later. Was it worth raising any caveats about information he himself could supply? He sensed, from his knowledge of Yinghua, that making demands, implying distrust, would be taken negatively. This wasn't a bargaining session. He was a petitioner, receiving hospitality and help. All the same, he was taking a huge gamble, a huge risk. He stared at Yinghua for a moment and then drew in his breath.

"There is some disagreement about this. My personal opinion is that public bees were used. Specifically, PMA bees."

Wang Na nodded. "Why you think this please?"

"It seems that a high level employee of the PMA here in Washington was working for Kronos, giving him the codes he needed to hijack their bees. She has subsequently died, probably murdered. And there are indications that other PMA offices have been penetrated by activists."

"But your colleagues, doesn't believe this?" Lin said. "Doesn't believe in threat from public bees?"

"No."

"Believes in special bees, private bees?" Wang said.

"Yes."

This provoked a minor upheaval, an outburst of chatter, between Lin and Wang and at the other tables. Lin stood up and tapped his hands together, as though applauding this industrious expression of interest. He moved over to one of the tables and had a word with Jiang Sing, the hard-willed woman from earlier, and then returned.

"And now, Mr. Doug Edie," Lin said, sitting down again. "I want you to try something else from Mr. Lou. Please have some more wine." He signaled to the waiters, who moved forward attentively.

Another interlude of eating and conversation followed, this one more protracted than the last. Doug found himself getting drowsy. He was fascinated to be in the middle of Yinghua's world, but it had been a very long day, and his concentration was faltering. He went to the washroom and splashed cold water on his face. He drank tea instead of wine.

The retinue of Chinese at the neighboring tables began to depart, bowing and smiling at him as they went. At last only Lin Xiaobao and his original companion, Jiang Sing, remained.

"I want to help you, Mr. Doug Edie," Lin said, the big smile embracing Yinghua as well, "but we have a small problem. We have to disappear the Chinese connection."

"What Chinese connection?" Doug said, glancing at the empty tables.

Lin laughed. "Yinghua right, you obviously smart man. Who were all those Japanese tourists? Ha ha ha. Now we just Americans eating Chinese. But seriously, I have to ask you to think about this. The information I need to give you is very top secret. You could start revolution with this information. And you could blame Chinese for revolution. You see, Mr. Doug Edie, we like to stay very good friends with United States government. If United States government know we have such information, they'll say, how did the Chinese get such top secret information? How come Chinese have information we don't have? What have Chinese been doing here in our country, poking about in our secrets? You understand this problem I'm sure."

"You want me to deny sources?"

"I want you to do more than that. I want you to *create* sources. I want you to find out this information for yourself. You or your FBI investigators. I want you to make clever deductions and go to the right people for answers. You are already half way there, we think, with your ideas of public service bees. I will give you some more ideas. I and my colleague Jiang will try and show you the shape of what you're looking for. We will give you a couple of names to whom you may address your enquiries. We think that a man as clever as you will fill in the gaps, and it will seem that you have pieced it together for yourself. And ah presto, we have disappeared the Chinese connection!"

Doug looked at the smiling Lin and his serious companion. "If Kronos chooses to target the mid-term election, I only have two days."

"Then you must work quickly, Mr. Doug Edie, and so will we. I will give you the military acronym for this very top secret information, but we would ask you not to use it unless you are running out of time. Of course it is quite possible that this program has no connection with your Kronos, we are not all in agreement about this, but you should look at it. It is buried deep amongst Pentagon officials of the last administration. It is called BEEKEEP."

CHAPTER 47

Zeb came awake with a start. He forced himself up on an elbow, generating a stab of pain in his head, and half-opened his eyes. The contours of a big unfamiliar room came into focus. Daylight was illuminating strange shapes crouched beneath protective sheets; with textured wallpapers, carved cornices, an embossed opening into a big bay window whispering style and wealth.

And bees. Was that what had woken him? The distant rush of air as a bee swarm moved in the room. For a second his flesh crawled and he moved a hand towards his left, towards the gun he remembered leaving within reach, and his eyes roamed the room, moved up to the ceiling. A jolt like electricity went through him and he fell back on the bed. Bees had formed big black letters directly above him:

HAIL, LORD KRONOS

Zeb closed his eyes and lay for a few minutes, letting his heart rate subside. The pain in his head was now a dull steady ache. Jesus Christ, he thought, I really am going to murder that guy. The day would come when Merko had nothing further to contribute, and then…

Yes, well, and then… Nice thought. In the meantime, unfortunately, Merko had a great deal to contribute. Zeb opened his eyes again. The insistent daylight, the strange room, seemed to be reminding him of just what a new world this was. He remembered the fierce excitement he had felt yesterday, so nearly nailing the Doug Edie monster, escaping the cops and the bees, launching himself at last into the revolutionary lifestyle, the void, the challenge, that had been waiting there for him for so long. Now it was all there in front of him, ready to be done: the surgical attack on the decadent rulers, the rallying of the young, the road to power.

He was already world-famous: now he would be the romantic hero, the new Che Guevara. Soon they'd be casting the movie. And when Doug Edie and Cap Olsen decided to go public, release his name, his real identity would be known. That would shake up a few people. Zeb Packer, that nice publicist, is in reality... Kronos! They'd wet themselves, those dumb clients of his, knowing who they'd been dealing with...

A faint, wistful regret percolated his mood, escalated towards a sense of desolation, even fear. He switched his attention to the pain in his head, the dryness in his mouth. What the hell had he drunk last night? There had been a lot of beer, he remembered, and Kate, or Pete, had been pouring chasers of bourbon. Merko, the sneaky bastard, had been tripping on his own weird stuff, which was probably why he was chirpy enough this morning to pull the Lord Kronos stunt. A mad and wild celebration of the fact that they were all now...

Again a dark shadow loomed, sending a chill over his thoughts.

Fugitives. They were all now fugitives. Heroic revolutionaries, of course, and even if they were caught, fame would give their captors a huge problem. But for the moment they would be living in metaphorical caves, hand to mouth. Even a house like this... a mansion in its own grounds not far from the potent symbols of Valley Forge, Pennsylvania... rented anonymously by Kate's classier supporters... protected against bees... even a house like this would be on databases somewhere as a target for investigation. Wherever bees couldn't gain access would be suspect. The only places to hide would be disguised and remote, an old mine, a hidden cellar.

His brain conjured up images of Che Guevara dying in the jungles of Bolivia, Osama Bin Laden shot like a dog in that miserable compound in Pakistan...

Zeb threw aside the sheet covering him and swung his feet down to the floor. A lance of pain hit him behind the eyes, but he ignored it and stood up. There were no rugs and the wood-block floor felt cold beneath his feet. He walked across to the big bay window and stared out. He was on the second floor and what he could see, beyond some grass and some statuary, were trees: tall, bare, gaunt, surrounding the house like a piece of the Valley Forge Historical Park itself.

He turned away and pulled irritably at the dust sheet on a piece of furniture. It was a multiple vanity unit, several mirrors, curving marble surfaces, gilded framing. He caught a glimpse of himself in the mirrors, a naked body, strong and shapely. He stopped and stared for a moment. The image settled him. He was there, real and potent, a person favored by nature. He had to survive.

He found his underpants and jeans on the floor beside the bed and pulled them on and went prowling out into the corridor. There were doors to other rooms and then a hallway with a big staircase curving downwards.

"Merko!" he shouted when he reached the bottom of the stairs. The house was silent.

He walked across the checkerboard marble and through an arch into a big living area. Glasses and beer cans still decorated a couple of the low white humps rising from the bare floor. Big stuffed chairs showed their shapes, the dust sheets pulled tight around their contours. Zeb continued through to the kitchen at the back, which had a green slate floor and plenty of walk-room around the central island. Big glass doors gave on to the back porch. Zeb headed towards the side of the house butting on to the garage. Merko had put his truck away in person last night, this morning he was fooling with bees, so maybe he was here with his truck.

Zeb opened a door and went up a steep flight of stairs and through another door. He was in a big room with skylights in the cantilevered roof and windows on two sides. A studio. The floor, in ribbed grey acrylic, was bare except for a pair of worn settees, some plastic chairs, a couple of easels, and a long wooden bench running along the wall under the windows. And two bee-hives.

And Merko.

Merko had on his chameleon jacket and glasses and was probably still tripping on chemicals, because he looked at Zeb with his dumb-assed, why-are-you-bothering-me? look. He was sitting at the bench and had assembled some comms and computing equipment around him and was taped up for brainwave control.

Zeb watched him for a moment, half-relieved that he was alert and functioning: in the truck yesterday he'd seemed pretty spaced out, which was maybe not too surprising in view of the nationwide manhunt and reports of roadblocks around Washington; maybe now he'd settled down.

"Staking out some territory, uh, Merk?" Zeb waved at the room.

Merko shrugged, his attention back with the images on his glasses. "Maybe you could get my snakes over here."

"Oh yeah, oh sure." Zeb stared at Merko to see if he was serious. "We'll just take a ride into Washington and pick them up some time."

"Maybe they're dead. You didn't check them, did you?"

"Yesterday? You do remember what happened yesterday, Merk?"

"You said you'd look after them."

"Is this why you decided to scare the shit out of me this morning?"

Merko turned to look at him, his mouth half-open. "I wanted you to feel good when you woke up." He seemed genuinely surprised at Zeb's irritation. Red question marks floated up his jacket like balloons.

Zeb closed his eyes and breathed deeply. "Where are they now?" he said. "the bees?"

Merko nodded at the hives. "Their mission was to wait until you got out of bed."

Zeb wandered over and stared at the iridescent domes. "You sure it's safe to run these things around the house? We're not exactly in the wilds of Michigan."

"It's okay. I did some tests. This place is sealed up tight. Not just against bees... everything. Wireless telcom goes in and out via dedicated relay servers. I had to open some new channels for satellite uplinks. As for MAIMCOM sensors, they'll get nothing."

"What happens when somebody decides to investigate?"

"Kate says we'll get a warning."

"That's handy." Just how far, he wondered, was Kate's self-confidence justified?

He turned back to the hives. Merko, at least, he trusted. "You know what would make me real happy? Get these things to construct a kind of halo or crown a couple of inches above my head, with 'Kronos' written around it. Can you do that?"

"For how long?"

"Until I tell them to quit."

Merko began nodding his head in the familiar way, but his eyes were opaque: Zeb couldn't tell whether he was working on the problem, or off on some unrelated mental odyssey.

"Okay, think about it," Zeb said. "Meanwhile, reassure me. You're getting hooked up with our teams across the country and you're making enough sense for them to understand that this is the hub, this is the control center. Briefings go out from here. Reports come in to here. We are Kronos, the lord and master of Operation Platinum Sting. Is that the picture, Merk?"

Merko shrugged.

"You've got it safe, haven't you, Merk? The Key of Power?" It was one of Zeb's biggest nightmares: that something happened to Merko, or that he did something careless and couldn't recover the key that he himself had created.

"Of course." Gunfighters blasting away in all directions appeared on Merko's jacket.

"Okay. Let's all get together in an hour or so and review things."

Merko nodded.

Zeb turned and started for the door of the studio.

"Wait," Marko said.

Zeb turned back. Merko was staring into the distance.

"What?" Zeb said.

"*Wait*," Merko said irritably.

Zeb stood still, wondering what kind of bombshell Merko might be about to deliver. Then he heard a faint hiss and tiny shadows danced for an instant on the walls opposite the windows. Merko was looking at him now, pleased with himself. Zeb reached up above his head and felt around: yes, the very soft tickle of bees.

"How the hell did you do that?"

Merko smirked. "They don't really like it, though."

"What?"

"It's undignified. Below their capabilities."

"Merko, these things are just..." Zeb cut himself off and walked out the door.

Back upstairs, advancing along the corridors of the second floor, he started opening doors, checking rooms. He found Kate on his third try. She was asleep on a big brass bed, black hair splayed out on the pillow. The room, like his own, was bare of rugs and drapes, reduced to bland impersonality by the waves of white enveloping the furniture.

He sat down at the foot of the bed. Kate's body, like the furniture, was draped by a sheet. He found an ankle under the sheet and shook it. Kate retracted her ankle sharply and sat up, wide-eyed with alarm. Seeing him at the foot of her bed didn't seem to relieve her distress. She pulled the sheet back up to her neck and stared at him.

"What the hell have you done to your hair?" she said.

"Like it?" Zeb said.

"Oh my God. It's bees."

"Just Merko, paying his respects."

"And you encouraged him, no doubt. My God, Kronos, you've finally gone over the edge, haven't you? Into rampant egomania."

"I like to think of it as a status check."

Kate slid back down the bed and put her fingertips to her forehead. "Would you please go away until I get the pieces of my head back together?"

Zeb stood up. "I'll do better than that. I'll get you a cup of coffee."

"Knock, next time you want an audience."

Zeb pointed at his head. "Kronos doesn't knock, sweetheart."

He went out of the door and down the stairs to the kitchen. The feel of Kate's ankle in his hand, the sight of the sheet slipping down to the top of her breasts, had stirred in his mind a question: would sex help to control her, subdue her? His instincts told him no. He'd slept with her a couple of times in the old days, and he knew that when it came to sex, Kate was the user, and her partners were the ones who were subdued.

He grasped the mugs of coffee in one hand and went back up to Kate's bedroom. She was lying as before, under the sheet, eyes closed. She opened them and blinked a couple of times when he sat down on the bed. She reached out for the coffee. He gave her the mug and helped reposition the pillows behind her back. The sheet fell down to her waist and this time she didn't hurry putting it back. Zeb didn't react. He sat and waited while she took a few sips of coffee.

"Zeb Packer is Kronos. Jesus, that's hard to get used to. You always were an uppity bastard, but I didn't have you figured for a grandfather killer. Make that a failed grandfather killer."

"I didn't have you figured for a killer period. Last time I saw you, you were piddling around with the M3R, going nowhere. What happened?"

Kate dropped her eyes. "Oh, you know... saw the light... got religion... long story, Zeb." She raised her eyes again, gave him a hard look. "Anyway, I caught up. Decided to play hardball."

"You did okay."

"I think I did more than okay."

"I think you're probably right. Which is why I'm pleased to have you on my team."

"Oh yeah? What team is that?"

"Maybe you should think of Kronos as a brand-name. You've joined my brand. Bought the franchise."

"Or maybe what I've done, Zeb, is I've *acquired* your brand. You were a bit lost out there. And right now you're feeling safe and comfortable in *my* little sanctuary, serviced by *my* people. Where would you be if I turned you out?"

"Where I'd be, sweetie, me and Merko, and maybe Pete Johnson as well, is in my *own* sanctuary, sending out messages to your people that they'd better join up with Kronos quick, or there'll be no Platinum Sting and no revolution. And you would probably be dead."

Kate looked at him, lips pursed. Zeb could see that his threat had briefly dented her confidence. "Going to set those Kronos bees on me, are you, Mr. Nice Guy?"

"Whatever."

"You weren't so good at dealing with grandfather Doug Edie, the way you told it."

"Doug Edie had the benefit of FBI protection. Whereas my brother Jason, let's say, didn't have those advantages."

"Your brother Jason? That guy with a small boy who used to come by the Connacher place now and then?"

Zeb nodded.

"You killed him? You killed your brother?"

"Jason was the guy who let you know about Doug Edie. He figured out his grandfather had rejuvenated himself, and worked out his identity. I reckoned he was a liability."

Kate was staring at him. Zeb guessed she was trying to hide her shock, cloak it in tough-guy indifference. "No wonder you haven't got much of a team. You've killed them all off."

"You're the one who wants to kill off lots and lots of people."

"That's the old. What else can you do with the old?"

"You can sideline them. Deprive them of wealth and power. Let them choose death if they want it. The important thing is to shift power back towards youth."

"They won't go for it! They'll just trample us into the ground!"

"Not if we play this right. We've got to radicalize and unite young people. We'll be too big a force to ignore. You think I enjoy killing? Maybe I do, in the sense that a hunter enjoys hunting. The point is, I understand it, I know what it does. Every old person you kill, you generate a dozen implacable enemies. That's no good. You want to inspire fear, but not universal revulsion. You want to choose bad people to kill, not good people. People stained by power, not innocent people. That's the beauty of bees, as against the bomb. You choose the ones who matter, and you terrify them. It's selective. The mass of old people don't feel threatened. With any luck we'll get what we want without the kind of civil war you seem to believe in."

"You think the one-niners are going to hand over the government, the military, the whole package, without trying to destroy us first?"

"Yes. Slowly, piece by piece, but yes."

"Listen, wise guy," Kate said, throwing up her free hand in frustration, "if the mass of old people don't feel threatened, your phrase, why should they support actions to dismantle their privileged world?"

"Because they know it's right. They know the system is unfair. And they *will* feel threatened. I was guilty of hyperbole. If their leaders and legislators are dying, of course they will feel threatened. Not by violence, maybe, but by the loss of order and stability. They'll prefer to compromise and give us our rights."

Kate gave a snort of derision. "Jesus, Kronos, first you tell me you killed your brother, now you're talking about a moral imperative. That's really kind of rich."

Zeb kept his body still, held her gaze. "You called me Kronos. Can I assume you've come round? Taken the pledge?"

"What you can assume is that I've taken a pledge to get you out of my fucking room while I get some clothes on."

Zeb stood up and took Kate's mug and backed away from the bed. "I never refuse a polite request."

"Good." Kate threw her sheet aside and stood up. "And keep those bees out of my hair." She walked around the bed.

Kate's naked figure was as good as Zeb remembered, but he looked only at her face. "Which kind of hair in particular?"

"All of it!" Kate snapped, heading for the bathroom.

"Hey listen," Zeb said.

Kate slowed, turned reluctantly.

"We've got immediate planning issues. Maybe we should bring forward Platinum Sting."

"What?" Kate faced him fully, reached up and ran a hand through her tangled hair, as though to make sure it was all there.

"Like we've been saying, Doug Edie is still out there."

"What the hell can he do?"

"I don't know. Depends what he's figured out."

"We can't go tonight."

"Why not?"

"You know why not. A lot of the designated targets are politicians. They'll be all over their respective states campaigning. And there are logistics issues. Getting equipment in place."

"All the same, we should talk about it. Merko's going to give us a status briefing in about half an hour."

"I'll be there."

"Bees, attack the lady."

Kate froze and stared at a point above his head, a moment of horror caught in the expression of her eyes; then she shook her head in fury, turned and continued towards the bathroom door.

Zeb laughed.

"Bastard!" she screamed as she disappeared from sight.

CHAPTER 48

D oug slept fitfully and got up late, but after a shower and breakfast he was relieved to find that the pain from the bullet wound on top of his skull had eased, and his memory of the previous evening at the *Shanghai Quest*, hazy at first, had begun to clarify. Yinghua's Chinese friends, whose sources within the U.S. government seemed alarmingly good, had made an astonishing assertion: that the Pentagon under the last president had authorized a Trojan horse in all bee firmware, which allowed a military takeover of bees in an emergency, and which had been given the codename BEEKEEP.

It was intriguing, and opened up lots of possibilities; it perhaps provided the missing piece of the puzzle, the mechanism by which Kronos had turned PMA bees into killers. The military would certainly want to bypass the civilian restraints and fully weaponize any bees they took over. Cap's connections at NSA were currently working on identifying the nerdy youngster he had met with Zeb; and if such a link were proven, they had a route via which the BEEKEEP firmware might have been accessed by the terrorists. That in turn might give them the firepower to convince Ponting that he was backing the wrong horse.

When Yinghua joined him for coffee, he said, "So those were your Chinese friends. Should I trust them?"

She gave him a measured look, and settled down close beside him. "I never met Lin Xiaobao before. But yes, I think we can trust him."

"He's the best friend the United States ever had. Can that be true?"

Yinghua shook her head impatiently. "Doug, no, of course not. China is a rival power. China aspires to world dominance. Of course he's not a friend of the United States."

He sighed wearily. He reached out and put a hand briefly on Yinghua's. "Sweetheart, it's a good thing I trust *you* so completely, because otherwise I'd be a little confused."

"We can trust his information. We can trust him to help us. But of course he has his reasons."

"And what are they?"

"You don't know?"

"At the moment I don't know anything very much. Except that I love you."

Yinghua was silent a moment. "Now I'm feeling guilty."

"You don't need to feel guilty."

"This whole world… China playing her clever games… I've dragged you into it. I'm used to it. I know the sub-text. But I don't want you and me always to be sucked into it. I thought you had to know those things, that information."

"I did."

"In China, Doug, Alan… In China, the old are respected, the old, in fact, are the rulers, but there's a different balance. Old people, except for Party members, of course, still die in China. That is accepted. Which means more room for the young. The young are the future in China."

"What you're saying," he said slowly, "is that Lin prefers a United States run, as at present, by the old and the decadent, rather than a United States re-invigorated by youth.

"I'm afraid so," Yinghua said quietly.

Doug found himself remembering his discussions with Kate Nakamoto, in which he had argued that young brains, new brains, were needed to regenerate society with new ideas. He had believed what he was saying at the time, but now he wasn't so sure, his own hopes for the future opening up new perspectives, clouding the argument.

"He may be wrong," he said.

"Yes," Yinghua said. "Of course he may."

◇◇◇

Their bijou house was split level, the rooms small but warmly decorated in subtly-changing shades of orange and cream. Doug got dressed and took a call a few minutes later from Cap Olsen. He went down to the living room and put Cap's image on a wall screen.

"Take a look at this," Cap said. "It's a simulation from DNA."

A stylized head and shoulders appeared on the screen. Character was lacking, but the structure of the face was immediately recognizable to Doug. "Congratulations," he said.

"Merko Milovic is the name."

"Merko. Yeah. That rings a bell."

"You know what the giveaway was? Okay, he stood out, like you say, because of his eccentric brilliance, but the clincher was this: his personnel record had disappeared from the database. Corelli said that was impossible. No doubt about it: this kid is smart."

Doug spent a few minutes telling Cap what he had learned about the military Trojan Horse, without referring to it as BEEKEEP, and explained how he thought this Merko Milovic character might have hacked into it as a way of fully weaponizing PMA bees.

Olsen frowned at his desk, taking all this in. "Let's say you're right, and this Trojan Horse thing is there, in all bees... Who would know about it? Some top military brass, right? General Ponting for starters."

"Yeah, the head of MAIMCOM would have to know."

"So why is he putting his career on the line and backing the other option? Not PMA bees, but rogue bees with a pipe into MAIMKEY?"

"First, he probably doesn't believe my intelligence about the Mickelburgers and their PMA connections is any good. Second, he's not reckoning on someone as smart as Merko. And third, he may have an unrealistic view of the security, the impenetrability, of his secret program. I don't know. Maybe he wants to create a spectacular foul-up for the President at election time."

"And dump the military in the dirt by association? Ruin his career? I doubt it. Even me, I lose sleep over how I'll come out of this, and all I did was put the grandfather of Kronos on the payroll." Cap shook his head irritably and looked up. "Forget I said that. Where do we go from here? Are you saying we should somehow put pressure on Ponting to come clean? My guess is he really doesn't want to talk about this secret military program to someone like Christine Diaz."

"Wouldn't there be a few officials from the last administration who would know about this? Could you put out some feelers?"

"So I've got Corelli to square, and now I've got a military Trojan Horse to investigate. You know what? You're going to have to rejuvenate me just so I can keep up with you."

Doug decided that underneath the grumpiness, Cap was largely reconciled to his interventions and would take the new leads seriously. That was borne out half an hour later when he got a call from Blake Silverman. Blake explained that he was an FBI special team member, and that he had been referred to the illegal children issue yesterday by Cap. He had a bright, inventive mind, which occasionally got a little ahead of itself, but he had clearly understood the significance of the phenomenon.

"Did you know a third illegal has turned up?" he said. "In Seattle?"

"No. That helps a lot. Three data sets are a lot better than two."

Blake had contacted a consultant who had done a lot of work for the PMA. "This guy understands swarm data files inside out, having been part of the team that developed them."

"Does he have any idea how the data files could have been sabotaged?"

"He says it wouldn't be easy. There are various cross checks that would catch anything simple. In fact he wants some input from you: what sort of thing you have in mind."

"What did you tell him about me?"

"I said you were a young guy with direct inside knowledge of the Mickelburgers and Mars Three, who's helping us analyze the illegal children events. That above all we're trying to find a predictor for which other PMA offices might be doing this."

"Yeah, okay. Sounds good. Can you bring him in now? But I'd better be disguised, voice and features."

"Can do."

They talked for over an hour. Doug pitched some ideas he had been mulling over, mostly to do with the DNA of the illegal children, which he thought might contain a special marker. Mostly he got shot down, but he persevered and the consultant agreed there might be something in his ideas that would be worth pursuing. Blake told him they needed an answer tomorrow.

Doug brought Yinghua up to date as they ate lunch. "These people who know who I am... except you... I get the feeling that they see me as some kind of freak. An insult to nature. I even get an echo of that when I look in the mirror. I think: that can't be me. I'm not like that inside. It's like I'm a frog who's been turned into a handsome prince, but who knows, deep down, that he's still a frog."

Yinghua turned to look at him, fine lines of worry on her forehead.

"Why don't you see me like that?" he asked her. "Like a freak of nature?"

"I was in love with the frog," she said. "So I'm not going to object when he turns into a handsome prince. Or anyway, a not-bad-looking student. It's the person underneath who counts."

"Just so long as the person underneath doesn't start changing too: the plastic brain, always adapting."

"I think, maybe," she said, her dark eyes fixed on him, "that you expect too much, too soon. At present, you are a freak, because you're the only one. People can't help looking at you in amazement. And yes, you probably start to adapt. Wait until there are a few of you, then a lot of you. Wait until you blend in with those of us who don't get older in the first place."

"Cap thinks there are going to be three kinds of people, the young, the old, and the rejuvenants, and we'll all hate each other."

"Initially, maybe. But the old will get younger and the young will get older. We'll blend into a common look, a common sense of who we are."

"And children? Like Sam?"

"There'll always be children. We'll never beat death completely. They'll just be..." Yinghua hesitated, dropped her gaze. "Rare."

He watched her for a moment and then reached out and took her hand. "I want you to know that I'm very sorry that the older, less mature, version of myself saw fit to let you go. Even if he thought he had his reasons. The younger version of myself will never let that happen."

She smiled faintly. "There you go. A good adaptation." She responded to his hand, but didn't, for a moment, look up. Something in her expression made him uneasy. She disengaged her hand and picked up her coffee cup.

"You mentioned Sam," she said at last. "As it happens, I spoke with Trudie earlier."

"Okay." He sensed her diffidence and kept his tone light. "How are they?"

Yinghua seemed to gather her thoughts. "Trudie is as you would expect: she's trying to guess the winners next Tuesday so that she can invite them to a party."

He acknowledged that with a half-smile and a grunt.

Now at last she looked up. "She wants me to look after Sam through the election. She just has too much on, and anyway, he's asking for me."

Doug nodded, seeing the logic of that, yet also aware of a selfish desire to hang on to Yinghua's calming presence. "Are you sure that's wise? I thought we agreed you were safer here than anywhere else. And if Sam is with you... maybe he's..."

"I told Trudie I'd go to her place. They've bee-proofed the house, remember, since the last Kronos attacks. And there'll be a police presence through the election."

"Okay."

She was watching him, her expression ambiguous. "It'll be better for you too, not having to worry about me."

"When will you go?"

"Tomorrow."

"And return when?"

"We'll have to see what Tuesday brings. Wednesday, I hope. Maybe by then we can all go home."

He stared at her, not sure that he any longer understood the concept of going home. "Then we'd better make the most of today."

CHAPTER 49

Time was playing tricks, Zeb thought, as he walked up the grand stairs from the main hall, light flooding down from the cupola on the roof; it was early afternoon still, but it felt as though they had been here in this house forever, the big spaces, the sequestered furnishings, soaking up their manic hopes with careless indifference.

Merko had just revealed to him that Kate had been trying to get into his pants. Merko being chased around these hallowed halls by a horny Kate had a comic flavor which made Zeb smile briefly; but he understood what she was doing, and behind the smile his thoughts were cold.

"Tell her that Kronos demands celibacy," he had suggested to Merko.

Merko nodded rapidly and then dropped his head with a worried frown. "She's ugly."

"Okay, tell her she's ugly."

Zeb knew that Merko was unlikely to give way to Kate: the way he told it, when she had visited his room in the night, he had screamed and curled up in a ball. But it made him mad: Kate thinking she could re-align the balance of power, get an inside track with Merko. That was sneaky, and he'd have to deal with it.

He stopped at the top of the stairs and put his hands on the rail and stared down at the checkerboard marble below. It was all up to him. He had to bring everything together, forge an organization, impose direction. It was no good just killing a bunch of people. This was a once in a million opportunity to kick the complacent bastards when they were already a little bit down, dent their confidence; and to mobilize the huge power of youth.

This is what you must do: you must tell your representatives that democracy must be returned to Americans; the leaden weight of your old and tired governance must no longer strangle the creative vitality of the young, who today scarcely bother to vote because their vote, their constituency, is barren! This cannot happen in a fair society! Kronos will attack your legislators and your officials until you respond with justice!

Zeb realized that he was speaking out loud, as though the hall below him had filled with a responsive, even admiring crowd, whistling and cheering and shouting encouragement. He indulged himself for a few more seconds, raising his arms, taking the applause, then he banged his hands down on the rail, glowered angrily around, and turned away.

He pulled the folded plastic screen from his back pocket and glanced at it, checking a couple of phrases, even as he moved briskly onwards through the upper hallway, heading for a bedroom in the eastern wing. He stopped before reaching it, stood frowning and tapping the plastic on the palm of his hand, turned around and retraced his steps down the stairs. He glanced in the kitchen and then went down the stairs to the basement.

He found Peter Johnson in the empty swimming pool, running up the ten foot wall at the deep end, with the aid of special shoes and gloves. He walked around the pool and sat down on the edge of the coping and watched Johnson go down and up a couple more times. He had abandoned his crown of bees, understanding that the joke was over, the point made; but he missed it. It had illustrated his control of the things that mattered.

"You know something?" he said, as Johnson reached the top of another cycle and paused. "You must be the god-damned fittest guy I have ever known."

Johnson settled himself in a sitting position, legs hanging down into the pool. He took off his boots and gloves one by one and threw them into the pool with studied indifference.

"Yeah," he said, staring down into the pool.

Zeb waited.

"There's a game tonight," Johnson said at last. "I should have been playing."

Zeb stayed quiet.

"I go through all the bullshit, all the stuff about not putting the team first, not putting the fans first, all those brain-rotted, geriatric, so-called fans... the stuff about being more trouble than I'm worth, bad for the game, too much ego... all that crap... and now... I'm out of it. Just... gone. Without a fight. Rolled up my career. Can you understand that?"

"But for a purpose, right?"

Johnson slowly turned his head, gave him a brief look. Zeb moved a little along the rim of the pool and put his hand on Johnson's shoulder.

"You believe that all this shit you've been taking... all the shit we all put up with... it doesn't have to be. You believe this whole, stitched-up, ageist, con trick of a society can be *changed*."

Peter Johnson, hands on the edge of the pool, arms rigid, seemed to stiffen. Zeb took his hand off his shoulder. "You the grandson of this guy," Johnson said quietly, still staring down at the floor of the pool. "That right?"

"Alan Connacher?"

"Alan Connacher, Doug Edie." Johnson flashed him a glance. "Man, have I got a bone to pick with you."

"Tell me."

"I go in there, risk my neck, tell that guy not to use that rejuvenation stuff. And then that's what he does. Himself, personally. And you let him get away."

Zeb took a deep breath, let it out. "That's right, Pete... I let him get away. What can I tell you?" Zeb paused. "He was one out of twenty-six. A fluke. A system error... Listen, if you think it was a family dispensation, a reprieve... No way. Worst mistake I ever made. And him landing up with you guys like that... I apologize. I don't often apologize, Pete, but... listen to me... I apologize."

"You let him get away *again*."

"Yesterday? Kate tell you that?"

"She said something."

Zeb was feeling a small germ of anger, but he repressed it. "I don't want to just tell you bad luck all the time, Pete, but I tracked him down to a safe house and I put a missile in there. That should have been enough, don't you think? The son of a bitch got out of there with about one minute to spare."

Zeb didn't mention the safety jackets that would in any case have saved Doug's life, nor the second chance he'd been offered out in the street.

"I would have come with you," Johnson said.

"Hey. *Now* you tell me." Zeb reached out and gave Johnson's shoulder a pat. "You guys were already on the road. It would have been too risky."

"Any chance of finding him again?"

"Are you offering?"

Johnson stared at him. "He was *young,* Zeb. Like, perfect. What are we going to do if... if *all* of them..."

"I know."

"So sure I'm offering. I've got a score to settle."

Zeb was thinking quickly. Maybe there was a chance that Pete could find Connacher. Maybe it was worth the risk. Connacher was still dangerous. More than that: Connacher, alive, made him bubble up with fury, just thinking about it. And it would leave Kate isolated, less of a disruptive force.

"Let's talk about it. We'd need a way to get you to Washington, or say Baltimore, and a way to keep you hidden while you re-opened a network."

"I can do that stuff. I know the right people."

"What stuff?" a voice said. Zeb looked up and saw Kate making her way around the pool. "What are you plotting?"

"Pete's got an idea. We ought to talk about it."

"Just so long as we talk about it together. What's this?" Kate had swung around behind him and plucked the plastic screen out of his pocket. She held it in both hands in front of her eyes and danced a pace away from him. "The writings of my Lord Kronos? The gospel according to Saint Zeb?"

Kate's hair, black and curly, streamed from her head with electric force, framing the pastry face, the bright oriental eyes.

"It's the Kronos communiqué," Zeb said. "The follow-up."

Kate lowered the document, looked at Johnson.

Johnson shrugged. "I don't know anything about it."

"Read it later," Zeb said.

317

Kate immediately raised the screen again and began scanning it. "What does it say?"

"It says we're reasonable people and we want constitutional change."

"Kronos, Kronos, Kronos," Kate said. "I don't see any mention of Mickelburgers."

"Get real, Kate. Kronos is the big name out there."

"Jesus, you are so fucking arrogant."

Zeb heard Merko's voice in his ear, pitched high with anxiety. He turned aside from Kate and said, "Tell me."

"The cops are in my place."

"What?"

"Taking it to pieces. Messing with my snakes."

"You're sure? You're sure it's cops?"

"Who else?"

Zeb thought for a couple of seconds. "What will they learn?"

"Nothing. It's a question of what do they know. They know who I am, that's what they know."

"Merk, just take it easy. I'm coming up."

Zeb turned back to Kate and Johnson. They were staring at him.

"Cops?" Kate said.

"At Merko's apartment. Merko says they won't find anything, but that isn't the point."

"What is the point?" Johnson said, his face tight.

"Come on," Zeb said, starting quickly up the stairs. "We'd better go find Merko."

"What is the point?" Kate yelped angrily at him as he rounded the top of the stairs and strode into the kitchen.

"The point is," he flung back at her as he crossed the kitchen, "that the cops know who he is, which means that Connacher, who met him once, must have worked out his identity."

Kate wailed from behind him: "*That's* why you had to kill him."

"Now you got it."

Zeb was into the garage annex now, and he took the stairs two at a time and pushed through the door into the studio. Merko, at the workbench, gave him a frightened glance. Zeb was aware of Kate and Johnson following him into the studio and closing up behind him.

"What have you got?" Zeb said. "What's your source for this?"

Merko began nodding his head in a worried rhythm. "They disabled the alarms. But I've got sensors providing feedback on the snakes. Maybe they didn't want to look inside the cages."

"And there's absolutely no-one else it could be?"

"These guys are searching. Everything. Been there an hour. I only just picked it up. Like I said, who else but cops?"

Zeb rested a hand on Merko's shoulder. Merko flinched. "Okay, Merk, this is not your fault. Any way these guys can trace your comms link, assuming they find it, to here?"

"Nope. It's ordinary telcom stuff."

"So, keep tabs on it." Zeb gave Merko a final pat and swung back to the others. "We got to go tonight. No more stalling."

Kate was flushed from climbing stairs, her hair wilder than ever. "What are you saying?"

Zeb began striding in a loop around the studio, his anger and energy no longer containable. "I'm saying that Connacher can work it out! What Merko did at NSA! What kind of bees we're using! I'm saying they can close us down, ground all bees, whatever the hell they think will do it! I'm saying we go tonight!"

"We can't go tonight!" Kate fired back. "I've been talking to the guys in the field and they say no way! We haven't got targets, we haven't got equipment!"

"Merko?"

"Yeah, yeah," Merko mumbled, head down. "Got to stick to the schedule."

"You see, wise guy?" Kate said. "I'm not always wrong."

Zeb ignored her, paced another loop, forcing himself to think. He stopped in front of Kate. "Pete says he'll go to Washington and look for Connacher."

"That's crazy. Pete stays here."

"I want to do it, Kate," Johnson said. "That guy has fucked us over from day one."

"You won't find him. The FBI have got him under wraps."

"But there might be a way." Zeb raised his arm and snapped his fingers a couple of times, eyes half closed. "Connacher's going to want to know what Merko was doing at NSA, right? And you guys are bound to have sources at NSA. So between you guys and Merko..."

"Between us, what? We find Connacher for you. And save your ass again. You know what? Stuff your communiqué." Kate threw the plastic screen, which she was still holding, in his face. "I'm going to write the fucking communiqué! You guys find Connacher." She headed for the door.

Zeb jumped after her and grabbed her, one arm around her waist, one arm around her neck, and carried her back to Merko's workbench.

"Do you know how easy it would be to break your neck?" he hissed into her ear.

He held her a moment, tightening the pressure on her neck; then he released his grip, kneed her away. Kate stumbled to the ground, skidded on the smooth floor, re-grouped on all fours. She slowly sat back, legs under her, stared in fury and frustration at Zeb.

Zeb watched her steadily, his own anger now under control. He saw the look in her eyes change, fear at last taking hold. "We need your cooperation," he said.

She glanced at Johnson.

Johnson looked back at her sadly. "He's right. We do."

"But I tell you what," Zeb said. "If Merk says we stick to the schedule, that's what we do. He knows the mechanics better than all of us. But you, Kate, are going to give your time, and your people, to finding Connacher. You will leave the communiqué, and other matters of leadership, to me. Got it?"

Kate looked up at him and held his gaze for a moment. Then she gave a grudging nod.

CHAPTER 50

There were three people already present in the Fort Meade conference room, two of them young. Cap introduced him as Frank Murphy, an FBI agent. As Doug shook hands and made eye contact with the youngsters, he realized he was once again in an ambiguous situation. They would see him as one of them, which might be an advantage; but they would also see him as someone involved in countering doomer activism, which might not.

They sat down and John Corelli, who had brought him through security as Doug Edie, served coffee and then joined them, sitting at the head of the table. He nodded at the youngsters. "Gerry and Paula both work in a high-intensity, experimental team project, kicking around ideas in information analysis, bee control theory. Both are Princeton luminaries, Gerry in mathematics, Paula in robotics." He nodded at the third man, who was short and wiry with attentive eyes. "Taylor supervises. All of them have worked with Merko, whom they would describe as what?" He glanced around quickly. "Somewhat anarchic, formal education limited, but maybe the brightest of the team, maybe the brightest in the whole damn building?"

The three nodded their assent.

Doug was studying Gerry and Paula. Paula had a lot of curly brown hair, which kept her face almost hidden from sight. Gerry was more extroverted, his face good-natured, but he leaned forward on one arm, head down, fingers of the other hand tapping restlessly on the table.

"I guess you guys know why we've asked for your help?" Doug said, addressing them.

Gerry made an evasive kind of acknowledgment, Paula didn't react.

"Just to recap, I met Merko in the company of someone we think has a link to Kronos. That means he might be the guy we're looking for, the guy who has sabotaged MAIMCOM security systems."

Gerry nodded.

Cap Olsen said, "I can add that we've been through Merko's apartment, Merko himself not there, of course, but we found the DNA of our Kronos suspect. So there's not much doubt that Merko is involved, both in the last attacks, and also in any future attacks they might be planning."

"So do you guys have any thoughts on that?" Doug said. "Any ideas how Merko might have programmed bees to get round the MAIMCOM defenses?"

"On the face of it," Gerry said, giving Doug a nervous look, "that would be really really tough."

The girl suddenly looked at him and said, "What does your job involve? I mean, it's obviously a good job, but does it involve..." She broke off and looked away, as though startled by her boldness.

"Spying on doomers?" Doug said.

She squirmed in her seat. "Something like that."

"No. I'm a technical analyst. My contact with the Kronos suspect was... accidental... personal."

"Oh. Oh. Okay."

"Happy?" Cap said.

"Yeah. I just..." She shrugged, retreated back into herself. Then she jerked into life again. "If we come up with something, are you going to... interrogate us like..."

Doug understood the reference to MAIMCOM's sequestration and interrogation of NSA personnel. He glanced quickly at Corelli.

Corelli said, "No. We never had any connection with that. In any case, the President has made it clear to General Ponting that those interrogations will cease. We asked you in purely to help us understand Merko and hopefully prevent any future killings."

Gerry looked embarrassed. "We want to help," he said. "We don't think killings are going to, you know, do it for the youth community."

"Neither do I," Doug said. "So... can I just run through the security architecture?" His glance around included Corelli and Taylor. "NSA designs the security module, which includes all the stuff that makes bees safe for the public, behavioral restrictions and controls, et cetera… and which is used in all public service bees? You also generate the daily MAIMKEY which you send by landline to all bee installations across the nation, and of course to MAIMCOM?"

"Right," Corelli said.

"Does anyone here in NSA have sight of the MAIMKEY?"

"Nobody. It's one hundred per cent automated."

"As you probably know, there's a theory going round, favored by MAIMCOM, that MAIMKEY somehow got out, into a rogue pipe, at least at the time of the Kronos attack."

Taylor spoke for the first time, impatience in his voice. "That just doesn't make sense."

"What do you think?" Doug said to the youngsters.

"Don't know," Gerry said. "From my perspective, very unlikely."

"Paula?"

The girl looked up, pulled nervously at her hair. "The thing is, Merko was interested in MAIMKEY. I'm sure of that. He once said to me that quantum encryption wasn't quite as clever as people thought it was."

"Jeez," Gerry said. "Really?"

Paula glanced at him, her gaze briefly determined. "I don't think he wanted anyone to know that, but I think... as a girl... he kind of didn't take me seriously. It just kind of slipped out."

"Did he mention it again?" Doug asked. "Elaborate at all?"

"No."

He looked around at the others. This wasn't what he wanted to hear, but he knew that his job was to uncover facts, not favor one theory or another.

Taylor said, "He wasn't serious. Some of his speculations were crazy, and this was one of them. MAIMKEY is rock solid."

Paula frowned behind the hair, and Doug prompted her again. "Paula?"

She shook herself, looked around half-fearfully. "I just think he knew something. It didn't sound like he was speculating."

"Okay, thanks. That certainly could be useful." Doug was aware that Cap was looking at him, not with a smug sense of satisfaction, but with surprise: is it true, you got this wrong? He avoided eye contact and added, "The other thing we wanted to think about is the security module. There's a possibility that instead of using his own bees and somehow diverting MAIMKEY to them, Kronos used public service bees and re-programmed them with his own missions. In which case he had to get around the controls in the security module so that the bees could kill people. Did Merko have reason to study the workings of the security module?"

"Merko didn't need reasons," Taylor said. "He got into anything that interested him."

"Anyone know if the security module was one of the things that interested him?"

"Probably," Taylor said.

"Gerry?"

"Merko was always way ahead of me on anything that took place at the behavioral level. I think he had the workings of the whole damn bee mapped out in his brain. So yeah, I'm sure he understood the security module. But as far as I know he never worked on the code."

"So you don't think he was ever in a position to make changes?"

"That would be impossible," Corelli said. "You can't just change the code and not hit a million roadblocks and queries."

"Paula?" Doug said. "Do you think there's any way Merko could have sneaked in a worm of some kind? Maybe disguised as something else?"

She shook her head in a kind of shudder. "Absolutely not."

He glanced at Taylor and Gerry, but they didn't offer an alternative opinion. He was beginning to feel frustrated and defensive. Cap was looking at him again. There was something here he was missing, probably, but he didn't have sufficient knowledge of bee architecture to ask the right questions. Nor could he refer to BEEKEEP, because he'd given his word, and nobody here would know anything about it anyway.

"One more thing," he said, forcing himself to concentrate. "MAIMCOM obviously has final control over the package that gets issued to the contractors who fabricate the bees. So they have their own technical teams and development labs. Do you know what else they add to your security module? Obviously the code that governs the IFF challenge and the exchange of MAIMKEY. Anything else?"

"We don't get to see the final source code, I can tell you that," Corelli said. "It's heavily defended. Military secret, all of that. But we know from the size of the compiled code that there's a few extra things in there."

"So you have access to the compiled code?"

"Oh yeah," Taylor said. "That's what goes out to contractors. We use it for simulations."

"So," Doug said, looking round, "the same question: did Merko spend a lot of time playing with the compiled code?"

After a moment, Gerry said, "Merko was a very secretive kind of a guy. He was tolerated in the team…" He gave Taylor a quick glance. "…because he occasionally came up with brilliant insights, but I'm not sure anyone really knew what he was doing. But like I said before, he knew the architecture inside out, the firmware, I mean, which includes that MAIMCOM package… so yes, I'd say he must have spent time with the compiled code."

"Passively, of course," Paula added. "There's no way he could make changes."

Doug looked around, but the others were nodding. He sat back with a frown. It was looking bad. If these guys were right, and Merko had no unidentified back channels, he had to have figured out the existence of the BEEKEEP Trojan Horse by studying the compiled code, and he had to have got himself access to it by adding something to the source code of the security module in such a way that nobody noticed; both of which sounded difficult, maybe impossible.

"Okay," he said. "So short of some mind-blowingly obscure technical ingenuities, the only idea we have is that he might have been able to tap into MAIMKEY. In which case, where is the pipe?"

"Not really our field," Taylor said. "Speak to the cabling engineers."

Doug tried a couple more angles, but nothing significant emerged. There were handshakes all round, and then Corelli guided them back towards the entrance.

Cap Olsen, walking beside Doug, said, "Being right all the time is annoying, but in your case I'd kind of got used to it. What the hell happened back there?"

"I don't know."

"When will you know?"

Doug didn't have an answer to that, and he let it go.

◇◇◇

Back home in the safe house, sitting over a cup of coffee, Doug couldn't decide in his own mind exactly how the probabilities had shifted. Had he really misread the evidence, got the conclusions wrong? Was there something in Syracuse, or earlier, that he hadn't noticed? Or did it simply not matter? Cap had drawn his own conclusions from the meeting, and would no doubt swing round to Ponting's view. He'd been written out of the narrative: nobody was listening to him and the truth was no longer relevant. He should rest and relax, make up for weeks of stress, and wait for events to unfold.

He watched some news stories about the election, arranged by his genie according to his known interests. He was surprised to see that Kronos was getting some attention: doomer organizations were reviving the manifesto which Kronos had publicized at the time of the first killings, which included a change in the voting age, cutting off those over seventy, and an option for those over ninety to choose euthanasia and pass on childbirth rights to a chosen heir. Young people gave their views, with a lot approving of these ideas. A few believed that the midterm elections, Kronos's deadline, would see a further outbreak of violence.

Zeb would be happy about that, Doug thought; or maybe he'd placed some of this material himself. Outside the youth media, there were a couple of serious discussions about the Kronos phenomenon, and some stories of politicians who had raised the issues during campaigning. None of these were agreeing that the constitution should be changed. Were they placing themselves at risk, several commentators wondered, by drawing attention to their anti-Kronos, perhaps anti-doomer, policies?

His genie also reminded him that he was registered to vote; which he could do by telcom link at any time. And since DC had finally become a state a few years ago, there were two senators and a congressman to be decided in the ballot.

Thanks a lot, Doug thought. Since I'm a young man, of course I'll vote for the youth candidates, even though they're standing as independents, and will surely lose.

He canceled the news feeds and walked up a level to the kitchen and ordered lasagna. He stared for a moment at the half-empty bottle of wine from which he and Yinghua had been drinking the previous evening, and then drew a glass of water from the machine. As he ate, he began to feel that he was losing touch with something very basic in his psyche, like the belief in his own viability, his participation in a meaningful passage of events.

He told his genie to post an image of himself on the nearest screen, and he saw a side view of someone, sitting alone at a table, eating. He eyed it for a couple of moments, and then raised his arm. The image raised its arm at the same time. He lowered his arm, and the image matched his movement. But he found himself unconvinced. It seemed he had a solid existence, but perhaps it was a fake. He told the image to go away, and it disappeared. Or had *he* disappeared?

He put his plate and tumbler in the processor and went up the few steps to the next level, where he stared at his face in a bathroom mirror. The face existed, apparently, but it was a face with which he felt only a tenuous connection. He contorted the features into grins and grimaces, but they didn't look like *his* grins and grimaces.

Who are you looking for, he thought; the kid who murdered his brother?

He took off his pants and examined his legs for bruises: the stigmata, he thought, of his youthful guilt. There was no sign that anything new had developed. He was almost disappointed: bruises might have put him back into a familiar pattern, with a familiar procedure to correct them.

He lay down on the bed and tried to steer his mind away from its downward spiral. He was tired, his efforts to defeat his grandson, that strange and dark embodiment of himself, had failed. He was at risk, he knew, of triggering one of those depressive states that had troubled him throughout his adult life. He clenched his teeth and tried to rally. All of these things he was trying to figure out would one day be resolved. He was safe in the care of the FBI. Yinghua also was safe, and would return when she was ready. He had to stay functional, because there might be something he was still required to do.

And then what? And then Doug Edie would disappear in a puff of smoke...

He drifted into an uneasy sleep. He was disoriented when his genie woke him. Paula Fields, the girl from NSA, had called FBI Headquarters, asking for Frank Murphy. After a few moments of confusion, he sat up wearily, saw his bare legs, and swung off the bed and climbed into his pants. "Is she using video?"

"No."

"Okay. I'll take it." He didn't want to speak to Paula, whose information had not been welcome, but a surviving sense of obligation made him decide he had no choice. He fastened the belt of his pants and sat down.

A hesitant girl's voice said, "Mr. Murphy?"

"Frank. Yes. Tell me."

"You remember me?"

"Of course."

"It's just that... there were so many people there this morning... I wasn't always taking things in... The point is, I think I may have remembered a couple more things about Merko."

"Okay. The elusive Merko... What kind of things?"

"Well... they could be important."

"I mean, do they materially alter your view of his work, his involvement?" He realized there was impatience in his voice, but he couldn't shake off a background sense of irritation, of unwelcome disturbance.

"Well... I don't know... Maybe."

"I'm listening."

"It's a little difficult right now... I kind of need to talk it through and I thought you might understand it... do you think I could meet you later?"

Oh God, he thought, a nutcase. Was it possible she had conceived a personal interest in him? Surely not.

"Are you at the FBI right now?" she said.

"As a matter of fact, no."

"But if I came there later... where, Headquarters building...? At, say, six? Could you be there? Could I go through it with you?"

He hesitated. At least there was no security issue at FBI HQ; but he wasn't feeling sociable or properly connected with the issues she would raise.

"Cap Olsen himself would probably be glad to see you."

"But he's old, isn't he? I'm sorry, I guess that sounds rude. It's okay, if you don't think it's important, I won't bother."

He sighed. Nothing would come of this, he felt sure, and the girl might indeed be a nutcase, but he couldn't deny her the chance to speak.

"I'll be there," he said. "Headquarters building, six o'clock. Come in the main entrance and ask for me."

He lay back and closed his eyes and tried to prevent his irritation from getting out of hand. A leaden weight was pressing down on his forehead. It took him half an hour to rouse himself and send a message to Cap Olsen, telling him that Paula had requested a conversation and that he needed an interview room. His genie relayed a message from Cap, asking if this conversation was likely to be significant. No, Doug replied. He could have added: because in my present condition I won't be a sympathetic listener, and I probably won't understand what she's talking about.

◇◇◇

He arrived at the J. Edgar Hoover building at ten to six. Night had fallen, but the main entrance on the corner was well lit. He half expected to see Paula hanging around outside, intending to intercept him and drag him off to another venue: but although there were a couple of women, reporters possibly, standing by the potted trees, and a small knot of young tourists a little further along, there was no sign of the nervous face and the curtain of wavy hair that he remembered.

He went inside and checked at the desk that an interview room had been reserved for Frank Murphy, aka Doug Edie. The agent on duty verified the situation with Cap Olsen, and he sat down to wait. It had occurred to him, in his irritated hunt for an excuse to avoid this encounter, that Paula was not the scatterbrained innocent that she seemed, but was instead a devious activist who had maneuvered him into being in a certain place at a certain time. If that turned out to be true, her comments about Merko would also be suspect. But Paula was obviously well vetted by NSA, and the FBI Headquarters was the wrong place to choose if some kind of an attack was planned. The defensive surveillance inside and out was such that any assault, with or without a weapon, would be countered microseconds after it began. No, if Paula was being devious, she had to persuade him to go somewhere else, and there was no sign she was going to try and do that.

At six fifteen, his irritation growing, he made a connection with Paula's telcom genie and asked where she was. The genie said that Paula wasn't available to speak with him, and apologized that it had no further information to offer. He waited another ten minutes and then decided to leave. He sent a message to Paula's genie to say that he was giving up on her, and told Cap Olsen that they had a no-show. As he went out onto Pennsylvania Avenue, he realized that if Paula was the devious doomer he had previously proposed, the plan might be to follow him back to his safe house. In which case, he had conveniently told her exactly when he was leaving FBI Headquarters. Increasingly furious, he alerted his genie and embarked on all of the routines he had learned for shaking off a tail.

He was in the middle of walking through a mall, going in and out of shops to identify and lose any pursuers, when he got a message from Paula, relayed by her genie in her mildly pathetic voice: she was very sorry, but she had been delayed, and then she had got thinking, and she wasn't sure that what she had to say would really be worth listening to. He increased his pace, his frustration and anger wound higher by an ugly sense of guilt: so it's my fault, he thought, or that's what she wants me to think; I intimidated her, revealed my skepticism. But did she really have anything interesting to say?

He was still fiercely debating the issue when he arrived home. As his fury died down, the familiar gloom took over. He forced himself to order some food, and ate without tasting it. Paula was an oddity, he thought. Nothing she might have remembered was going to change the fundamental tenor of her earlier testimony. Nor did this farce about meeting really indicate that she was an activist obeying orders: it was too crude, the opportunity to follow him home too obvious. He had certainly countered that, even if they'd tried it, and even if they were using floaters and other forms of overhead surveillance. So forget her, he thought. The die was cast, and Ponting was the man in charge of preventing bee attacks. Doug Edie could fade into oblivion.

Yinghua called soon after he finished eating. He was slumped in a chair, staring at a plastic download of the Washington Post. He listened as she gave him news from his daughter's household. Trudie's husband's seat was not one of those being contested, and Senator Lightfoot had remained in Washington. He and Trudie were caught up in general campaigning and socializing, and Yinghua was at that moment alone with Sam. She was relieved not to be spending much time with Trudie and Andy: neither of them was aware that Trudie's son, Zeb Packer, a frequent guest in their house, was Kronos. Yinghua was finding her secret knowledge a difficult burden to bear, knowing that in time she would have to admit to her behind-the-scenes role. Andy, she thought, would explode or collapse when the news about Zeb became public, and Trudie would be worse, motherhood and career both in shreds.

Yinghua had encountered the Senator fleetingly over lunch, and his remarks about Kronos had made her shiver: partly because of their poignant innocence and lack of realism. Kronos had no chance of repeating his spectacular attacks, the Senator thought; bee defenses and controls wouldn't fail a second time. Of course some of his congressional friends, campaigning in their home states, were privately nervous, aware that they were offering no compromise, no concessions, on the age-related issues raised by Kronos, and aware also that the election was the final deadline; but Andy thought they'd be okay; if Kronos tried anything again, "The bastard will hit stuff he never realized we had."

Doug listened and sympathized, but his link with Yinghua seemed curiously diminished. It was as though he had shut down, run out of energy, in every area of his life, including this most important of relationships. He gave her a short account of the NSA meeting, but edited out his doubts and frustration, let the outcome stand as an endorsement of Ponting's defenses. He didn't mention Paula's abortive follow-up.

"You look tired," Yinghua said.

"Yeah. But I'm okay. I'm just glad it's not my responsibility any more."

"Do you want to say hallo to Sam?"

"Sam?" He was aware of an inner retreat. "As what? As your boyfriend?"

"Just as a friend."

"I think I'd rather not talk to him until I can tell him who I am."

"Oh. Okay." Yinghua promised to call him again the next day.

He felt vaguely irritated with himself for not even wanting to see Sam's face on the screen, and he sat for a long time staring into space, pondering his deficiencies, allowing his apathy to grow.

He got an unexpected call later in the evening from Blake Silverman.

"You want the good news, or the really good news?"

Doug tried to rouse himself. "You got something?"

"What we've got, I would say, is a real breakthrough."

"I thought Cap had lost faith in all that stuff and put you onto something else."

"Are you crazy? Cap thinks you're god. How can you lose faith in god? Of course he also thinks you're a pain in the ass, but hey, you can't have everything."

He said nothing, not convinced that Cap thought he was god, and his brain still encumbered with negative emotions.

Blake went on, "I've sent the data to your genie, so you can go through it however you want. Basically, as you suggested, there is a little section of DNA that is unique to these three kids, the illegals. It looks like human DNA, but it isn't. That leads to a rather simple, but clever, worm which can be introduced into the local PMA data files, presumably by an infiltrated doomer. The worm makes PMA bees ignore anyone with DNA containing that non-human section. It wasn't easy to find it, but once we did, we used the powers of PMA headquarters system management, granted to us by Susan Schwartz, to search all of the data files in the local offices. And bingo."

"How many offices are involved?"

"Forty-four. Including the three we knew about. As I say, the list is with your genie."

"What's the geographical distribution?"

"All over. Slight preponderance in the north-east and the south-west."

He felt a distant longing, like nostalgia, for the time, hours and hours ago, when this news from Blake would have given him the sense of breaking open the final dimension in the bee attack threat; whereas now, in all probability, it merely confirmed the existence of a lot more illegal children.

"It's a great effort," he said. "The problem is... well, you know what the problem is. Our meeting at NSA this morning makes it look like Ponting is right and I'm wrong. I don't think finding out how these kids were concealed is going to move the dial."

"Understood. But I figured you'd be glad to know. At the very least the FBI will get the credit for digging out a whole bunch of these illegal kids."

And a whole bunch of very unhappy mothers, he thought with a sigh.

CHAPTER 51

Merko was relieved that his principal deity and patron, Kronos, had given up his wild idea of bringing forward Operation Platinum Sting and had restored the original countdown to today, Monday. It gave him more time to wrestle with the forces that seemed to be crowding their way in to his tightly-controlled world: the fractious and divisive Kate; the inflamed spirits of his personal swarms; and bigger gods, in devilish forms, threatening to unseat his protector Kronos and ensnare him in their evil work.

As the afternoon progressed, Kate was downstairs most of the time, rallying her followers. Zeb paced the studio or sat at a screen or went down to check on Kate. Merko was able to sink into a state of quasi-mystical concentration, in which he darted around through his cyber world and created code which eased his anxieties and secured the state of his inner world, as ruled by Kronos; code which he didn't fully perceive as having real world consequences.

"Hey, Merk, we got it. The timed entry."

Zeb was back in the room, but Merko was far away and Zeb's comment didn't at first penetrate.

"Merk?"

Zeb's heavy hand on his shoulder brought him back to earth. For a shocked moment he thought that Kronos the god had penetrated his world and seen what he was doing. He struggled to stop himself trembling.

Zeb removed his hand, apparently oblivious. "You hear what I said, old buddy? We got that Connacher freak dead on the money. Time and place. That's what you need, right?"

Merko hunched defensively over the bench. "Right. So track him back home."

"Me?"

"I showed you this stuff. You did it before, remember?"

"Kind of. I need you to remind me."

Merko looked up, covering his guilt with irritation. He saw at the edge of his glasses that the time was just after six o'clock. There was still a lot to do. "So, what, this is Connacher going into the FBI building?"

"Right."

"You got the time to the nearest tenth of a second?"

"Five fifty-one and seven point eight seconds."

"Okay. You need our recording of PMA surveillance data. I'll load it for you. Enter time and place. Identify Connacher as the guy who goes into the FBI at that time. Then put his movements in reverse time and track him back to where he came from. Got it?"

"Got it."

Merko made the link for Zeb, and then slipped back almost immediately into his mystical world of gods and conflict. Zeb's intrusion had heightened the sense of urgency. People were going to die. Lots of people. But it wouldn't be his fault, because he was merely the servant of Kronos, and Kronos was worthy.

He barely heard the whoop from Zeb. "Hey Merk! I got him!"

A couple of moments later he felt Zeb's hand on his shoulder again. He gritted his teeth.

"Hey buddy. You're not listening to me, are you? I said I'd got him."

"Why wouldn't you get him? I told you what to do."

"Yeah, well, it's nice to be right, huh? Pete, you there?"

Merko felt the heavy weight of Zeb's hand lifting from his shoulder. He half-listened as his voice droned on.

"Worked like a charm. You guys really came through on this... yeah, no real doubt... It's a place in Adams Morgan. Pretty much fits the bill for an FBI safe house... Listen, Pete, my advice is to stay away unless you really have to get involved. The FBI'll be all over it... Maybe you can handle the swarm yourself... Yeah, your own Baltimore people... Merko's great Key of Power is going to be disseminated very soon... I'll tell Kate this is job one, and you're directing it. Wham, this nemesis granddad of mine is history... Yeah sure, talk to her yourself. But I think she knows she's got to do what I say."

Zeb fell silent, but Merko could feel his presence behind him. "Are you going to leave me alone to work?" he said petulantly.

Zeb walked over to where his screen was unrolled on the bench and stared at it for a moment. Merko was sinking back into his world when Zeb said, "You ready to send this Key of Power?"

"Give me a few more minutes."

"For what?"

Merko shrugged. "A couple of details." He was just managing to sustain his concentration, and the last thing he wanted to do was let it go at this point. If he left stuff undone, it would all go wrong and unsanctioned death would be scattered abroad, like pollen in the wind.

"I've got an idea," Zeb said.

Merko closed his eyes.

"What about sending a conditional key? A time-limited key? Valid for this operation only."

"We've talked about this," Merko mumbled.

"We have?"

"We can't do it that way."

"Why not?"

"The Key of Power is in the firmware of the bees. You can't change it. I did it that way because I wasn't planning all this stuff."

Zeb sighed, moved back a pace. "We talked about it, uh?"

"Yeah."

"Because you know what we're doing? We're handing power over to Kate and her Rose Mickelburger Faction. Which, okay, I'm going to turn into the Kronos Army. But all the same... Why throw away a source of power?"

Merko was still keeping his mental world alive, the gods in his universe still arguing over what to do with the mortal with the unique power, and how the worthy one should be identified.

"Merk?"

"What?"

"Can't we do something?"

"No. Anyway, the power won't last. I told you already." Was that true, Merko wondered? In the world inside his head, the power was forever.

He felt Zeb's hand on his shoulder again, the touch lighter than before.

"You want something? Coffee?"

"No."

Zeb went out and Merko flipped back to his private world. When Zeb returned with Kate, twenty minutes later, Merko was ready, but surprised, not sure exactly what he'd done. He remained seated at the bench, the other two one each side of him. Kate was still subdued, her expression wary. Zeb had that irritating half-smile. Merko suddenly felt frozen with terror.

"Are we linked to all the teams?" Zeb said.

Merko remained frozen a moment longer, his eyes on Zeb. Then he felt a kick from his gods in the cyber world. He turned away. "Yeah. The video link will come up as well. All we need is a sign."

Zeb immediately looked suspicious. "What?"

"Everyone out there... who has learned respect for Kronos... they want a sign... that Kronos approves of Platinum Sting."

"Merk, I hope you know what the hell you're doing. What kind of a sign?"

"A grand sign... from the god Kronos."

"Are you two serious?" Kate said, her pallid face showing spots of color. "This is crap. A waste of time. We don't need any sign from Kronos."

"A sign, uh?" Zeb said. "A majestic sign, showing the might of Kronos. What about this: my servant Merko, laid out on his own bench, throat ritually cut, blood mingled with his processing devices. Will that be okay?"

Merko shook his head quickly. "The sign must come from Kronos."

"I am Kronos!" Zeb shouted. "I don't need a sign! Everything I do is a sign!"

"You are the earthly embodiment of Kronos. We need a sign from above."

"Jesus Christ, Merko, if this is serious..." Zeb's look was lethal.

Merko felt a sudden and inexplicable burst of courage. He took off his glasses, and stood up, pulling at the sensors attached to his scalp. If Kronos killed his servant Merko, that was the way it would be. "I'm not involved any more. Kronos himself will send the key. It's in the hands of the gods." He shambled towards the door.

Zeb leaped after him. "Merk, so help me – "

Kate ran after them and grabbed Zeb's arm. "Back off, you Neanderthal! This is a stunt, can't you see? Merko is telling you to do something flamboyant, summon up your crown of bees, whatever, and then he'll beam the video out to my people and make them all go aaah. Pathetic, but we have to humor him or we're fucked. So work it out."

Zeb stared at Kate, and then back at him. He was breathing hard. Merko wasn't happy with Kate's intervention: he wanted Zeb to make the link.

"Is she right?" Zeb said, his voice menacing. "You want me to do something that proves I'm Kronos? Lord Kronos, the god?"

Merko spread his hands. "But I don't know what it is."

"Merk, you fucking created it, whatever it is, you must know what it is."

"No. I did it, but I wasn't permitted to know what I was doing."

Zeb stared at him intently. "Merk, if you've chosen this moment to lose your sanity, then I think maybe I'll join you." Zeb shook his fists like a madman. "WHAT THE FUCK ARE YOU TRYING TO DO TO US?"

Merko felt his eyes moving under Zeb's furious gaze. Back to the corner of the room where...

Zeb froze, watched him, then suddenly strode over to one of the hives. He looked back at Merko, eyebrows raised.

Merko shrugged.

Zeb wagged his finger at him, as though telling him he would pay for this deviousness. "Bees, instruments of Kronos," Zeb said, his tone ironic, impatient, "come out and show your power. Show the power of Kronos to the world."

Merko stared at the hive, his heart beat suspended: would that do it? He wasn't sure, now, what he'd programmed, how general he'd made it. But the flickering of tiny shadows told him that bees were gathering.

Zeb waited, his gaze shifting from Merko to the hive, until he too picked up the signs. He gave Merko a final glare and then spun away and took up a stance in the middle of the room. Merko watched him with relief and a touch of awe. Zeb had got it. More than that, Zeb was rising to the occasion, functioning as Kronos.

Zeb began to speak: "Welcome to our teams and our agencies across the nation. This is a great moment. I am Kronos and I speak for youth. I am about to deliver to you the power devised by my servant Merko, a power we can use to crush the old and win justice for our cause. Use it well. And now, as a symbol of our struggle, I give you Kronos!"

Zeb threw his arms upwards, fists bunched. Merko felt himself gagging for breath, as he waited for the results of his semi-conscious handiwork. Then the Kronos crown, now in brilliant gold, sprang to life over Zeb's head, and golden digits radiated from it in fiery snakes of light, data symbolically flowing into the ether. Merko sank down onto his knees. A sign had been given. He was the humble functionary, nothing more. He dragged himself to his chair at the bench and pulled himself up onto it in weary relief.

He heard Kate saying angrily, "Jesus, Kronos, I don't know which one of you put that together, but it was a cheap trick. Next time..." There was a pause. Then she went on in a different tone: "Okay, I'm getting messages. Looks like we're in business. Yasmin says they've got the key..."

CHAPTER 52

W hen Doug Edie came awake, he felt disoriented, out of place. The room was unfamiliar. He stared at a piece of flat blue glass, hanging on the wall in front of him, trying to decide what era, what style, it represented.

He perceived at last that he was slumped in an armchair, stiff and cramped after hours of sleep. He pushed himself upright. The creamy plastic of the Washington Post download had spread itself flat on the rug.

FBI safe house. Adams Morgan. Doug Edie. Wasted days, a wasted mission. A valueless identity.

"Time?" he muttered.

"Tuesday morning, zero two thirty seven," his genie responded.

He settled back again in the chair. He should go to bed. Instead, he stared at the glass ornament.

Where, exactly, are those PMA offices? Those forty-four PMA offices?

It was an intrusive thought, which, for a moment, he barely recognized as his own. Why would he think about PMA offices in the middle of the night? But he had been sleeping; processing off-line; his brain had been sifting through the data; and sometimes his brain knew what it was doing.

"You've got the data from Blake Silverman?" he said.

"Yes, Doug."

"Display the forty-four PMA offices on a map of the United States."

"Done."

He stared at the colored display, at first with detached interest, and then with increasing engagement. There was, as Blake had told him,

340

a greater density of red dots along the eastern seaboard, around the cities of the Great Lakes, in Texas, and in California; areas where young activists were likely to be entrenched.

"Enlarge Maryland and Virginia," he said.

He had noticed three red dots in the DC area: on the enlarged map, he identified these as Columbia and Annapolis to the north and east; and Fredericksburg to the south. Columbia and Annapolis were within easy range of Baltimore, Kate's operational base.

"Give me an estimate of flight characteristics of PMA bee swarms. Speed and range." A sense of agitation was growing at the back of his mind. To this point, he had ignored his personal situation, but the memory of being attacked by bees and descending to the depths of his pool had never entirely gone away.

"All public sector bees can reach about fifty-five miles an hour when flying in aerodynamic formation," his genie told him. "Range varies. Some bees with energy absorption properties are thought to be viable for several days, although not when continuously in flight."

A half-hour away, Doug thought. There are bees at local PMA control centers, control centers possibly infiltrated by activists, less than half an hour away.

He pushed himself to his feet. The depressive weight in his head suddenly dispersed. He no longer felt detached or sleepy. Instead he was quickly tracking back through the arguments, the evidence, that had convinced him of the involvement of PMA bees in the original attacks. Had he really got it wrong?

There were facts that said no: like Merko and Zeb not knowing that their attack against him had failed; like Naomi, in Syracuse, linking the activist infiltration of the PMA with the new Kronos operation.

And opposed to that was the evidence of Paula and Gerry at NSA. Young people. Doomers. People apparently validated by their superiors, but nevertheless people whose loyalty could not be completely guaranteed.

Paula's abortive trip to the FBI... what had that been about?

He went up to the kitchen and got a cup of coffee and took it down to the sitting room. He asked his genie to check on the status of Cap Olsen and Blake Silverman. Cap was at home trying to get some sleep, but Silverman was on a watching brief at HQ.

"Any news?" Doug asked him.

"No reported attacks, if that's what you mean." Blake's voice was tired and gravelly.

"I wouldn't bother you, but there's something I'd like to check. Maybe you know I was at HQ yesterday to meet Paula, the girl from NSA. She didn't show, but I'm beginning to wonder if there was some non-obvious reason why she wanted me at HQ. You've got surveillance data for the main corner entrance, right?"

"Wait a minute." There was a brief pause, and then Blake's voice sounded stronger. "Say all that again."

Doug repeated his preamble and question.

"Yeah, okay, we do that kind of surveillance."

"Can you send me the data? I got there close on ten to six last night."

"That might be difficult. I tell you what, I'll check it myself. Gives me something to do. What are you looking for?"

"I'm not sure. Suspicious persons, suspicious activity, anything that seems associated with my arrival at the building."

"Got it. I'll get back to you."

Doug sipped his coffee and prowled around the sitting room, thinking about Paula, the comments she had made at the meeting, the sound of her voice when she had called him. The truth was, it had all been plausible and in character. He was probably getting alarmed over nothing.

His genie told him that Silverman was back. "There's nothing very obvious. At the time you arrive, there's a mixture of people out in the street, most of them going somewhere, not apparently paying any attention to you or the entrance. There's a few who look like tourists, more stationary, including a small group of youngsters who appear to be waiting for something. They're not very close to the entrance, and they don't seem much interested in it, although one of them is looking at you as you go through the door."

"Just looking?"

"I've run the sequence a couple of times. She has one hand in the pocket of her raincoat and there's detectable movement of the hand as you go through the door. Probably coincidence, but it's possible, I suppose, that she activated something. Obviously no bombs went off, so I don't know what that could have been."

"Did you identify this girl, or any others in the group?"

"No, but we're pretty sure that none of them are known to the FBI."

"Can I have a look? Just that particular girl?"

"Yeah, okay. Give me a second."

The surveillance data included shots from several angles, and high resolution. Doug watched the girl closely, her intent face, the barely visible movement of the hand in the pocket. It wasn't Paula, but he had a feeling he had seen this girl before. The hair was different, maybe other things, but the features... Suddenly he saw her, in his mind's eye, with Kate and the others at a cubechess match, and as part of the group at the sports bar. He had never spoken to her, but he was certain of the context: this was someone who hung around with Kate and Johnson, a Mickelburger.

Which meant she knew him from real life, not just videos or simulations. She'd recognize him more easily in a situation like this: Pennsylvania Avenue at a busy time of day.

Doug stood rigid for a moment, wild ideas chasing each other around in his mind. He sat down abruptly and told Blake what he believed he had discovered.

"You sure?"

"Ninety percent. But unfortunately I don't recall her name."

"Any idea what she was activating in her pocket?"

"A clock," Doug said.

"A clock?"

Doug paused, following through the spontaneous jump in his thinking. "Does any agency collect overhead surveillance data?"

"Not us. The CIA, maybe. The PMA? As a matter of fact, I think I've read that the PMA analyzes people movement in cities as a way of optimizing bee deployment."

"So we're back to the PMA again. Look, Blake, see if I'm crazy. If the PMA collects surveillance data from some form of high altitude cameras, it will be, by law, of insufficient resolution to identify individuals, correct?"

"That would be hard to do anyway, from directly overhead."

"Right. But that doesn't mean that they can't discriminate individuals as discreet units, discreet trackable units, right? So suppose our friend Merko has hacked into this data and records it. Now... If he

343

knows the exact time I arrive at FBI HQ, the exact time I step through the door, it should be possible to identify me as a discreet unit on his surveillance recordings. And he can then..." He broke off.

"Doug?"

"Shit," he said, his voice low, his heart rate rising, "the bastards know where I am."

"How so?"

"I went from here to the FBI. I was stupid. It doesn't matter that I used a cab. They can track it back. Once they've identified the dot on the cityscape that's me, they can track it back to here."

A short silence. Blake said, "My brain still isn't entirely functional, but I think I follow you. If it's any consolation, we're keeping an eye on the safe house. We should be able to help."

But not if they send bees.

"Look, Blake, time may be short. Number one, if I'm right, we now have a link between Paula and the Mickelburgers. Which discredits everything that she and Gerry said at NSA. You need to brief Cap. Specifically, you need to tell him that Ponting's defenses may shortly be revealed as crap. Number two, the forty-four PMA offices you discovered, the ones with the worm for concealing illegal children, are suddenly a lot more important. They could be the ones from which Kronos is going to hijack swarms and mount his new round of attacks. What does Susan Schwartz know about that?"

"Schwartz? Nothing. I'm not sure she even knows we've identified forty-four offices as compromised. I told her simply that you had the full confidence of Cap Olsen, and that we needed to do some searches on your behalf."

"Okay. So I guess it's up to me to convince her that her agency might be involved in a new Kronos operation. Can you tell Cap to set up some kind of conference as a matter of urgency?"

"Sure. He'll enjoy that."

Doug hardly heard the sarcasm. "Number three. You might have noticed that Columbia and Annapolis are among the suspect PMA offices. That means all of us here in DC are potential targets. Again, Cap needs to know that."

"Now that the General's defenses are crap."

"That's my assumption."

"Maybe we should all hang out with the General at MAIMCOM HQ. At least that's one place with good bee defenses."

"Is that where Ponting is right now?"

"I don't know, but I'd guess so."

"Tell Cap he should join Ponting, or go to the White House, if he wants to be safe. You too."

"I'm still waiting for my invitation to the White House."

"Then join the General." Doug paused, his mind continuing to range over the immediate tactical decisions. "Okay. Main thing: brief Cap Olsen, and let me know the result. One last thing. Those safety jackets you had at the last safe house: will I find those here?"

"Should do. Probably in several locations. Just try opening cupboards."

◇◇◇

Doug found the jackets in a cupboard under the stairs on the first floor. He spent a few minutes reading the instructions contained within the packaging. Bees were not mentioned, but the protective dome built almost instantly around the head 'would resist most forms of physical and chemical ingress'. The internal oxygen supply would last up to ten minutes, and as long as the tube was in the mouth and oxygen being drawn, the chemical softening of the protective dome would automatically be delayed.

There are no defenses against bees.

Keeping them out of his eyes was useful, but he had to assume that once a swarm had been souped up by the BEEKEEP intervention, they would attack anywhere, biting whatever part of the body they could reach. He went up to the bedroom and opened the doors of the fitted closets. Yes, the FBI had kindly thought to provide spare clothing, even winter undergarments. He put these on, changed into heavy socks and sneakers, and tucked his pants into his socks.

And felt like an idiot. Nobody was worrying about him now, not even Zeb. Yes, he had come up with Merko, but that had been countered. He was no longer a threat. Then why was this girl in Washington? Why had Paula set him up?

Reluctantly, he put on the safety jacket. He checked the breathing tube and the release mechanism. The instructions had told him that the protective dome would interfere with wireless transmissions from the head area. He spoke to his genie:

"If you lose my signal for more than a few seconds, assume that I'm under attack and make emergency notifications. Cap Olsen and Blake Silverman would be top of the list."

"Yes, Doug."

He remembered again being attacked by bees in his home: the sensation of being enclosed, trapped, helpless. They must have used advanced trauma therapy at the hospital, he realized, because the drowning that had followed seemed hazy, hard to recall, almost benign. But it really wasn't benign. The whole thing had been anything but benign.

He wanted suddenly to run. He had good reason to confront Ponting, they ought to let him in to MAIMCOM. He could argue strategy, force home the point about PMA bees, get Ponting to change course before it was too late. What the hell was he doing waiting around here, an easy target?

He was hanging around here, he thought, trying to quell the incipient panic, because he didn't really believe his own arguments; and he doubted that anyone else would, either. It just wasn't likely that everything lined up the way he was proposing. There were too many assumptions. The chance of bees striking him again was tiny. What he should do was settle down and make calls to the necessary people, starting with Olsen and probably Schwartz. Ponting was going to be tougher, and he would need better evidence than he had so far. Evidence, probably, of bees getting through his defenses.

He walked over to the window and stared out at the street. A stupid thing to do, he thought a moment later: with the light behind him, he was a perfect target of another kind; maybe Zeb had given somebody a couple of his missiles, or one of those head-shot guns. He moved back, but he had noted, at least, that the street was as quiet as a disused movie-set: nobody out there watching, no sign of bees.

CHAPTER 53

Yasmin brought her all-terrain vehicle to a halt and stepped out into the moonlight. She was small and almost as glossy as the expensive vehicle beside her: her black hair moved in sleek waves, her camouflage-pale blouse and slacks hugged her body as she moved, and she was adorned with rings of gold on her wrists and around her neck.

The tree-lined track she was following had opened into a small natural clearing. A broad arc of stars was visible above. She stared around at the dark shadows beyond the clearing with defensive hostility: there'd better be nothing wrong with this place, or someone would pay. It was, in fact, familiar territory: a part of central Long Island, south of Commack, where the homes of wealthy and mildly-paranoid New Yorkers occupied a few acres apiece, and where country lanes with names like Bread and Cheese Hollow Road ambled amongst the woodlands. No lights from any of these homes were visible from her chosen clearing; and she knew, from the surveys of her acolytes, that even in daylight the trees were sufficient to blot out the sightlines. She also knew from a realtor friend that the property to which the track gave access was unoccupied and for sale, and that protective surveillance of the buildings didn't start for another twenty yards.

She stood still for a moment, testing the silence. A cold breeze fanned her cheek and dead leaves stirred at the side of the track. Nothing else moved. Satisfied at last, she got back in the vehicle and nodded at her two male companions. They got out and went to the back of the vehicle and began to uncover and align the communications dish which was bolted to the open box section. She put on display glasses and monitored their progress. This was going to go right, every step and stage, or she'd be thinking seriously about summary execution for incompetence. And that included herself.

Yasmin had been brought up in California, and had never known anything but wealth and luxury; but her parents, arriving as children from another world, had been authoritarian, coercing her with harsh methods into their own cultural and religious patterns. She had learned to hate them for that, nursed her secret rebellion, moved to New York, immersed herself in the radical politics of the doomers; and then had become authoritarian in her turn, demanding discipline and exact obedience from those she recruited and brought under her command.

When Kronos himself had appeared on her screen with gold shooting out of his head, talking as though he was some kind of supreme leader, it had been, yes, inspiring in a way, but also troubling. He wasn't really a god, certainly not a Mickelburger god, and setting himself up like that looked like overreach. She'd been relieved to get a follow-up memo from Kate, assuring them all that they were the people who counted, and that they would soon be running this operation themselves.

Yasmin fixed her mind firmly on the Merko procedures. She guided the work through the first two stages, getting the dish linked to the satellite, and then establishing a satellite communications footprint over Commack. The men got back into the vehicle. Now they could start what Merko called 'swishing': sending out 'respond-now' signals, in rapid sequence, using the local protocol, and appending one of the series of swarm numbers which Barry had sneaked out of the Commack control center.

They'd been cycling through the swarm numbers for about twenty minutes when a response signal came back. Yasmin clenched her fists: a swarm of bees, up there in the darkness, was about to be abducted by a higher, stronger power. Maybe Kronos's golden digits made sense after all. She could see the swarm in her mind's eye, formed into its own dish, holding its place, balancing against that cold night breeze. She exchanged a glance with Barry, who nodded... So... we send Barry's local validation key and... *Yes.* They were validated, in control. A gust of excitement flickered up her spine.

Run Merko's package. Her eyes moved, head nodding slightly, bringing up symbols on her display. *Run, run, do it.*

She watched for messages, sent commands, authorized functional changes. And Merko thought this stuff was simple... This wasn't simple at all, it demanded full concentration... First, change the communications channel and follow to the new channel and switch to a new local key... then run Merko's special sequence, using his absurdly-named Key of Power, which removed the security constraints and weaponized the swarm... then finally...

The new mission. She took a deep breath.

A mission which was several missions in one. Her special list of targets, together with a methodology, practically a revolutionary philosophy. Because unlike the swarms in Kronos's Washington spectacular, this swarm, and the next, and the next, were not going back to their owners. They would fight on to the death; fight on as Mickelburgers.

Yasmin watched the display, remembering the work, the simulations, making sure the flickering symbols showed the right progression. She was rigid with tension now, could feel her skin under the smooth sheath of her slacks turning slippery with sweat. But it was all flowing onwards like a perfectly-choreographed dance.

"It worked," Barry said, awe in his voice. "We got ourselves a swarm."

"What else?" Yasmin said, her voice sharper than usual. "Come on, guys, let's keep concentrated here, this stuff happens fast." But her display told her that the handshake was already down, the swarm primed and on its way.

She felt suddenly drained. And for the first time, she made a connection between herself and what the swarm had set off to do.

This swarm was going to kill people.

She felt as though she was being physically sucked downwards, the ground opening around her. She put her hands on her knees and squeezed hard. Come on, this is no time to get philosophical, just do it. Think where we'll be before the day is done.

She looked out of the window to the west, towards the skyscrapers of Manhattan, and tried to imagine herself as an avenging swarm of bees.

She took her hands off her knees and told Barry they should begin swishing for the next swarm.

CHAPTER 54

Special agent Trish Ibanu still enjoyed her job, even though at 93 it took some work to pass the physical, and even though the Field Office put her on nights more than she thought was justified. Maybe they thought because she was black and six foot tall and weighed in at 190, folks would see her as just too scary in the daylight.

Her companion today on the early morning shift was a scrawny white kid whose brain ran too fast for his own good, but who could at least drive the cruiser. Right now he was moving the thing along just short of the speed of sound. It seemed that a real important guy in an FBI safe house had lost wireless contact with his genie. Which didn't sound like that big of a deal, but Director Olsen himself had told them to get there fast, so that's what they were doing. She had an uneasy feeling that bees might figure somewhere in the situation. That's what everyone was talking about, how the election could be the moment when Kronos struck again. She remembered the last time, three months ago, when the whole damn city was in a state of panic.

The kid pulled into a street in a manner that left her squashed against the door of the cruiser and then applied the brakes in a manner that threatened to put her through the windscreen. They were outside the door of a nice row house in Adams Morgan. The door was blue and up a few steps from the street. She and Rick stared at the dashboard screen. They were getting surveillance shots from front and back, and several fuzzy interiors. It looked peaceful: there was illumination on the second floor, but no sign of movement inside or outside the property, nor any broken windows.

Bees didn't need to break windows.

"We going in?" Rick said.

"*I'm* going in. You get ready to haul my ass out of there when I holler."

Trish retracted the door of the cruiser and levered her way onto the pavement. She stared at the blue door. Those Kronos bees three months ago killed the poor sucker they'd chosen and then vanished. They didn't attack the investigators. So your ass is covered. So get in there.

The blue door suddenly opened inwards and an alien staggered out. Trish's heart started pumping in a crazy rhythm and she almost fell over. Jesus God, what is that? The figure swaying precariously on the walkway at the top of the stairs looked like an ordinary man dressed in winter clothes except that there wasn't a head; not a real head; just a bulbous mass, greenish in places, with a surface that... *moved,* for Christ's sake... this bulbous, blackened thing was kind of... *alive...* like a giant fruit cake covered in...

Bees. Oh, mother of God. This guy was...

The figure was feeling around like a blind man, reaching out for the railing. Trish suddenly decided she was not going to throw up, she was going to do what a special agent was supposed to do.

"Rick! Bee attack! Call in!"

She was moving as she spoke, taking big steps across the pavement, and heading up the stairs, arms outstretched, grabbing the heavy clothing of the man and shouting something at him, she didn't know what, anything so he knew she was there. She saw now that the bees were not just wrapped around the green bulge of the head, but also were in camouflaged little clumps on his clothing. With his free hand, the man was striking at these, but there was something feeble and helpless about his gestures. She sensed abruptly that he was going to collapse, and she swung close into him and grabbed him under the arms. Shit, the bastard was sinking, letting go, and he was big. She flexed her leg muscles and shouted at him again, and began to maneuver him down the steps like a side of beef.

Blind as he was, he must have sensed that her intentions were friendly, because he made an effort to take some of the weight onto his own legs. It wasn't exactly a graceful tango, but they made it down to the pavement without falling over. The bees didn't attack her. Maybe they thought she was on their side. And she might as well be, because she'd done nothing to get them worried. She saw now what she'd been too slow to see at first: the guy was wearing a safety jacket, and his head was inside one of those protective domes created by the safety jacket when it went off. That protective dome would self-destruct, turn to dust, after a few minutes, and then the bees would go for his eyes, his nostrils, and it was all over. Gal, you got to chase them away and get him in the cruiser.

She maneuvered him across the pavement, her mind racing, but she couldn't remember ever hearing of something that would blow away or burn up or electrically zap bees in a way that didn't also zap the human to which they were attached. And if there was such a thing, it sure as hell wasn't FBI standard issue. Bees were zapped by the military, and only when they'd been lifted clear of the action.

These bees, probably, wouldn't even say hello to the military.

Turning her head, she saw that Rick was half way out of the vehicle.

"Get back inside!" she hissed. "Open the rear door!"

Maybe if they drove at speed, this guy's head out of the window... It wouldn't work, they'd just attack his body, but it might buy some time, and Rick could sure as hell do that stuff.

The rear door concertinaed open. Rick was back behind the wheel. She was about to use all her strength to throw her charge onto the rear seat, when she paused. Maybe there was something else she could do here. Maybe it was the wrong thing to take the bees into the vehicle.

"Ask them what we do now!"

"They don't know!" Rick responded immediately.

Trish braced herself, brushing a hand at the bees within kissing range beside her, still hesitant, but not sure what she was waiting for. Suddenly there was a sound all around her like tiny drills in metal. The end-game, she thought. They'll kill us both. A second later she realized that the bees had vanished. No, not vanished, they were up above her, forming a shape...

Gal, move your ass.

She put her big hand on the now-bald green dome beside her and pushed it down and into the cruiser, as though she was dealing with an arrested felon, keeping her other arm around him and pushing hard with her feet. He gave enough of a cooperative push to help both of them sprawl onto the rear seat.

"Seal us up and go!" she yelled.

Rick was quick enough, but only just. The rear door zipped across, the window tightened into a transparent pane, and she saw the houses moving as they picked up speed: but against the weak light from the street, a dark shadow had gathered, settling on the window beside her. She stared at it in disbelief.

Yeah, well tough, she thought, trying to preserve the rush of relief she had felt as the door had closed; see how you like it in a convoy at a hundred miles an hour. Truth is, you're going to be one sorry swarm of bees... You're going to have one very bad hair day... So leave us alone now.

Obligingly, the dark mass slid down the window and out of sight.

Trish heaved her body around on the seat and turned towards the man sprawled out beside her. He was limp, perhaps unconscious. The dome on his head had split open and was starting to degrade. She could see black hair. She reached over and felt for a pulse in his neck. Alive, for now, but they ought to get him to hospital.

Of course they'd have to shake off the bees first. Otherwise they couldn't open the door of the cruiser. Hospitals, as far as she knew, were not expected to deal with patients covered in bees.

And then she thought of something else. Maybe the bees could find a way of getting in to the vehicle. Even at a hundred miles an hour. Maybe *especially* at a hundred miles an hour.

CHAPTER 55

General Lee Ponting walked up the broad stairway from the subterranean levels and into the atrium on the first floor of MAIMCOM Headquarters. At this time of the morning, normal functions mostly in suspension, the high, vault-like space looked empty and pretentious; but a couple of his men had chosen to gather at the guard-rail of the main visitor display and watch the default simulation in the pit below.

The General had been in the building through the night, catching a couple of hours sleep before and after midnight, and spending the last hour touring the lower levels, where some of his best technicians were on duty. He had briefed the President the previous evening, and now, he told himself, the situation was contained, the necessary and logical things had been done. It had been a struggle, but police chiefs across the nation had cooperated, and he was confident that his dataset included virtually every swarm identification number currently in use: over 800,000 of them. Any swarms flying without a valid number would find themselves rapidly taken out by the MAIMCOM defensive system. Just to be sure, he had increased the check rate by a factor of three, at least for the next six hours.

He should be feeling confident. Instead he had a profound sense of imminent catastrophe. It was like the Iraq thing, the sudden and irrational outbreak of group emotion which had led to the death of a dozen innocent civilians. Something you didn't see coming could just explode around you.

General Ponting moved forward towards the display pit, exchanging a few words with his subordinates, and pausing to look at the brilliant animation spread out below. United States territory from coast to coast hovered in relief and color, sparks of blue light erupting and fading like fireflies, thousands in number, forming a glistening matt in areas of high population. Each blue spark was an indicator of normality: a bee-swarm which had responded correctly to the IFF MAIMCOM challenge.

"A great sight, sir." It was the Army uniform, a woman, who had spoken.

"Making America safe," he said. "Let's keep it that way."

"Yes sir, General."

The two intermediate ranks saluted and turned away and headed for the stairs.

The General lingered for a moment. He was half hoping to see a spark of red amongst the blue: a sign that a swarm had failed the challenge, and had been destroyed. It would mean, probably, that his system was working, that a Kronos swarm had been successfully interdicted. But the sea of blue pulsed on, unbroken. So maybe, he told himself, there would be no attacks; maybe the Kronos threat had been exaggerated.

"FBI Director of Security Cap Olsen for you, General," his genie said.

He felt an immediate echo of his earlier premonition of doom. He straightened up and began walking. "Tell him I'll be with him in a moment."

"Yes, sir."

He walked through the atrium to the main entrance hall and took the elevator to the fourth floor. The lighting in the reception space was subdued, and the lecture theatre and briefing rooms were dark. To his right was the security portal to Senior Command. The Headquarters building was heavily defended around its outside perimeter, and as a secondary precaution was divided into cells. Like the overall building, each cell was bomb-proof, radiation-proof, and bee-proof. He placed his hand in the slot beside the security portal and waited for the door to open. He was vividly aware that he was only in command of MAIMCOM because his predecessor, General Anderson, had been a victim of the previous Kronos attacks. But Anderson had been at home, and his situation here at Headquarters was very different. If the security of the overall building had been breached, a complicated algorithm determined which doors would open rather than stay closed, which doors that were normally open would close, and what kind of alarm would sound.

No alarm sounded. The door opened. He stepped through the portal and the door closed behind him. He was now better protected than in any other part of MAIMCOM.

The conference area immediately surrounding him contained high-tech work stations. A senior technician was standing at a bank of large screens. The corridor to his right led to a gym, a medical station, food and drink facilities, and a small common room. To his left was a ring of six offices opening on to the conference area, the inner walls of which could be set to any required level of transparency. The usual choice was eighty percent transparent. Two of the offices were occupied, to judge from the lighting patterns and the blurred shapes within: his senior aide, and a colonel seconded from the Marine Corps. His immediate deputy was getting some sleep at another protected location.

He went through to his own office, which was large enough to accommodate a small conference table, several slow-growth decorative sculptures, and a quartet of posture-sensitive leather recliners.

"I'm with you, Cap," he said as he sat down at his desk. "What gives?"

He waited a few seconds while his genie prompted Olsen and relayed his comment.

Cap's voice, when it came, was quick, strained, as though he was dealing with several things at once. "Hey, Lee. I take it you're in a secure location. Your genie wouldn't say."

"I'm shut away in MAIMCOM."

"Good. I may have to ask if I can join you."

"Did I hear that right? You're not in a protected location?"

"I'm in a safe house downtown. But it's not bee-protected. More important, there's been an attack. My guy Doug Edie, Alan Connacher, is in a bad situation."

"Are you serious? Bees?"

"What else."

"But he's alive?"

"I know, he should be dead. He used a safety jacket, and we somehow got him inside an FBI vehicle. This is happening while we speak."

General Ponting felt a coldness stretching down his arms into his fingers. His worst imaginings, rising up out of the mire, clutched at him... He grasped at detail.

"Are you sure? Cap? I mean, are you sure he didn't panic? Maybe he assumed that some ordinary PMA swarm, come to check him over, was going to kill him and so he fired up his jacket... Which made them stick around..."

"Hold on, Lee..." Silence for a few seconds. "Lee? I have a link to our agents in the vehicle. If I can, I'll bring Doug into the conversation, but at the moment he's not able to speak... The problem they have is that they believe the bees are still with them, maybe trying to gain access through the air filtration system, even though they're traveling at speed. We've got a couple of experts working on whether that's possible or not, and how long it would take... But to answer your question... Our agents are sure this is a real attack, because the bees were biting him through his clothing, which is why he's currently too sick to speak."

"Maybe he ran out of air from the jacket. That would make him sick."

"Lee, there's background I should give you." Ponting could hear increasing stress and impatience in Cap's voice. "I only got this stuff a half hour ago, and then I was trying to figure out the angles, so there was no time to tell anybody. But here's the deal. Doug was supposed to meet Paula Fields at FBI HQ yesterday at six o-clock. She had something important to tell him. You remember Paula? The NSA girl who validated our ideas about Merko Milovic diverting MAIMKEY?"

He didn't like the way this was going, but he grunted an acknowledgment.

Cap remained silent.

Ponting said, "Carry on, I'm with you."

"I just got news that Doug is conscious, asking a couple of questions. Anyway, Paula didn't show for the meeting. But what we now know is that a Mickelburger was staking out FBI HQ at the time that Doug arrived. Don't ask me for detail, but that apparently gave the Kronos gang access to data that told them where Doug had come from. So they knew where to send the swarm. Secondly, this means that Paula is busted. She's no longer a credible informant. Which throws out the stuff about Merko, in fact makes it look like purposeful misdirection.

I have to tell you, Lee, that even before he got attacked, Doug said that your defenses were probably not going to work."

"And I have to tell *you*, Cap, that you're jumping to a hell of a lot of conclusions." He was rising from his chair as he spoke, and moving around his desk to stare out at the blurred conference space. Who was he going to bring in on this? That technician out there? The really bad part of this, which some vigilant cells in his brain had telegraphed straight into consciousness, was that if Paula and others at NSA were actively on the wrong side, what did that say about MAIMCOM? Was he sitting on the same foundations of clay, the same systematic betrayal? Of course his immediate colleagues were one-niners like himself, but they all depended on the technical input from the lower, and younger, ranks.

He felt his chest growing tight, his breathing more rapid. The hell with that. He wasn't going to weaken, he was in charge of this agency and he'd take the incoming flak. Which was, as he'd just pointed out, of questionable accuracy. There was no point yielding too much ground just yet.

"Cap?" he said into the ongoing silence.

After a couple of seconds, Cap's urgent, quick-fire, voice was back. "The best thing is to get Doug in on this. Hold a moment."

He waited for a few more seconds, then Cap said, "He's with us now. Doug?"

Ponting heard low vehicle noise, retained by the comms system to give context. He had never met Alan Connacher, let alone his new incarnation as Doug Edie, and he found it hard to get a sense of the man who now began speaking. The voice was low, unsteady, but driven by something which sounded like a mixture of stress and arrogance.

"General Ponting is in on this?"

"Yes. Present."

"Okay, General... I assume you have a basic outline of this event, so I'm going to try and tell you..." There was a brief pause, then the voice returned, a little stronger. "I'm going to try and tell you what you need to know."

"I'll stop you if I need to clarify something."

"I suggest you just listen. I don't know how long we've got."

The General drew in his breath, his irritation growing. He said nothing.

Doug continued in short phrases. "The important thing is this... I've been asking the agent who got me into the vehicle about what happened... I was very lucky... Before she got me in the vehicle, the bees... stopped attacking... went away, disappeared... she thinks upwards... that's how she kept them out of the vehicle... so that was almost certainly a MAIMKEY check... maybe you increased the frequency... Am I right you'll have a record of that, General? Given that we have time and place?"

"You want to prove there was a MAIMKEY challenge?"

"What I want, General... Because you're not just checking MAIMKEY now, are you? You're checking the swarm number... to see if it's valid."

"That's correct."

"And it *was* valid, because the swarm wasn't destroyed."

"That's correct."

"So that's the first thing. Your system isn't working."

"One is hardly a valid sample size from which to draw that conclusion."

Doug's voice rose into an exasperated growl. "Your system isn't working, General. If you can't get a handle on that, you're going to wind up killing a lot of people."

"Among them yourself, I suppose?"

"Yes."

"And yet you sound very much alive."

"You're implying that because I'm alive, I wasn't attacked. You're clutching at straws, General. I know this is tough. It means ditching your defense plan and moving to another one. But you've got to get hold of the facts. I didn't imagine this attack. Ask the agent sitting beside me. Ask her about the bites on my body and the bees trying to get into the vehicle."

"I'm sure she's a good agent. I'm sure she thinks that bees are trying to get in to your vehicle. But is there any real evidence of that? I'm not saying you imagined the bees, Doug, but I think it would be entirely understandable if you mistook an ordinary inspection for an attack. You were attacked before, weren't you? Died, in fact. That is one hell of a trauma."

Lee Ponting thought he was staying calm and rational, given the provocation from a know-it-all civilian, and the stress inherent in the situation. He wasn't prepared for Doug's next comment:

"Cap, we're wasting time with this guy. He needs people to die before he's going to act. Can we cut him out and go over to the PMA Director? We need her cooperation to get data from these 44 PMA offices."

Cap said, "Doug, slow down, give it one more minute. Tell the General what you started to tell him. The important thing."

Doug's voice, which seemed to be picking up energy the longer he spoke, said: "Okay, but make the connection with Schwartz, because I don't know how long I've got. General, the point is we have the place and the time at which the attacking swarm was challenged, and that data is being sent through to your genie by my FBI companion as we speak... Now, like I said, you presumably keep the data on these IFF challenges... Is that correct?"

"Yes."

"So you should be able to search through that data and get the swarm number of the swarm that's attacking me. You will find it's a valid number, a PMA number, but if you check with the PMA, you'll discover that the originating PMA office is not local to DC, but is more remote, probably Columbia or Annapolis. That's your first clue that this swarm is not on a routine mission. Now, if you want to help save my life, you can *delete*, got that? *delete*, that swarm number from your dataset of valid numbers, so that next time that swarm gets challenged, it will be destroyed..."

He clenched his jaw and said nothing.

"Okay," Doug continued, "I'm not holding my breath about that, both because you probably won't do it, and also because the agents in the vehicle with me tell me they can hear noises in the air-con outlets suggesting the bees are in there cutting things up, in which case they're surrounded by heavy metals and stuff and probably won't receive the MAIMCOM challenge... But it's the principle that counts. I've identified 44 suspect PMA offices which may have been penetrated by activists, and we're going to get the numbers of all the swarms run from those offices from PMA Director Schwartz. I assume the data you have isn't differentiated by local PMA office... General?"

"No. I think not."

"Okay. We'll get it for you. Again, to be clear, *delete* those swarm numbers from your dataset, so that all such swarms will be destroyed when challenged."

Again he didn't respond.

Doug's voice was tiring. "I sure as hell hope your genie's recording this, because I'm not going to say it again."

The General had settled back against his desk, slow-burning anger undermining his self-control. This guy was not only an arrogant smartass, he was also missing the inherent flaw in his reasoning. "I appreciate the lecture, Doug, Connacher, whoever you are, but you're talking about PMA bees without acknowledging the main problem with that: PMA bees can't do these things; they can't attack people, penetrate vehicles, or anything else of an anti-social nature."

Doug's voice rose up in renewed irritation. "Oh come on, General, you know the score: these PMA bees have been weaponized by tapping into a secret military program, a Trojan horse sitting inside every bee out there."

He felt his body going rigid, his fists clenching tight. "I don't know what you're talking about."

"We don't have time for this crap, General. The name of the program is BEEKEEP, and you absolutely do know all about it."

He ignored the shock, the sense of air going out of his lungs, and pushed himself into a standing position. Before he could speak, Cap's voice, surprised, irritated, said:

"Doug? You talked with someone?"

"Yeah, I talked with someone. It doesn't matter who. I know about BEEKEEP, I know it's a program introduced under the last president. This stuff has to be out, on the table. Are you trying to protect your secrets, General? Is that what all this nonsense is about?"

He wondered later whether, if Connacher was there in front of him, he would have shot him. That would certainly have fairly expressed his frustration, his justified outrage. BEEKEEP was *necessary*, for the security of the nation. The external threat from the Asian giants had never gone away; and the way things were developing, the internal threat might become even more severe. So it had to stay secret. If this flawed, weak, President heard about it, she'd axe it.

"First I have to warn you that communicating sensitive information of this kind to civilians outside the designated loop is a serious offense, and you are therefore at this moment breaking the law. Or you would be if the information was correct."

"General, I don't give a fuck about breaking the law." Doug sounded as though he was now in a state of fury of his own. "Have you still not connected the dots? This is what Merko was doing at NSA. He was deciphering the MAIMCOM sections of code and figuring out how to turn on BEEKEEP. Have you got it now? PMA bees, BEEKEEP-enabled. And we can stop them, if you'll throw off the military straitjacket and put two and two together." Doug went on in a lower voice, "Cap, like I said, we're wasting time. Can you lose this jerk and link us up with Schwartz?"

Cap's voice, half-apologetic, said, "Sorry, Lee. But the guy is smart. It's worth thinking about what he said."

General Ponting was left trembling with rage.

CHAPTER 56

When General Ponting finally withdrew from his auditory field, Doug resisted the urge to slump back against the FBI cruiser's upholstery and give way to pain and anger and defeat. Cap was still with him and they had a job to do, no matter what kind of archaic military mindset was impeding them.

His body, encased in thick clothing, and dotted with swollen bites, felt as though it was twice its usual size and getting bigger. The biosynthetic agents injected by the bees continually threatened to subvert his conscious thought processes. Maybe it was just as well the General had made him mad: at least the stimulus had kept him awake and functioning.

The bees would get him soon. That was obvious. The General would do nothing, and anyway the bees were too deeply buried inside the vehicle to register on the MAIMCOM detectors. Or maybe Trish was imagining all that about bees at the window. Or maybe he was imagining Trish imagining all that. He thought he could hear a keening sound like the dentist's drills they used in his childhood, reverberating out of the air inlets, but that could just be in his head.

Trish was shaking him again.

"What did you find out about the dentist?" he said, forcing himself upright. No, that wasn't right. He tried to repel the mental fog. "I mean the air filtration system... the vehicle's..."

Cap was evidently still with him, because it was his voice that replied. "According to Quantico, there's some tough materials in there. It should hold up the bees for a while."

Doug turned his head, tried to focus on any passing landmarks. "I don't know where the hell we are, but is there a protected building close? Where they've got proper entrance controls? The White House, maybe? I could cover my eyes and your guys could help me get to the door."

"I'll get Blake on that."

"Then let's concentrate on... on the PMA data... Any word from Schwartz?""

"No. Not yet."

The driver turned his head and said, "Sir, I'm heading west, for the Beltway. Is that okay?"

The young kid at the wheel had seemed to Doug at moments like a grinning demon, an acolyte of Kronos, but he had fought aside these unfounded delusions. "The Beltway won't help. Keep us downtown."

The vehicle lurched and swung right, then swung right again. Trish held onto him and he fought off an attack of nausea.

Cap's voice suddenly exploded in his ear. "Jesus Christ, it's happening... It's happening all over again... I cannot believe we let this..." A short pause. "Doug, I got to jump into this. Blake will stay with you. That fucking idiot Ponting..."

"Cap?"

A small delay, and then Blake's voice: "I'm not with him, Doug, but it seems... it seems... yeah, Boston Field Office... shit... hysterical woman... wife of Senator McCauley... the same shit, the same fucking shit..."

"Bee attack?"

"Yeah, eyes gone, nothing recoverable... Our worst nightmare... Jesus, how many more of these are coming down the pike?"

"Lots." Doug felt his own eyes stinging. He flinched, felt a momentary wave of faintness. No, there were no bees in the vehicle and that noise was inside his head. He shook himself.

"Listen, Blake, you and I have to stay with the Schwartz thing. We have to get that PMA data. With a bee attack proven, Ponting has to back down. If you can't get Schwartz, get somebody else. You have the connections."

Blake didn't answer.

Doug clenched his fists, still encumbered with winter gloves. "Blake?"

After a few more seconds, Blake's voice returned, full of urgency. "Tell your driver to head for MAIMCOM Headquarters. As fast as he can. I just learned something fucking unbelievable."

Doug instructed the kid, who responded with another gut-wrenching maneuver. Pushed by fresh adrenalin, his brain was now wrestling its way out of the fog, starting to engage. What had Blake found out about MAIMCOM Headquarters? It was obviously a state of the art, bee-proof, facility, but was it maybe something more than that? Had some of the BEEKEEP mentality leaked through into the design?

The top brass knew about BEEKEEP, for sure: which meant they'd get worried about defending against weaponized bees, their own or the enemy's. They'd know that weaponized bees could piggy-back on vehicles, even penetrate vehicles. So if they had garages within the secure perimeter, they would know they had to clean not just personnel who entered from the street, but vehicles as well.

And Ponting knew about that?

Doug felt his anger reviving, burning at a new level. "Blake?"

After a moment, Blake's voice said, "Sorry, Doug, more stuff coming in, this is a fucking crap shoot. New York, Manhattan... Congressman Healey jumped out of a brownstone, three floors up. Obviously trying to escape bees, which came down anyway and finished the job... Something coming in too from the next time zone, Chicago... suspected bee attack but no details..."

"Listen, you'd better convince Cap he should join me at MAIMCOM HQ. Not only will I need help nailing down Ponting, but he probably isn't safe where he is. Does Ponting know I'm on the way?"

"I'm working on it. But Cap is notifying the President, and I think your safety is sufficiently high priority that Ponting's not going to have any choice."

"I assume you found out that MAIMCOM HQ can sanitize vehicles."

"Like I say, fucking unbelievable the guy doesn't even mention it. His underlings are giving me crap about only military vehicles being eligible, but every death reported is making that less and less tenable. Got to go, Doug. Hang in there. I'm going to get you cleared for MAIMCOM entry within the next five minutes, or die trying."

Doug felt his whole body coming awake, and a new kind of fear growing. Maybe there was a chance, after all... if there were no delays... if the bees were lost up the wrong pipe... Maybe he'd get close, and then...

He stared out of the window and realized that he was looking at the superstructure of a bridge. In the blackness below, he could see lights reflected off water. They were already crossing the Potomac, and MAIMCOM HQ was in Arlington, so they were minutes, seconds, away.

Trish said, in tones of harsh complaint, "They going to do something about these bees?"

He turned to look at her, suddenly emotional about the big, motherly woman who had saved his life and wanted to go on fighting. "That's the idea." In quick phrases, he filled in some detail about what was happening, and had a halting exchange with the youngster, between the scariest of his driving maneuvers, about what they might find at MAIMCOM Headquarters, and what they should aim for.

"Nearly there," the kid said, hunched over the wheel, siren at full blast, a couple of early-morning commuters scuttling for the curb.

"Blake?" Doug said. There was no reply.

A building appeared directly ahead, softly glowing, apparently disconnected from the ground, like a big alien spaceship about to land.

Come on, Doug muttered to himself, a generalized plea to all involved parties: *make this happen.*

Something brushed softly against his cheek. His gloved hand was half way there before his conscious mind reacted. He jerked forward, eyes darting left and right. He could see nothing in the gloom, but now there were several flutterings against his face, a faint tweak at his wrist under the glove.

"Bees," he said. "Testing me out."

Blake's voice: "Shit. You sure? Tell the military General Ponting is approving this. They've *got* to process you."

The driver said, "'Visitor Parking'... 'Authorized Base Personnel'... 'Military Vehicle Inspection and Cleansing', okay, that's us."

The building was looming close beside them, dark, featureless, except for a few circles of opal light. They swung left and down a ramp, siren still sounding. Doug could see nothing around him, the bees, if they were there, staying low and camouflaged. But the tickling against his cheek continued, seemed to get worse. He waved his hands, spat out air, his heart rate climbing.

Suddenly they were in an area of strong illumination, and he could see shadowy specks floating around him like motes of dust, gathering in density. Outside the vehicle, only briefly catching his attention, were figures in Army uniforms.

The driver killed the siren and opened a hole in his door space and began talking rapidly. Trish had taken off a shoe and was batting at the bees in front of his face, and also shouting at the uniforms.

Blake says, he articulated in his head, *Blake says General Ponting...* but he didn't manage to speak. He closed his eyes tight as the tickling grew more aggressive and began pulling off his gloves. Why hadn't he thought about air? Maybe there was an emergency source in the vehicle. Too late. He expelled the air in his lungs in a vigorous blast, shaking his head backwards and forwards, and then sucked in through almost closed lips. His hands now free, he clamped the heels of palms over his eye sockets, and pulled his wrists together to close his nostrils. But already the bees were biting him on his exposed hands.

He didn't know what the soldiers said in response to the desperate threats of Trish and the driver, but at last the vehicle began to move. Forward, thank God. He sensed the brilliant light fading, heard a swish and a clunk behind. He clamped his lips together, his lungs already demanding fresh air. The assault of the bees was gathering force: it seemed like a cloth made of diamond-sharp needles was pressing against his face and hands; and with each second the injected chemicals were driving the strength from his muscles.

He felt himself falling slowly against Trish, his hands coming away from his eyes, his mouth opening to breathe, a half-welcome numbness spreading around his body. *Got to talk with Schwartz,* he told himself. *Mustn't go to sleep. Got to talk with...*

But Trish seemed to be hauling him out of the vehicle, and her body was full of static electricity. There were sparks between them and his hair was doing funny things. He fell onto a hard floor. The inside of his mouth tasted of ozone. He spat out tiny pieces of grit and drew a couple of trial breaths. He opened his eyes. What the hell had happened? He put a hand up to his face and felt carefully. Lumpy, but no bees. Was he alive, or just imagining? Where the hell was Trish? The space around him, he began to see, was as clinical as a morgue. A morgue with robotic arms and pipes and strange shapes on the ceiling. A huge coffin, just for him.

He pushed against the floor and turned slowly over. The FBI vehicle. So he wasn't crazy. Not even dead. He reached out and touched a tire. When he turned back, he wasn't alone. Army uniforms were lifting him onto a stretcher.

"Got to talk with Schwartz," he muttered.

CHAPTER 57

A midst all the fury and anguish created by the new wave of bee attacks, Cap Olsen was aware of one small comforting point of stability: his guy, Alan Connacher, the smartass he'd risked his career for, was right after all. *Lee Ponting*, the self-righteous prick, might end up as landfill: but he himself, and the FBI in general, were probably going to do okay. As long as bees didn't get them.

Cap was sitting at a table in a small row house in Georgetown. One of the big wall screens in front of him showed President Diaz at her Oval Office desk, with other participants in her recently-convened conference arranged in boxes around her. As well as himself, these included John Corelli from NSA, Martha Lundquist, the New York Police Chief, and a rolling list of temporary participants. The Mayor of Chicago had just given them a moving account of the death of an Illinois senator.

Cap was distressed that Susan Schwartz, the PMA Director, could not be located. He liked her and she was badly needed to hustle through the PMA data they required. She lived alone outside the Beltway in Kings Park. Nobody knew exactly what she'd done to defend herself. Bees from local law enforcement were investigating, and police personnel were following up. Cap expected a report at any moment. Meanwhile, White House staffers were tracking down her deputy, just in case, and hoping to bring him into the conference shortly.

A second wall screen in front of Cap's table was selecting and displaying news stories about bee attacks. He also had an interactive display rolled out on the table, showing FBI operational involvement. Six deaths had now been reported to law enforcement agencies. Only two of those had so far been publicized in the media: that of the New York congressman, jumping out of the brownstone, and the more recent case of a State Department minister who had been killed in the airport in Atlanta. Young people were reacting to the news by showing up at the crime scenes, even though it was still not quite four in the morning.

Cap was too busy to think much about his personal situation, but his wife told him that a swarm had visited their home about fifteen minutes ago, checked her over, and then disappeared. He didn't think the swarm would be able to track him to Georgetown, but given that the activists had found Doug, and might know about the safe house he was in, he knew he had to take action: at least, he thought, he should climb into the waiting limousine, where he could still take part in the conference, and be ready to go somewhere; but he hesitated, caught up in the urgency of the discussion.

Messages on his roll-out display told him, to his relief, that Doug had survived the bee attack. The FBI agent at the scene, Trish Ibanu, said that he'd been bitten a few times, but she didn't think it was as serious as the previous attack.

General Ponting joined them live near the end of the Mayor of Chicago's report. Cap watched him closely. He looked calm, considering that his tactical measures, prepared over several days, had just been blown out of the water. Cap was still simmering with anger over Ponting's failure to offer his MAIMCOM facilities to Doug as soon as the attack was known to him.

When the Mayor signed off, Cap said, "Madam President, I think you're aware that my technical adviser, Alan Connacher, has survived the bee attack against him, following a last minute agreement with General Ponting over the use of his defensive facilities at MAIMCOM Headquarters. Since he is key to our assessment of the present situation, I strongly urge you to allow him to join our discussion."

Watching her image on the screen, he was glad to see that in spite of the new burdens weighing down her features, she still looked fully and intelligently engaged. She turned her gaze to her left for a couple of seconds, and then looked back into camera. "I take it he's sufficiently recovered to talk to us?"

"General?" Cap switched his attention to the box containing the image of General Ponting.

Ponting's face was fixed in a mask of careful control. For a moment he seemed to prefer to leave the mask in place, rather than allow speech to disrupt it. Then he dropped his gaze, swallowed, and looked up.

"We've done our best for him, of course, but my latest information is that he's still unconscious."

"Unconscious?" Cap said in surprise, concentrating his attention on Ponting's expression.

"Unfortunately the bees penetrated the vehicle and were able to bite him. Not his eyes, which he was covering, but his hands."

Cap was hit by a sudden wave of suspicion, and also the sense that he'd missed something, misjudged the situation. "My information is that the bites weren't serious."

The General shrugged and spread his hands, as though sad that he didn't have better news. "I'm afraid our young friend has taken a lot of punishment this evening."

Was it possible? Ponting couldn't be trusted to look after Connacher? The man who had shown up his mistakes, and discovered his military secrets?

Of course it was possible: *there is no limit what people will do to protect their own interests.*

He found himself rising to his feet and rolling up his display. "Ma'am, if I may... I will stay in aural and, where possible, visual contact... but it's become apparent that I'm not secure where I am, and if the General will permit me, I will make the move across to MAIMCOM."

Giving the screen a final glance, he caught Ponting's frown of annoyance, quickly covered over. "Of course," the General said. "We'll be glad to see you, Director."

"Thank you..." Cap turned and made for the door. "Again, with the General's permission, I will assess Connacher's condition and see if I can bring him into the conversation. Meanwhile, Madame President..." Cap closed the front door behind him and trotted down the short pathway to the street. A doorway in the rear of the limousine opened with a soft beep, as bodywork panels reconfigured. "Meanwhile, I'll have my colleague Blake Silverman standing by. He understands Connacher's work..."

Cap glanced quickly around, a futile action unless bees were caught in silhouette against a streetlamp, and then folded himself into the rear seat of the limousine. He reached up to his ear and briefly suppressed the wireless link. "MAIMCOM Headquarters," he said. The doorway swished together and sealed. The vehicle took off. His genie worked fast, and in a few seconds the screens facing him displayed the same information he had been viewing in the safe house. He locked his gaze on the image of the President. She was speaking:

"...another three deaths, I'm sad to say, so we'll catch up on that, and then I'd like to have a comment from General Ponting on this urgent question of our defenses."

Three deaths? Jesus, this thing was accelerating. And moving west, he learned, as the stories unfolded. Two were in the east, both congresswomen, but the other was in Denver, a well-known former Secretary of State. Mountain time, two hours behind. One of the congresswomen had ignored the warnings and been attacked in her home; the other two had apparently been tracked by the bees to temporary bolt-holes. All three victims had suffered irreparable brain lesions. It was their worst nightmare, playing out across the nation.

He broke off from the conference to brief Silverman. On his return, General Ponting was speaking:

"...other possibilities we would have to consider. In particular, Madame President, and I'm sure Director Olsen agrees with this, there are indications that security in all of our agencies is not as strong as we would like. He told me himself that Alan Connacher's whereabouts may have become known to the activists because of leaks out of NSA. Even in MAIMCOM, where we put a very high priority indeed on recruiting the right people and keeping them loyal, we can never be totally sure that we don't have a spy in our midst. So maybe our new defensive system was known about to the enemy, and in that case it would be vulnerable. Even one valid swarm number, given to all their illegal swarms, would enable them to answer the new MAIMCOM challenge successfully and avoid destruction."

There was a brief pause, and then Christine Diaz said, "If I hear you right, General, you're still denying that these attacking swarms are PMA swarms, hijacked away from their normal missions."

"That's correct, Ma'am, I still regard that as unlikely."

Cap felt a rush of irritation. God, this guy was slippery!

The President continued, "As I understand it, Director Olsen, the PMA theory is the one your adviser was working on."

"Yes, Ma'am. And we think we can prove it. General, did you find out the number of the swarm that attacked Connacher?"

Ponting hesitated, his expression unfriendly. "Not yet... We're not sure it's important at this stage..."

"Believe me, General, if Connacher wanted it done, it's important. Madame President, if the General will nominate a member of his technical staff, Silverman can work with him on this."

"Do it, General," the President said. "We need to throw everything we can at this."

"Yes, Ma'am."

"Meanwhile," she went on, "two more dead. One of them Sarah Bailey, a senator not up for re-election, killed right here in this town. Several of you will know her for her committee work on defense issues. A great public servant... This is a miserable night, and all of us stand indicted for not preventing it. So, General... Is that in hand?"

"Yes, Ma'am."

"Give me a name, General," Cap said.

Ponting's voice was taut with irritation. "I've asked my senior technical officer, Colonel Reznichek, to assign the task."

The President said, "Since you don't sound confident of a good outcome by that route, General Ponting, I must ask you what you think we should be doing instead."

Cap withdrew briefly from the conference to pass the message to Blake. He stared out at the passing lights and asked his vehicle when they would arrive at MAIMCOM Headquarters. "Six minutes, sir," the vehicle told him.

On his return, the General was saying, "...obliged to recommend, Madame President, against all my military instincts, that you adopt the strategy that you yourself proposed: that is, instruct all agencies running bees to shut down operations with maximum possible speed. When our monitors show that the number of swarms still in action has declined to an acceptable level, we will destroy everything out there. That will include the swarms that are killing people. This involves some wastage, obviously, but in my opinion we're at the point where this is the only responsible thing to do."

"You told me last time, General, that it would take you twelve hours to modify your systems for that purpose."

"We've already done that work, Ma'am. A simple over-ride procedure will enable us to destroy all bees, even if they respond with MAIMKEY."

Cap said, his anger renewed, "Madame President, I wouldn't want to stand down all FBI bees, without warning, when such a thing is almost certainly unnecessary. You'll compromise hundreds, maybe thousands, of situations across the nation in which bees are making a necessary contribution to law enforcement. You'll also send the wrong message to those people out there who are trying to do us harm."

"You're referring to Kronos and his activist allies," Diaz said.

"Maybe youth in general. I think it was General Ponting himself who spoke of riots and property damage. Does he think the armed forces have enough men on the ground to maintain public order if bees are withdrawn?"

That provoked a lengthy response from Lee Ponting, and a promise from the President that she would shortly be hearing from the Chairman of the Joint Chiefs. As his vehicle pulled up outside an amber-colored arch, structured in the midst of a wash of warning colors, he heard her giving more bad news: another five reports of bee attacks had accumulated in the brief space of time since the last update; and one of those related to the PMA Director, Susan Schwartz, who had been found dead in the back yard of her home. Total deaths had now reached fourteen.

Cap got out onto a cobbled forecourt, lit by the amber arch. He could see the upper floors of the building, but at ground level the outlines were soft, almost invisible. Armed soldiers, possibly robotic, stood on each side of the arch. He walked into the arch and found himself in a high-ceilinged space, intelligent materials providing misleading boundaries. He was aware of SAIMs, bees' larger cousins, making a deft and almost undetectable examination. A moment later a door opened ahead of him and he passed through into an imposing hall, an atrium to his left.

An army major saluted and said, "Welcome to MAIMCOM, Director Olsen, the General asks you to wait for a moment at our visitor display." He led the way into the atrium.

Cap saw a guard rail circling a large sunken space, with blue light emanating from the display below. His wireless contact with the outside world, cut briefly during his passage through the entrance, had been restored. He could hear the comforting sound of the President's voice.

He took a chance and jumped in, speaking loud enough for the Major to overhear. "This is Director Olsen, Madam President, forgive me for interrupting, but I'm now in MAIMCOM Headquarters. General, I'm going immediately to see Alan Connacher, conscious or not, and then I'm going to see Colonel Reznichek. No form of delay is acceptable."

There was a very brief silence, and then Ponting said, "Take it easy, Cap, we're not conspiring against you."

"Good." He cut off his aural input to the conference, and started walking quickly towards the stairs. "Let's go, Major. It's all arranged. Is this the way to the sickbay?"

"Sir, I'm not sure..."

"Yes you are, Major. I repeat: is this the way?" He turned his head to look at the man scurrying along behind him.

"Sir..." The Major seemed to hesitate and listen. He ran up alongside just as they reached the stairs. "Yes sir. I'll show you."

They trotted down three flights of stairs and walked along a corridor. The Major opened a sealed door on the left. Cap followed him into a spacious room with grey walls, clinical lighting, and two beds. Even Cap could tell that the medical robotics arrayed at the bedside and around the room were basic by modern standards. The man on the nearer bed was dressed in FBI-issue winter clothes and was stretched out on his back with his eyes closed. Cap moved forward quickly and stared at his face: it reminded him of the older Alan, drowned in his own pool, dead but not dead, waiting for help and resuscitation. He reached down and raised an arm, which was limp, and looked closely at the back of the hand: there were bite marks, but as far as he could tell, these were not dangerously aggravated. There were no prostheses attached to Doug's body, nor any sign of other clinical interventions. Did they just bring him here and dump him?

He let go the arm and turned. "You've got no physician on duty?"

The Major shook his head. "A medical orderly. I'll get her."

"And ask Colonel Reznichek to join me down here."

The Major seemed again to hesitate.

"Quickly," Cap said.

The Major bobbed his head and disappeared.

Cap listened for a moment to the White House conference: Schwartz's deputy had finally logged on and was getting up to speed. He checked that his own vocal input was suppressed and bent over the body. "Doug?" he said quietly, close to his ear. "I won't allow you to back out like this. We need you. There's more to be done. Whatever that bastard did to you, don't let him get away with it."

The steady breathing didn't change. Cap felt for a pulse in his neck and counted off the beats. Slow, but at least it was steady.

A middle-aged woman entered the room. Cap turned away from the recumbent Doug Edie and studied her. She wore a clinical smock with sergeant's stripes at each shoulder. She had strong features and carried herself well, but her eyes betrayed uncertainty, perhaps something more.

"Sergeant, thank you for your help, run me through this quickly. How was your patient when he arrived here at your facility? How would you describe his condition?"

"Clearly compromised, but not really serious... uh..." She turned her gaze briefly towards the bed. "Much as you see now."

"Unconscious?"

"Yes."

"Macro diagnostics okay?"

"Nothing to suggest trauma."

"This is what... half an hour ago?"

She nodded.

"Did you give the patient any medication?"

A quick glance at the bed. "No. We did not."

"Nothing? Nano-diagnostics? Cellular repair infusion?" He held it a beat. "Anything involving suppression of normal functions?"

"No." She dropped her eyes. "We don't have a nano-diagnostic capability here."

Cap glanced around as though in disbelief. He turned back to the woman, and the Major, who was hovering just behind her. "So, what's the plan? You've got a physician on the way? How come he isn't here by now?"

The woman shrugged uncomfortably. "I wasn't instructed to call a physician."

Cap threw up his hands. "Have I got this right? You have in your care a very important civilian, whom the President of the United States is anxious to interview, who was attacked by bees, who is lying there practically in a coma... And you do nothing? No physician, no advanced diagnostics, nothing? What the hell is going on?"

The Major said, "Director Olsen... I'm sorry if our lines of communication..."

"You do understand that high-level officials are being murdered, across the nation, about every three minutes? Your lines of communication have functioned sufficiently for that, I suppose?"

Shock registered on both of their faces.

"And you do understand that this patient of yours has important information which might help to stop those attacks?"

The Sergeant shook her head. The Major pursed his lips as though searching for ways of contradicting this intelligence.

Cap took another step towards them. "Sergeant, I'm going to ask you again. This is extremely important. Did you administer any medication to this man? I don't care who authorized you, or why you thought you were being asked to do it, I just need to know the truth."

There was fear in her eyes now. She shook her head twice. "But he's young!" she burst out. "He can't be..."

"On our side? But he is. And he's not even young. So I ask you: is it reversible?"

"What?"

"Is it reversible... the medication that General Ponting or General Ponting's fall guy told you to give to this man, to render him comatose... Is it reversible?"

The Major began, "Director Olsen, I don't think – "

Cap was suddenly overwhelmed with anger and impatience and the frustration of being stonewalled. He only just stopped himself reaching out and grabbing the Major by his crisp army uniform and shaking him.

"*Is it reversible?*" he hissed.

The Sergeant sank down on a bedside chair and put her hand to her mouth. "I think so," she said.

"*Then do it!*"

"I need – " the Sergeant began.

The Major cut in. "Sergeant, this is insubordination. You will do and say nothing further."

"But we're – "

"Nothing! You're dismissed."

"Hold on, Major," Cap said, his voice, driven by fury, finding a new level of menace. "I don't think you understand the situation. The President of the United States is at this moment presiding over a conference to determine how we respond to these bee attacks. She very much wants to talk to this man here, who may be able to stop them, but who, because of the idiocy and misplaced loyalties of your commanding officer, has been well and truly fucked over and removed from the action. I think you know that I am her envoy in this building, and I think you know that the President of the United States outranks not only anyone in this building, but also anyone else in the entire military. So what do you want to do? Do you want to do as I say, or do you want me to interrupt the conference, explain to her that some two-bit major has decided to ignore her wishes and keep the man she wants to talk with in a comatose state?"

The Major stared at him, eyes wide with indecision. His face had turned pale.

"Don't keep me waiting, Major. I don't want to interrupt the President again, but if I have to, believe me I will. I will ask her to issue orders to you direct. I think you should keep in mind that she doesn't much care for General Ponting, because General Ponting has dropped her deep in the shit over the current round of attacks. I think she'll care even less for one of his staff who has collaborated in keeping one of her advisers in that kind of condition." He pointed at the supine form on the bed.

The Major was still suffering, grinding his teeth and staring by turns at Cap Olsen and the man on the bed.

Cap watched him and said in a quieter tone, "Genie, put me back into the President's conference."

Suddenly the Major exploded in self-justifying activity, whirling around and shouting at the wall: "Duty Captain? You there? Major Fossett. I need a paramedic team asap, in sickbay two, transfer of patient to first floor sickbay one, then scramble the duty physician, we need him yesterday, patient needs resuscitating immediately. Got that? Patient needs to be conscious and lucid for a presidential briefing. These orders represent the wishes of the President herself, so move your ass..."

Fossett swung back to the Sergeant, who was staring at him with her mouth half-open. "You got all that? For the moment I'm going to overlook your insubordination and poor judgment. You are back on duty. Stay with the patient, make sure he's looked after, any delays, problems, let me know."

"Yes sir." The Sergeant drew herself up and tossed off a salute.

"Director Olsen, I can only say, you'd better be on the level."

"I am on the level, Major. There isn't much choice, when you've got one death every three minutes. Where's Colonel Reznichek?"

"The Colonel said you'd have better data sources available if you'd come to his office."

Cap looked at him for a moment. His instinct was to stay with Doug, make sure that these slippery bastards did what they said. Ponting was surely not beyond organizing something devious, given that his back was now against the wall.

"Okay," he said. "But I want updates from you personally every couple of minutes. If I get the idea you're stalling, I'll send my guy to Bethesda, and my report to the President."

He gave Doug's recumbent form a final glance, exchanged a look with the Sergeant, and then followed Major Fossett back along the corridor and down a floor. The visitor display was serviced at this level, and open doorways on the left of the curving hallway gave access to the machinery beneath the simulation of bee challenges above.

Colonel Reznichek's office was full of display screens and idle equipment of uncertain age and utility. The Colonel himself looked more like a hobbyist collector of exotic species than a military man. He got up and came around his desk and shook hands.

Major Fossett excused himself, flicking a courteous, or possibly ironic, salute at both of them before disappearing.

Reznichek began talking in a low voice on his way back to his chair. "I've talked with your colleague, Blake Silverman. He's right. Because of the data we're now collecting from all MAIMCOM challenges, we were able to identify the swarm that attacked your investigator. The number in hex is..." Reznichek looked at one of the screens on his desk. "Nine, D, B, two, five, zero, A... Since we know broadly speaking the source of these numbers, I can tell you it's a PMA number."

Cap eased himself down on a chair. He was relieved but not surprised. "What's your take on that?"

The other man stared back at him, eyes wide and intense. "I know we're under severe time constraints, but can I confirm a couple of things? New bee attacks have begun, not just in Washington?"

"Correct. The furthest west so far is Denver."

"And you believe it's PMA bees, hijacked swarms?"

"Colonel, I'm not smart enough to believe anything. It's what my guru, the guy you've been trying to silence, told me was probable."

Reznichek dropped his gaze and nodded, his shoulders slumping. "What I'm about to say will probably end my military career, but do you remember that both our agencies had spent bees to analyze after the first round of attacks?"

"Sure."

"You didn't get any useful information?"

"Nope. Ours were dead."

"Maybe we got lucky. Maybe because we specialize in bees we've got better methods. Anyway, we got a good indication, statistically fifty-fifty, that they were PMA bees."

"What?" Cap thought that his opinion of the General and his agency had already reached rock bottom, but he managed a new wave of anger and disgust. "And you sat on that?"

"The General suppressed the result. I was never sure why."

"I know why, but I can't tell you. One of the General's big military secrets. It explains how PMA bees can kill people."

"Ah. There is a mechanism."

"Yes. And as for your military career, Colonel, don't lose hope. It's the General who's going down. At least if I have anything to do with it. So, bottom line, the evidence for PMA bees is strong on all sides."

"Yes. I would say so."

Where the hell is Major Fossett, Cap wondered, I should have had about three reports by now. He told his genie to make a direct link with Blake Silverman.

Silverman, it turned out, had just sent the same message. "What's going on?" Cap said.

"I got the new PMA guy to check our swarm number for us," Blake said.

"And?"

"Sorry Cap. It's not from one of the forty-four."

"Say that again: it's *not* from one of the forty-four identified by you and Doug?"

"No."

Cap closed his eyes and felt the energy draining out of his body. "Shit," he grunted.

CHAPTER 58

Z eb felt as though he'd been standing for hours in the middle
of the living room of the Pennsylvania house, posture rigid,
jaw clenched, watching reports of the bee killings on the
big wall screens. The growing crowd of youngsters outside the dead
Congressman's residence in Manhattan and at the airport in Atlanta
was a development he hadn't anticipated, and he had a sense that it
was pregnant with promise but possibly premature, even dangerous.

A few feet away from him, Kate was half-drunk with excitement,
and wine, and maybe some other stuff: she was shouting encouragement
at the youngsters, criticizing the commentators, as though she was
watching a violent hockey game. He remembered his own high, first
time around, and his need to communicate with someone: now, in
theory, it was different; since Merko's stunt, his face was known to
lots of activists, but he still didn't feel he could reach out and share the
moment. These were Kate's people, over whom he had yet to impose his
leadership. As for Kate herself, what he needed was a loyal chief of staff;
instead of which he'd got an anarchic meddler, with her own dreams
of glory, and the political sensitivity of a two-year-old.

The youngsters in Manhattan, lit by street lamps and media floaters,
were beginning to accumulate into a real demonstration. A couple
of sign-writing petards were launched, the letters cutting fiery slices
against the dark Upper West Side frontages. There was cruel sarcasm:
'HAPPY ELECTION DAY, CONGRESSMAN!'; and bland exhortation;
'VOTE YOUTH OF AMERICA AND GIVE US A VOICE'.

No reference to Kronos, Zeb thought, feeling the absence deep in
his gut; not even to his program for constitutional change. He had

always hoped that his nationwide fame would make all activists, not just Kate's people, fall in behind the Kronos banner, and promote his goals; but that wasn't happening yet.

Kate cheered when the petards exploded into life, and began skipping and dancing around the room, threading a way between the heavy furniture, still covered with sheets. "We're winning, we're winning. And of course it's my organization that's getting these guys out on the streets... this revolutionary mob... All down to me. So look on my works, ye mighty Kronos, and despair..."

He looked at her in anger and astonishment. "Wait a minute. You're saying you or your cadres *planned* this? *Organized* it?" He flung out a hand at the wall screen.

"Of course. Why not?"

"Nobody could know these deaths would get publicized."

"Well d'oh. We just had to be ready."

"For all of them?"

"All of them."

He took a couple of paces towards her. "Not that I believe you, necessarily, but wouldn't it have been a good idea to tell me?"

She danced away behind a big upholstered shape. "Now don't get contentious, Kronos, we're doing great, we're winning, what the hell does it matter to you what the Mickelburgers do as follow-up?"

His genie's voice sounded in his ear: "Peter Johnson for you." He took a deep breath and turned aside. What does it matter? he thought. What does it matter? Jesus, I can't wait to strangle this idiot.

"Pete?"

Johnson's voice was weary but thick with emotion. "It's true what I told you. They got him into MAIMCOM HQ. He's alive."

"Connacher?"

"Who else?"

"MAIMCOM Headquarters?"

"Yes."

Zeb felt like screaming into the void. What did it take to make this ancestor of his go away? He was like some indestructible cartoon character, dead one moment, running round making mischief the next.

He said, "You got an informant in there?"

"MAIMCOM? Yeah. Cubechess player. One of their top technicians."

"And you trust him? I mean this is really true."

"Oh yeah. He's the real deal, in there, leaking information, right at this moment. And get this. He thinks he can probably sneak a swarm inside MAIMCOM Headquarters, if it's done right."

Zeb wanted to say: *Don't bother, Pete, my granddad is immortal. Not just rejuvenated: immortal.*

Instead he said, "I thought MAIMCOM was sewn up tight."

"There's an anomaly at one particular air intake, where deliveries of food and drink come in. Of course there are defenses inside MAIMCOM as well as outside, but my guy thinks these can be avoided for a while, at least, if we play it right."

"Hold a second." He turned to Nakamoto. She had skittered back to the wall screens and was cheering on the demonstrators. "I need a swarm," he said.

She glanced across at him. "What? The great Kronos? The great Kronos hasn't got a swarm?"

"Pete's opened up an important opportunity."

"My swarms are busy."

"Your swarms are my swarms, honey, and I don't give a fuck if they're busy. Get me a new one."

"Still can't kill your grandfather?"

Zeb turned away. "Pete? I suggest you use your Baltimore team again. That has the advantage of being outside the illegal children network, which Connacher may be on to. Kate is being stupid, but tell them to pull out an existing swarm or get a new one and stand by. Tell them that if Kate offers any objection, we'll cut them out of the system."

There was an explosive sound to his left. Kate was shouting: "You can't do that! Don't listen to him, Pete! We've got the keys and the protocols, we control our swarms!"

"Kate," he said quietly, "you haven't been keeping up, have you? Merko runs the communications system, Merko controls the satellites, and without the satellites you're out of the game. We also have the keys and the protocols, because we monitor everything that goes through the system, so play along with us, or you're dead."

Kate was staring at him with her usual fury, but she didn't speak.

"Okay Pete, I think she understands the situation, and I don't think she'll offer any opposition over Baltimore."

Pete said, "I guess you realize that if we get a swarm inside MAIMCOM, we can also take out a few more. Think about that. The Commander and his deputy would be obvious targets. The word is that the guy from the FBI, Olsen, is there as well."

"Olsen? Jesus. What are they all doing?"

"My guy isn't senior enough for that. But he's pretty sure that some changes have been made in the IFF interrogation procedures."

"They're trying to find our swarms. Which they'll do in the long run, but we need to slow them down. So put all you have into this, Pete. Tell me when you've snagged a swarm. Meanwhile I'll brief Merko." He scowled and thought: you can't survive another attack, Granddad, you really can't; even immortals run out of luck in the end.

When he turned back to the wall screens, Kate was still staring at him, as though hoping her eyes were brain-destroying lasers.

"You're *wrong*," she said. "You're doing this *wrong*."

"What's that, sweetheart?"

"These killings." She gestured at the screens. "What we're seeing here... *proves* what happens when one of these *hate* figures... these one-niner lords of creation... gets killed *in public*. You get a response, you get doomers showing up, you get activism, you get a god-damn fucking *revolution*, that's what you get, Kronos."

"I thought you said you organized all that."

"We helped, sure. But it can happen anyway."

"So you think that's what we should be doing more of?"

"I think it's just... *pathetic* that you can't see the possibilities. You don't need to waste time in targeting special people, congressmen, whatever... You just send out swarms and..."

"Kill old people?"

"*Yes!*"

"One after the other?"

She shook her head violently, as though freeing herself of his pusillanimous refusal to face facts. "At least until they're forced to shut down bees completely. *Then* they can't stop us."

Zeb watched her, trying to read her thoughts. "Why don't you understand the basic politics? If you kill old people at random, rather than the ones responsible for the present situation, they'll hate us and fear us. We might have a fantastic street party and do a lot of damage, but then what? We're a minority, Kate. We *need... some... support... from the old.*"

She stared at him, mute and hostile, and then pretended to lose interest, returning her attention to the wall screen, waving her hand at it and enlarging the display area.

He felt a flash of annoyance, an impulse to jump on her and break her neck, but he restrained himself, occupied with a deeper question: what was she planning? More important, what were her cadres around the country planning? And why the hell hadn't he seen this coming?

He gave her stubborn profile a final glance, and went off in search of Merko.

CHAPTER 59

Doug Edie first became conscious of bright lights and raised voices. He clamped his eyes shut again, not ready for strange people and new places. Was his body and mind functional? He could waggle his toes, nothing was hurting, and his heart rate seemed steady. After a few moments, he opened his eyes again. He tried to sit up, and felt the bed stiffen and hold him.

"Take it easy," a gruff voice said. "You've been out for a while. Medics are bringing you back."

As his vision steadied and ranged further, Doug saw army uniforms, a man close beside him in a suit, and a white-coated woman. Looking down, he discovered that probes from various sites on his body were bundled through his lightweight garments to a wheeled robot nearby. The white-coated woman was looking at a hand-held display.

Looking again at the pugnacious man in the suit, he suddenly felt the information begin to flow, like a cipher turning nonsense into meaningful data. This guy was FBI, Cap Olsen, the one he needed to do this urgent thing, which was a thing to do with bees, of course, like the bees which had attacked him...

He found himself reaching out towards him and trying to rise, but Cap put out a hand and restrained him.

"Hey. Give it a moment. You're still weak."

"What happened?" Doug said. "We had to get the data... PMA data..."

"We got the data... some of it... minutes ago... and the Colonel..." Cap jerked his thumb at one of the army uniforms, "got the number of the swarm that attacked you. But there's a problem." Cap raised his eyes to the woman on the other side of the bed. "How's he doing, Captain?"

"He's coming up okay. Go easy, that's all."

Doug said, "The swarm wasn't from either..."

The man looked at him sharply, as though remembering something about him, and shook his head ruefully. "Columbia or Annapolis. Right. Or any of the other forty-four."

Doug closed his eyes, fighting off a spell of dizziness. "Where was it from?"

"Baltimore."

Doug kept his eyes closed, allowing his brain to resonate around this, and the memories to clarify. "Ah... yeah... sneaky... you see what they're doing? Protecting home base."

"Protecting home base?"

Doug opened his eyes and moved up almost to a sitting position. He was himself startled by the sudden vigor of his mental processes. Stimulants kicking in? "It doesn't matter right now. The point is that Johns Hopkins is in Baltimore, so Baltimore PMA is almost certainly penetrated. It doesn't change the argument about the other forty-four."

Cap said, "So have we still got a plan? Because the ruling power upstairs, your friend General Ponting, is trying to persuade the President to stand down all bees."

Doug's exertions had made him feel faint. His head was dropping forward, but he forced himself upwards again. "That's not going to work. Have there been more killings?"

"We're up to thirty-three. Given delays in reporting, my guess is at least fifty, maybe a hundred."

Doug found himself struggling to get to his feet. The robot beeped and moved in closer, as the probes tugged at his body. "Jesus, Cap, we have to get going on this. Ignore the General. Have we got a PMA guy we can work with?"

"Doug, I need to plug you into the President's conference. She calls the shots, and she wants to hear from you. You're the guy with the dope on the terrorists, you know the way Kronos's mind works, she'll listen to you. Can you handle it?"

"It's a waste of time," he said. "She'll think I'm protecting my grandson."

"I don't think so. She's pretty smart. And we need her authority if we're going to over-ride the General. We can't do it without MAIMCOM, right?"

Doug gave a little nod, not caring who he spoke with, but worried that other things would stall.

"Listen... while I'm doing that... We need somebody at each of our forty-four PMA centers, forty-five including Baltimore, to get all of their swarms currently on missions to call in. Pretty obviously, the hijacked swarms will be working on different comms channels, so they won't call in. After five or ten minutes, you have a list of swarms that are not responding, and these will almost certainly include the ones we want to destroy. That would greatly reduce numbers and make the PMA happier about what we're doing."

Cap gave him an inscrutable look and said, "Genie, relay what Doug Edie has just said to Blake Silverman, and ask him to take action. Colonel, can you help with this?"

The Colonel nodded and headed for the door.

◇◇◇

Doug was relieved that the President didn't delay him unduly, and asked only sensible questions. He and Cap had been relocated to a secure interview room by Major Fossett, and they were able to watch the other conference members on a wall screen. These were now six in number, in addition to the President.

General Ponting said, "Okay, it's true that the swarm that attacked Mr. Connacher responded to the MAIMCOM challenge with a PMA number. A Baltimore number, to be precise. But the point is this: responding with a PMA number does *not* mean that this was a PMA swarm. I've already explained that word of our new defenses might have leaked to the enemy. So they realize they need to supply their swarms with numbers, and where better to find such numbers than the PMA in Baltimore, a place we are informed was the heartland of activism? They could surely rustle up a sympathizer who could give them a batch of valid swarm numbers."

"So have you obtained the full set of Baltimore swarm numbers and removed them from your lookup table, General?" Doug said impatiently.

Ponting ignored him. "Madame President, we should proceed immediately to an orderly shutdown of all bees, and hope we can start destroying whatever is left after an hour or so."

Cap and others reiterated tactical objections to the grounding of bees.

Doug sat down at the table in the interview room, furious and fatigued by Ponting's red herrings. Cap was already seated. Doug allowed his attention to wander to an adjoining screen, which Cap had set up to monitor news feeds. The picture appeared to show a subway station concourse, tiled floor, square pillars clad in advertisements, fixed and floating signage: the New York subway, he realized, as he saw N, Q, and R, signed in one direction, and A, C. and E signed in another; only New York, surely, used these letters to denote subway lines. It looked like a live picture, but at just past six o-clock in the morning, a big station concourse, which he began to suspect was Times Square, should have been full of people; instead, it was empty.

His attention held by this oddity, he watched as the camera, probably a floater, panned across and fixed on a heavy woman, splayed out flat on the tiles. Doug felt a frisson of shock and surprise. The camera moved around, changing the angle of view to a side-on shot. There was blood on the tiles near the woman's head. He recoiled in recognition: her face was partly obscured, but the smear of blood looked aligned with her eyes. This was an attack. A bee attack. Right here in the subway.

He leaned forward, now totally concentrated on the news channel pictures. The next shock came a second later. The camera was moving on, rising up and looking beyond the woman's body, and there, six or seven yards further on, was another splayed-out bundle of clothes, this time a dark suit, its owner stretched out on his back, arms straight and stiff beyond him, as though reaching out for help. The bearded face, in particular the eyes...

He must have made noises, because he sensed Cap stiffening and moving his head, and then he too began to exclaim.

Doug muttered, "Genie, audio on screen two," and listened to the commentary:

"...have succeeded in blocking access from most of the street entrances, but passengers who can't get out are beginning to panic.

Meanwhile, trains continue to stop, with doors still opening at several platforms and passengers fighting to get on or off."

The picture jumped to another floater-borne camera, which was skimming the heads of a massed throng of people, some trying to go down some stairs leading to a subway track, others trying to go up, anger, desperation, incredulity, incomprehension on their faces. Several were shouting warnings, trying to point at something up the stairs. The floater carried on to a subway platform, a train waiting, doors closed, people pressed up against it.

"To repeat," the male commentator said, "we are looking at scenes at Times Square subway station, where in the last few minutes three, possibly four people have died, it is believed, but not definitely confirmed, from an attack on the eyes by a rogue swarm of bees... So far, our cameras at the scene have not detected or photographed the swarm, but we have other cameras on the way which should be able to find it. The epicenter of panic, we can tell you, is now the mezzanine floor where another individual seems to be under attack... This scene is extremely disturbing, please exercise caution about viewing... even in the context of the attacks now taking place across the country, this is surely a new level of barbarity..."

Doug averted his gaze and checked what was happening among the conference participants. News of the attacks seemed to be filtering through: the President herself had turned her gaze away and was staring at something with a pained and angry expression; General Ponting was pictured standing up and moving around his desk; Cap Olsen, both on screen and beside him in the flesh, was crouched forward on his chair, talking rapidly, presumably to his FBI colleagues.

Doug glanced quickly at the other screen, but the news channel had evidently censored the raw pictures, and was showing a graphic of the present attack in relation to the other attacks in the subway. The news anchor was offering, in hushed and horrified tones, a few details of the victim's rapid demise, and made the further observation that all the victims, who had now been identified by subway police SAIMs, were over the age of eighty, but otherwise had nothing in common; in particular, none of them was a government official or an elected politician.

Doug was gripped by sudden fury: who the hell was behind this stunt? Zeb? His psychopath grandson? Surely not. Zeb had a game plan: shake up the government machine, and leave everyone else alone. Kate's people?

He told his genie to connect him with Colonel Reznichek. "Colonel? Have you seen what's happening in New York?"

"Yes. It's triggered a MAIMCOM alert."

"You have MAIMCOM defenses in subways?"

There was a tiny hesitation. "This is top secret, of course, but to hell with that. Yes, we have systems that operate in subways. New York is obviously one of the best."

"So this atrocity swarm will have been challenged?"

"Yes... I presume so... Times Square... I was already working on extracting the data... Five... six swarms have been challenged in the last five minutes. All of them legal, of course."

"So no means of knowing which one is running amok?"

"No."

"But you have the swarm numbers?"

"Yes. If General Ponting authorizes me, I can destroy all six."

"Wait a minute." Doug closed his eyes and thought hard. "If you do that, you also destroy the evidence. That is, we won't know whether our method of picking the Kronos swarms is working."

"This Times Square swarm is going to go on killing people, Mr. Connacher. At a rate of, at a guess... one every minute and a half."

"I know that, Colonel, but there's a trade-off. This is something new, a swarm that just kills old people, one after the other. It's scary as hell. Suppose it's a new tactic, a new mission format? There could be dozens of swarms doing this. That's hundreds of deaths. To save those people we need to know if our method works or doesn't work. Where are you with the data from the PMA centers?"

"Mostly it's here... I'm just collating it... Yeah, we've got swarm numbers from most of the forty-five MAIM-farms... it looks good... the right sort of quantities..."

"One of the MAIM-farms is near New York, right?... Because we already had an attack in Manhattan... on the congressman..."

"Yeah... Wait a minute... Commack... on Long Island..."

"So you have the missing swarm data from Commack?"

"Yes... seven swarms... numbers are here."

"Is there an overlap with the Times Square challenges?" Doug was desperately trying to concentrate on the conversation with Reznichek, while keeping an eye on the screen showing the situation at Times Square. If they were going to stop these crazy, escalating, attacks, then they needed this to come right. "Is one of the swarms you've identified in Times Square one of those missing from Commack?"

"Jesus... I should have got this... Wait a minute, I have to combine this data for a machine comparison... And it looks like... Jesus. Yes. You're right. There's a Commack swarm in there."

"Then that's the villain. And we can prove it. Destroy that swarm and if the Times Square killings stop then we're there. Not even General Ponting can stop you destroying all the others on that list of missing swarm numbers."

"Agreed. But I need the General's authority to change the IFF lookup table."

"Even to remove one number?"

"Yes."

"Christ." Doug stood up and banged one hand against his head, renewed frustration and fury taking hold. "You mean we've got to go through all this with the General? Make him understand the detail?"

"I think if I tell him the essential story, he'll agree it right away. He might insist on destroying all six, but I could destroy this one first and delay the others. Then, as you say, we've got proof."

"And you can act on a verbal okay?"

"Yes. We have a procedure called genie-authentication. But I can't get through to him."

Doug was aware that Cap Olsen had sat up straight and was now watching him. "Cap? You know where the General is?" Looking up at the conference screen, he saw that the General's box was still empty.

Cap said, "He was supposed to be on his way down here. I think he wants to do a deal."

"A deal? What the hell does that mean?"

"It means he knows he can't stall us any longer, and he wants to cover his ass."

"BEEKEEP?"

"Probably. Swear us to secrecy, that kind of thing."

"God, that guy is a waste of space." Doug strode to the door of the interview room and flung it open. He was in the vaulted atrium, the visitor display in front of him. There was nobody in sight. He turned left and half-ran across the wood-block floor towards the main entrance hall, glancing back at the stairway down to the lower floors. Still no-one. What the hell was going on?

At the entrance hall he glanced left, and saw first a clustered knot of three soldiers bending over something on the ground. He skidded to a halt and stared. The thing on the ground was a man. He took another pace forward. No, impossible, he was *inside* MAIMCOM. Safe, defended. But the uniform of the man on the ground had stars on it. And General Ponting was no more going to collapse from ill health than he was. With guilt and disbelief, he sent a darting gaze from one side of the hall to another, up to the ceilings and across the wall, searching for a faint iridescence, a giveaway shadow. Then he turned and ran.

CHAPTER 60

Staring out of the studio window, Merko could see nothing but hostile blackness. Every reported death was like a stiletto piercing his flesh, ratcheting the tension inside him to new levels. He had made a dash for the washroom and thrown up twice. Kronos was a worthy god, fighting a worthy cause, and he was merely the agent, the loyal acolyte, but even so... the shock, the revulsion, the anger, building up out there across the country was going to engulf them all and there was no means of escape. He tried to picture himself back in the city, with his snakes, listening to a new band, solving an exciting problem. Had that world ever existed? How had he fallen prey to these strange cosmic forces, whose gear wheels, it seemed, had caught the edge of his earthly garments and wound him into this crazy violent universe?

He turned on a local music channel to steady the anxiety that coursed through him in unpredictable waves; but instead of familiar performers, familiar sounds, he saw the worst thing possible; bodies, one after the other, splayed out on the tiles of a subway station. He stared, gagged, tried to believe he'd caught a piece of a movie. No, this was death by bees, something that his systems must have mediated and allowed. Guilty pictures sprang to life on his chameleon jacket: himself with long arrows skewering his body in all directions.

But wait a moment, his frozen brain told him at last: this wasn't the work of Kronos; this wasn't part of the sanctioned plan; this wasn't Platinum Sting. These were just... *people on the subway.*

Old people, it was true, but people just the same. Not the enemy. Someone's grandparents.

What did that mean? It meant that someone thought he was smarter than Kronos, and could disobey Kronos; it meant that someone out there had taken up with a rival god, a callous and uncivilized god, and that order and authority was being lost; so he would write a program to find out who that was; what swarm, what mission, was killing people on the subway; and then he could bring the wrath of Kronos down on that heathen god...

Except, of course, he already knew who that heathen god was: *the traitorous one... the ugly one... the canker in their midst...*

Merko was suddenly full of furious anger, all the tension and guilt of the preceding hours focused on a new target. He leaned forward and concentrated on his displays, thinking his way through the commands and conditions he wanted, storing them, loading them. There was a hiss as dormant bees charged themselves up and emerged from their hive, a misty shadow heading straight for the door.

"Merk?" Zeb's voice sounded urgently in his ear. "You seen what's going down in New York?"

"Yeah. I seen it."

"This woman is fucking out of control! This is a putsch!"

"Yeah, I thought it was her. Where is she?"

"I don't know. She snuck off a few minutes ago. Scared what I'd do to her, I guess."

"She's defying Kronos. That's not allowed. I sent out bees to round her up."

"Good thinking. Bring her down to the living room, okay? And come yourself. We need to find out exactly what the hell she's done and how to undo it. This meddling bitch is destroying everything we've achieved so far."

Merko sat rigid, lips pressed together. He didn't want to go down. He'd give Zeb the commands he'd programmed into the swarms, and let Kronos defeat the rebel.

But that wouldn't work. Kronos had spoken.

He got up and pantomimed a sword fight, with himself victorious. He raised his fists to heaven and allowed the forces of Kronos to beam down into his body. Then he left the room and clattered down the stairs.

The living room was lit with a background glow from the walls, the shrouded furniture, it seemed to Merko, poised ready to jump on them. Zeb's attention was on a couple of bright wall screens, his look of thunderous fury worthy of an Olympian. Merko said nothing, averting his gaze from the screens, watching behind him.

"They got her?" Zeb said.

His nod was rendered void by a wailing sound like a cat in heat from the stairs. A disheveled Kate, spitting with rage, erupted into the room and flung herself in the direction of Zeb, falling down against a covered chair with whimpers of pain before reaching him. The bees, in golden Kronos livery, hissed around her with custodial concern, making swirling thrusts against her face and other parts of her body. Seeing Merko, another wail escaped her and she tried to raise herself for another attack, but the bees, nipping at her like sheepdogs, drove her down into a defensive crouch, arms over her head, obscenities streaming out of her mouth.

The look Zeb gave him told him he'd done well.

"So how do I pull these things off her?" Zeb asked.

Merko put his hands out, palms down. The bees drew back from Kate's body and formed a golden halo above her head. She looked up cautiously, breathing still rapid, eyes full of hate.

"And how do I start them up again?"

Merko raised a clenched fist briefly above his head. The bees flowed down again and Kate raised her arms, screaming in rage and pain.

"Show respect," Merko said, the bodies on the subway still driving him. "Get on your knees and bow your head before the Lord Kronos."

Kate didn't move.

"On your knees, sweetheart," Zeb said with a smile of controlled menace. "You are in big-time shit. Boy, are we going to fuck you around."

Kate dropped her head and gritted her teeth. She was sprawled on all fours, hugging the floor. She muttered something but didn't move.

"How do I increase the pressure?" Zeb said.

Merko raised his clenched fist twice. The bees seemed to vibrate into new shapes and greater activity. Kate made gurgling noises.

Zeb put out his hands, palm down. The bees withdrew into their harmless halo.

"Don't raise both fists at the same time," Merko said.

"What happens?" Zeb said.

"She dies."

"She dies!" Zeb cried out. "How tragic! How sad!" He moved forward and put his foot on her shoulder. "Now do what he says and kneel in front of Kronos!" He pushed and Kate fell backwards. She scrabbled around and righted herself and stared up at him, panting with rage. She raised a finger. Her voice, restricted by shortness of breath, jabbed at him:

"Now you listen to me, you over-hyped ego-maniac. You think you're in charge, but you're fucking not! I told you before, this is my territory, this place is on loan from my people. If anything happens to me, you're finished, both of you."

Zeb waved this aside. "You're deluded, my little princess. If anything happens to you, you're the one who's finished. Your people are currently part of the biggest youth revolt ever seen in America, ever seen in the world! They're not going to kill the goose who lays this golden egg, this golden Kronos. They're going to embrace him, follow him! And so will you." Zeb raised both fists to shoulder level. "So before I really lose my temper and do something unfortunate, will you please tell us what the fuck is going on in New York."

Kate tensed, gritted her teeth. "Nothing that isn't going to benefit us."

Zeb raised one hovering fist. The bees swooped down and Kate gave an angry scream. "Nothing that isn't going to benefit us!" Zeb echoed. "You've got a swarm killing anonymous old people on the New York subway..." Zeb waved at the wall screens, "...which is being aired around the country and is losing us friends and supporters about as fast as if we'd signed a cooperation treaty with invaders from Mars... and to which you will probably add other stunts around the country of the same crazy kind... and you think that's going to *benefit* us?"

Zeb leaned over her writhing body, put his hands out palms down, waited for the bees to retreat, and then squatted beside her, as though ready to continue the torture with his bare hands.

Kate beat her fists on the ground and moaned in frustration and pain: "Why can't the great fucking Kronos understand that this is the *best way*? We'll never get another chance like this. This way there's a rallying point for our guys to get out there and defeat the enemy. *Why can't you see that?*"

"Because the great fucking Kronos is fortunately not as stupid as the stupid fucking Kate! If the old guys were out there killing young guys, then yes, we might be out on the streets, fighting back, we might have a revolutionary situation, but the old guys are not going to do that because *they're not that fucking stupid!*" Zeb lashed out with the back of his hand and knocked her sideways. "Not even if you force them to stand down bees, because it's bees killing old people, not young guys killing old people, and young guys won't start killing old people until old people start killing them! Which they won't. Can you get that through your thick fucking head?" Zeb hit her again and then raised his fist. The bees swooped down. "So you will now tell us exactly what you've organized, which teams, where, are going to switch to this crazy nonsense, so that Merk can cut them out of the system and get us back on track. And believe me, sweetheart, fuck me around any more, and you are one dead Mickelburger."

Zeb settled back on his haunches and watched his prey.

Merko looked on in agony, satisfied that Kronos was dealing at last with his enemy, but terrified that things would still go wrong, that counter-forces would strike. And embodying his fears, he noticed suddenly that the wall-screens had quietly shifted from showing news to showing people: women, in fact, young women, women he immediately suspected were the activist allies of the heathen god, Kate; two on one screen, two on another, and then two more on a third. The Furies, he thought, as he took in the anger on their determined faces; come to remonstrate with their brother Kronos.

"My Lord," he croaked.

Zeb looked up and followed his gaze. Merko was relieved he showed no response beyond disdainful irritation.

Zeb raised himself to a standing position and put out his hands palms down. Kate rolled over, breathing deeply, and looked up at the screens.

"So this is your hard core," Zeb said. "Glad to meet you. I take it you guys are responsible for the breakaway action in New York and maybe elsewhere. You're exactly the ones I want to speak to. This is a disaster which is going to undermine everything we're doing and it will earn us the permanent hostility of the majority of citizens in this country. You may think that's good revolutionary practice, but it isn't. It simply makes sure that we lose. It's got to stop, and if you don't stop it, we will."

Merko studied the faces on the screens. There were a couple of frowns, a half smile. What worried him was the absence of respect, the absence, even, of familiarity: these women would be getting an image of Zeb from one of several cameras, and it meant nothing to them; they stared back in haughty anger, no sign that these were acolytes, followers of the Lord Kronos. With a sick feeling in his gut, he realized also that he recognized none of them: these were not the technicians he had worked with, from whom he had demanded obeisance to Kronos, and to whom he had sent images of the golden, transcendent, god; and who had mostly been male. These women seemed to be on a different level, and confident of their own power.

Zeb, Merko thought, hadn't noticed that yet: he stood proudly watching the screens, as though he expected immediate capitulation.

Kate said in a newly-invigorated voice, "Yasmin, tell this throwback where he really stands in the new order of things."

A sleek woman with waves of black hair quite unlike Kate's, whose image was on half of the middle screen, said, "First, if you or your bees touch Kate again, we'll exact a worse punishment. Trust us on that. It may not be immediate, but it will be inescapable. Our network will get you."

"That would be the Rose Mickelburger network."

"Yes."

"I didn't know you were a female cabal."

"We're not. A few men are with us."

"Oh good. You can practice the full gamut of emasculation on them. The problem is, Yasmin, and the treacherous Kate here, and the rest of you, you're not in a position to call the shots. We control the technology. If you want out, go, get lost, but either way, I'm going to shut down any unauthorized Mickelburger operations that you try and sneak into the program. They're harmful to the bigger cause. Better think about it."

Kate had pulled herself up onto the dustsheet-covered arm of an upholstered chair. There was blood on her cheek from Zeb's blows. "No, you'd better think about things, Kronos. Do you really imagine that this technology advantage of yours is going to last beyond the next day or two? Once they figure it out, MAIMCOM, NSA, and all the others, it's never ever coming back and you're history, totally fucked. So forget all this Kronos is great, Kronos is a god garbage. You're back to Zeb Packer, wanted terrorist, with no friends in the god-damned entire universe. But if you're nice to us, we might help you survive, and maybe use you and Merko as technical contractors... Yup, thems the breaks, sweetheart. Try and take it like a man, not like the spoiled brat you really are."

Zeb stared at Kate, and then the women on the screens, with contempt. "You're crazy. Totally lost the fucking plot. Heading straight for the wall." He clapped his hands together and raised his voice. "You will not start a revolution like this! You're just mobilizing the enemy!"

A chorus of protest came back from the screens.

"And our strategy goes on," the woman sharing a screen with Yasmin shouted with sudden fervor. "We've got a swarm hitting one-niners in Philly, and another about to go in Houston."

"And Boston!" another one shouted. All the women were suddenly cheering and shaking their fists.

Merko stared at Kate, at the ecstatic, energized expression on her face, and lost control. He screamed and raised both fists in the air.

"You can't do this, you can't defy the Lord Kronos!"

He stayed locked in that position for several seconds, bending towards Kate, arms straight up, everyone making a noise, and then he staggered back in shock. Everything went grey, distant, as though he'd entered a dream world. He closed his eyes, dropped his arms, backed into a piece of furniture, half fell. He stared at the rug, didn't look up, but saw in his mind's eye the bees invading Kate's orifices, setting about the work of destroying her. He shuddered and almost fainted.

Zeb was shouting something.

When Merko raised his head, he still didn't look at Kate, or at Zeb, but instead turned to the screens: the women's faces were wide-eyed, shocked, agitated; a couple were still shouting, at him or at Zeb or maybe at the other women; he couldn't tell. He risked a quick, sidelong glance at Kate, and flinched; yes, she was a mess, a bloody mess. He dropped his head, nauseated, not sure he had really done what he had done, nor why he had programmed the command to do it, but satisfied in some small corner of his mind that he had finally executed the end-game.

The shouting died down. He heard Yasmin's voice: "...end of the road for you two. Your sanctuary is no longer protected. Bees or cops will find you. And then, of course, *we'll* find you, so don't get too comfortable in jail."

A moment later, the first alarm sounded, somewhere inside the house. Looking back at the screens, Merko saw that they'd reverted to news feeds. The women had gone.

Somebody grabbed his arm and shook him. He looked up in shock. Zeb stood there, like Kronos, golden fire in his eyes. Zeb would kill him, but that was okay too. He'd started the new cycle, the renewal.

"Why?" Zeb screamed.

Merko dropped his head. "So Kronos can rule. She was bad." He waited for the blow.

Zeb's rough grip on his arm suddenly fell away. "Come on. We got to get out of here."

Merko didn't move. He took a deep breath. This was where it got difficult. "No. I've got to go through the data, stop the bad killings. They'll harm Kronos. And they're not right. You go. Take the truck. It has some defenses."

"Bring the gear. Work in the truck."

"No. There isn't time. And I need the satellite links." He turned, stumbled away towards the hall, stopped and faced Zeb. "Go. Now. Kronos must survive. I can find out where bees and cops are and send you the data. You can make it."

Zeb looked behind him at the now still form of Kate, at the bees in their golden holding pattern, and bellowed, as though challenging his own gods, "This is fucking insanity! How did we get here! Where did it go wrong?" Then he took off at full speed, racing towards the kitchen.

Merko followed, up the stairs, into his aerie, where he stood, trembling, listening for the distant whine of a motor. Would Zeb change his mind, return to deal with his slippery lieutenant, set fire to the house, cover his tracks? Minutes seemed to go by before he saw a glow of light at the window and heard the sound of tires fading away down the long driveway.

He sat down at the table and slumped forward, head resting on his arms. The alarm was still sounding, far away, but otherwise the great house surrounding him seemed quiet, almost peaceful. He couldn't believe he had taken such an extreme and deliberate action, killed the miserable girl, driven Kronos away. He would pay in lots of ways. Zeb would figure it out and find a way to destroy him. NSA would exact their own revenge for what he had done to their systems. It was all going to land on top of him. He'd betrayed Kronos, and the gods would punish him.

But it was over. Almost. If he was sane, if it had happened. He'd done it and it was over.

Just the final thing: he had to work on this data. Figure out all the missions, stop all the killings. Not just Kate's madness, all of them. He felt a surge of energy, put on his glasses, plugged himself into his systems. It was a big job. He needed to retrieve all of the comms protocols at all of the PMA centers that Kate's people had hacked into, all of the satellite channels they had switched the swarms into, and send out an emergency recall to all the swarms.

It took him a couple of minutes to understand that something was wrong. All of the links he had originally opened to his satellite channels were dead. He took off his glasses and threw them aside. Obvious. What was he thinking? Kate's people controlled the alarms, the bee access, the systems. They'd shut him out, closed everything down. He was entombed.

He sat rigid, skin crawling. It was a big mistake. He should have stopped the killings *first,* then attacked Kate. But he hadn't the courage for that. She was the evil force, she, personally, had driven him to act. That was the way it had to be. Destroy the evil one, and *then...*

He'd tell the cops when they arrived. He'd tell the cops everything. They could stop the killings.

His head dropped slowly back onto the table and he closed his eyes. He jerked up again a moment later. He was supposed to help Zeb, warn him where the cops were. But he couldn't. And the gear in his truck was gone, because Zeb had taken it.

He stared fixedly at the dark window. Let Zeb figure it out, he thought. He was smart enough; and there was nothing his servant Merko could do.

His ex-servant Merko.

He lowered his head back onto the table and let the weariness take over.

CHAPTER 61

D oug didn't know where Colonel Reznichek hung out, but he thought he remembered a reference to the lower levels: so when he ran, he chose first to escape the vicinity of the General's body, and then, as he crossed the atrium, he headed for the broad stairway which spiraled downwards to his right.

"Colonel?" he barked. "If you're still hearing me, I should tell you that General Ponting has been attacked, probably by bees, probably causing death."

After a couple of seconds delay, the Colonel responded, his voice high and tense. "Connacher? Wait a moment... I'm overloaded here... Did you say Ponting is dead? I've got an emergency procedure starting up... Shit... yes... command is transferring..."

Doug stopped abruptly on the first landing down and tried to concentrate. "You've got a new commanding officer?"

"Yeah, it says so... You say the General is dead? Yeah, his deputy, Major General Ross Patel is now in command..."

"Colonel, this is of crucial importance. We've got swarms killing people across the country, not to mention one here in this building. You must persuade this new guy to authorize you to change the IFF lookup table on the basis of the PMA data. *Now.* Will he listen to you?"

"I'm putting a maximum priority request through as we speak."

"Great. And tell him to stay in a secure place."

"Where are you?"

"I'm on the stairs. Forget about me. Just get that lookup table changed. Please."

"I'll do my best."

Doug wanted to resume running down the stairs, but he realized that was probably futile: if he and others were going to escape the swarm of bees that had killed Ponting, he had to use the defenses with which the MAIMCOM building was surely provided.

Assuming, of course, they were functioning. A swarm wouldn't be here in the building without insider help. Which meant nothing could be relied upon.

He remembered suddenly that he had left Cap Olsen in the interview room. He turned and ran back up the stairs to the atrium and turned right. An army corporal still stood outside the second door along. Doug nodded at him and opened the door. Cap was there, expression intense, sitting at the table and interacting with the screens. Doug went in and glanced at the main screen: the presidential conference was still in progress, although several of the boxes showed participants doing their own thing or absent. His own box had been closed down.

"You heard about Ponting?" he said harshly.

Cap looked at him, shook his head.

"Dead. Bees."

Cap froze in shock, muttered to his genie, then said to Doug, "Here? Inside MAIMCOM?"

"Yes. And yes, we're both vulnerable. If you know any technical guy here, we should speak to him, get some ideas what to do. Not Reznichek. He's working with the new Commanding Officer on changing the lookup table."

Cap stared at him, said, "Major Fossett, please," then added to Doug, "There's another swarm killing one-niners at random. In Philadelphia. Also in the transit system."

"Shit. Better pray for Reznichek."

A man in uniform appeared on a screen. "Director Olsen. I've been wanting to speak with you. General Ponting has been killed by bees."

"I know."

"Sickbay One reports that a swarm was there, checking personnel. In fact I was checked myself."

Doug swore to himself, glanced reflexively through the still open door. "Doug Edie here, Major. No attacks?" he said.

"No, sir."

"I think we can conclude that they're looking for me and Director Olsen, and maybe your new Commanding Officer. Anywhere secure we can go?"

"No, sir. I mean yes, sir. Headquarters is divided into bee-proof cells, and I could escort you to the nearest, but I can't guarantee the integrity of our systems at this time."

Doug waved at Cap and turned towards the door. "Then we'll head outside. Can you get us a vehicle?"

"Yes, sir. I'll requisition that right now."

Doug wasn't sure that a vehicle was the quickest option, but at least he knew it had worked for him before. He went out into the atrium and started for the hallway. He might be heading back towards the swarm, but if he and Cap moved fast enough, they might escape while the swarm was still checking personnel.

He glanced behind him and saw Cap, not as close as he had expected, but stalled near the duty corporal, waving his hands in front of his face. Doug felt the strength go out of his legs. He couldn't see the bees yet, but he instinctively knew they were there: they must have been checking the corporal as he came through the door.

He heard a grunt of irritation and dismay from Cap, saw him pivot around, start to move. He got his own sluggish legs in motion at last and ran back to Cap, placing a reassuring hand on his shoulder. He could see the shadowy glint of the swarm now, in a holding pattern around Cap's head, still checking his identity. The corporal nearby was at attention, feet unmoving, face turned towards Cap in a look of uneasy indecision.

Doug turned towards him. "Soldier!" he shouted with as much authority as he could muster, "We need your tunic. Please!"

The corporal stared at him, a picture of doubt and incomprehension.

"This man is being attacked! Your tunic! Take it off!" He pulled at an imaginary garment on his chest. "Now! Now!"

The corporal began to react at last, jabbing at the quick-release buttons on his jacket. Doug turned back to Cap. "We'll get you out of here. Put the heels of your palms tight into your eye sockets and hold them there."

Cap gave him a final baleful look and did as he was told. Doug could see that the bees had made their check and were swirling into attack mode. He winced as he remembered what it was like to be jabbed at by a thousand needle-sharp missiles.

"Cap? I'm going to tell you in a moment to lower your hands while I put a protective jacket over your head. Okay? As soon as you feel the material is in place, put your hands back over the eyes and press it home."

Cap nodded awkwardly, keeping his palms over his eyes.

Doug reached for the tunic, which the corporal was holding out to him, and juggled it so that the open front was facing Cap. "Now!"

Cap dropped his hands, Doug flapped the jacket across his face, displacing some shadowy dots, and then wrapped it around his head. "Hands!" he called out, but Cap was already getting the heels of his palms back in his eye sockets. Doug pulled the tunic tight, clamped the material together at the top of Cap's head with one hand, and put his other arm through Cap's arms and around his throat in a half-nelson, pulling the tunic tight in to his neck.

"Soldier... open doors for us... get us outside."

The corporal set off, and Doug nudged Cap into motion. "Can you breathe?" he said into Cap's ear.

Cap grunted something, which he decided might be a yes. He got Cap into a shuffling run without either of them falling over. The bees, he knew, would already be working their way into Cap's clothes, eating holes in the fabric, starting to bite and inject chemicals. He had maybe half a minute before Cap would be dead weight, his hands no longer pressed to his eye sockets.

The two of them staggered through the main hall, picking up a couple more military helpers. Doug recognized one of these as the Major they had spoken with from the interview room. "Vehicle?" he flung at him.

"Not yet arrived, sir."

"Let's get him outside anyway."

They went through two automatic doors and an air barrier, Cap still mobile enough to shuffle along beside him, like an arrested felon in an arm lock. Doug found himself on the illuminated pavement beside a strangely insubstantial building, a cold breeze sharpening his senses. Was this a good idea? Cap was beginning to groan from the burrowing onslaught, and one of the soldiers, seeing him slump downwards, had stepped in to give him some support. Still pulling the tunic tight to his face, Doug could see Cap's hands trembling and weakening in the fight to keep the material pressed in to his eye sockets.

Still no vehicle.

"Back in through your main defenses, Major!" he called out. "You guys carry, and I'll try and keep some protection in place on his eyes."

Two soldiers jumped forward and grabbed Cap, one each side, as he began to fall. His hands fell away from his face. Afraid he would break his neck, Doug removed his arm lock and tried to grip the tunic above and below his neck. With a horrified sense of despair, Doug saw that the material of the tunic was breaking down and tearing, and pulsing black blobs were settling into the cracks. With a shout of urgency, he pressed his fellow rescuers into a lumbering run.

With a whirring noise that startled Doug, the bees suddenly abandoned their prey and disappeared.

It took him a second to remember the pattern: an IFF challenge. At last. "Go, go!" he shouted. "Get him inside!"

They had at least ten or fifteen seconds before the bees would resume their work. And if the building's bee defenses were working, here at the pedestrian entrance, Cap would be safe.

The soldiers bore their burden easily, running in disciplined formation with Cap held between them. They disappeared into an arch of amber light. Doug stood his ground, looking up into the faint light of dawn, overpoweringly curious, and feeling the first glimmer of hope. He could just make out a dark dish, about twenty feet above him. He braced himself. When the bees returned, they would try to get through that amber arch. If they failed, then he was probably their next target.

The bees coalesced into a tight arrow and disappeared. Still he stood there, head back, watching.

Suddenly there was a shower of tiny sparks, high up, like a celebratory firework. This time, the weakness in his legs was irresistible. He sank to his knees and put his head in his hands.

◇◇◇

Cap was in Sickbay One, unconscious but not seriously hurt. Doug had been joined by Colonel Reznichek and several others at the main display pit in the atrium. In the midst of the sea of blue, occasional flashes of red were appearing. Mostly these were on the east coast, but a few had also registered in California and the mid-west. A secondary display showed the total count of swarms destroyed, and the location. The figure was currently thirty-seven, and the locations included Times Square and downtown Philadelphia.

"You deserve a medal for this, Colonel," Doug said lightly to Reznichek.

The Colonel turned his round face towards Doug. "What I deserve," he said slowly, "is a good night's sleep."

They watched as three more swarms were destroyed. Doug turned away at last. He knew he had to speak with the new PMA Director and warn him that swarms could still be abducted from the forty-five centers, and that new missions should be aborted for the time being; but first he asked his genie to connect him with Ma Yinghua.

CHAPTER 62

This time around in the Oval Office, Cap Olsen was gratified to note, the President treated the occasion as informal and abandoned her desk and joined her guests amidst the soft furnishings. It was a little before eight o'clock in the morning, and the steward had served coffee and freshly-baked strawberry croissants. Despite intense fatigue, and some itchy spots where the bees had penetrated, Cap was staying afloat on adrenaline and an absolute determination to show his face before his nation's leader. He felt he hadn't eaten for days, and he took a couple of swift bites out of a croissant. It tasted delicious.

The President had also wanted to express her appreciation to Alan Connacher, alias Doug Edie, and Cap had been obliged to bring him along. Cap didn't begrudge Doug his moment in the sun, but his presence made him slightly defensive and uneasy, as though his own role in recent events would somehow be lessened in comparison. At worst, he would be made to look positively slow and out-of-touch. But the downside, he thought, was limited, and the upside was good: his decision to recruit Connacher and give him important responsibilities had been validated ten times over. Connacher, whose work had helped to terminate an increasingly disastrous situation for the President and the nation, was FBI, his man; and as long as Christine Diaz remained in office, his job, surely was safe. He might even graduate to Secretary some day.

That was assuming Connacher didn't come across as the mastermind behind everything, making him look like a total schmuck. Not to be ungrateful, but it was pretty sneaky of him to save his life like that yesterday. Just because he'd saved Connacher's life a few weeks before that. Just to get even. It almost seemed like he'd set it up, figured it out, to get free of the one-way obligation. He looked across at Connacher, sitting near the President, his head drooping with fatigue. What the hell, he thought, smiling faintly at his own curmudgeonly attitude: the problem was, the two of them were now bonded for life; and he didn't know whether he could stand that youthful face outsmarting him forever.

"You know what makes me sad?" the President said. "All of these young lives, so fatally off track, given over to this…" Words failed her. She looked at her guests and sighed. "So where do we stand? I take it there's no risk of a further outbreak of killings?"

Cap swallowed with difficulty and said, "We think not, Ma'am. All of the PMA centers known to have been penetrated by these terrorists have been the focus of intense investigations, and we've made dozens of arrests. Kate Nakamoto is dead, and the technical genius behind the attacks, Merko Milovic, is in custody and cooperating fully. Our sense is that the move by certain Mickelburger hardliners into the kind of operation we saw at Times Square, continuous random killings, has alienated a lot of the less radical membership. As for Kronos himself, Zeb Packer… I'm afraid he's escaped, at least for the time being. We suspect he had a well-planned exit strategy, and has fled the country. But we don't see him making any kind of a comeback."

"The nation is grateful to you and your team, Director Olsen."

Cap blinked a couple of times, suddenly undermined by emotion. "Frankly, Ma'am, we got a little lucky. And with the sad exception of General Ponting, we had good support from the PMA and MAIMCOM leadership."

The President turned towards Doug Edie. "And from this young man, from what I hear… maybe we'll learn more of your story in due course… although I confess what I really want to say to you at the moment is: my, how you've changed."

Doug looked blank. He took a quick sip of coffee. "Madame President, I… I'm not sure that…"

"Perhaps you've forgotten giving evidence to a senate committee on which I was serving. This is going back a bit."

"Of course, I remember…" Doug still looked blank.

"I also know your daughter and have met you several times at your daughter's home."

"Right. Of course." Doug struggled to sit up. He seemed to be having difficulty in getting his brain to function.

"I feel for her at this time. Does she know that her son is Kronos?"

Doug half-closed his eyes. "No, Ma'am, not as far as I know."

"I'll give her what support I can. But to return to your situation, Mr. Connacher, what I'm trying to say is that I would never have recognized you in a million years."

Doug at last gave a faint smile. "No, I see. We, uh... We had to make some changes." He waved a hand towards his face.

"Are they permanent?"

"No, I hope not. In fact, they're life threatening."

"Life threatening?"

"We don't fully understand the problem, but it takes the form of something like tissue rejection. The new genes that define my face, hair color and so on are interfering in some way with the old genome still present in nerve cells and bone."

"Are you telling me you're a walking talking symbol of the young-old conflict?"

Doug's smile broadened slightly. "Yes, Ma'am, I guess you could say that."

"What are you going to do about it? I mean the life threatening genes, not the young-old conflict."

Cap could see that some measure of energy and attention was returning to Doug's expression. Despite the intense fatigue which they both felt, it was hard to ignore the President. And clearly Doug had a lot of personal interest at stake here. He was leaning forward in his seat to engage more closely with her.

"Well, Ma'am... currently I'm surviving with medical treatment. Which can possibly be improved. But I would like to attempt another rejuvenation, to return to my Alan Connacher identity. At the moment, to be honest with you, I feel a little lost. For example, you mention my daughter, whom I happen to know has a high regard for you, by the way... well, my daughter doesn't know that I'm alive. She's lost one son. And at some point, as we were saying, she will find out that her other son is Kronos. That's a... that's a very difficult situation for her and therefore for me."

Cap Olsen, seeing the President nodding and displaying the grandmotherly sympathy for which she was known, decided he should make a point. "Madame President, nobody knows more than I do the sacrifices which this man has made… he deserves our fullest help in rebuilding his life… but if Doug Edie…" Cap waved a hand in his direction… "if Doug Edie returns to being Alan Connacher, he will be a target not only for these people he's just brought down, who could well be plotting revenge right at this moment, he'll be a target for every youth extremist in the country. I'd like to say we can protect him, but how can I guarantee that?"

Christine Diaz looked at Doug with a concerned expression. "What do you say to that, Mr. Connacher?"

Doug's expression had darkened and he seemed now to be wrestling with strong emotions. "Madame President, I don't want to trouble you… I know this is something that I'll have to work out… It is made more complicated by the fact that I will be living, I hope, with someone for whom I have very strong feelings… Obviously, I shouldn't, I couldn't, subject her to the kind of risks that… that Cap is talking about…" Doug seemed for a moment too choked up to continue. Then he added, "But I will say this, Ma'am, that if it wasn't for her, if it was just me, I would go back to being Alan Connacher, and to hell with the risks."

The President nodded slowly. "I understand the dilemma, and I'm glad it's not mine. Mr. Olsen, what would you advise?"

Cap took a quick sip of coffee. "Doug unfortunately needs another change of identity. Too many people now know who he is. We should get a team working on the gene problem so we can give him a change of appearance without medical consequences. Then he needs a relocation and a fresh start. I know it's hard to give up a career, but he's smart… God knows he's smart… and he'll build a new career. We can give his partner a similar change of identity. It's the only safe way."

"And what about Trudie? Can we bring her inside the loop?" Doug said.

"No. You know that's not possible. Neither Trudie nor your family in California. Nobody. Nobody, period. They've been through the trauma of your death. They're adjusting. You've got to leave it that way."

Doug dropped his head, frowning unhappily, and said nothing.

The President said, "If you're determined to reclaim your identity, why not come and work in the White House?"

Cap heard this with a sense of shock, immediately sensing the risks and the problems, but it took him a moment to work out acceptable reasons for his opposition. Meanwhile Doug had raised his head and was staring at the President.

"You could head a commission," the President went on, "investigating the full effects and implications of rejuvenation. As a rejuvenant yourself, you'd be uniquely qualified. I also think that, looking and acting and living as a young person, you have the chance of forming a bridge between the young and the old. The great majority of young people totally reject the extremist platform, and might see you as someone they could relate to."

Cap could no longer keep quiet. "Madame President, with the greatest possible respect, that is not the way the FBI would characterize the mood of youth in today's world. Doug would be seen as a symbol of one-niner intransigence and power, an intruder into their space, and hence as a target. And by bringing such a security risk inside the White House, you'd jeopardize the safety of other members of your staff."

"We're used to security risks, Mr. Olsen. What I'm saying, Mr. Connacher, is that by joining the White House staff, you'd benefit from the protective umbrella of the Secret Service, which is, no disrespect to the FBI, the best in the business."

Cap Olsen bowed his head and managed to remain silent. Doug seemed stunned, but also revived by the offer.

"I'm deeply honored by the suggestion, Ma'am," he said. "Would you mind if I talked it over with my partner?"

"Bring her in to meet me, Mr. Connacher, and we'll talk it over together."

Cap stared at the two of them and nearly moaned out loud.

CHAPTER 63

"If you were dead," Doug said, "your Chinese controllers would be neutralized. They'd never bother you again."

They were in a taxi on the way to Trudie's house in Georgetown. Yinghua, whose expression was uncomfortable, verging on mutinous, was silent for a moment. "Maybe they'd find out."

"What? That you weren't dead?"

"They found out about BEEKEEP."

It was Doug's turn to pause. "That's true."

"Anyway, we agreed it would be much too distressing for Sam. Me dying. Quite apart from my own family."

"Sweetheart... I know what we agreed. And I agree with what we agreed. I just don't want to think of you... and Sam, if that works out... being exposed to... your Chinese people, and my youth extremist people."

"We'll have the protection of the Secret Service. Isn't that right?"

"If I go to work in the White House, yes."

"Isn't that what you want to do?"

"I don't know. It depends on you."

"Alan, you'll have to decide that for yourself."

"Yeah. Okay."

Yinghua reached out a hand to squeeze his arm, and turned her head to stare out of the window.

Since his visit to the White House with Cap Olsen, Doug had spent two days and nights trying to relax and catch up on sleep. When the results of the election began to come through, he was relieved that support for the President, and for anti-Kronos policies, was evident;

she increased her majority in the lower house and gained two seats in the Senate.

He went into hospital for some more post-trauma therapy and a full check over. He attended a briefing at the FBI. Some of the arrested activists were talking, and the round-up of others continued. Cap was friendly enough. Doug had a sense that his own role was being subtly air-brushed out of the history of the counter-attack, and he couldn't fault that as a policy. The less that anyone knew of his role, the better. But it made it harder to cope with all the personal upheaval, the family trauma, the void in which he seemed to be floating. He felt like an astronaut adrift in space, looking down at the inviting but unreachable world filling his field of view.

He and Yinghua moved into yet another FBI-monitored house. He enjoyed being with her, and in spite of the uncertainties, the inactivity, he avoided drifting into a depressive state. There were moments of fear and tension; he had nightmares about bees; he even wondered a few times whether Zeb was out there, still in the country, plotting revenge against his grandfather; but in spite of all the ugly memories, he had the sense that he was regenerating, recovering, that his old brain was reworking bits of his life, knitting itself together.

He and Yinghua talked about how they could live. He sensed her frustration as every option seemed hedged around with difficulty and risk. They were in agreement on one thing: if Trudie wished it, Yinghua should try and adopt Sam. But this would induce the most serious problem of all: the risk he would create for Sam. Yinghua, he knew, loved Sam and felt responsible for him. Doug wondered once or twice whether he himself, despite being the great-grandfather, was more trouble than he was worth; but Yinghua pushed this idea aside, promising him that however long it took, they would become a family in the end.

Yinghua turned away from the window and again put a hand on his arm. "Honey, don't take this the wrong way, but…"

He recognized the tone of voice and tried to look receptive, meeting her gaze full on.

"…you know the way this is going to work out… you know what we have to do."

"You mean," Doug said, "if you adopt Sam."

"Especially that. But even if I don't."

He held the receptive look, although he sensed a drop like an air pocket looming ahead.

"We have to live apart. Just for a while."

He nodded slowly, as though this was a sensible conclusion. "How long is a while?"

"A year or two? Maybe less. We'll just have to see whether..."

"Whether I can stay alive."

"You're going to stay alive," Yinghua said firmly. "I need you alive, okay?"

"Okay."

"But we have to see whether the new situation, the new circumstances of our lives..." She stopped. "We'd see each other as much as possible."

"In secret?"

"That might be wise."

"Okay."

"I know you don't like it."

"I don't like it because I love you. But the worst thing for me would be to put you, or maybe Sam, in danger. So I accept it. It's the right solution."

"Honey, look at me."

Doug raised his eyes.

"I love you too, you know that, don't you?"

Doug nodded.

"We have to think of the future," Yinghua said. "We have to take it in stages. We're going to be together a long time, aren't we?"

Doug put an arm around her and drew her close. "Yeah," he said, his voice unsteady. "We are."

The taxi drew up outside the Georgetown row house. Doug engaged in the brief payment ritual with the taxi and he and Yinghua got out and walked up the short pathway to the front door. It was late afternoon on a cool November day, the sky iron grey, the light fading. The police presence, which Doug understood had been provided for all senators and congressmen during the election period, was no longer in evidence.

Trudie opened the inner door, after they had announced themselves and gone through an ID check. Doug was shocked at how old she looked, her face thin and drawn tight on the bones. She welcomed Yinghua with a kiss, but there was no animation in the gesture, none of the usual theatrical warmth. Her eyes, when she turned them briefly on Doug, were exhausted. There had been no word in the media, yet, about Kronos's real identity, and if Trudie suspected anything she had made no reference to it; but she looked like an empty and defeated shell.

She led them through the ostentatious hall and up the stairs to the family room, complaining distractedly that Andy was working as usual and that she didn't see much of Zeb or Russell these days.

Sam was bunched at one end of the long couch, clutching a pillow as though it was a soft toy, staring at them over the upholstered arm. He jumped down when he saw Yinghua and ran over to her and gave her a hug.

"Did you come to see me?" he said.

"Of course I did. Are you okay?"

"Not really really okay, but…"

"Hanging in there."

"Yeah."

"Good for you. I want you to meet my friend, Doug."

Sam turned and gave Doug a long look and then took hold of Yinghua's hand. "I don't like him," he said.

Doug was taken aback. He advanced cautiously and squatted down in front of Sam. "Anything I can do to change your mind?"

Sam considered that, leaning against Yinghua's leg. He shook his head.

Doug realized that to the boy he might seem like a threat: someone who also loved Yinghua. "Why don't you like me?" he said quietly.

Sam looked him up and down and thought for a moment. "Your hair."

"What's wrong with my hair?"

"It should be red. Not black."

Doug felt his mouth opening in astonishment. He closed it and glanced at Yinghua. She was looking equally surprised. What had the boy picked up, he wondered: a gesture, a distinctive body chemical, a turn of phrase?

Yinghua stepped forward and put a hand on Sam's shoulder. "Come on, Sam, let's go for a little walk. Doug wants to talk with your grandmother."

Trudie, who had sat down on the couch, said plaintively, "Oh sweetheart, please don't leave me."

Yinghua looked across at Trudie. Doug could see that Yinghua wanted to go across and comfort her, but instead, she glanced quickly at Doug and held herself back.

Sam suddenly stepped forward and pointed a finger up at Doug. "You see? Grandma doesn't like you either."

"Sam, that's enough." Yinghua put a restraining hand back on Sam's shoulder and looked again at Trudie. "Doug has a couple of things to tell you. He has some news of your father."

Trudie looked sharply at Doug, her face fearful, expectant, but also a second later withdrawn, as though she didn't really want to get into such a sensitive area with a near-stranger.

"Come on, Sam," Yinghua said, "let's go and take a look at your sculptures."

"They're not *sculptures,* Yinghua," Sam said, taking her hand again and drawing her towards the door, "they're nano-generated models."

Alone with Trudie, Doug stood still, momentarily at a loss. His daughter seemed absorbed in her own misery, her body language defensive. It was the kind of sulk with which he was familiar, but on this occasion she seemed truly beaten down. By what, exactly? Her father's death, Jason's death. Well, perhaps he could change some of that.

"Can I get you a drink?" he said at last.

"Why not? Sure." She gave him an almost desperate glance. "Gin and tonic."

"Without lemon, I think."

She gave him another quick look. "How do you know that?"

Doug drew back his lips in a bloodless smile, but said nothing. Nor did he attempt to disguise his familiarity with the bar as he moved across and ordered Trudie's gin and tonic and a small scotch for himself. When he returned to the couch with the drinks and sat down a couple of feet away from her, he had her attention, although her curiosity was still mingled with defensive anxiety. She took a large swallow of the gin and tonic.

"May I call you Trudie?" he asked.

She nodded.

"And may I tell you that I care about you, and that what I have to tell you will seem, I hope, like good news rather than bad."

She had turned towards him and was clutching her glass in both hands, staring at him over the rim. "We know each other, don't we?"

"We do."

"You're not who you seem."

"No."

"Sam guessed who you are."

"Maybe."

Trudie shuddered and turned away from him and held on to her glass as though it was the only solid thing in her world. "Tell me. I'm not going to think about it, I'm not going to guess. Tell me."

Doug leaned back against the upholstery and took a fortifying breath. He could sense his daughter's brittle mood and he didn't want to give her unnecessary shocks. "First I ought to tell you what happened to your father, Alan Connacher. You think of him as a victim of the Kronos attacks, but there was an FBI guy with him when the bees arrived, and he managed to save Connacher's life. Or rather, he prevented the bees from doing any damage. Connacher was drowned, but he was resuscitated later at an FBI medical facility. Death was briefly induced again, so that you could identify the body, but again, no harm was done. He survived, completely okay."

Trudie had put down her glass and was now crying softly into a handkerchief. She didn't look at him and he wondered if she had understood what he was saying. Keeping his voice steady, he went on to tell her how Connacher, at the request of the FBI, had rejuvenated himself at his own labs, changed his appearance, and taken a new identity as a graduate student. He gave her a little of the story of Connacher going undercover and helping to pre-empt the new round of killings.

He thought that by this stage she must certainly have guessed the truth, if she hadn't already guessed it from the beginning. But she still didn't react, didn't fall into his arms, or shout at him, blame him for the agonies of bereavement which she had suffered. She seemed beyond emotion, snuffling, hunched over, immersed in her own tragedy.

At last, as though aware that her absence of response was unsustainable, she put down her glass and pushed herself to her feet and took a pace away from him. Then she swung around, her expression angry:

"No, no, no! How am I to relate to this... this... suit of flesh that you're showing me? This kid of twenty-five with black hair... How am I supposed to see my father in there? I can't do it!"

Trudie seemed furious not just with him, but at the entire, menacing world, with which she could no longer cope.

He got up slowly and stood before her, hands half-outstretched. "Trudie..."

"I'm not going to pretend, I'm not an actor any more. Of course I love my father, but you aren't my father. It may feel like it to you, but you're not my father!"

Doug felt fear penetrating his body like arctic cold. Was this the way it was going to be? Always rejected? Just because he looked different? Because he looked young? Even Cap was scared of him, jealous of him. Yinghua accepted him because she had got used to Doug Edie first, but even she...

"Trudie... listen..." he said, dropping his hands, softening his voice. "I've gone too fast... you need some time to get used to this... don't you think? Especially when I change again, go back to being Alan Connacher, it'll be easier... Just... give it a chance. You'll find I'm the same person. I still love you like a father. I remember your whole life, as a father does. I remember you on the beach at Cape Cod, demanding that I give you a ride on my shoulders. I remember your first high school dance, when I had to sew you into your dress. I can understand you, or... I can try to understand you... as a father does. My role doesn't have to change, just because my face has changed. Our unique connection with each other is in our brains. Just give me time."

Trudie raised her eyes at last, and Doug saw with relief that their expression had softened. Suddenly she flung herself into his arms. "Oh Dad, oh Dad... you're back... I can't tell you, I can't tell you..." Then just as suddenly she pulled away. "No, I can't do it! Not yet..." She began to retreat from him, hands half raised in entreaty. "You can understand, can't you? It needs time, like you said. Just give me time, please..." She gave him a final anguished look and fled from the room.

CHAPTER 64

Doug stood stock still for a couple of moments, wanting to follow his daughter and comfort her, but seeing the futility of any such effort. He sat down at last on the couch, picked up his glass, swallowed the remainder of his scotch. His hand, as he set the glass down, felt weak and unsteady. Okay, it would take time: but surely in the end what he had told her was true; his youthful shape couldn't destroy the bond between them. For a moment she had understood that, and surely as she grew accustomed to him, she would understand it more and more. There was no need for despair, neither with Trudie, nor with the other friends and family members with whom he would eventually begin to reconnect.

But he nevertheless sat slumped in gloom, until Sam pushed open the door and made a cautious entrance. He stood fiddling with the doorknob and glanced once at Doug.

"Hi," Doug said, trying to keep his tone of voice light.

Sam said nothing but moved a couple of paces into the room.

"Would you like a drink?" Doug said.

Sam shook his head.

"Would you care to sit with me for a moment?" Doug said, indicating the couch.

"No," Sam said. But he idled forward a couple more paces.

"Why do you think I should have red hair?" Doug tried.

Sam gave him a look, but the mischievous energy that had driven him before seemed to have died. "I don't know," he said.

Doug gave it up and remained silent. Sam slowly made his way to the end of the couch away from Doug and knelt down and leaned forward, his elbows on the cushioned seat.

"Yinghua and Grandma are talking," he said.

"What are they talking about?"

"Me," Sam said. He rested his head in his hands, his expression thoughtful. "I might go and live with Yinghua."

"Would you like that?"

Sam raised his head and nodded several times. "Yeah. Grandma has bad moods, you know."

"Things have been difficult for her, I think."

"Yeah. My father died. I may never see him again."

"I'm very sorry about that."

"And then Conchita left. That made her worse."

"Conchita left?"

"Yeah."

"When was that?"

Sam sat back on his heels and counted on his fingers. "Three days. Three days ago."

"Wednesday?"

"Yeah."

"Why did she leave?"

"Grandma said she wanted to go home."

"But? You thought?"

"I don't know... Conchita was crying... Like she..."

"Like she was being told to go?"

"Yeah."

Doug felt a crawling sense of alarm gathering in his mind. Wednesday: the day after the election, the day after the terrorist attacks; Conchita asked by Trudie to vacate her accommodation at the top of the house, apparently against her will. Trudie's bad mood, her obvious nervous tension.

"Sam, you know that bees can't get into this house, don't you?"

Sam nodded. "Yeah. I get extra checks at school."

"Do you know whether Grandma can shut that off? I mean so that bees would be able to come in?"

"There's a special box. But only Grandma and Grandpa Andy can use it."

"You mean I wouldn't be able to use it?"

Sam shook his head firmly. "It's a special box."

ID-restricted, Doug thought; as you would expect. Another thought struck him: internal surveillance. It had become habitual to him, since going undercover, to do regular checks with a floater, and he hadn't yet become secure enough to give that up. He felt in his pockets and found a floater and released it into the air. Sam watched it arcing up and whirling from place to place like a demented bee. Of course his action in releasing the floater might cause existing surveillance or monitoring equipment to switch off, or stop transmitting, but he could at least be sure that nothing was relaying his conversations from now on.

"Cap Olsen," he said to his telcom genie, and heard the usual acknowledgment. As he waited for Cap to come on the line, he leaned over towards Sam and said gravely: "Sam, do you know where your grandma and Yinghua are?

"They're in my room. That's my dad's old room."

"Okay." The floater had now signaled a clearance to his telcom genie. "Would you go and ask them to come here? Tell them it's urgent and important."

Sam looked at him for a moment, his head on one side, as though trying to decide whether or not this was just a game, and then nodded. "Okay." He ran off.

Cap's gruff voice came on the line. Doug outlined his concerns. "I should get confirmation in a minute or two."

"Son of a bitch," Cap said. "I thought we'd covered this stuff. Every possible hideaway. You know what? No, never mind."

"I may be wrong. I'm probably wrong."

"I'm going to mobilize some bees. Leave the line open."

"Okay."

Sam did his job. Trudie and Yinghua entered the room. Sam had perhaps said more than Doug had asked for: Trudie looked traumatized; the color had gone from her face and she was staring at Doug with almost malevolent intensity.

"Where's Sam?" Doug asked Yinghua.

"I said he should stay in his room."

"Okay." Doug stood up and advanced towards Trudie and met her gaze. "Trudie, I'm sorry, but I can't not ask you this: is Zeb in the house?"

Trudie broke down in sobbing and subsided into a cream-upholstered chair.

Doug repressed a stab of sorrow and concern. He bent towards her. "Sweetheart, I'm sorry... He's here now? In Conchita's room?"

Trudie looked up at him and dropped her head in a tiny nod of acquiescence.

"Cap?" Doug said, straightening up and turning away.

"I'm here."

"Confirmed. Probable location the maid's bedroom on the top floor."

"Bees on the way."

"Okay. Give me a few minutes."

Doug squatted down in front of his daughter. "Trudie... listen... we've got to turn off the bee screening system."

Trudie was wringing her hands, pressing them into her lap, her expression despairing. "I'm his mother... you're his... I don't know what you are... his grandfather."

"And he'd kill us both if he had to."

"No... Of course he wouldn't... He's in some kind of trouble, I know... he said so... but he wouldn't..."

"Trudie, you know this, really... you must know this... Zeb is Kronos."

"Oh God. Oh God, no. He can't be." She didn't raise her head, didn't meet his gaze.

"You know he is."

"He told me he'd got involved with bad people, that it wasn't his fault."

"Trudie, sweetheart, he's told you what you wanted to hear, given himself a sanitized role, noble motives. You know you love a good story. But he is Kronos, a mass killer, and there's no escape for him. Not here, not anywhere. We have to let the police take over."

"Am I to be the one to destroy him?" Trudie sobbed. "My own son?"

"You won't destroy him. The safest place for him right now is in jail."

"You don't know how he is. He's weak. He's ready to be destroyed!"

"Then he's brought that on himself. Trudie, you can't keep him here. You'll become a co-conspirator. Are you going to give up your Washington life? Everything you've worked for? Your marriage, influence, status?"

"I'll give up anything," she said, as though trying to convince herself, but she didn't meet his gaze.

Doug leaned down and took her arm. "Come on. Let's do it now, while we've got the chance."

Trudie looked up at Yinghua, hovering close by.

Yinghua came forward and took her other arm. "Your father is right, sweetie. You have to do this."

Trudie nodded in resignation and allowed herself to be helped to her feet. Doug went ahead, and Yinghua guided Trudie, who seemed half-blind and unsteady on her feet, down the long curving flight of stairs to the main hall. This was a space sometimes used for small receptions. There were two pieces of classical Roman sculpture towards the back, a Jackson Pollock splash of color above the original fireplace on the far side, and two tall windows facing the street. Persian runners decorated the wood-block floor. Doug had no idea where the control box for the bee screening system had been fitted, and Trudie, reaching the bottom of the stairs, seemed confused.

"Can't we just open a window?" Yinghua said.

"The windows are sealed," Doug said. "If you break a window, there's a backup barrier. We have to switch the thing off."

Yinghua was still holding Trudie's arm. "Trudie? Where is the control box?"

Trudie looked around and seemed to focus. She started towards the small outer hall leading to the front door.

A voice came from above. "Hey, folks. Let's forget that, shall we?"

Doug looked up. The landing at the top of the stairs overlooked the hall. Zeb was standing at the rail, looking down. He was unshaven, his hair unruly, his casual pants and shirt ill-fitting. His expression, as far as Doug could read it from a quick, raking glance, was bored, almost sleepy; there was no intensity there. Drugs? But his words had been clear, not slurred. His right hand was hanging loose by his side. He was holding something in it, something partially obscured by the railings. Doug stepped cautiously back a couple of paces, his right hand instinctively raised towards Yinghua and Trudie. The thing in Zeb's right hand was the chunky, sand-colored gun he remembered from their last encounter. Doug cursed to himself, furious that he had allowed this to happen, not sure how he could have avoided it.

There had been a gasp from Trudie, and as he looked now to his right, he saw her clinging with both hands to Yinghua's arm, looking up in horror. Yinghua had turned to look towards Doug.

"You're doing it to me, again, Granddad," Zeb said, his voice resentful, but not hate-filled. "Making things difficult for me."

"There's no hope for you, Zeb. Bees are outside. The FBI is on the way."

"Yeah. I guess it is. I could still do some damage, though." Zeb made a small movement with the gun. "Especially to you, Granddad." His gaze moved on to Yinghua and Trudie. "But nobody's safe with me around. You'd better call your friends and tell them to back off."

Doug hesitated a couple of seconds, then he said, "Cap? You there?"

"Yeah."

"We got a situation. "

"So I gathered."

"Zeb has a gun."

"Okay."

"Bee defenses are still in place. We didn't get that done. You'd better hold off."

"Okay."

"Really hold off."

"Okay."

Doug looked back up at Zeb. Zeb seemed almost relaxed. His week-old beard obscured his features, but there was a look of complicity in his eyes as he returned Doug's gaze. Doug wasn't sure what that meant, but he was reminded of the Zeb he knew, the Zeb he liked, the grandson who had worked with him in his business.

Trudie, however, must have sensed, perhaps for the first time since he had sought sanctuary in her home, the killing intent behind her son's languid stance. She suddenly burst out, her voice a despairing wail: "What did we do wrong? How did you start on this... how did you *think* of this... this killing... this mass murder?"

Zeb frowned, as though caught out cheating on his exams. "I just wanted to be a hero, Mom. Okay, a very big hero. A hero who made the rules. A hero who lived like a king. But I believed in the cause. I still believe in the cause. Youth gets treated like shit. I just wanted the respect of my peers."

"A hero doesn't kill his family," Trudie threw at him.

"Who says? A hero does what he has to do. It's the result that counts. I didn't really want to kill my family, I didn't want to kill Val either, but I saw the necessity. And I had the ability to do it. Where did those genes come from, eh? That's what you're wondering. Not from you, Mom. Not from you, Granddad. Maybe I got some of the ambition from you. You can be pretty focused and single-minded. But you're not a killer. No, it was my father. And his father before him, the one I killed for his money. I'm really surprised he didn't see that coming, considering what he and his son were like. Bastards, both of them. Eh, Mom? Mom knows all about that. I never figured out exactly what they'd done to advance their careers, but I'll bet there's a homicide or two involved there somewhere. Dad introduced me to cruelty. Thought he was teaching me a useful lesson, and I guess he was. Kind of backfired on him, though. He thought he'd spawned the devil. Which helped get him out of your life, Mom. You've got that to thank me for."

"I didn't know, I didn't see it, how could I know?"

"You couldn't know. You were a movie star. You weren't living a real life."

"You're saying it was my fault?"

"It wasn't anyone's fault. I am what I am."

In the brief hiatus that followed Zeb's existential statement, Doug saw, with a shock that seemed to punch the breath from his body, a figure, small behind the railings, making its way with a hop and a skip across the landing to where Zeb was standing.

"Uncle Zeb! Uncle Zeb!"

Out of the corner of his eye, Doug saw Yinghua move forward and he put out a warning hand.

Above them, Zeb transferred the gun from his right hand to his left hand and ruffled Sam's hair. "Hey Sam. How's it going?"

"I'm living here now, Uncle Zeb. Ask me a question."

"Are you going to fight for young people when you grow up?"

"Not *that* kind of question, Uncle Zeb."

"Okay. Thirty-nine divided by four."

But Sam had now been distracted by the object in Zeb's left hand. "What's that?" he said, reaching around Zeb's legs and pointing.

Zeb lifted it up and away. "It's kind of a gun, Sam. A very clever gun."

"Does it kill people?"

"Oh no. It's for games. We're having a little game here. You want to play?"

"Sam," Yinghua called up, "come on down here. Please. Uncle Zeb doesn't have time for games."

"I want to play."

"Not now."

"Are you going to be on my team, Sam?" Zeb said.

"Yeah."

"You got to stay up here with me, then. Okay?"

"Yeah."

"Whatever I do, you got to trust me, okay?"

"Yeah."

"Sam, come down," Trudie called, her voice unsteady.

"Just one game, Grandma."

"See that man down there," Zeb said.

Sam peered down through the railings. "Yeah."

"I call him Granddad. That's a joke."

"Cause he isn't your granddad."

"Cause he's so young."

"Yeah. He's really really young. And I don't like him because he's got black hair like me, but he shouldn't."

"Good. You'll enjoy the game then. First thing I do is…" Zeb drew back his left hand and lightly tossed the gun down towards Doug.

Doug caught it without thinking, his first thought relief, his next thought queasy doubt.

"…give him the gun," Zeb finished. "Okay, Granddad? You ready to play?"

Doug looked up at the two above him. "No. Let's quit right here. I'm not going to use this gun."

"You have to use the gun, Granddad. Or else…" Zeb reached down and put an arm round Sam and stood up and twirled him around. "…or else I throw Sam over the railings."

Yinghua gave a gasp. "No."

"And that applies if anyone tries to run up and rescue him."

"Let me go, Uncle Zeb."

"It's part of the game, Sam. I have to hold on to you."

"What the hell are you trying to do?" Doug said.

"I'm just trying to create a good ending. Must be my mom's dramatic instincts. You destroyed my ambitions, Granddad. You brought me down. You and that treacherous bitch, Kate. But you know what? I blame you. Kate was just dumb. Didn't understand her limitations. But you? I know you did what you had to do, but on the other hand... I'm your grandson. Shouldn't you have cut me some slack?" For a moment Zeb's expression hardened into bitter anger. "Anyway, I want you to finish what you've begun. You're the one I've chosen to administer the coup de grace. Use the gun, Granddad."

"No!" Yinghua yelped. "You might hurt Sam."

"No, no, no," Zeb said. "That gun is much too clever for that. It won't fire if it's aimed at a kid. Just point the gun in my direction, Granddad, and you'll hit me."

Doug felt panic brewing at the back of his mind. "Are you saying I should have let you kill more people? Hundreds of them?"

"I'm saying that as a grandfather you could have seen me as someone special. Someone who could change history. And maybe for the better."

"I recognized your potential, but..."

"But you're one of them. An old guy. Come on, Granddad, if you think I'm evil, do the deed, save the world."

"You're hurting me, Uncle Zeb," Sam said plaintively.

Zeb still had Sam tucked up under his right arm. "Hang in there, Sam, it's part of the game." He spun around again, Sam's legs swinging out over the railings. "Wheee!" Zeb sang.

Doug's mind was racing. Could he kill Zeb? No, he couldn't. He felt that conclusion like an iron law clamping itself down over his body. This was his grandson. Or, as it had begun to seem, his brother. He couldn't kill any more brothers. Especially not in front of Trudie, the grieving, traumatized mother. Yet he had to: he had to raise the gun and shoot, to save Sam, and to keep the love of Yinghua. Except that his muscles wouldn't obey.

"Why give up?" he half-shouted at Zeb. "Go to jail and see it through. You could stay alive for years. The mood in the country could change. Think of all the terrorists who have lived to be pardoned."

"I'm just not that kind of guy, Granddad. Maybe I thought I was, once. I thought I was Che Guevara. But I'm not. I don't want to live in jail, I don't want to live in some miserable foreign hell-hole, waiting for the knock on the door. The point is, I'm not an idealist. I believe in the cause, yes. But I don't believe that the cause is bigger than I am. So pull the goddamn trigger!"

Zeb stared down at him, arm still tight around Sam, who had begun to struggle now. Doug saw that Zeb was losing patience, that the courage he had gathered to drive himself forward and give up his own life might spill over into destructive fury. But still he couldn't kill him.

"Yinghua," he said quietly, without taking his eyes off Zeb. She was a couple of paces to his right.

"I'm counting to five," Zeb called out. "One…"

"I'm giving you the gun," Doug said. He still didn't turn, didn't know whether she nodded, whether she heard.

"Three… four…"

Doug reached out blindly with his right hand, felt Yinghua take the gun, and leaped back towards the main hall.

Zeb gave a roar of fury, spun around like a discus thrower, and let Sam fly over the top of the railings. Doug measured the arc of Sam's flight and ran, saw he was too close in, veered, threw his arms up, spun around, and took Sam's body full in his face. As he fell backwards, he got one of his hands on Sam's head, another hand close to Sam's hip, and as he hit the floor he was able to keep Sam on top of him, breaking his fall. His head exploded like a clanging bell. Sam yelped and rolled away.

Doug managed to turn and raise his head enough to look back at the stairs. An enraged Zeb was running down them at reckless speed. Only then did he hear a shot. Zeb's legs stopped working and his upper body fell forward, his momentum carrying him down to the woodblock floor.

The woman standing with the gun in her hand was his daughter Trudie. Yinghua held her as she collapsed in wracking sobs.

EPILOGUE

It was the kind of routine that Alan Connacher had begun to get used to, but still found frustrating and embarrassing: first the women in D Block were returned to their cells, then his Secret Service companions took him through the basement and up in a goods elevator to say hallo to the Warden; and finally he was hustled into a barren-looking room with no windows and lots of surveillance devices, where he waited for fifteen minutes while prison guards and a head-covering of identity-protecting SAIMs brought his chosen guest through the corridors for interview.

Naomi had lost weight, and her hair was pulled back in a tight, utilitarian bob, but there was still something in her expression that suggested the large-scale personality he remembered from his previous visit to Syracuse. She hadn't, it seemed, been crushed by prison life, and the behavior reports he had read showed her as cooperative, but also as a woman who had the respect of the other inmates. She was a natural leader, and had lobbied successfully for improved educational facilities.

She sat down quickly and gave him a business-like look, eyes open, inviting him to explain himself. Like almost everyone else in the facility, she had not been told of his visit, and her face gave no sign of recognition.

"I'm sorry about all the secrecy," he said. "I'm Alan Connacher."

He thought she would make the connection and he braced himself for her response. This interview could end right here, if she decided she would have no dealings with an undercover snitch.

She nodded briskly. "Okay, yeah. I think I saw you on the Today show."

He waited a moment, but she showed no further reaction beyond mild curiosity. It was true, of course, that he had never been publicly associated with Doug Edie, in fact Doug Edie's existence had been written out of the record, all of the historical data created by Cap and his team destroyed; but he was sure that amongst the activist community, the Rose Mickelburger Faction in particular, his old name lived on.

He hesitated, then decided that if she was one of the few who had stayed out of the loop, it would not be a serious breach of security to bring her inside.

"You might remember me as Doug Edie."

She pulled back in shock, looked at him hard. "But you don't look... Oh my God. Now I understand."

"Nobody told you?"

"I heard about Doug Edie... I just... I mean, the guy who came to deliver stuff... I never knew his last name was Edie... But you don't look anything like him... you don't even look young."

Alan nodded slowly. "I did another rejuvenation, using my original genome. I'm still young, in functional terms, but I found a way to introduce the appearance of ageing... into my face."

Naomi stared at him for a moment, her expression cool, but not, Alan thought, transformed by revulsion or hatred. Her tone of voice was acid: "So now you're a fake on all sorts of levels. You're basically an old guy who's made himself young. But instead of looking young, you're pretending to be old. Although you don't look old exactly... more like mature."

"That's a nice way of putting it."

"I'm not trying to be nice. I'm trying to be nasty. But for some reason..." She broke off, scowled, and dropped her gaze.

"Naomi, I came here first of all to apologize. Of all the people I met when I was undercover, you were the one who was the most... positive, life-affirming, normal..."

"That's me. Miss Useful."

"...and also the one I felt most guilty about betraying... especially since it was your trust, and relatively unguarded remarks, that helped me to make some important connections..."

"I'll give you this: you were very convincing."

"That's because I believed what I was saying. I was close to crossing over."

"Really?" She looked at him doubtfully, then dropped her gaze. "The funny thing is... So am I. When the killing really got going, especially that stuff on the subway, I began to think this wasn't the answer."

"I'm hearing that quite a lot, from young people I talk with. Which is kind of why I'm here. I want to offer you a job."

Naomi pulled back, her expression clouding over. "I'm not informing on my friends. That isn't going to happen."

"Not that kind of job. A real job. You weren't involved in the abduction of swarms, so you could be out of here in a year. Less, with my help. Meanwhile there's stuff you can do from jail."

"What's the job?"

"I'm putting together a group of young people to serve on a presidential commission. You'd talk to schools, clubs, societies, make presentations, argue with old guys, help to shape policy. The goal is to find a way of giving some genuine power back to the doomer age group. President Diaz recognizes that the political establishment has become decadent and self-satisfied. Even the Kronos option of new voting arrangements could be given consideration."

"Rejuvenation? The fascists at the PMA?"

"Everything is on the table. Although in the case of rejuvenation, I should point out that it's a temporary issue, affecting only us one-niners. Your generation is already benefiting from longevity treatments which will mean you never get old."

"Assuming that's what we want."

"Yes. But there's very little sign of you turning these treatments down."

"And what about you?" Naomi said, looking at him shrewdly. "You've lived a lot longer than us. Are you still up for it? Immortality?"

He hesitated, dropped his gaze. This was something he had found time to think about a lot. "My views about that are still developing," he said at last. "Being young doesn't solve anything. At one time I wanted to be young for its own sake, I thought I could start again, avoid certain mistakes. But that didn't work. Unless we make real assaults on our humanity by changing, augmenting, redefining our brains, which doesn't appeal to me, by the way, we are stuck with the ugliness of imperfect, perhaps repetitive, lives. Maybe such lives will one day become wearying, and we'll be prepared to give them up. The problem is..." He raised his eyes and fixed his gaze on Naomi. "...anyone with large and interesting horizons, some degree of good fortune, doesn't see that day coming soon."

She appeared to think about that for a moment, and then looked up with a mischievous smile. "So we'll have to get rid of you by lottery."

"That's a policy you could certainly propose."

"Interesting people could get a bye into the next round. You're still quite good-looking, you know. Although Doug whatshisname was definitely a hunk."

Alan burst out laughing. "Is that a yes? You'll take the job?"

"Why the hell would I say no?"

◇◇◇

The Secret Service got him out the same way they had got him in, and installed him in the back of a limousine. His spirits began to rise as they left the industrial landscape of Syracuse and headed north-east for the Adirondacks. It was Friday and his week in Washington was over. He had thrown himself into his work for the President, but he had begun to chafe at the claustrophobic world of White House politics, and was trying to figure out a route back into entrepreneurial science. Rejuvenation was still a highly contentious issue, his own status, even as a man not pretending to youth, difficult to manage: but there were medical offshoots of his technology that he thought he could exploit; and the death threats were dwindling.

It was early summer, and the green open hills, gradually giving way to lakes and woodlands, sparkled with promise. He put down the briefing papers he had been trying to read, and watched the scenery unfold. He found it hard to recall the dark days of his Doug Edie existence, when all paths forward seemed blocked. There were still risks to be faced, precautions to be taken, but with the help of the President's Secret Service, and Cap Olsen's FBI, he had recovered the sense of a life worth living.

The limousine turned off the highway and followed a narrow paved road through stands of birch and poplar and pine; and then made another turn onto a dirt track with signs proclaiming 'Private

Property', 'No Entry', and 'Guard Dogs in Use'. After half a mile nosing through leafy brush and roof-scraping limbs of spruce, they emerged into a clearing. Facing them was a small log cabin with a steep shingle roof and a porch. Through the trees to the left, water glinted white in the sun.

What Alan noticed first was the familiar red SUV parked over by the woodpile. He felt his whole body relax, as though he was already floating in the waters of the lake.

He had the door open as soon as the limousine drew to a halt. Getting out, he paused briefly to sniff the pine-scented air; then he waved his thanks at his escort and ran up the steps of the porch, eager to start the weekend with his great grandson and his wife-to-be.

www.ingramcontent.com/pod-product-compliance
Lightning Source LLC
Chambersburg PA
CBHW070627180626
46817CB00006B/2070